STOCKTON
Township Public Library
Stockton, IL

THE TRUEST PLEASURE

ALSO BY ROBERT MORGAN

FICTION
The Blue Valleys
The Mountains Won't Remember Us
The Hinterlands

POETRY
Zirconia Poems
Red Owl
Land Diving
Trunk and Thicket
Groundwork
Bronze Age
At the Edge of the Orchard Country
Sigodlin
Green River: New and Selected Poems

NONFICTION
Good Measure: Essays, Interviews, and Notes on Poetry

ROBERT MORGAN

THE TRUEST
PLEASURE

ALGONQUIN BOOKS OF CHAPEL HILL
1995

Published by
ALGONQUIN BOOKS OF CHAPEL HILL
Post Office Box 2225
Chapel Hill, North Carolina 27515-2225

a division of
WORKMAN PUBLISHING
708 Broadway
New York, New York 10003

Library of Congress Cataloging-in-Publication Data

Morgan, Robert, 1944–
    The truest pleasure: a novel / by Robert Morgan.
        p.   cm.
    ISBN 1-56512-105-8 (hardcover)
    1. Farm life—North Carolina—History—20th
century—Fiction. 2. Married people—North
Carolina—Fiction.   I. Title.
  PS3563.087147T77 1995
  813'.54—dc20   95–22740
                                                              CIP

10 9 8 7 6 5 4 3 2 1
First Edition

I would like to thank the staff at Algonquin Books for their unstinting help with details both artistic and practical, and especially Shannon Ravenel for her inspired and inspiring work as editor of this and many other books.

FOR MY SON BEN

THE TRUEST PLEASURE

CHAPTER ONE

The first Pentecostal service Pa ever took me to was held in a brush arbor up near Cedar Springs. The preacher was a fiery little man named McKinney from Tigerville, South Carolina. I was just seventeen and curious to see what was going to happen.

"Is this the kind of service where women roll on the ground?" my sister Florrie said.

"Sometimes they do," Pa said, "if the Spirit moves them to."

"Who do they roll on the ground with?" my brother Locke said. He was always making jokes and making light.

"Won't do to mock other people's worship," Pa said. He had attended Pentecostal services when he was a prisoner at Elmira, New York, during the Confederate War. He was just a boy, and they had prayer meetings in that awful camp where they sung and danced to keep warm by the froze river. When I was a girl he would tell about it, about one prisoner who was a preacher and could make anybody speak in tongues just by looking at him. That preacher could raise hisself high in the air while preaching so he was talking from way above. "It made us forget we was cold and hungry," Pa said. The preacher's name was McKinney and he was the papa of the one now holding services at Cedar Springs.

"McKinney said he would survive the camp if he had to live on icicles and cockroaches, and looks like he did," Pa said.

Preacher Jolly at the Baptist church had condemned the brush arbor meetings. He said it was the devil's work to come into a community and stir folks up and have them talking out of their heads. He said preachers like McKinney got folks all confused and quarreling and then went on their way. Preacher Jolly said the baptism of fire was just rot and the only baptism to count was water symbolic of the blood. He said anybody attending the brush arbor services was liable to lose their letter in the church.

The more people talked against the Pentecostal Holiness meetings the more curious I was to attend. My mama before she died was an Old Regular Baptist and I remember hearing her argue with Pa when he attended a revival in South Carolina. I was just a girl and hardly understood what they was talking about, but I knowed it made her angry for Pa to go to Pentecostal meetings.

"The Spirit speaks to people different ways," Pa had said.

"Ben Peace," Mama answered him, "I don't want my children to ever witness such shameful goings-on."

They had quarreled about the meetings for weeks, until the revival was over. And the next year she died of the fever.

My brother Joe was courting Lily then and they went with Pa and me in the wagon to Cedar Springs. It was Dog Days, before fodder-pulling time, when they had revivals back then. To get there in time we had to start when it was still daylight.

"It's a way for Ginny to get out of doing dishes," Florrie said as we left. She always did say the most cutting thing.

"Who does the dishes when you're out with David?" I said.

"At least I ain't going to disgrace myself by hollering and rolling on the floor," Florrie said, and flung spoons in the dishpan.

"Ain't you?" I said, and slipped out before she could answer. She had already bragged to me that she had laid down with David and I didn't pass up many chances to tease her about it.

When we started out in the wagon you could hear grasshoppers clicking in the weeds. They sounded like a million timepieces ticking. And jarflies sung back in the oak trees like baby rattles shook so fast they blurred. By the time we got to the river road the crickets was ringing in the grass. It was the big black crickets called meadow moles and they rung all over the pasture hill and in the brush along the road. They sounded like tiny chisels pinging on rocks. "Six weeks till frost," Pa said, as he always did when he heard a meadow mole.

There was horses tied to trees and wagons in the field around the brush arbor. The MacBanes had built the arbor out of poles, and nailed pine limbs on the poles. It looked like a green chapel carved from shrubbery. The arbor smelled of resin and sawdust and shavings spread on the ground. Some folks had brought their own chairs, but most set on benches of rough lumber.

We set near the middle of the arbor. Lanterns had been hung on either side up front, and there was one lantern on a pole in the center. The katydids got loud as a grist mill in the trees by the time it was dark. "Where is the preacher?" I whispered to Pa.

"He will come," Pa said.

There was an altar in front and a pulpit of rough pine. One of the MacBanes, I think it was Hilliard, climbed up on the platform and said, "We will raise a hymn." The MacBanes ever was the best singers in the valley, and Hilliard was supposed to be the very best, after his uncle Ben. His voice was so pure you felt it was the true voice and all others was just mocking it.

"The Spirit speaks first through music," Hilliard said, and begun lining out "Revive Us Again."

"Amen, b-b-brother," someone called. It was Joe.

Hilliard sung slow at first. He said a phrase and then sung it. He said another and sung that. "You all sing with me," he said. "The Spirit is right here with us in these woods. I can feel it. Can't you?"

"A-a-a-amen," Joe stammered.

As we sung I begun to notice something. Everything around me was changing in some way. The lantern light was still the same, and the people the same, and the smell of the pine resin was still the same. But it was changed too. It was sweeter. And I thought how time was more intense and sweetened by music. I felt closer to the people. They was still the same but I saw them different and better. I had on my same white blouse, but it begun to glow in the lantern light like pearls or opals.

When the song was over we heard somebody running. They come lickety through the leaves and trees outside. It sounded like somebody running for their life. And just as I was wondering who it could be this man leapt out of the dark into the brush arbor and right up on the pulpit.

"The devil was chasing me but I beat him," the man shouted. Everybody laughed. It was Preacher McKinney. He wiped his brow with a handkerchief, and stood right on top of the pulpit. "Got to move fast to outrun the devil," he said. He paused and looked around. I felt froze. I couldn't take my eyes off him.

"Thank you, Jesus," Lily said beside me.

"Do you know what it is?" the preacher said. "Do you know what it is that is so sweet?" He paused again and looked from one side to the other. Then he looked right at me. "It is the fellowship of time with eternity," he said. "It is the communion of flesh with spirit; it is this world rubbing up against the next."

His words was thrilling. He was saying just what I had often felt, what I had thought and only half understood before.

"We cannot put off these rags of flesh," the preacher said. "But we can wear them in the Spirit and close to the Spirit. We don't have to be dirty and miserable. We don't have to feel sorry for ourselves. We don't have to be lukewarm. We can live in the light and close to the light. For the spirit is here, right now."

It felt like the burdens of my life started falling away. All the tedium and work, all my quarrels with Florrie and my sadness after Mama died, my disappointments because I had big hands and feet and because the boys stayed away. My worries about what things meant and what I read in books got suddenly trifling.

I looked at the preacher and he looked right into my eyes. It was like I was about to say something but couldn't. There was words at the tip of my tongue but I couldn't speak.

"You can have the baptism of fire," Preacher McKinney shouted. "The baptism of water is not enough. You must have fire. And once you have the fire you cannot fall from grace. The dryhides and the washfoot Baptists won't tell you that. They'll tell you one dip in the branch or mudhole and you are guaranteed a seat in heaven. They talk like their plunge into the dirty creek is a ticket to paradise."

He stopped and wiped his brow with a big white handkerchief. He turned to the other side of the congregation. "Well I'm here to tell you hell is full of washfoot Baptists," he said. "And the water is dried off them quick in eternal torment. You've got to fight fire with fire. Just like you caseharden a nail to make it stronger, or fire a pot in the fiery furnace to make it last. It takes the second baptism to see you through."

"A-a-amen," Joe shouted. He jumped up and put his hands on either side of his mouth as if calling a long distance. But what come out was a chatter and buzz. I thought he was stuttering, but he was speaking too fast. It was the opposite of stuttering. He must have spoke half a minute and I did not know what he said.

"Bless you, brother," the preacher said. "The Lord has made you a vessel of his word. Bless you all, my darlings in Christ."

Lily begun to shake beside me. She shook like she had been through a cold river and then stood up in the wind. The look on her face was froze, but her body jerked. She bounced in every part of her. Without seeming to try, she walked out into the aisle. I stood back to let her go by. She walked up the aisle twitching and wrenching herself sideways.

"Bless you," the preacher said. "The Spirit is in you also."

As she walked toward Preacher McKinney, shivering and shuddering, Lily did not take her eyes off him. She held her head stiff, while her whole body was dancing in spasms and seizures.

"Bless you, honey," the preacher said. And as he said it she dropped to the sawdust like she fainted. I stood on tiptoe to watch. She fell to the ground and kept jerking for a few seconds, and then she started rolling. She rolled from side to side, as if struggling to get loose from bonds. She kicked in the sawdust as if pushing away from a bank or shore.

"The Spirit is right here," the Preacher said. "It is not in some dryhide Baptist church and not in Greenville. It is not in some fine building, and not in Washington, D.C., or New York City. It is right here in this brush arbor tonight, and it is here to change our lives. It is here to baptize us forever."

Lily had cut all ties to being stiff and vain, to being prideful and full of self-regard. Usually she worried all the time about how she looked. She even put on airs a little. She was vainer about her clothes than any woman in the valley. But on the ground she spun and swam as if in a river of spirit, beyond ordinary concerns, selfish desires.

This is a new level, I thought to myself. This is a new dimension in our lives. And yet it seemed an old dimension too, something I had forgot since I was a girl. I could remember letting go that way when I was little. This is a new beginning for you, I said to myself. From now on things will be different.

Pa had took out his handkerchief and was waving it. Tears streamed down his cheeks, but he did not make a sound. He held the handkerchief over his right shoulder and waved it, like he was signalling to somebody, or shooing away flies.

"Send a message to the devil to stay away tonight," Preacher McKinney said. "Let's tell him he might as well go back to hell. He ain't got no business here."

I looked at Preacher McKinney's eyes and he looked at me. My neck locked like steel and I couldn't take my eyes away and I couldn't close them. I didn't know I was saying anything, even though I felt my tongue move. But it felt like I was raising above myself, even while I stood still.

Everybody had turned to look at me. And the preacher said, "Bless you, sister, the Lord has made you a vessel for his Word tonight. Through you has flowed the sweet honey from the rock and in your mouth is the light of stars."

A great burden was falling away and I was at ease for the first time in years. The striving and struggle dropped away. The worry and the need had washed away. I felt poised on the instant, and happy in the very nick of time. I need not worry that my hands and feet was not beautiful and my lower lip puckered out when I was thinking. It didn't matter that I had never had a real boyfriend though I was almost seventeen, or that Florrie had been with David and I hadn't hardly been kissed.

And the little irritations would not matter either. I would not be concerned with the cold mornings when I had to go out to the cow stall to milk and the cow would kick me with a filthy foot. And I would never have to worry about the blues that made me feel lower than the earthworms. And I did **not** need to feel guilty for not fixing myself up every day the way Florrie and Lily did. From now on I would practice charity naturally and give to those in need what was in my power to give.

I stepped into the aisle and walked toward the preacher on tiptoe. I did not jerk as Lily had. I kept my eyes on Preacher McKinney and took short quick steps. Lily was setting in the corner wiping her eyes, but I did not look toward her.

"This sister is in the Spirit," the preacher said. He reached out and placed his hand on my head and I begun to shudder and melt. I quivered throughout my bones and sunk toward the sawdust like jelly. I wanted to sink in the ground to show my humility. I wanted to fall and float right into the earth under the horizon.

And as I hit the ground I felt myself spun over. The only way to show humility was to wallow like a mare. I had to stretch out and shed my vanity. I spun and rolled as if carried by a flood across the room. Turning, I felt pulled underground, deeper and deeper into humility. Only by turning could I reach the center.

I touched the edge of the brush arbor and as I begun rolling back I felt the fire around me. The flames bathed and caressed me. The fire scorched away all pride and dirt of willfulness and the pain of vanity. I was lower than anybody in the room, and it was only by lowering myself that I could be cleansed. The fire burned and cooled me at once. Flames stretched through my thoughts and across the sky millions of miles like endless sunsets one after the other. The fire reached the edge of dark space and brushed up against stars.

"You've got to fight fire with fire," the preacher shouted.

I whirled and whirled and saw that everything was spinning. Days was spinning and the earth was spinning and the sun itself was turning. Everything was curves and circles.

Everything turned and returned. Each speck of me had been cleansed by turning.

This is the sweet geometry of light, I thought. This is the algebra of spirit and time. This is where flesh becomes clear as a lens and dust shines like Christmas candles. Carrion is radiant and new potatoes glow like babies. Lightning bugs pepper the dark. The coldest rock is on fire and icicles too. The sky is a blue fire and time runs its flame through everything.

When I stopped rolling I was too weak to do anything but lay in the shadows at the edge of the brush arbor. Sawdust and shavings stuck to my sweaty face and neck and my hair was tangled around my forehead. Sawdust was stuck to my legs behind my knees, but I didn't care. I felt emptied out and full at once.

"It is a privilege to be here tonight," Preacher McKinney was saying. "In all my years of preaching I have never seen such an outpouring of the Spirit. We are blessed with a rare gift."

There was shouting all around and a man, I think it was one of the MacBanes, hopped down the aisle and around the altar like he was crippled and hadn't walked for years but couldn't help hisself. "Thank you, Jesus," he shouted, "thank you, Jesus."

"What a taste of Glory tonight," the preacher said. "What a great big tin tub of honey has been dumped over us."

I heard somebody else speak in tongues, but couldn't tell who it was. The voice was so stretched it didn't sound like anybody I knowed. There was a stream of syllables like bubbles gargled and blowed from a pipe. Then there was more, and still more.

"Bless you, sister," the preacher said and looked at me, and I saw it was me that had been speaking. I didn't even recognize my own voice. The syllables stopped as fast as they had started. The last one fell off my tongue like a big final bead.

"Everybody come forward," the preacher said. "Everybody come get down on their knees in front of the altar."

I tried to pull myself up on my knees.

"The Spirit and the bride say come; let whosoever will take the water of life freely," the preacher said, quoting Revelation.

I fell back on my butt I was so weak.

"Help the sister up," the preacher said. One of the Jenkins men reached out and helped me raise to a kneeling position.

"Everybody on their knees," Preacher McKinney said. "It's the only way to face eternity, right here on your knees in the dirt and sawdust." Everybody come down and dropped to their knees, all close together. I was between Tildy Tankersley and the Jenkins boy. We crowded shoulder to shoulder.

"Now everybody put their arms around each other," the preacher said. I put my left arm around Tildy's neck and my right on the Jenkins boy's shoulder. We got so close together it felt like everybody had their arms around everybody else.

"'By this shall all men know that ye are my disciples, if ye have love one to another,'" the preacher said. He got down on his knees and put his hands on the necks of two people right in front of him. I think it was Joe and Lily.

"Lord, we will get right down here in the dirt in our humbleness to you," he said. "We ain't got no pride, and our strength comes from you. Without you we're no more than dirty rags. We that was once lost are now found. We that was filthy are now cleansed and saved with fire. Thank you, Jesus."

"Thank you, Jesus," we all said.

·

"Now hug each other closer," the preacher said.

It was the most wonderful feeling as we all drawed each other to us.

"Hell itself cannot stand against love," Preacher McKinney said.

I was aware somebody had put a hand on my breast and squeezed it. But in the packed-together crowd I couldn't see who it was and I didn't much care. We was so close everybody was touching somebody. We swayed as one body when the preacher prayed.

"This is what people was made for," Preacher McKinney said. "We was put here to share in the joy of Christ's love, and to know Him through love."

I don't know when I first noticed the smell of smoke. The scent of coal oil burning in the lanterns had been there from the beginning. And there was the scent of pine needles heated by the lanterns. But suddenly I caught the odor of smoke. At first I thought it was just a lantern, or the smell of pipe smoke on one of the men. But it was a dusty papery smoke. Everybody looked around at the same time and saw the hair of smoke pouring through the arbor, and heard the crackling.

It was such a shock it took us a few seconds to respond. People unlocked their arms and begun twisting and struggling to get up. Some helped each other and some crowded toward the door. "It's a fire!" Tildy screamed.

In a daze we all begun pushing toward the door. It was purely dark outside, but I could see the fire glow on the trees.

"Where is the spring?" Joe said.

"It's way up on the hill," Emmett MacBane said.

"Closest water is the branch," his brother Tilden said.

"Anybody got a bucket?" Pa said.

"It's the baptism of fire," a voice shouted out in the woods, and there was laughter.

"Where's the bucket of drinking water?" Emmett said. It appeared somebody had stole the bucket and dipper from the stump in front of the brush arbor. But it was too late anyway. The pine brush on the walls and roof of the arbor had caught like tinder. The fire soaked right through the walls almost as soon as we got out. There wasn't much we could do but stand there watching the arbor drown in flames. Within a minute fire had reached into the frame and opened the walls. We could see the benches burning, and the pulpit and altar. There wasn't a thing we could do except gasp as the roof started falling a piece at a time.

"We will build it back," Emmett said.

"We will build it back even bigger," Tilden said.

"The Lord's work will not be stopped," the preacher shouted to the darkness. The fire lit the trees far into the woods, but blinded by the flames I couldn't see a thing.

I don't remember much about the ride back down the river road. After the heat of the service, and the rage of the fire, the cool air felt good at first. But I soon begun to shiver in the dark and wish I had a coat. Joe lit the lantern but it didn't help much against the night chill. We creaked and rattled along the rough road under the stars. I brushed pieces of sawdust and shavings off my dress and out of my hair.

"You had a true baptism, Ginny," Lily said to me. "I could tell it. I could tell you was in the Spirit."

But now that we was out in the dark I didn't want to talk about the service. It felt wrong to talk about it.

When we got to the house it must have been past midnight. We had left Lily at her place up near the ford. Florrie and Locke had gone to bed and there wasn't even a lamp on in the living room. The katydids was so loud in the trees around the place it was hard to believe the house was there at all.

While Joe unhitched the horse and led him to the stable, Pa gathered kindling and cobs to start a fire. Because it was so clear, the night had got cold. I shivered and suddenly felt awful hungry. "Make the fire in the stove," I said. "Build a fire in the stove and I will fix some biscuits and coffee."

"I'm mighty hungry for cornbread and butter," Pa said.

"Then I'll make some cornbread," I said. I got meal and buttermilk and salt and soda and mixed them up in a batter by the time Joe come in. Pa had the cob fire roaring in the stove and the kitchen started to warm up. I poured the batter into a pan and put it in the oven. The water for the coffee begun to boil.

"He's the best I've ever seen since Elmira," Pa said. "He's as good as his daddy was."

"He's as good as Lilburn is," Joe said, "and I always said L-L-Lilburn could outpreach and outshout anybody in Dark Corner."

I wondered what they was going to say about my part in the service. Now that we was back home I felt even less like talking about it. It didn't seem right to discuss what had happened, not because what went on in the brush arbor was shameful, but because it was too sacred to talk about.

I put a cake of butter on the table and we had hot cornbread and butter and cool molasses and coffee with cream in it. The butter tasted better than ice cream on the hot bread. And the strong coffee matched the buttery sweetness of the molasses.

"The MacB-B-Banes will build another brush arbor," Joe said.

"They should build a rock church," Pa said. "Except then it would get just like all the other churches."

"They could meet in somebody's house," I said.

"It's not the s-s-s-same if you gather in somebody's parlor," Joe said. "You need a sp-sp-special dedicated place."

I saw what he meant, for I didn't even want to talk about the service, and what happened to me, now that we was among ordinary things. I wasn't ashamed. But it wouldn't be the same to have a service right in the living room. It would be hard to give yourself to such a meeting. Maybe I was a little embarrassed. I flicked another crumb of sawdust off my dress.

"Why it's two o'clock in the morning," somebody said. It was Florrie standing in the doorway in her nightgown, frowning.

"Do you want some cornbread and molasses?" I said.

"I just got up to see who was making all the fuss," Florrie said.

CHAPTER TWO

Everybody always said I was the most high-strung of the Peace children, but the hardest working. Sometimes I work because I can't stand not to be doing something, because I don't know where to look or where to put my hands. Other times I'll get so interested in a job I can't think of anything else. It will be like I forget I am me, and just think of the job, of what my hands is doing. That's when I feel the best, when I don't even think about myself, but about what needs to be done. I guess that's when I'm most at myself, when I don't even worry about it.

People say I got the "Italian" look from the Peaces and the Richardses. It's true I have Pa's black eyes and hair. But I got Mama's fair skin and height. People talk that way all the time, like they know why people look the way they do. But I don't think we know much about why people are what they are. Some children don't take after their parents at all. And I sure can't see traits going back several generations, to Italian, a trace of Italian, blood, or Indian blood, all the way to South Carolina, and Pennsylvania, and back to New Jersey and Wales even before that. I think we are just like God made us and we don't ever know much about our ancestors or what they did.

They always said I had a way of my own, and that much I'll agree to. I never did want to be anybody else. Some said it was because Mama died when I was young, and I never had anyone to bring me up but my sister Florrie. There was nobody else to show how a girl ought to be. Some said it was because I fought with Florrie from the time I was a youngun and didn't have a chance to learn manners. Others said it was after Pa took me to the meetings that I got mixed up and nervous. And still others said it was because I read too many books that I acted quair.

But from the time I was just a little girl I always did pitch in if there was somebody sick. I visited the shut-ins and took plates of chicken to the bereaved. Even as a girl I went to poundings for somebody that had their house burnt and took a pound of coffee or of sugar, or a piece of ham meat. I wasn't more than fifteen when I helped wash and lay out a corpse. It was old Miss MacDowell up on Rock Creek that dropped dead while she was rendering lard. I helped put her on the cooling board and clean her up and even washed her hair.

People liked to say I was a worse bookworm than Pa and I reckon that was true too. Even as a girl I subscribed to the *Moody Monthly* and *American Magazine*. Pa took the Toledo paper and I read that too. And we got this magazine from Ohio called *The Telescope* that I went through every page of. I liked to read early in the morning before daylight. I'd get up and make coffee and read in the kitchen when the house was still quiet. That was the time I liked best, for it was cool in summer and too early to milk the cows. And in winter I'd get the fire going in the stove and have coffee and read before daylight, before Joe and Locke, my brothers, got up. Florrie never did wake up till she had to.

People always liked to have Florrie around, because she was fun and told jokes. But the truth is she was a little silly, always talky and boy crazy. I hate to say it, but a lot of women and girls appeared to me just plain shallow. They didn't have a thing on their minds but gossip. And Florrie always was a little lustful. She married early and liked to say that I was becoming an old maid. I never tried to discuss with her about men, but, like I say, she let me know several times she had gone with David before they got married. I couldn't help but wonder where they had done it, for both our house and the Latham house was always full of people. I guess I was really a little jealous of her.

From age fourteen on I had gone to picnics with young folks from school and walked home from time to time with a boy after church. That's the way we did things back then. A boy was interested, he walked you home after meeting. But I had only one beau before I met Tom. He was the schoolteacher for a term, named Simcox. He was from Asheville, and like all teachers back then he boarded around the community. That was part of his pay. When he boarded with us him and me got to talking. We talked way into the night after I washed the dishes. He had read more books than anybody I ever met, and he knowed all about Egypt. Everybody else had gone to bed, and we set there talking while the fire died down. The talking got slower and it was getting cold in the room.

Finally he stood up like he was going to bed. I stood too, and he looked at me. He pulled me to him and kissed me, not a deep kiss but just a meeting of lips. I didn't know what to think, but it felt good. I didn't want him to stop, but he pulled away like he had done something wrong. And he wasn't looking when he stepped back right into the churn. I had set the milk by the fire to clabber. He tried to catch his balance but the churn tripped him. Down he went and the churn tipped over and sour milk poured over the hearth and over him. Some even splashed in the fireplace and hissed and smelled like scorched sour milk will.

Pa and Locke come to the door to see what was the matter.

"The churn tipped over," I said to Pa. I wanted to laugh, but I didn't. Pa and Locke went on back to bed.

I looked at Mr. Simcox like I was about to bust out giggling. But he wasn't laughing at all. His face was all red and looked sweaty. I think him and me could have made a go of it if he had been able to laugh then, when he was getting up and wiping off the sour milk. I liked him a lot. But he took it too serious, and we never did get closer after that. Oh, we walked up to the spring at twilight and back several times. And we set by the fire talking about every kind of thing you could think of. But we never did relight the spark. He had got too embarrassed. Some men don't ever forgive you if you see them in a pickle. Locke teased me something terrible for months, saying, "When is Mrs. Simcox going to have supper ready?" and "Is the learned Mr. Simcox going to join us?" When the school term was over Mr. Simcox went back to Asheville and I never saw him again.

I thought I was too tall for the boys to like me. I put up my long black hair as was the fashion then, and wore my white blouses. I reckon I read too much.

Pa was always an easy mark for peddlers. They would come through in those days with packs on their backs, or in buggies. Most was recent comers to America that spoke with accents. Pa loved to talk, and welcomed them for dinner, sometimes for the night. And he nearly always bought something. He said I was too suspicious of strangers, especially ones selling something.

One of them was Ahmed, from Palestine, who had arrived in Greenville only a year or two before. On his first trip through the mountains he carried everything in his pack, a few pieces of cloth, needles, thread, thimbles, small vases of brass and pewter. His English was barely understandable, but his patience and cheer was endless. I was breaking beans on the porch the first time Ahmed arrived.

He walked into the yard sweating and out of breath, but he took off his pack and begun showing his wares. He brought out one piece of silk or linen after another, and holding them to the light would say, "Is a nice, madam, no?" He kept repeating the words and showing the scarves and strings of lace, while I went on breaking beans. Finally he reached into the bottom of the pack and brought out an afghan with apricot and gold and green workings on it. "And now for the woman of taste," he said.

He asked ten dollars for it. I offered five.

"Madam, I have wife and many chindren in the old country who must come to 'is country." He spread the afghan over a chair. "For such work it would be a sin to take less than nine dollars," he said. I offered him five again and kept snapping beans.

"Is impossible," he said. "You want me to starve, and all my little chindren?" He folded the afghan and placed it on the pack.

When Pa returned from the field at dinnertime Ahmed and I was still talking on the porch. He had dropped his price to seven dollars, but I refused to give any. I think it was the work of stringing beans that made me so firm, for I did want the afghan.

Pa introduced hisself and invited Mr. Ahmed to stay for dinner. They set on the porch and talked while I fixed bread and taters and roastnears to go with the beans. The peddler brought out his wallet and showed Pa a picture of his wife and children, brothers and sisters. When he made enough money, he said, he was going to have his own store in Greenville and "sell nothing but the best." In fact, even now he sold "nothing but the best."

Before he eat, Mr. Ahmed brought out a little book and read from it, after Pa said grace. Pa asked if that was the Bible.

"Yes, yes, the words of the prophet."

"Do you believe in Jesus in your religion?" I said. I knew it wasn't exactly the thing to say, but I wanted to know.

"Yes, yes, he also was a great prophet."

"Then you do believe in the Lord?"

"Yes, yes, in the great lord, Allah." Mr. Ahmed went for the cornbread and new beans and taters. But he would not touch the buttermilk, asking instead for water. The roastnears he eat with special relish. Afterwards he spread the afghan on the cedar chest in the living room. "And for you, kind lady, only six dollars and a half," he said.

I shook my head.

"But is worth ten. How can I live?" he said.

"Ginny can be stubborn," Pa said. "Here, I'll give you six and a half."

"No, you won't," I said. "Five dollars is all it's worth."

But Pa got the money from the leather purse he kept in his

closet and paid Mr. Ahmed in silver dollars and one half-dollar. "Ginny's a good girl, but stubborn," he said to the peddler.

The first time I met Tom Powell it must have been at church. Most people like to claim they fell in love when they first saw each other. I reckon that's the way they remember it, because that's the way they think it should have been. But I have to be honest. The first time I saw Tom I was just curious.

What I recall seeing first was the big blond mustache Tom had. It was at the church picnic, and in sunlight his mustache shined like crystal. I thought, That man is built awful strong, and his mustache makes him seem even bigger. He wasn't much taller than me, but he looked stout, like he was used to lifting logs and splitting rails, which I found out was true.

They had put watermelons in the spring to cool, and then after dinner, and after they had sung hymns in the hot church for hours, Pa and Joe and other deacons sliced the melons. It was late August and the watermelons was so ripe they split with a crack when you touched a knife into them. I offered a piece to Tom, and thought, How is he going to eat through that big drooping mustache? I handed him a fine slice, and I was curious.

"Thank you," he said and took the dripping melon. It was the nineties and he had on a flat straw boater hat and one of those suits with narrow lapels and a shirt collar tall enough to choke a body. He even had a cane which he hung over his left arm.

I was busy passing slices to everybody, old folks and young-uns, but I wanted to keep my eye on the new feller to see if he got his mustache wet. I handed a special piece with no seeds to the song leader, and I cut another slice for Preacher Jolly.

When I turned back around I didn't see Tom at first. He had got under the shade of one of the big oak trees. And he had took out his pocketknife and was calmly cutting little pieces and putting them in his mouth. He wasn't getting a drop of juice on his suit or mustache. That was my first lesson in how careful he was. Didn't anything hurry him. And he had found the best spot in the shade while most folks was busy talking and sweating in the sun and little kids spit black seeds on each other.

"Howdy," I said.

"How do," he said. "I'm Tom Powell."

"Where you from?" I said.

"I work over at the Lewis place," he said. You could tell he wasn't used to wearing fine clothes. His face was sunburned and his hands was rough. In the collar and cuffs he looked stiff as a man in the pillory. I felt sorry for him, knowing he was ill at ease. I had never felt sorry before for a man like that.

"You ain't been to church before," I said.

"I go down to Crossroads," he said. Under his Sunday clothes he looked powerful the way a horse looks powerful. His shoulders was so broad it seemed he could lift the corner of a house.

"You should come back to visit us," I said. I couldn't believe I heard myself saying it.

He looked at a stain of melon juice on his pants. Careful as he'd been, the piece had dripped. "What a shame," I said.

"Ain't nothing," he said.

"Come down to the spring and you can sponge it off," I said, "quick, before it dries."

"Where is the spring?" Tom said.

"It's just a ways down this road," I said.

We started walking toward the spring. That's what courting couples did after church in those days. The road by the spring was maybe half a mile, but in several places it went under trees, and there was side trails off into the pines on the pasture hill. The excuse was always that they was walking to the spring for a drink. Older folks smiled when they saw young people go that way, and kids giggled and sometimes hid in the thicket and throwed rocks at couples kissing under the white pines. Many a marriage got started on that walk to the spring.

Tom and me ambled down the road in the August heat. It was cooler in the shade, but deerflies and gnats was out. I had on this big hat with flowers on top. It was the kind of floppy hat women wore back then. I brushed flies and gnats away. It didn't seem dignified to slap at them. But in the shade above the spring the air was whining with bugs. A breeze come up. After a hot day in August it will oftentimes blow in a storm.

We had been so busy talking, or I had been so busy talking, I hadn't noticed any clouds over the mountain to the south. I raised my hand to brush a gnat away and hit the rim of my hat. The breeze snatched it and lifted it above the road and into the trees below the road. Tom reached after the hat and missed.

Wind knocked the hat right down through the trees toward the spring branch. It looked like a big white and pink bird flopping through the woods, bouncing off limbs and saplings.

"Oh no," I said. Tom was after it like a hound after a rabbit. He run down through the brush and hemlocks, trying to catch the hat on his cane.

"Let it go," I hollered. "Come back."

But he had started out after my hat and he was determined to get it. He disappeared in the hemlocks going toward the pasture. I was embarrassed all this trouble had happened over my silly hat. I picked my way around the hill toward the fence, trying not to catch my Sunday skirt on briars or holly bushes. It was a good ways to the edge of the pasture.

Pa had been one of the first to put in barbed wire. He said it was easier than splitting rails, and would last longer too. He put the barbed wire around the pasture where he kept the bull.

By the time I got to the fence Tom was already in the pasture. Wind jerked my hat in little hops over the grass, and he kept trying to pin it down with his cane. Every time it looked like he had caught it the breeze jerked the hat further along.

"Don't matter," I hollered.

Just then the bull come around the rise. He started running right at Tom, straight ahead in a beeline. Then Tom saw the bull. He jumped up and started for the fence.

"Hurry hurry hurry," I hollered. I stood at the fence and pushed the top wire down so he could jump over it easy.

The bull stopped for half a second, then charged as if shot from a cannon. Tom was maybe a hundred feet from the fence, and it appeared he was stretching to reach the strands while his feet was way behind pushing on the grass. I never saw a man reach so far, with the hat in one hand and the cane in the other.

I pushed the top wire further down and he kind of turned sideways and hopped across the fence still holding the hat and cane. He made it except the pants on his left leg caught on a barb and ripped a tear maybe a foot long in the cloth. The bull run right into the fence and stuck his head through, snorting.

"Get away, Bill-Joe," I said. "You get away."

My hat had pieces of grass and little bits of trash stuck to it. Tom handed it to me like something I might not even want.

"You shouldn't have gone to such trouble," I said.

His face was red from the heat and from the running. And I guess he was embarrassed too. His straw hat had been lost by the branch, and his blond hair was all messed up. The tear in his pants was so big I could see white skin through it.

"I'm sorry," I said. "This old hat wasn't worth it." I had ordered the hat from the catalogue from Chicago for exactly $2.98. And now it was dirty and probably couldn't be wore again.

"I better look for my hat," he said. While he was poking around in the brush down by the branch I glanced up at the sky. A cloud passed over the sun and it got dark all of a sudden, like you had put a light out. Something snapped in the air straight above, and there was thunder at the very top of the sky. Then there was a flash over the mountains, and booms faraway.

"It's going to rain," I hollered. He had found his hat in the branch and was wiping it off. The wind come harder all of a sudden, as if it sprung out of the shadows. There was a big flash, and then a boom off the sides of the mountains, and I heard this roar. It was a sound I knowed only too well, having growed up across the river from the mountain. Sure enough, the top of the ridge was already white with rain. Rain at a distance looks like fog that stretches down, pulled straight down.

Just then lightning snapped like a sheet tearing in the sky above us. Rain was marching down the mountain across the river valley. "We're going to get soaked," I said.

"How far is it to the house?" Tom said.

"It's around the hill there," I said and pointed.

We started running along the fence toward the road from the spring. Thunder banged like boulders dropped on a roof. I took Tom's arm and pulled him along. He seemed a little dazed by all that had happened, by the thunder and roar of the coming rain.

A big poplar was up ahead. It was the yellow poplar beside the strawberry bed, the one we used to call Joe's Poplar because he would slip away from hoeing strawberry vines and set in the shade there. It was one of those poplars that seem to go up to the sky and look like they've been there since the beginning of creation. I pulled Tom toward the tree.

Rain crossed the river and was coming in walls of gray over the fields and hemlocks by the house, advancing up the branch.

The rain hit us not ten steps from the poplar. The drops felt big as nickels and quarters as they stung my neck and shoulders. We dashed through the red dirt and stood close to the trunk of the poplar, out of breath and already wet. The drops had soaked through my blouse. Big drops hammered on the leaves above us.

"How come rain is so cold if it comes from where lightning is?" I said.

"Maybe falling cools it off," Tom said.

I shivered as more drops soaked through my blouse. I had let go of his hand when we got under the tree. We stood up close to the sooty bark of the poplar.

"This rain will wash the dust off the corn," I said.

"Have to wait a week longer to pull fodder," Tom said.

A cricket, the first cricket I had noticed, started chirping at the foot of the poplar. It was a big black meadow mole with a mellow note. "Six weeks till frost," I said. I looked at Tom and he leaned over and kissed me. He put his hand under my chin and his mustache tickled my nose and the sides of my mouth. But his lips was firm. Just then a big cold drop hit me on the forehead and run down my nose. We pulled apart and laughed.

There was a flash, like the air was stung. It felt like the air prickled and crackled. Lightning had hit a pine on the hill. Thunder shoved us and we saw the pine tree catch fire as it busted all to pieces. Limbs and big splinters went flying. A smoking piece of wood landed in the mud just in front of us.

Rain blowed in right under the poplar then, and lightning hit a tree further up the hill. "We better get away from here," I said, "before this tree is hit."

"Ain't no place safe," Tom said. The air had a sharp smell, like scorched resin and hot sap in wood. But there was something like bleach too, or smelling salts that burn your eyes.

Lightning kept hitting like it was walking around us. And the thunder made us feel inside a big drum. "Let's go," I said and took Tom's hand. We started running, and rain hit my face in splashes that could have been throwed from buckets.

There is a strange feeling of protection when you are out in a storm. The rain and wind drive you deep into the shelter of yourself. Even with rain crashing on your face it's like you're way inside and watching the storm.

The road to the house swung round the hill, toward the barn, but the shortest way was to cut through the pasture. Once we got past the bull pasture we climbed the slick rail fence and run by the molasses furnace.

Lightning hit other places higher on the hill. Fire appeared to leap out of the trees to meet the bolts coming from the sky. "The Lord help us," I said, and pulled Tom along the wet trail.

But just when we got past the molasses furnace I heard this other roar. It was the sound fire makes when chimney soot catches. Or it sounded like a train going through a tunnel.

"Wait!" Tom said, and pulled me back. I don't know how he saw what was happening. He jerked me back so fast I almost slipped on the muddy trail. And then I saw this bucket Pa had left by the furnace go flying in the air like it was swung on a rope. And next a barrel for water to rinse the skimming ladle went soaring up in a curve. The roof of the furnace shed shot up and away.

It come to me this was the end of time, but instead of the souls of this world took up in Rapture it was the things of this world carried off into the sky.

"It's a twister," Tom said, "a little twister. Run!"

"I ain't running," I said. I planted my feet in the mud and faced the ugly thing. If it was my doom I might as well look at the thing fair and square.

Tom stayed with me. I guess he figured it wasn't any use to run either. He held up his stick as though it was a sword. The twister come on closer, and it was like looking into a furnace of burning water. The wind raged with madness. My hat was jerked off and sucked into the wind. The handkerchief in my sleeve was pulled out and flung into the black whirl. My blouse was covered with spots of mud and my face was too. My hair was wet and my skirt was soaked. My blouse had pulled out at the waist and my Sunday shoes was wet and muddy.

As the twister crossed the branch we could hear it sucking up water. Even above the roar of the rain and wind it sounded like the sky was swallowing through a big straw. All the water that fell as rain was being pulled up to the sky again.

"No use to hurry now," I said. We walked through the pasture, splashing in big puddles. Tom's suit was covered with mud and his new collar had melted. I held his arm and we walked like a couple promenading through the streets of Greenville. "Perfect weather for a stroll," I said.

When we got to the house Pa was standing on the porch, just out of the drip. "Was you caught in a flashtide?" he said.

"We got chased by your bull," I said, "and by the Devil hisself." Tom and me busted out laughing. Looking at ourselves on the porch, there wasn't anything else to do.

CHAPTER THREE

While Tom and me was courting, my brother Locke come back from the army on furlough, and his first night home we stayed up late. Locke was always a mighty talker, when he got going. He had served as a nurse on a hospital ship at Havana, and he had lived in Washington, D.C., and in the Philippines. He brought me a toy rickshaw from Tokyo. I fixed dinner for the whole family.

"Do you go to church in the army?" I asked him.

"Most of the time there's no church to go to," Locke said. He had never attended services with much enthusiasm when he was home. I was just needling him a little, to see what he would say.

"I read the Bible from time to time," he said, "and a book a friend gave me called *Science and Health*."

"Why that's Christian Science!" Pa said.

"It's interesting," Locke said. "It makes a lot of sense."

"I've heard it's h-h-h-heathenism," Joe said.

I poured more coffee for David and Pa and a little for myself.

"It's not heathenism," Locke said.

"Then what is it?" Pa said.

"It teaches thought is more important than anything else," Locke said. "Afflictions of the body are mostly in the mind."

"That's foolishness," Florrie said. "Locke, you always did have a quair streak."

"Have you studied it?" Locke said to her.

"No I ain't, but I don't need to. If I'm constipated it's not in my mind but in my guts."

"How can you criticize what you haven't read?" Locke said.

"I thought you wanted to be a doctor," Lily said, "and was studying medicine." She stuffed her handkerchief in her sleeve.

"I *am* studying medicine," Locke said, "every way I can."

Everybody at the table was silent for a second. It was early summer and still not dark outside. A whippoorwill started calling from the trees out near the barn.

"You have seen a lot of the world," David said.

"What do the Rocky Mountains look like?" Lily said. "I have always wanted to see the Rocky Mountains."

"They are mighty pretty," Locke said, "and mighty rocky." Everybody laughed. "But when I crossed them on the train I wasn't thinking about scenery. I was feeling too hungry."

"Don't the army f-f-f-feed you?" Joe said.

"They gave me money for the trip, but I spent it all in Washington. I bought medical books, and it took the last dollar I had to buy the train ticket for San Francisco."

"What did you live on?" Florrie said.

"I had forty-three cents left and bought some cheese and soda crackers in the station. I was going to make them last all the way to the Pacific Ocean. I figured if I set quiet on the train and watched the scenery and drunk plenty of water I could make it to the ship. But it takes almost a week to get from one coast to the other. I rationed myself to five crackers and a slice of cheese each meal. When the other people went to the dining car I stayed in my seat and ate soda crackers and hurried to the fountain for a drink of water."

"You must have got constipated," Florrie said.

"I got constipated and I got all tight with gas," Locke said. "But that wasn't the worst of it. By the time we had got past St. Louis and approaching Kansas City all my crackers and cheese was gone. I had to cross the whole West with nothing to eat."

"Did you pray?" Lily said. "For something else to eat?" She patted the lace collar of her lemon-colored dress.

"I prayed that the trip would be over and I would get to my ship. I set in a kind of daze all the way across Utah and Nevada. You never saw such an empty place. Sometimes I looked out at the stars above the icy peaks. Once I looked down and saw the sparkle of a stream way below as we crossed a trestle that seemed half a mile high.

"I must have dozed off, for suddenly I woke to a kind of humming and roaring. It was completely dark outside the window. I had the feeling it was time for daylight, but there was nothing but blackness outside. The roar was like a high wind.

"Suddenly the train shot out into daylight and I saw the sun on peaks above. We had been going through one of these snow sheds the Chinese coolies built to keep the deep snows from blocking the train. We had been in a kind of tunnel made of timbers.

"We come down into the valley and passed all these orchards. It was late summer and you could see people picking peaches. Far as you could look was one orchard after another. We stopped at a little town for about a minute and this woman got on and set down across from me. She put a bag beside her and took out this golden ripe peach. It was the biggest peach I'd ever seen.

"She spread a handkerchief over her lap and took a little knife out of her purse and begun to peel the peach. It was so ripe juice run off the knife even as she lifted away the long curl of skin. I watched her eat the peach in slices. When she finished that peach she took another out of the bag and begun to peel it.

"In less than an hour we got to Sacramento and the woman left her seat. She put the handkerchief and peelings in the bag and left it. I waited for her to come back, and tried to figure how many more peaches there might be in the bag. The train started pulling out and still she had not come back. I waited until we was almost outside the town, and looked up and down the aisle, then grabbed the bag. Under the peelings and wet handkerchief there was five more peaches, big and ripe and firm. I held the bag on my lap and ate one like it was an apple. Juice run down my chin but I didn't mind. When I finished that I had another. By the time we reached Oakland I had eat them all."

"And your constipation was cured," Florrie said.

"It sure was," Locke said. "It sure was."

"Who wants some popcorn?" I said.

"Did I ever tell you about the time I tricked Brother Joe?" Locke said.

"About a th-th-thousand times," Joe said.

"Tom hasn't heard it," I said. Tom had been setting at the corner of the table and hadn't said a word.

"It won't take but a second," Locke said. "Remember the ditch in the lower end of the field, before Pa put the pipe in there? Joe and I was coming back from fishing and it had got dark."

"I've heard this story," Lily said. "It's a mean story."

"Well David hasn't heard it, and neither has Tom," Locke said. He took a sip of his coffee. "I had a string of fish in one hand and my pole in the other. And when I got to where the ditch was I took a little jump, like I had crossed the ditch, and said, 'Watch out for the ditch, Joe.' Then I jumped the trench in a long leap, quiet as I could. Behind me Joe took a leap from where I had told him to and landed right in the water."

"Wasn't you nice?" Florrie said. She looked at Tom. "That's the kind of family we are. You better watch out for Locke."

"I g-g-got even," Joe said, "when we dug for zircons."

"He made me dig the pits, because I was the little brother," Locke said.

"You all dug holes all over the pasture and mountainside," I said. "And didn't find a thing."

"I wasn't looking for zircons," Locke said. "I was an explorer, like Columbus. I was looking for the route to China."

"Looking for a way to get out of hoeing corn," Florrie said.

I brought out a plate of cookies and lit the lamp at the center of the table. "When are you going to get out of the army and settle down?" I said.

"When I find a girl that suits me," Locke said.

"How are you going to meet a girl off in the army?" I said. "And what girl wants a feller with such crazy ideas and a lack of faith?" I had said more than I meant to.

"I have faith," Locke said. "I have plenty of faith."

"Ginny wants you to come back to the river and attend brush arbor meetings," Florrie said.

"I didn't say that," I said.

"It wouldn't be a bad idea," Pa said. Pa never did like to tease or argue about religion. He had a horror of disputation.

"I saw somebody that was demon-possessed when I was in the Philippines," Locke said.

"I've seen a few people that was demon-possessed closer to home," Florrie said.

"No, this man was a demoniac, like in the Bible," Locke said. "They had locked him up like he was a lunatic. A doctor who had also studied for the ministry took me with him to the prison outside Manila. We was supposed to treat the prisoners. It was a part of the army's plan to pacify the country, to send doctors and nurses out to treat the people. I was asked to go because I had studied tropical diseases.

"We went through this jail examining inmates and giving out pills. There was murderers and prisoners of war, terrorists and political prisoners. The Philippines are full of terrorists. We looked at bullet wounds and people with TB and malaria and jungle fevers you've never heard of. There was people with sores caused by funguses and ringworm, and people with gangrene. Everybody seemed glad to see us until we come to a cell where the man started screaming, 'Stay away from me. Stay away.' He had taken off his clothes and was climbing the bars like a monkey."

"Maybe he was d-d-d-descended from Darwin," Joe said. Joe was always worrying about Darwin and the theory of evolution.

"This demoniac spit at us and hollered, 'Stay away from me, stay away.' He cussed up a storm. You never heard such oaths. The strangest thing was they said he didn't even know English, and here he was swearing so I could understand him."

"What did the doctor do?" Tom said. Tom set up in his chair and put his elbows on the table.

"He demanded that the guard let us into the cell," Locke said. "The doctor walked right up and held out his hand to him. 'Be still,' he said. The doctor looked into the demoniac's eyes and the afflicted man could not take his eyes off the doctor's face, though he twitched and blinked.

"'You will come out!' the doctor said, like a sergeant giving an order. 'You will come out and leave this man in peace. You will come out and leave him forever.' And the look on the prisoner's face changed. He seemed like a different person. When he opened his eyes he smiled at the doctor and didn't seem afraid at all. He shook hands with the doctor and he shook hands with me. But do you know what was the strangest thing?"

"He decided to join the army?" Florrie said.

"He couldn't speak a word of English, or understand anything we said. Once the evil spirit left him we couldn't understand what he said. The guard had to interpret for the doctor. But the man was smiling and happy when we left him. I heard later he slept for three days he was so exhausted from the possession."

"What denomination was the doctor?" Pa said.

"I never asked him," Locke said.

"The Lord can heal anybody," I said.

"Was there any swine for the demon to go in?" Florrie said.

The whippoorwill was louder now. It had come closer to the house with its mournful croak and screech.

"That's supposed to be the voice of the dead," Locke said.

"Who are they talking to?" Lily said.

"Maybe us," Locke said. "Maybe they're telling us something."

"What tommy-rot," Florrie said.

"Whippoorwills love graveyards," Tom said. "I've noticed that."

"That's b-b-b-because it's peaceful there," Joe said.

"Spirits could be anywhere," Locke said. "Haints, if there are haints, don't have to live in one place."

"I thought you wanted to be a d-d-doctor?" Joe said.

"I do," Locke said. "But maybe not a regular kind of doctor."

"You could be a doctor like your uncle," Pa said. Pa had always got on well with his brother-in-law, Dr. Johns.

"All you have to do is learn to drink more," Florrie said.

"His pharmacopeia is simple," Locke said. "Whatever liquor is available." We all laughed, even Pa.

"He picks herbs and simples just like Mama used to," I said.

"And then soaks them in liquor," Florrie said.

"That's how you make a tincture," Pa said.

"That's how you make a hangover," Florrie said.

Locke turned to Tom. "Where are your folks from?" he said.

"From over near the line," Tom said. His face turned red. I could tell he did not like to be questioned.

"His folks come from South Carolina before the war," I said.

"Everybody's folks come from South Carolina before the war," Locke said.

"We lived over near the Lewis place," Tom said. Everybody was looking at him.

"Our grandma Richards was a Lewis," Locke said.

"But she married a Richards," Florrie said.

"How did the Richardses get to North Carolina?" Tom said, like he wanted to start Locke talking again so nobody would ask him more questions.

"The Richardses have been here a long time," Pa said, "longer than the Peaces or the Johnses."

"They come from down in Rutherford County," Florrie said. "But that was a long time ago. Who knows what happened that long ago?"

"Before that they come from Pennsylvania, and way back yonder they come from Wales," Locke said.

"I thought they went first to Saluda," Florrie said.

"No no, they come to Saluda from Mountain Creek in Rutherford County," Pa said.

"Word is they was the first on Green River," Locke said.

"Except for th-th-th-the Indians," Joe said.

"Our great-great-great grandma was named Petal Jarvis," Locke said. "She thought her husband Realus was bringing her to Tennessee. But he wound her around through the mountains till she was lost and then told her it was the Holston when they settled down near Saluda."

"Just like a man," Lily said, and punched Joe on the shoulder.

"She had to stay up all night once to keep a panther from coming down the chimney," Locke said. "Her husband had gone off and left her by herself. She burned up all the furniture."

"And she give birth to her first child that night," I said.

"By herself?" Tom said.

"He left her all by herself," Locke said.

"Tom's Pa died in the war," I said. I didn't want it to sound like we was bragging on our family too much.

"What battle did he die in?" Locke said.

"He died in prison camp, in Illinois," Tom said.

"That camp was as bad as Elmira," Pa said. "A third of the boys at Elmira died in eight months."

"Where was the doctors?" Locke said.

"They didn't have any doctors," Pa said. "All the doctors was on the battlefield. And the doctor assigned to us sold the medicine and supplies instead of giving them to the prisoners."

I poured popcorn in the pan on the stove and put the lid over it. The first pop was like the report of a little gun, and then there was a second bang. The room was silent for a moment, and there was another thump in the pan, and then two at once.

"Popcorn w-w-waits for the Spirit to move it," Joe said.

"How did you become a nurse?" Tom said to Locke.

"It was the only thing he could do," Florrie said.

"That's right," Locke said. "I was too lazy to stay on the place and help Pa and Joe. And I was too poor to go to college, and too dumb to be a politician or a lawyer. So when recruits were give bonuses to go to Cuba I signed on."

"Locke helped nurse Mama when she was dying, even though he was only eight or nine," I said.

"I found my talent was for emptying bedpans," Locke said.

"I don't see how you can stand it," Lily said, "being around sick people and filth all the time."

"I guess you have to be a caring person," Florrie said.

"Or get so hard nothing bothers you," Locke said. "How can you help people if you're always wrought-up because they are sick? You've got to keep your head even when they are out of theirs and suffering and dying. I found that when I enlisted and was sent to the hospital ship at Havana. I was nineteen and I didn't know anything but a little folk medicine. They put me on a ship that was nothing but a death ward. It was so hot and muggy the harbor stunk. That ship was full of hundreds of dying men."

"All those was wounded at San Juan Hill?" I said.

"There was almost no wounded. Most of the boys had yellow fever and malaria, with a few other tropical diseases thrown in, and cholera and dysentery. I said, Locke, you're not going to be able to get through this."

"You got through it," Florrie said. "You even got a medal."

"That all came later," Locke said. He set back in his chair and chewed popcorn. The whippoorwill had moved to the arborvitae by the front porch and was louder than ever.

"That thing gives me the chills," Lily said.

Tom looked at his strong hands and clasped them and unclasped them. "What did you do?" he said to Locke.

"I looked at those dark wards on the ship, and I wished I was back here on the river. And all those sick boys out of their heads and dying made me feel hopeless and useless. Everything was going to pieces there. A patient was dying, and they was holding smelling salts or something in a bottle to his nostrils. Another patient was screaming out of his head, 'The devil is eating my hair. Please help me, the devil is eating my hair.' And suddenly this sick man right behind me started throwing up. He retched over his sheets and mosquito netting, and over the floor. You could tell he was too sick to care. I found a mop and bucket at the end of the ward and drew water from a faucet.

Pouring in a little antiseptic I hurried back to the bed of the nauseous patient. He was throwing up again. I held a bedpan under his chin and put my left hand on his sweaty forehead. He was white as a mushroom.

"As soon as he had stopped and laid back I pulled off the soiled sheets and spread clean ones under and over him. Then I begun mopping around the bed. I was sweating in that awful heat as though under water. But the bed and floor was fresh and clean. I got hold of myself through hard work. Wasn't anything else would get me through. I had to help out and I had to clean up what I could. I have never worked so hard before or since as on that ship. I was more than myself, and better than myself. It seemed I become the work, and was no longer me at all.

"From the doctors and other nurses I borrowed what books I could. On my own I studied anatomy and pathology and the drugs in the dispensary, and I talked with anybody that was willing about surgery and internal medicine. That's why I read *Science and Health*, because I wanted to read anything that was new to me. I felt I might learn from anything. I felt strong because of my work and curiosity. I could take criticism and admit my own ignorance. I was getting enough confidence to make me humble."

Locke paused and it was quiet around the table for a few seconds. "Once Locke starts talking he won't stop unless you hit him over the head," Florrie said.

"I become a talker in the army," Locke said.

"You was always a big talker," Florrie said.

"You become a good nurse, I bet," David said.

"You're only as good as the job you're doing," Locke said. "It's not as though you build up credit or a permanent ability. A surgeon is as good as the cutting he's doing at the moment."

I could see that caught Tom's attention. He had been listening all along, but really woke up when Locke started talking about raising yourself above yourself through work. "I guess all work is that way," he said to Locke.

"Maybe so," Locke said. "But I know it's true for nursing."

"It's a wonder you didn't catch something yourself," Pa said, "around all those sick people."

"Hard work is the best immunity," Locke said. "And I'm careful to wash my hands and not touch my nose or mouth when working. Of course I wouldn't want to work around a TB clinic."

"When are you going to get married?" Florrie said. She took the last of the popcorn from the bowl.

"When I find somebody that will have me," Locke said. He helped hisself to another cookie.

CHAPTER FOUR

Tom come back to visit again the following Saturday night. I soon learned he did not like to go out in crowds, as though he was afraid the public might steal something from him. And later I learned he did not like staying up late at night, as if the dark was evil and dangerous and the only safety was in sleep.

He could not remember his pappy. His pappy had gone off to the war and never come back. Tom and his sister Becky and his ma had to look after the place in the hard years after the war. His ma had to plow with the horse same as a man, and get in firewood. Soon as Tom could he was helping her butcher hogs and gather corn in the wagon. When he was eleven or twelve he hired hisself out to work for Colonel Lewis over at the Lewis place.

When Tom showed up that Saturday evening I invited him to set on the porch. Pa liked to rest there in the evening and talk until it was dark. Like Locke, Pa loved to talk more than anything else, except to go to preaching. Him and Joe and Locke could make up stories and tell jokes for hours.

"H-h-how are you?" Joe said to Tom.

"Howdy," Pa said.

"How do?" Tom said.

"Your pa was named Tom too," Pa said. "I remember him."

"He was named Tom," Tom said. Tom looked at his shoes, and he looked out at the pines beyond the branch.

"He was in the Sixty-fourth Infantry as I recollect," Pa said. "They did some terrible fighting in that battle not too far from Chancellorsville, but after Chancellorsville. I can't remember what it was called. They got pinned down and the smoke was so thick they couldn't tell friend from foe."

"Was that The W-w-wilderness or the Seven Days?" Joe said.

Tom did not answer. I could not tell if he didn't know what brigade his pappy had served in, or if he just didn't want to talk about it. His face turned slightly redder. I figured the thing to do was get him off the porch, for I wanted to be alone with him and talk to him myself.

And besides, I wanted to touch him. He was the first man I ever felt that way about. It was something about the way he was made. He was so strong and compact. I saw he was made more like a pony than a horse, not tall but powerful and calm in his strength if he didn't have to talk and explain anything. He wanted to work and do. I could see it was a pain for him to talk to strangers, and tell about hisself. He was comfortable with his strong hands and broad shoulders. I felt if I could touch him I would feel calm too, and things might work out in the future. He had got his suit mended. I reckon it was the only suit he had.

"Let's walk out to the Sunset Rock," I said. The sun had gone down but there was a glow in the west, over Chimney Top and the ridge at the head of the river.

"You-all stay away from twisters, Ginny," Pa said.

"We'll just stay away," I said, and laughed.

It was one of those evenings in late summer when you can feel fall in the breeze. The air thrills, like when you touch silver in a drawer. The grass and weeds get cold and damp soon as the sun goes down, and you smell the corn leaves ready to be pulled as fodder and cured. There is the smell of old weeds with dust and dew on them. Even while there is a glow in the west a star comes out like a bright face watching you.

"What is the Sunset Rock?" Tom said. We walked out the road behind the log barn.

"It's a place on the west side of the pasture hill, where I used to watch the sun go down when I was a girl." I didn't tell him I still went out there sometimes after milking, to see the full spread of the western sky when it was gold and red.

"Who named it Sunset Rock?" he said.

"I named it when we was kids," I said.

Crickets in the weeds sounded like little silver notes. When we walked by they stopped, but soon as we got past they went on singing. The katydids was starting to make a racket in the trees on the hill and there was a jarfly off in the oaks by the river.

I made as though I slipped on the wet grass and took Tom's arm. He put his hand on mine. A shiver went through me. He gripped my hand and waist. Tom had confidence in hisself, in anything to do with his body. I don't think I had ever touched such certainty. He was at home with hisself in a way I had never seen, at least once he got away from Pa and Joe. He wasn't all anxious and worried like I was, and he wasn't trying to think of something witty or wise to say like Pa was. Maybe he thought he wasn't able to be witty and wise and didn't even try.

The trail around the hill come out of pines to this big rock. Though the air was cool the rock was still warm from the day's sun. We climbed up and set like it was a warm hearthstone. Flies had gathered there to the heat and they buzzed around us.

"How much land do you own?" Tom said, looking up the river valley.

"Pa owns to the bend in the river," I said, pointing.

"And how far down does he own?" Tom said.

"His property goes down to the mouth of Schoolhouse Branch," I said. I could see his interest, how his thinking was going. But it didn't matter to me. Maybe it should have, but I didn't care. Tom didn't have any land of his own and it was natural he would be attracted to this fine bottomland. It made sense that he would fall in love with the land as much as with me.

"We own from the river all the way to the top of the ridge yonder," I said, and pointed to the summit where Pa put his peach and apple orchard.

"The ridge is the right place for peaches," Tom said, "to keep them from budding too early and getting killed."

"The line runs all the way to the church," I said. "Pa give the land for the church."

I leaned closer to him. "Pa is going to give me the house and the big flat bottom," I said.

Tom didn't say a thing, but I could feel him thinking. It excited me because he was excited. And because I understood him. I had never felt before that I understood a man that well. I was afraid of him a little, but I knowed what he was thinking. When I was around other boys I felt how big my hands and feet was, and how tall I was. And how I read too much. But when I was with Tom I felt attractive. I couldn't have explained it.

"I come out here to look up the valley and feel close to God," I said. Tom did not answer. "Sometimes I just repeat Bible verses in my mind. This is a good place to think and pray. After Mama died I used to come here and set for hours."

"What was that?" Tom said, and turned toward the north. I looked but didn't see anything but the stars coming out over Olivet Ridge. It was on the way to getting dark.

"We'll step on a snake going back," I said.

"Not if we go slow," Tom said. "Give them time to get away."

"Snakes are blind this time of year," I said.

"They ain't," Tom said.

"That's what I've heard. Snakes crawl blind in Dog Days."

"I seen a pilot the other day, and it could see well as ever."

"Then why do people say it?"

"Cause they like to scare theirselves, I reckon."

Just then I saw something in the north. It was like a spike drove in the sky. Sparks shot from the point. There was another, like a nail on fire an instant. And another, and another.

"Meteors," I said. "This is August, when meteor showers come."

This line of fire streaked in the north and cut across the sky. It was coming right at us. The light got bigger, and then melted into sparks. There was a puff of sound.

I tried to think of something I had read about meteors. What famous thing had been foretold by a shooting star? I leaned against Tom and shivered. It was dark now in the west. The only light was from the stars, and the katydids got louder than ever.

"What makes them shoot so fast?" Tom said.

"They're pieces of rock from way out in space," I said. "They burn up when they hit the air." I went on, remembering what I had read about meteors in *The American Magazine*.

"How could air make rocks burn up?" Tom said.

"Cause they are moving so fast."

"I don't believe it," Tom said. But from the way he said it I could tell he must be grinning.

"It's true," I said, and laughed.

Just then a bigger flare shot out of the northwest and stretched all the way over Pinnacle Mountain and Chimney Top and disappeared in the south without ever burning out.

"What if one was to hit you?" Tom said. In the dark he was talking more than I had ever heard him. That was the first time I saw he liked to talk in the dark. And I remembered that before Mama died, when I was a girl, I used to hear her and Pa talk in bed way in the night. I had forgot about it till that moment.

"People have been hit," I said. "Rocks have fell out of the sky through people's houses. A woman was ironing in Cincinnati and got hit on the head by a rock that come through the roof."

"Was she killed?"

"No, I think she was bruised." But I couldn't quite remember, except about the meteorite coming through the top of the house.

A point of fire appeared in the sky almost straight above us. It just glowed there like a coal giving off sparks, as if somebody had hung a lantern that kept getting brighter.

"It's coming toward us," I said.

The point got bigger and brighter, like somebody was blowing on it. I couldn't tell how far away it was. Sometimes it looked just overhead. The light swelled and flared. I gripped Tom's arm and wondered if we should run. But which way could we run?

"It's coming," I said. But Tom didn't answer; he looked up as if he was watching a bird flying.

I turned my head away, and then looked up again. The light was bigger and whiter. It was whitehot. As far as I could tell it was aimed straight at us. "What are we going to do?" I said, and grabbed Tom's arm even harder. I had read that if a meteor was big enough it would destroy the world. It would be like a bullet hitting a peach. A hole would be punched in the earth and all the water and fire would pour out.

When I looked up again it appeared the ball of fire was just a few hundred feet above us. It had swelled till it was the size of a washtub and bright as the sun when it comes up. "Here it comes!" I said. "Lord help us. Is this the Rapture?"

But just then the ball of fire busted into a thousand pieces. It was bigger than the fireworks you see on the Fourth, a million times bigger. Sparks and pieces of fire went streaming and showering every which way. Rags of fire shot across the sky, falling on all sides. It's going to catch the woods on fire, I thought. I reckon my mouth was open with awe and surprise.

The tatters of flame falling on every side of us went dark, either quenched or falling beyond the mountains. That was when I saw the meteor was further away than it appeared.

"Whew!" I said, and breathed. I must not have took a breath for a minute. The pasture and woods looked darker than ever.

I couldn't even see Tom, but felt his calmness in the cool air. It was like a smell that I couldn't describe. It wasn't just the soap he had washed up with after working all day, and it wasn't just the smell of his fresh ironed shirt which had got a little sweaty on the walk over from the Lewis place. He wasn't at all startled or flustered.

"Wasn't you scared?" I said.

At that instant a big light shot out of the north, bigger than the meteor we had just seen. It come low over the Olivet mountains throwing sparks like little shooting stars. It was skidding to the west. At first it was red, and then yellow and white. It was streaming and fizzing off light. My first thought was it was going to set the trees on fire it was so low.

"Where's it going?" I hollered. "It's the end of the world. It must be Jesus coming." But Tom just looked at the streak like it was a June bug playing in front of us. The fire got bigger and bigger. It appeared to be going to land in the pines, or in the river.

"It's the end of time," I said.

But the rags of fire disappeared over the trees and the night was dark again. I was blinded and couldn't see a thing for a few seconds. Then the stars come winking back. And I heard crickets in the grass and katydids on the hill. Tom set there without saying anything, and I now could hear the waterfall over at the Johnson Mill. Nothing had noticed the sky exploding except me. Tom was listening to the night sounds as usual. I hugged him close and put his arm around me. That's when I fell in love for sure. After that I just couldn't help myself.

Now people say women always fall in love with danger, that if they're not scared by a man they can't really love him. I know there's some truth to that. They say women like a man that will order them around and take charge of everything. And even a man that will threaten them. I've heard a woman brag that her husband said he would kill her if she tried to leave him, and that thrilled her because it showed how deep he loved her.

But I guess I was born different. What made me fall in love with Tom was to see how calm he was when the sky exploded and fell down in flames. He didn't have anything to say about it. He watched like it happened every night. Maybe I was so nervous and confused in my mind his calm felt mysterious and dangerous. I know you can say a thing any which way to make it sound like it makes sense. But all I know is how I felt. He didn't threaten me at all far as I could see, except it appeared he could see through me. He saw how I did things in spells of feeling, and that I was scared in ways I didn't hardly understand.

"I thought we was finished," I said. "I thought it was the end of time, and Jesus had come for sure."

"Nothing is the end of time," he said.

"It says in the Bible time will come to a stop at the Rapture," I said.

"That's what some people say," he said.

"You don't believe what you read in the Bible?" I said. I didn't know that Tom could just barely read. He hadn't gone to school but a few months in the hard times after the war.

"I don't believe everything people say about the Bible."

"But you believe in the Bible?" I said. "You believe in the signs and wonders?"

"I don't believe everybody's opinion about the Bible."

I should have been worried right there, but I wasn't. I was falling in love, and in love you see things the way you want to.

"Do you reckon it is a sign?" I said.

"What is?"

"The meteor. What do you reckon it foretells?"

"Don't know," he said. "A sign of what?"

I put my head against his. His hair smelled of sweat in the hot sun, and some kind of rose oil. "A sign for us?" I said.

"Could be," he said.

And that was our engagement. Those two words was his proposal. That was when we agreed to stay together. And to me it was as romantic as if he had got down on his knees and took off his hat and recited lines of poetry.

I could feel the heat of the sun on his neck and face. Tom had the kind of skin that was always a little flushed. It made him look more alive than others. He worked in the sun and was always a little sunburned where his hat didn't protect him. He felt warm as a stove. It was like his face give off a kind of light.

"We better go back," I said. "I bet Pa has made a pot of fresh coffee. We can have coffee and biscuits and molasses."

Tom got off the rock and lifted me down. The air was chilly now and I shivered. Everything was wet with dew.

"What if there's a copperhead?" I said. As we started back on the trail it felt like there was copperheads in front of us.

"I'll walk in front," Tom said.

"So you can rile a snake and then it will bite me," I said. It was an old joke.

"I've got on heavier shoes," Tom said.

I wanted to hurry, but the thought of snakes made me go slow. I was pushed ahead and held back at the same time. But Tom walked real slow, listening before he took a step. Pilots don't make a sound, except when they crawl. Crickets stopped when we got close, then started up again behind us. I held Tom's arm, and it was like he was working and searching. Walking without stepping on a snake was a job and he was going to do it well. Everything for him was work. To me everything he did was wonderful.

"What is that?" Tom said, and stopped.

There was a rustling in the grass. I held my breath and listened. It sounded like a mouse running. But all was dark, and I couldn't see Tom in front of me. "What is it?" I said.

"No!" Tom said, and jumped back, kicking in the dark. He stomped the grass, and I heard something flopping around.

"What is it?" I said.

He stomped on the ground like he was trying to put out a fire. "Stay back," he said.

"What is it?"

He kicked at something again. "I can't see," he said.

Then he started on down the trail and I followed him. It seemed he was limping a little, but I couldn't be sure. I didn't hold his arm anymore, but stayed a foot or two behind him. He seemed to drag his foot in the grass.

There was a light on in the house, and Pa had left the door open so a streak of lamplight fell across the porch. Tom climbed up the steps and stood in the light. "Get me a stick," he said.

There was a pile of stovewood on the porch and I brought him a piece. He slammed the wood down hard on the porch near his foot. I strained my eyes in the dim light and saw a snake there, a little snake. The tail was twitching.

Pa come to the door and asked what was it.

"Bring a light," Tom said.

"Where did the snake come from?" I said.

Pa returned with the lamp and held it down close to Tom's leg. I bent over to see better. There was a little copperhead laying there with its back broke. "Did it bite you?" I said.

It was the strangest thing you ever saw. The snake fangs had gone into the leather of Tom's shoe and I guess they had got stuck. Then when he jumped back and started kicking and stomping, the head had got tangled in his laces. I reckon he had half killed the snake by stomping on it. And then he dragged it all the way to the house because he couldn't see what had happened.

He held the snake down with the piece of wood and untangled and untied the laces. Where the snake's fangs had gone into the leather it was all wet with venom. It looked like somebody had poured syrup on the shoe. Of course there was dew on the shoe also, and pieces of grass and clover blossoms.

When the snake was loose from the strings Tom mashed its head with the stick of wood.

"I never saw such a little pilot," I said.

"It's a young snake," Tom said.

"Young snakes are just as poison as big ones," Pa said.

There was two tears in the leather where the fangs had gone in. "I wouldn't touch that place," I said.

"It won't hurt unless you have a cut in your skin," Tom said.

"Come on in," Pa said. "I just made a fresh pot of coffee."

The light hurt my eyes when we went inside. I blinked like I was waking up. The smell of fresh coffee filled the house. Pa always did know how to make the best coffee. I think he learned during the Confederate War when coffee was so scarce you had to make every bean count. There is nothing like the smell of coffee. It fills the air and suggests richness and confidence, earth and harvests. It makes you feel like taking hold of things.

"I never seen nothing like that," Pa said, looking at Tom's shoe. "You got lucky."

"I was," Tom said.

Joe had long gone back to his own house across the hill. While Pa commenced to tell about the rattlesnake he saw as a boy that laid in wait for people on a high bank and could jump across the road, I started to make biscuits to go with the coffee. I already had the dough made up, and I just rolled it out, cut the biscuits, and baked them. I had made the dough because I thought Tom was coming. Or I had hoped he was coming.

The men kept talking, or rather Pa kept talking and Tom did the listening. I saw right off they could get along.

"It was common during the war," Pa said, "for boys to wake in the morning with snakes laying on their blankets. They crawled there for warmth I reckon. A snake ain't got no heat of its own. Gets chilled it can't hardly move. A cold snake is sleepy and won't bite you. You could pick up a cold snake and lay it on your cheek and it wouldn't bite you."

"A snake gets too hot it dies," Tom said.

"I reckon a hot snake bleeds to death inside," Pa said. "A snake gets too hot its veins melt. I seen one trapped in a sand pit by the river one time and it died by dinnertime from the hot sun. I reckon it just baked inside."

"Have some biscuits," I said. I put the plate of hot biscuits on the table, and brought plates and knives and a jar of sorghum. I poured a cup of coffee for each of us and brought a pat of butter from the back porch. I used my fanciest painted dish which usually leaned on the top shelf.

"That's a pretty dish," Tom said.

"Locke sent me that from the Philippines," I said.

I set down and we drunk the rich coffee and eat hot biscuits. Biscuits are good in the morning, but even better late at night. We passed the butter back and forth, and the jar of molasses.

"Hard to make it come out even," Tom said, after he had eat three or four biscuits.

"What do you mean?" I said.

"To make the butter and molasses and biscuits come out even," he said. "So you don't end up with some left on your plate."

"Then you just have to keep eating," Pa said. We all laughed. We was feeling merry like people do when they have good food and fellowship. You start to get a little drunk I guess when you have rich coffee and sweet biscuits.

"Can't stop until the biscuits are all gone," I said.

"These molasses was cooked too long," Tom said.

"How do you know?" I said. I quit laughing and looked at Pa.

"Cause I make molasses for the Lewises," Tom said. "These molasses is good, but a little bit thick."

"Pa makes good molasses," I said.

"No, Tom is right," Pa said. "I did overcook these a little bit. The cows got out, remember, and I had to round them up. When I got back the batch had cooked too long."

"Better overcooked than undercooked," Tom said.

CHAPTER FIVE

Sometimes when I was young I could almost taste the future. At times the sense of tomorrow delighted me so I could barely think of the present. Every instant was a threshold to the next, and every place I stood was the beginning of a new long journey.

It was a mood I had often, this thrilling sense of time arriving and arriving in an endless flood of blessing. I was wealthy in time. The next minute and the next hour, the next day and the next year, was shining with promise.

My sense of the future was more like New Year's than any other holiday. Christmas was thrilling with its carols and candles, brilliant wrappings, cakes and cookies, oranges and spirit of giving, its mystery of birth and lighted trees, and hush at midnight. But it was after the holiday was over, after the tree was down and the mistletoe and turkey's paw thrown out, the gifts put away and wrappings folded to be used next year, and the last of the cakes and hard candies eat, that the best pleasure come. It was the return to the ordinary, to everyday life on New Year's Day, that moved me most. With the decorations put away and the trimmings, there was such openness in the house. There was a spirituality in the absence and emptiness. The morning of New Year's Day the light was different.

I would get so excited I walked in the pasture without a coat just to feel the sweet wind, and newness of the air. I was so happy the holidays was over and we could return to ordinary days, the opportunity of day following day, that I glided over the grass. The ground looked washed clean by rain or snow, and the broomsedge and pines looked waxed and polished.

I can remember shivering with the mystery of space around me. It was too good to dream of that there was so much space to move through and breathe and use. That's when I felt closest to God, when the air was towering above and curving around me. I looked up the river valley to the far mountains, and I pondered the warm nest of myself in the whipping breeze.

Sometimes I run through the pasture and into the pine woods beyond the hill, then along the river where winter pools was low and clear. I run on the trail above the barn and through the orchard and along the ridge above the spring. And then I would go inside and set in the dim bedroom to calm myself. It took several minutes before I could look at things up close again.

But I would also calm myself thinking about the future. I thought how I didn't have to do anything to make the future arrive. It just come to me, as if floating on a long river.

But when I was about fifteen the strangest thing happened. I was a tall awkward girl with these big feet and big hands and everybody kept saying, "Ginny's growing up to be a pretty girl" and "Ginny's going to be a tall woman." But they kept saying it year after year, and I come to see they meant I was ugly now but I might look better later on.

Except as the years passed I kept looking the same. I knowed things was supposed to happen to a girl to make her grow into a woman, but I wasn't sure exactly what. Mama had died when I was nine, and all I had was Pa and Florrie to tell me about things. Pa never did like to talk about female things, and Florrie was already courting and ignored me as much as she could.

But I felt something was wrong, though I didn't know exactly what. And I certainly didn't know what to do about it. Florrie liked to say things like "Ginny ain't never going to grow up as long as she keeps her nose in a book." I knowed that Florrie had her monthlies and she kept rags which got soaked with blood and which she washed on the back porch and hung to dry. And she talked about how awful she felt sometimes, and the pain she had. And she liked to take powders or a drink at times for the pain. I figured it would happen to me in time and I was scared.

Nothing angered Florrie like when she thought some blood had soaked through her dress and she had to run to her room and change. Sometimes she throwed things then and banged pots together, and talked about "the curse."

For a long time I feared what was going to happen to me, and then I feared nothing was going to happen. I waited month after month and I was still awkward and gangly and my chest flat and my hips narrow. I could tell Pa worried too, though he never said anything. He didn't know what to say to a girl about her body.

"How are you feeling?" Pa would ask from time to time.

"I'm fine," I would say. He asked so many times I finally said, "Do you want me to be sick?" He turned red a little bit.

But when I snapped at Pa he never answered back. And then I felt worse for flying off.

In the end I guess he asked Florrie to talk to me. She come into the bedroom and said, "Ginny, there's something I have to know, that Pa wants to know."

I turned to face her, already angry. It was like she was accusing me of some fault. "What have I done this time?" I said.

"It's what you ain't," she said. "Have you had any bleeding?"

"I bleed when I am cut," I said.

"I mean bleeding in your . . . you know what I mean," she said.

"Why?" I said.

"Because it's time. Because you are old enough," Florrie said.

"And what if I don't?" I said.

"Then you won't have children. Only a woman that has monthlies can have children."

It was like she was accusing me yet again of being wrong. I run out of the room and out of the house. I run all the way to the springhouse and stood under the hemlocks there and cried.

Florrie didn't say anything more for a few days, and of course Pa didn't say anything either. But after about a week Mama's brother, Dr. Johns, come by and said he wanted to talk to me. Everybody disappeared and left me alone with him. He smelled like whiskey, as he always did when making his rounds. Whiskey was the medicine he mostly prescribed, and he always took a little hisself. But he was my favorite uncle. He liked to tease me. He said if I kept reading books I would be a doctor myself some day. He said my black hair made me look like an Indian or a gypsy. When I was little he brought horehound candy in his doctor's bag. I imagined the candy smelled like the whiskey on his breath. I even wondered if horehound candy might make you drunk.

"Ginny," he said to me. He made me set on the sofa in the living room, and he set down beside me. He was no bigger than I was, and seemed like a little boy hisself except for his gray beard. He had a gold watch chain that flashed in the firelight. "Ginny," he said, "do you ever feel sluggish, or heavy, or a little crazy from time to time?"

"Only when I have work to do," I said.

Dr. Johns laughed, and looked me right in the eyes. "Do you ever feel pains in your belly?" he said. "Deep in your belly?"

"Only when I eat too many apples," I said.

"You're too smart for me," he said.

"You can give me one of your tonics," I said.

"I *am* going to give you a tonic," the doctor said. "I want you to take a tablespoon three times a day, before each meal."

He handed me this bottle of black stuff. It was like a thin syrup, and you had to shake it before taking any. It was the color of Co-Cola but it didn't fizz up when shook. I don't know what all it was, except some herbs Dr. Johns had concocted for his female tonic and he sold it all over the county when he made his rounds. There was so much whiskey in the mixture it tasted like a cordial, except it had an aftertaste of anise or licorice. When I took it I tried to imagine it was some elixir that would make me beautiful with full breasts and voluptuous hips.

The tonic warmed me and made me feel better. And sometimes I took two tablespoons before a meal just to make sure I got enough. It made me feel cozy and confident, and I was sure my problem would be solved. All the medicinal weeds and barks and berries Dr. Johns knowed about had been compounded in the tincture and I was certain it would help.

But the only effect I noticed from the tonic, besides cheering me up, was it was a mild laxative. I took it every day, until the bottle was gone, and nothing happened. Pa didn't say a thing, but he was watching. Whenever he asked how I felt I always said fine, fine. But I could tell how worried he was.

For once it seemed the future might not come to me. I was somehow trapped and could not go ahead and become a woman. I would not have a marriage before me, or children. I hardly knowed what I had done to deserve it. But I felt guilty, especially when Florrie said it was because I read so many books that I had not growed normally. "A woman wasn't meant to think so much, and to keep her mind on such rot," Florrie liked to say.

"I know what you keep your mind on," I said.

"Jealousness won't help you," Florrie said.

One day Pa told me to get ready to drive down to South Carolina. It was early spring.

"Where are we going?" I said.

"To see a doctor," Pa said.

"Which doctor?"

"An Indian doctor," he said, "named Dr. Match, that doctors women's problems."

I felt awful scared but I got ready. The truth was I was so worried I would have been willing to go anywhere if it could have helped. I saw myself soon becoming an eighteen-year-old and a nineteen-year-old that couldn't ever have children.

It was so early in spring the trees was mostly bare along the river. But once we crossed the line at Saluda Gap and started down the Winding Stairs I saw the poplars had leaves like little green flames. The sarvis was in bloom high up and the dogwoods lower down. It was like we descended to spring, for by the time we got to Chestnut Springs the trees was covered with green and yellow leaves and the woods was a blur of tender colors.

Pa turned to the left toward Dark Corner and we drove over Poinsett's Bridge that my great-great-grandpa had helped build. The hollers at the foot of the mountain are deep as pits and the mountains so steep they seem to hang out of the sky. The peaks far above was blue and the woods around us almost green. We passed a waterfall and Pa turned the horse onto a smaller road, just a track, leading out through woods and over a hill.

The road come out into this little valley, and I smelled smoke. It was a perfect nest of a valley at the foot of the mountain with new-plowed fields by a creek and houses and barns scattered here and there. First thing I noticed was a pit dug into the side of a hill with a ladder down into it. A man was climbing the ladder with a heavy bucket in his hand. He wore nothing but drawers, or maybe a cloth wrapped around his middle, the way Indians used to. And he had dark skin.

As we passed the pit I could see down into it. Below the layer of brown dirt and red dirt, and meally yellow dirt, was clay white as cream. It looked as if they was digging into pale butter. It was white as the clay Pa dug out of the branch and eat a bite of every spring for a tonic.

Pa stopped the wagon in front of a shed and tied the horse to a pine tree. Smoke rose from an oven that looked like a big mud beehive. In the shed two men in breech clouts was shaping clay on a turntable. I saw it was a place that made pottery, for there was pots setting all around the shed and in front of the oven. But what was astonishing was the size of the pots. Some would hold five gallons and some was big enough for a boy to hide in. I had never seen urns or jugs that big. It would take two men to lift some of them, as it was taking two men to shape one on the turning wheel. But the jugs and big jars also had faces carved on them, with jutting noses and bulging eyes big as taters.

The path to the house was lined with pots. All had faces on them, some with bulging eyes, some with terrible grins and grimaces. Flowers filled some pots, and painted sticks was stuck in others. The yard was swept and I didn't see any chickens.

The man who come to the door was dressed like any doctor, in a black suit and stiff collar. He had silver hair and silver rimmed glasses. But his skin was dark, and he wore a string of beads around his neck big as pebbles of different colors. And he had several rings on his fingers, all set with red and blue stones.

"Are you Dr. Match?" Pa said.

"I am," the man said. "Won't you come in."

"We are here about Ginny," Pa said. "She has this trouble . . . "

"I see," the doctor said, cutting Pa off. The doctor looked at me with his black eyes like he was studying a puzzle.

"I'll wait in the wagon," Pa said.

When Pa was gone the doctor guided me inside to a table. "Sit here," he said. "I want you to talk to Madame Sparrow first."

The room was almost bare except for some feathers and wood carvings on the walls. There was big pots standing in the corners. The table had wonderful designs painted on it.

A fat woman in a maroon dress come through the curtained door. Her gray hair was braided and coiled around her head. She wore earrings of colored stones like those on the doctor's necklace. "Please hold out your hands," she said.

She took the tips of my middle fingers and looked at my palms. Then she looked at my face as though it was a mile away. "You have been planning for the future?" she said.

"Yes," I said.

"But you are not ready for the future?" she said.

"No, I guess not."

She looked at my palms again. "You have lost someone dear to you," she said.

"Yes," I said.

"But you will have a great love, in the future," she said.

"I will?"

"You will have great joy, and sorrow, and then happiness again," she said.

"What kind of sorrow?" I said.

"I cannot say." She looked at my forehead and then at my hands again. She studied the palms and wrists. "You must not be afraid to change, even as the seasons change," she said. "Only as you change will you find happiness."

"What kind of change?" I said.

"You will find that out as you come to it," she said. She did not smile. She studied me as a prospector would a pan of gravel.

"Sniff this," she said, and pulled a handkerchief out of her sleeve. She held it to my nose and I snuffed. I don't know what was on that cloth. It might have been some drops or powder. But it made me sneeze the awfullest sneeze, and stars shot through the top of my head. I sneezed so I felt I had sprained my spine. Tears come and the room blurred and twisted around.

The woman, Madame Sparrow he had called her, got up and left. I wiped my eyes on my sleeve, but the tears kept coming. I didn't know why I was crying, but the water seemed to gush out of my eyes. The tears made the room dim and crooked.

Suddenly the doctor come back and set opposite me. He had a leather pouch in one hand and a bundle of feathers in the other. He waved the feathers at me as though he was making the sign of the cross, but I don't think that's what he meant to do.

"What do you think about?" he said.

I didn't know what he meant. "Lots of things," I said.

"Do you think about the future?" he said. "Do you worry about the future?"

"I do," I said.

"You must not worry about the future," he said. "What you worry about will not come."

"What should I think about?" I said. I sniffed and rubbed my eyes. My eyes was all hot inside.

"Think about the past," Dr. Match said. "Think about what has been, and think of pigeons. Imagine you are a pigeon."

"A pigeon?" I said.

"Think of yourself as a pigeon high on a tree or flying over the valley. Think of flying hundreds of miles, of flying close to the sun and over rivers." He touched the pouch to my forehead and the feathers to each of my shoulders. He looked at my eyes and past my eyes. It was as if he was trying to see behind my eyes.

"Do not tell anyone that you are thinking of a pigeon," he said. "It will not work if you tell. It will lose its medicine."

"Yes, sir," I said.

"And you must know your secret name," he said. "No one else can know this name." He leaned forward and whispered the name in my ear. And to this day I have never told anyone that name. I don't know if it matters or not, but I have never revealed to a soul the name he told me, though I have said it to myself at the hardest times ever since.

"Now you will take this," he said, and pulled a little jug out of his pocket. It was a jug like the big ones around the room and pottery shed, except it was no larger than an apple. But it had a face with bulging eyes on its side and a wooden stopper in the top. It was a perfect little jug, small enough to fit in my hand.

"Take a spoon of this before each meal," he said.

"Is it a tonic?" I said.

"You must not ask," he said, "only take it as I say."

"I will," I said. My eyes had quit crying and my head was beginning to cool. I could see him clear again.

"Remember," he said, "if you start to worry, think about the pigeon. And say the secret name to yourself, over and over."

The sunlight was blinding when I stepped outside. Pa stood on the steps and held out a silver dollar to the doctor. Then he tipped his hat and said goodbye. Dr. Match did not answer. He stayed on the porch and watched us walk back to the wagon.

It felt like spring had advanced while we was in the little valley. Driving back I noticed how big and soft the leaves was on the maples and sycamores along the creek. Some trees looked a darker green and even the tender green leaves had unfolded more.

Maybe it's the way memory can fool us, but the big change for me begun on that trip back from Dark Corner. The mountains looked different, and the sunlight on the steep slopes sparkled. The horse stepped faster going home, at least on the level places, and Pa's heart was lighter.

But maybe that's just the way I recall it. Sometimes I think we only recollect what we have remembered before. What we recall is having recalled something already, so our strongest and truest memories come from a chain of often recalled things, and in that chain, over the years, events get adjusted and sorted around and stretched to fit the way we see things along the way. There's no way to prove it, but I think that's how it works. And maybe I've run a lot of things together because they happened so long ago.

"Well, what did the Indian doctor do?" Florrie said when we got home. She never could hold in her curiosity.

"He didn't do much," I said.

"That tells me a lot, Ginny."

I felt more grownup because I had been away. I didn't feel like being bossed by Florrie that day.

"Did he give you any medicine?" she said.

"He give me something that made me sneeze," I said.

"I'm sure that will be a lot of help," Florrie said. She spread the wet dishrag on the rim of the emptied pan.

"It made me sneeze so hard I cried," I said.

"Did he sing any secret chants?" she said.

"He waved a feather in my face, and a little bag," I said.

"And Pa took you all that way for that?" she said.

For once I had the advantage of Florrie. Her curiosity, and the fact that she had stayed at home, made her weak. "I got my fortune told," I said.

"By the doctor?"

"By his wife, I reckon." I stacked dried dishes on the shelf.

"And what did she say?" Florrie said.

"She said I would have a lot of joy, and then a terrible sadness in my life. And finally a great happiness."

"That's an easy prediction to make," Florrie said. "For it will be years and years before you know if it's true."

I almost told Florrie about the secret thought of the pigeon, and the secret name. But I stopped myself. There was plenty about me that Florrie didn't need to know.

"He give me some medicine," I said.

"I should hope so," Florrie said. She got the broom and swept crumbs and ashes from around the cookstove. I showed her the little pot with the wooden stopper.

"That's a toy," she said. "That's something for a playhouse."

I told her about the pottery shed and the kiln and the clay pit, and the jars and jugs just like mine except they stood waist high. "Why would they make pots so big?" I said.

"To store corn in, and to hold water, I reckon," she said.

I remembered reading somewhere that they buried people in big jars in some countries, and that they placed offerings to their gods in big urns on altars.

"How much did this doctor charge?" Florrie said.

But I decided not to tell her anything else. She could ask Pa how much he paid Dr. Match if she wanted to.

That evening I took a spoonful of medicine from the little pot. It looked like the tonic Dr. Johns had give me. But it tasted different. I don't think there was much alcohol in Dr. Match's medicine. It was so strong it burned my tongue. It tasted like he had put the extract and concentrate of hundreds of plants in the mixture. The liquid had been boiled down and distilled, and boiled down again like an essential oil. As soon as the jar was opened its scent filled the room. I don't know what give it such a smell. The fumes flared up in a ghost that filled the air. I thought of the story of the genie in the bottle.

"That's just a little bottle," Florrie said. "What will you do when it's all gone?"

"If this don't work I guess I'm hopeless," I said.

But even that night I felt things happening inside me. Maybe it wasn't the medicine, and it was just time for things to change. But the effect was so quick I think it was the medicine. It was like little doors and hallways started opening inside me, and weights in my body begun shifting around. I don't know how else to describe it. I felt like some busy freight yard inside where cargoes was being sorted and loaded.

Next day I got itchy all over. It was a stinging itch and made me want to laugh. I laughed at my own jokes and at silly things

Florrie said. And I just laughed to myself over nothing at all.

"I don't think you are at yourself, Ginny," Florrie said.

"I'm fine," I said.

"It must be the Indian juice," Florrie said. "I'd sure like to know what he put in that."

"You can try it yourself," I said.

The itchiness turned into a kind of soreness all over after three or four days. My chest was sore, and my belly. It was a raw humming kind of soreness. And I started to feel heavy. After several days I felt full of lead, and the humming kept on.

"Do you feel bad?" Florrie said.

"I'm fine," I said.

"That medicine ain't working," she said.

But it was working. It was stirring things in me like some gas pain or heartburn had got hold of me. I wanted to be still, yet couldn't stay still. I wanted to set by the fire, yet it was too hot. I put a cool cloth on my forehead, but it made me shiver.

"What are you doing?" Florrie said.

"I'm going out to the Sunset Rock," I said.

"Better stay in the house," she said, "out of that wind."

There was a wind in the pasture. Even the trees on the ridge across the river was beginning to get green. Big clouds eased up over the top of the hill. It felt as if there was going to be a storm. I set on the rock but the wind was too cold. The grass was dark and trout lilies and trilliums bright along the edge of the woods. I climbed off the rock and walked to the river.

There must have been some hatch of flies that morning, for the air above the river was filled with sparkling things. They hovered in mist above the pool, until a gust swept them away. They returned glittering, like some visitation. Trash was caught in the brush showing how high the spring flood had been. I stood by the river and prayed, "Jesus, if you will let this happen to me I will always serve you. I will be faithful in your service."

That night the pain in my belly got worse. I was sore inside and something terrible was pressing against me. I wanted a hot drink and made myself coffee before going to bed. More than I wanted to sleep I wanted to ease the pain.

It was like the worst indigestion I had ever felt. I got in bed and laid curled up on one side. And then I turned over on the other, looking for a fresh cool place in the sheets. But the pain kept growing. I curled myself up tighter and it helped a little. It was like I had this cold in my head and all over.

I turned the other way in the bed. And then I remembered what Dr. Match had told me about the pigeon. I tried to think of a pigeon, of the noise it makes ruffling its feathers, of the lavender and green rainbows on its neck. I saw a pigeon leap off the gable of a barn and fly out over the valley. It flapped across the river and up over the mountain, so high the trees was like weeds below. And beyond the peak I saw the plunging hollers of South Carolina. The jumpoffs and valleys looked miles deep. I saw apple trees in bloom, and peach trees. I saw the old woman, Madame Sparrow, doing her wash, and smoke coming from the kiln.

And while I thought of the pigeon soaring I said the secret name Dr. Match had told me. I said it over and over, and looked out across the vast expanse of the foothills and mountains all the way to Caesar's Head and Table Rock. I saw Old

Callahan Mountain, and Tryon Mountain to the east, stretching away into the spring haze above the flat country.

When I woke there was this stickiness between my legs and under my hip. The pain was gone and I smelled blood. It was just daylight and I saw what a mess I had made when I pulled the covers back. My gown had blood on it and the sheets had a stain of blood. Some places the blood had dried and stuck to my skin.

It was such a mess I shuddered, thinking how much washing in cold water the sheets and gown would take. And I would have to do it with Pa and Joe and Locke watching. Everyone would see the blood stains and know what had happened. I got up and poured water into my washbasin. The napkins Florrie had give me was folded fresh and clean in the dresser.

It was awful to be in such a fix. And yet I felt wonderful too. I had come through to a new place. "Thank you, Jesus," I said as I washed the gown and sheets. It seemed I had achieved something, and I could touch the future again. I placed the little jug in the drawer with my clean linen.

CHAPTER SIX

L ike most big things that happen to me, my marriage just seemed to take place on its own. Though I must have made thousands of choices it felt like I didn't choose at all. Everything come to me. I know people like to say marriage isn't what it's cracked up to be and loving isn't anything like what people brag. But when it went good it was more than I could ever have expected. I have never felt better than when I was with Tom and we was getting along. I looked forward to the end of the day and going to bed. No matter how hard I had worked or tired I was, it was restful to be loved by Tom. No matter what has happened since I wouldn't trade those nights for anything.

Tom and me got married at the house. Preacher Jolly come down and pronounced the ceremony, and we took our vows. Wasn't any of Tom's family there. They wasn't sociable people. My brother Joe and his wife Lily come down, and my sister Florrie and her husband David, and we had fried chicken and watermelon later. Wasn't any infare party or dancing like some people have.

First thing Pa discovered about Tom was all the things he didn't do. He didn't hunt much, and he never did trap for mink and muskrat. He never fished except a little bit in spring.

He went to meeting on Sunday but never did attend prayer meetings during the week. He never did read books or magazines, and he almost never read the newspaper. He didn't like to talk politics, and he never did stay up late at night if he could help it. He never took a drink of liquor for pleasure, and he never smoked or chewed tobacco. He worked on holidays same as other days unless they fell on a Sunday. Nothing bored him as much as Sundays.

After the preacher was gone and I had cleared away the dishes we set around the table. Joe and Lily had brought us a lamp for a wedding present. It had crystal hangings that looked like big snowflakes. When it was lit the lamp appeared hung with ice. Pa give me a hundred dollars, and Florrie had made me a quilt. The house was quiet. I guess Pa decided it was best to leave us alone. "Time to go milk," he said, pushing back his chair.

"I'll help you soon as I change," Tom said. It was clear Tom wanted to get out of his dress clothes and find some work to do. He rubbed his hands together like he was washing them. They looked dry and powdered they had been scrubbed so clean.

"Then I'll run up to the spring," Pa said. "When I get back we can do the milking." Pa often said he was walking to the spring when he had to relieve hisself. By the time he got back Tom had already changed clothes and took the buckets to the milkgap.

"Pa, you might as well set down," I said. "Tom's done gone to milk." Pa went out and set on the porch. After that he let Tom and me do all the milking.

That night it got chilly and Tom built a fire in the fireplace. I think he did it mostly to have something to do. There was kindling already in the box in the kitchen, but he took the lantern out to the woodpile and split some more. He carried in several sticks of oak that had been seasoning in the shed.

"We don't need too big a fire," I said.

"I'll just make a scrap of fire to take the chill," he said.

"A fire feels friendly after dark," Pa said.

I took longer than usual cleaning up the dishes and drying them. I wiped every single spoon and fork and placed them in the drawer. I set the dishes in the cupboard and placed the rest of the cake in the safe. After throwing out the dishwater I swept the kitchen and mopped it with the last of the hot water.

By the time I set down the fire in the living room was trotting like a fox. The flames danced on the grate and the house was fragrant with seasoned oak. The late summer coolness had gone.

"A fire relaxes you," Pa said, "whether you're inside or out."

"A fire makes you feel at home," I said.

Tom poked at the logs and made the flames leap higher. "People will naturally gather to a fire," he said.

I thought how true that was. People will locate theirselves around a fire, and feel confident and comforted. That's why altars in the Bible always had fires. That's why the hearth is the center of the household. Building a fire was Tom's way of establishing hisself in our house. It was his fire.

"I noticed in the war you never feel like fighting when you are standing or setting by a fire," Pa said. "At night we would camp in sight of the Yankees and cook our sloosh and warm ourselves while they done the same. We'd even holler back and forth at them and tease them and trade playing cards and liquor and such. Once the fires was lit everything got peaceful."

"A fire is a sign of respect," I said. "The Romans believed that gods lived on the hearth."

"That don't make sense," Tom said. "A hearth is in plain sight and you can see no god lives on it."

"Maybe the flames looked like little gods," Pa said.

"Or maybe the gods seemed to live in the draft, or the warm bricks," I said.

"People believe what they want to," Tom said. He had took off his tie and collar before, and his sunburned skin shone gold in the firelight. His hair was gold and his eyes sparkled. His shirt was dappled rose and peach-colored. He looks like a golden god and don't even know it, I thought.

"A fire is always interesting to look at," Tom said.

Pa pulled his watch out. "Time to wind up the cat and throw the clock out," he said. It was a joke Pa had been saying since I was a little girl.

"We should say a prayer," I said.

Pa and me got down on our knees by our chairs, and when Tom saw what we done he dropped to his knees too. I put my cheek against the chair and saw the moon through the window. It was in the first quarter and appeared to lean looking into the house.

"Lord, we ask your blessings on this family, and on our new member," Pa said. "As Ginny and Tom start out on their life together, we ask that you look down on them and protect them. And we ask that they dedicate their lives to your work."

When Pa finished we all stood and Pa took a lamp off the mantel. "I'll leave you all to lock up," he said. He reached out his hand to Tom. "Mighty good to have you in the house," he said.

After Pa was gone Tom set down and looked right into the flames. I wondered what he was seeing there. Some people claim to read the future in a fire. "Would you like some popcorn?" I said.

"Don't reckon so," he said.

"I could make some coffee and hot biscuits," I said.

"No, I'm still full from supper," he said.

He set closer to the fire and light stirred and swayed over his features. I shivered, as if it was cold. He stretched his boots out toward the flames.

"Whenever you get sleepy we can go to bed," I said.

"Pretty soon," he said. "I never was one to stay up late."

"I will go turn down the bed," I said.

"Ain't no hurry," Tom said.

I looked into the fire where he was watching and saw flames arching from either side toward the middle.

"People say they can read fortunes in a fire," I said.

"A fire is just a fire," Tom said and looked into the flames.

"I'll go on then," I said.

"Might as well," he said.

I had not touched Tom since the ceremony, when we kissed after Preacher Jolly pronounced us man and wife. I took a lamp off the mantelpiece to carry, and I placed a hand on Tom's shoulder as I walked by. Under the white shirt his muscles was hard as steel.

That morning I had cleaned the bedroom as it had never been cleaned in my lifetime. I had hung curtains made that summer and spread a new quilt on the bed. I dusted in corners and carried magazines and books to the attic. I made room in the wardrobe for Tom's clothes and I put a crocheted mat on the night table. With a broom I chased cobwebs from the ceiling. The bedroom was on the north side and was always the coolest room. I washed the window and polished the cedar chest and chest of drawers with oil.

After the heat of the fireplace, the cool bedroom felt good. I set the lamp on the night table and turned up the flame. The room was mostly in shadow, and the wardrobe loomed like a great empty door. It was the room I had been born in. It was right that it would be the room for my married life.

I turned down the bed as neat as I could so the fresh sheets was showing. The many colored squares on the quilt sparkled and looked shivery. I will never have this room to myself again, I thought. I had laid out my nightgown across the chest of drawers earlier, one I had made that summer of sateen with lace sleeves and collar. I took off my clothes and hung them in the wardrobe.

A door closed and I listened to see if it was Tom or Pa. But Pa was snoring in the next room. I stepped to the window and pulled the curtain back. All I could see was the quarter moon over the hemlocks and arborvitae. Men always go out to relieve theirselves before bed. I wondered how long Tom would be.

Once in bed I saw how bright the lamp was. I didn't want Tom to be blinded by the light when he come back inside. I turned down the wick and the room got soft in the yellow glow. My hair fell over my eyes and I pushed it aside.

It took forever for Tom to come back in. Finally I heard him close the kitchen door and slide the bolt, and then he poked the fire. He must have took off his boots by the fireplace and walked quiet down the hall for I started when the bedroom door opened.

"I left the lamp so you could see to hang your clothes," I said.

"No need to," Tom said. He walked to the table and blowed out the lamp. In the dark I heard him take off his pants. I wondered what he was going to do with them. Was he going to drop them on the floor to get wrinkled and stepped on? And then I felt him brush the frame of the bed and knowed he was hanging his trousers on the bedpost. I guess that was what he had always done at the Powell house and the Lewis place.

When Tom got under the quilt I moved over to make room for him, but I scooted too far and had to shift back. His skin was a little cool from being outside. The bed tilted to his side as he laid down, making the mattress feel different.

"What time do you get up?" I said. But he didn't answer. I thought maybe he hadn't heard. "What do you like for breakfast?"

"Shhhhh," he said, like he was afraid of waking Pa.

Tom was completely still, though he was close against me. He brushed my lips with his and his mustache tickled my nose. I giggled a little, and he giggled too. It was the first time I had heard him laugh all day.

"Shhhhh," I said, and put a hand on his hard shoulder.

It is strange to have someone else in your bed, I thought. But it didn't feel strange in the way I expected. I felt curious as a little girl. What is going to happen? I thought.

And then I felt my gown moving. It was sliding up under the covers. The soft sateen slipped over my knees and over my

upper legs. It was tickling, but it was a good feeling. The cloth
slipped over my skin whispering as it rubbed and pulled away.
It was like I was sliding free as I had not been in a long time.
The gown slipped over my hips and I thought, I haven't felt
this free since before I can remember. Long ago I had that kind
of naked freedom, maybe. My belly felt the center around
which everything moved. And I thought, This pleasure is me.
It is mine. For some reason I thought of tomatoes in the sun
and fresh chips from chopped oak. Tom moved so slow he
made me wait for every touch until it seemed like I couldn't
hardly wait any longer. Easy does it, I could hear him thinking.
And I kept smelling those warm tomatoes in the sun. What I
felt was both less and more than I expected.

We got married at the end of summer. It was the time for
cane cutting, molasses making, a job I always hated but
Tom seemed to relish. It was terrible work, stripping the cane
while it stood in the field, going down every row and breaking
your back. Then it had to be cut at the ground and carried to
the mill. I don't reckon there is any more boring job than feeding cane stalks bottom first to the rollers of a mill. You have to
be careful not to get fingers caught; otherwise you could do it
asleep. There is tens of thousands of stalks in a field and you
push them in one by one while the horse goes turning the mill,
leading hisself around. Yellow jackets get all crusted on the
trough running down to the pan over the furnace.

Now cane always seemed to be just big grass. You bust the
stalks to get the juice and cook it. But really you're fixing the
sap from grass. I grant you that sorghum has a smoky dark

taste that is special. And if you forget where it comes from it's
even better. But if they're undercooked, molasses are green and
look like juice squeezed out of crabgrass and taste that way too.

Tom had learned to boil molasses at the Lewis place. I reckon
it was work he took to from the first. He didn't seem to mind
stripping the rows of slender stalks, and carrying the stalks to a
pile beside the mill. He cleaned off the mill and oiled the
rollers where they had rusted since last year. He started at
daylight when the field and pasture was covered with dew. By
dinnertime the horse had wore a circle in the grass around the
mill, and the horse was wore out too. But Tom didn't even want
to stop for dinner. He brushed away yellow jackets on the
trough and when one fell in the sap he flicked it away.

The worst job by far was standing over the steaming pan,
skimming and stirring. Tom had piled a heap of stovewood by
the furnace and he kept the fire roaring. With the dipper he
scooped bits of trash and yellow jackets that had got in the
syrup.

Yellow jackets was worse that year than ever before. People
said it was because of the drought. Their holes in the ground
had not been flooded and all the young ones had hatched and
gone looking for sweet things. Apples that fell in the orchard
was tunneled and eat out by yellow jackets. Wherever you
peeled apples and peaches there was jackets buzzing in your
face. I got stung twice canning peaches. "Jassackets," Pa called
them and laughed. They buzzed around your lips and hands,
and around your eyes. Maybe they liked the taste of tears. I
didn't see how we could make molasses, there was such
swarms of them fogging around.

Tom dug a hole to put the skimmings in. It was soon filled by dipperfuls of foam and trash scooped off the boiling pan. It's hard to describe the color of molasses skimmings. They are like scum and slime, and sometimes kind of green and sometimes brown and almost pink. Yellow jackets crusted the hole and swarmed a yard high every time Tom come near it.

"You watch out for jackets," I said.

But he didn't answer. He was too busy skimming and stirring. The pan bubbled its sweet steam into the sky, and the steam mixed with the smoke of the furnace.

"And don't go and fall in," I said as he leaned way over the middle of the long pan. What comes to the surface **of** boiling sorghum is partly dirt and flecks of crushed stalk. If the syrup is to be clear you've got to skim them off. A kind of shiny suds foams at the top and has to be dipped off.

"Good molasses have the color of fresh coffee when you hold them up to the light," Tom said.

I scraped yellow jackets off the edge of the pan and throwed them in the hole with gobs of foam. Pa was feeding the mill and I helped at the furnace. Every time I scraped off a dozen jackets a hundred more appeared. I don't know where they all come from. There was jackets everywhere. I got stung again, and the horse got stung. Pa got stung at the mill. The long sweetening was calling every yellow jacket for miles. Honeybees joined the feast too, and where you see one bee you'll soon see a hundred.

But so far Tom hadn't been stung, even though he stood right over the pan. "Don't fall in," I said again.

Tom was stirring the pan so the syrup would be evenly cooked. Juice run in the upper end and I figured the syrup in the middle, where the pan was hottest, cooked first. Tom reached the dipper into the middle and only got more foam. He reached in again.

You know how it is when you go off balance and hardly know it until you hit something. I saw Tom's feet start to slip on the gravel and his stand give way. He tried to brace hisself but overreached with the dipper. Maybe the skimmer full of syrup was too heavy, or maybe he was dizzy from the steam.

I saw Tom falling, face down, right into the boiling molasses. The steam coming off the pan was thick as grease and he was pitching right through it toward the sap dark as licorice and root extracts. I don't know if I screamed or not as he fell. It was his neck and face I thought about, how the hot syrup would scald them. He must have squeezed his eyes shut. What I don't understand is how he got his elbows down in time to break the fall. I didn't even have time to reach out and catch him.

His elbows went into the boiling pan, and then his chest and armpits. It looked like he was drowning. This is what it is like to see a death, I thought. I will be a widow no sooner than I am married. His strong body will be burned to a blister, and I will never know my pleasure with him again.

I jerked Tom by the waist. He jumped back at the same time, and I flung him on the grass with the sorghum smoking off his arms and chest like the hottest compress you could imagine.

"Take it off," I screamed. "Take your shirt off." I tried to tear at the buttons, but the syrup burned my hands. It felt like he was covered with blistering slime.

Then the yellow jackets found him. They started buzzing in his face, and it seemed every yellow jacket in the valley come at once. It looked like he was wearing a shirt of them humming and crawling on every inch of him. Some caught in his mustache.

"Get the bucket," he hollered, and pointed to the pail of water we used to rinse the dipper. I picked up the bucket and splashed it over his face and shoulders. That must have cooled off the syrup and drowned a few yellow jackets, but mostly it made them mad. They boiled up like they was spitting at his face and started to sting him. "Oh!" he hollered, and tried to get at the buttons on his shirt. But the buttons was all sticky.

"Run away from them," I yelled. I fanned at the yellow jackets with my apron. I tried to think of what else I could do.

Tom started running across the pasture. I didn't know where he was running to, but I followed. And then I saw he was heading toward the river. There was a little field beyond the fence, and then the swimming hole where Joe and Locke used to go after working in the corn patch.

I followed Tom all the way to the river bank and saw him jump into the swimming hole. He dived in up to his neck, but the jackets kept hitting his face. He ducked into the cold water and stayed under a long time. I thought he wasn't going to come back up. I must have screamed and started into the river. Suddenly he raised his head out of the water and I saw the stream was carrying away hundreds of yellow jackets.

The water both hardened and melted the molasses a little. You could smell the smoky sweetness mixed with river water. Tom rubbed his face like he was washing it. I could see the red spots where the jackets had stung him on the neck.

But the yellow jackets was gone. Maybe there was one or two buzzing around his head, but he didn't even notice them. He acted dazed by the burns and stings. I reckon a bee sting always makes you shivery and cold. He shuddered in the icy water.

"Come on out," I said. I wanted to put tobacco juice or ragweed juice on the stings. He would need a drink from the jug to stir his blood. Nothing will stand up to venom like liquor.

But Tom climbed up the far bank because it was closer. There was birches on that side hung with grape vines from their tops. A high bank rose where we used to climb and swing out on the vines when we was younguns. Tom pulled hisself up the bank with a vine. I reckon he wanted to get in the sun, away from the cold water, and far from the molasses furnace and yellow jackets.

With the burns and stings on Tom's face and elbows and chest I wondered how we would manage our lovemaking. But when young people are in love they always find a way. We just went slow at first and took more care. And the care and limitations made it go even better. I felt I was bringing him back to health. We give a whole new meaning to the term "home remedies."

Another thing Tom liked to make was cider. He had never had his own apple trees before. Pa had set out two orchards right after the war, one on the top of the mountain and one on the hill above the house. In fall we had Golden Delicious, Red Delicious, Winesaps, Ben Davis, and a tree of big Wolf Rivers for pies and sauce. We also had a plum tree and a pear tree.

It took Tom less than a week to recover from the yellow jacket stings. Turned out the burns didn't amount to much. I guess his shirt had protected him and he had jumped back so fast the only real burns was on his elbows. But the places there formed scabs and begun to heal. I think he was lucky. He never was the kind of man who could set around for long. The day after he was stung he moped on the porch and didn't say anything when Pa and me went out to finish the molasses. The stings made him weak and the scratch marks on his side made him sore. He didn't complain.

I found Tom was the sort of man that had to be moving toward a goal or he couldn't stand it. I reckon it was the way he felt in control of things. And he wouldn't ever do anything else. He never did go hunting, and he never did drive stobs in the ground and play horseshoes. He liked to eat good, but he never did drink any liquor. Even Pa liked to take a drink from time to time, as I did myself, when it wouldn't hurt anybody.

Like I said, I found out early Tom liked the pleasures of the bed. He liked to sleep when he was tired, and he liked love things too. For somebody that didn't have anything to say he liked loving a lot. I reckon all men do, and most women too, for that matter. I don't have any way to compare him to anybody, but it occurred to me he did his talking through loving. Being with Tom was like taking part in a long conversation that could begin anywhere and might go this way and that, but was always surprising at some point. From what I've heard other women say about such things, including Florrie, I believe Tom was special. I believe he put his mind to loving the way he did to other work. Everything he did was careful and right, except for falling in the molasses. He worked his way along and most everything he touched turned out right. I even told Florrie how much I enjoyed Tom, which wasn't like me. And I later wished I never had.

Two weeks after he was burned Tom hitched up the wagon and drove to town to buy a cider mill. It cost him eight dollars, and took him another day to get it set up and oiled and working. Next he cut brush and shoveled the old road up the mountain so he could drive the wagon to the big orchard. It was the first time I could remember that we harvested all the apples. Usually we gathered some in sacks and carried them down the mountain. The rest got left for deer and birds and frost to turn to mush.

Tom went into the grove and picked every single apple. He put the different kinds in separate sacks, and he picked every good apple out of the grass. When he was finished the yellow jackets and birds had only the rotten ones and those half busted.

We wrapped the best apples in newspapers and put them in barrels in the cellar. All together we had more than twenty bushels, and Tom sold some at the village. But the apples he had picked up, those that had been stuck with straw or bruised, we washed for making cider. We worked every evening after he come in from the field, grinding fruit in the mill and squeezing juice out in the press. We sweated in the cool evenings, churning the apples into sweet smelling pieces, then screwing down the press to crush them. I loved to see the juice stream out the cracks of the press. You could smell every fresh spurt foaming gold and winky. I kept a pine limb to brush away yellow jackets.

Apples don't smell like anything else unless it's flowers. The white flesh of an apple turning gold when it breaks open smells like the essence of earth. The sap is an extract of all the sun and wind and rain of the summer. Cider already tastes like a kind of liquor, even before it hardens.

To keep the juice sweet Tom sealed the jugs with wax, and we set more than fifty gallons in the cellar. As I bent over, wiping pulp from the press board, my hair come partly undone and stuck to my neck. I had loosened my dress by a couple of buttons and could feel the sweat running between my breasts and under my armpits. I glanced up and saw Tom looking at my breasts. "Shame on you," I said, and slapped his arm. His face was red when he was working, but it turned a little redder. I had put on some weight since the wedding and felt bigger and softer and rounder.

Already that fall Tom had established a routine. He had trouble sleeping after four in the morning. He liked to go to bed early and get up early. When he rose he ground coffee on the back porch and had a cup before it got light. It was the only time he could set. Maybe it was his favorite time of day, as it was mine. He made a fire to boil coffee and he set there and thought. I'd have give anything to know what he thought about. Maybe he prayed, and maybe he thought about sacred things. But I think he planned what he would do that day, what had to be done, and what could be done that time of year. He was planning to improve the place, and he thought about roads and fences, terraces to firm up and gullies that had to be choked with brush. After stepping outside to relieve hisself he would set for half an hour. I believe he thought the fiber of the Peace family had wore out and he needed to get the place right again.

After the cider making was done Tom built a new springhouse. The actual spring was three hundred yards around the hill, and Pa had bored out pumplogs to lead water down to the yard. But the pumplogs was rotting and leaking and we had never had a decent springhouse. Tom ordered pipe from town to replace the logs, and he dug a basin big as the spring itself and lined it with rocks. He cobbled the outlet that run along the pasture fence down to the branch. I had never seen anybody work as long or steady. Tom had not done masonry before, but he planned the wall with such care it looked like the sure work of a journeyman.

Tom split big chestnut logs for the springhouse itself, and set those logs around the basin, under the hemlocks. When he put the cedar shingles on the building it was cool and dark inside. Water splashed out of the pipe and murmured in the overflow. On the hottest day it was cool in there, and Tom made a box to keep the milk and butter, eggs and cider. In winter it was warm under the low eaves, with the heat of the earth and springwater rising up. Nothing set there ever froze in even the coldest weather.

Between the smokehouse and the springhouse Tom fixed a wash place for me. And he built a table for the tub and washboard. He strung up a clothesline along the path from the smokehouse.

If Pa resented Tom taking charge of so much and doing so many new things around the place he didn't let it show. Pa was past sixty, and liked to set on the porch in the sun and talk, or by the fire after dark. He always did like to talk more than anything, just like Locke and Florrie. He loved to tell about what he had read, and what he had seen in Virginia as a young soldier. He had growed chin whiskers and suddenly his face begun to show age. He read the paper, and he kept up with the war with Spain. He read to Tom and me accounts of Teddy and his Rough Riders. That Roosevelt was a Republican made him seem even more a hero. Pa had always been a Republican, ever since he voted for Lincoln, him and all our family. After the war he hadn't changed to become a Democrat the way so many in the valley had.

I reckon Pa had got less and less practical over the years. It seemed at times he was just drifting, talking about his months in the prison camp up North. I reckon he wasn't interested in building up the place anymore, after his heart trouble started.

That first winter Tom added two stalls and a feed room to the log barn. He snaked logs in from the hill, and with Joe's help rolled them into place. It was a low barn, and the worst work was notching the logs and setting them in place. They bored holes in the logs and pegged them together. Tom built a fence around the barn, encircling the manure pile curing out front. Pa had kept the pile behind the barn, out of sight, but Tom pointed out that sun on the south side would dry the manure faster. And it would be easier to clean the stalls if the pile was closer and easier to reach with the wagon at spreading time. Enclosing the yard enabled him to put the roughage piles closer also. The stacks of corn tops rose above the barn roof. The cut ends stuck out into the weather, but the leafy tops inside stayed dry and sweet-smelling. Pulled a few at a time, the tops would last all winter, with only the butt ends blackened by the elements.

CHAPTER SEVEN

Whenever I mentioned going to the Pentecostal meetings Tom would stiffen up. At first I didn't know how to tell when he was mad, because he didn't say much. Everybody in my family would talk out their anger. But I come to recognize the way he would say even less, and not look you in the eye when he was mad. He would turn his head away, and sometimes his face would go red. And he wouldn't hardly answer when you asked him a question.

"Tom," I said, "worship is one of the finest things people can do. People have a hunger for worship same as they do for food and loving." I had heard Preacher Liner say something like that one time at a meeting and never forgot it.

"I go to church," he said. "I've always gone to church."

"But I prefer sometimes services where the Spirit moves, where the meeting is not dry and dead," I said. But I did not know how to explain how I felt at revivals when I danced or spoke in tongues. It was hard to put the feeling into mere words. "Most churches go through the motions of worship, like some duty," I said. "They have meetings like mournful chores to get through."

"I'd hate to judge other folks's worship," Tom said.

"That's what I'm asking, that you not judge my worship," I said. "Here, let me read what it says in Acts." I wanted to warm up the chilly space that opened between us when I mentioned the Holiness meetings. I was still hoping to make Tom understand.

"'And when the day of Pentecost was fully come, they were all with one accord in one place,'" I read. "'And suddenly there was a sound from heaven as of a rushing mighty wind, and it filled all the house where they were sitting. And there appeared unto them cloven tongues like as of fire, and it sat upon each of them. And they were all filled with the Holy Ghost, and began to speak with other tongues, as the Spirit gave them utterance. . . . Now when this was noised abroad, the multitude came together, and were confounded, because that every man heard them speak in his own language.'"

It was a passage that always thrilled me. I had heard it so many times I knowed it by heart. Just listening to the words made me feel lifted off the ground.

"But you don't need such doings here," Tom said. "Everybody on the river speaks the same language."

I saw that he did not understand. He heard things the way he wanted to.

"But language can mean a message," I said. "It means everybody hears the message they need. That's the miracle."

"I don't see the use of acting drunk and crazy," Tom said. "That won't help nobody."

"Peter answered that very charge," I said. "Listen to this. 'And they were all amazed, and were in doubt, saying one to another, What meaneth this? Others mocking said, These men are full of new wine. But Peter, standing up with the eleven, lifted up his voice, and said unto them, Ye men of Judaea, and all ye that dwell in Jerusalem, be this known to you, and hearken to my words: For these men are not drunken, as ye suppose, seeing it is but the third hour of the day.'"

"That was a long time ago in a different place," Tom said.

"But it's a message for today," I said. "It is especially for today. Listen to this. 'And it shall come to pass in the last days, saith God, I will pour out my spirit upon all flesh: and your sons and daughters shall prophesy, and your young men shall see visions, and your old men shall dream dreams: And on my servants and on my handmaidens I will pour out in those days of my spirit: and they shall all prophesy: And I shall show wonders in heaven above, and signs in the earth beneath; blood, and fire, and vapor of smoke.'"

I felt almost light-headed reading those words they was so powerful. It was the promise of prophesying, and signs and wonders, that stirred me most. I could hardly read them without tears coming. That promise was the richest thing we had.

My arguments was just making Tom quieter and stubborner, but I couldn't stop myself.

"People are here to praise the Lord and be joyful," I said.

"They wasn't put here to act like fools," Tom said.

"It's dangerous to call other people fools," I said. "The Bible says it puts you in danger of hellfire."

"If people act like fools why not call them what they are?"

I had set out to explain to Tom what a joy the Pentecostal services was, and here I had just made him madder. I couldn't let it end there, and yet I couldn't think of what to say.

"Let me read you this piece from *The Moody Monthly*," I said. I smiled to myself remembering Florrie's sacriligious joke. Every woman gets moody monthly, she liked to say.

But Tom didn't answer. He looked at his hands on the table and he looked at the floor. I could tell from the set of his shoulders he just wanted to be out working by hisself.

"The Lord wants us to be happy," I said, "not all troubled and angry. Not riled up most of the time."

I don't know what Tom believed, except that folks should go to church on Sunday. He never liked to talk about what he thought. I guess the way Pa and me and Joe talked and argued all the time made him quieter than he would have been.

"You mean like the Happyland colony?" he said. It was the first time I had ever heard him be sarcastic.

"I don't know much about the Happyland colony," I said. "It was mostly gone by the time I can remember."

What I did know was that a group of freed slaves from Mississippi or somewhere had come to the mountains after the Confederate War and built houses on the Lewis place. They was led by a preacher named Robert Montgomery. In the mountains Montgomery called hisself king and his wife Luella queen of the community they named The Kingdom of the Happyland. Some members worked at the Lewis place to pay their rent. But in the Kingdom everybody owned things in common. I had heard the king and queen had a fine carriage and wooden thrones they set on.

"I growed up near the Happyland," Tom said. "And when they had their meetings at night you could hear them hollering and screaming. They danced so hard they packed the ground."

"I guess they was happy not to be slaves anymore," I said.

"They was just ordinary people," Tom said, "except at their services they went wild. You never would have dreamed of such goings-on. They was supposed to be Christians but they hollered and leaped around like crazy people. Sometimes the women would take down their dresses and dance naked, shaking their-selves in the lantern light. They used skulls and blood in their services. I think some of it was voodoo. They would keep us awake till the small hours if it was a full moon or warm weather."

"Everybody worships different," I said.

"They would go crazy," Tom said. "They would hurt their-selves jumping over things. One feller broke his leg when he climbed a tree in a fit and jumped out of it."

"I guess that was just an accident," I said.

"Mama was ashamed for me and Sister to hear such ravings," Tom said. "She used to close the windows when their services got going. But once I slipped out and hid in the woods to watch."

"I bet you wanted to see those women take down their dresses," I said, and slapped his knee. Tom didn't even smile.

"It was heathen stuff," he said. "They shook like they was having fits."

"Don't nobody take off their clothes at our services," I said. "At least I've never heard of it."

"Once a woman got so worked up dancing she give birth to a baby," Tom said. "But the baby was dead. I seen it the next day laying on a table before they buried it."

"Maybe it was a miscarriage," I said.

"It was murder," he said. He looked at his feet and shook his head. "The thing was the Happylanders was ordinary people in the daytime," Tom said. "I worked with them and they worked good. They was good people, except their king led them wrong and made them worship him. He done it to keep them under his thumb."

"It might have been their greatest pleasure," I said.

"Worshipping him?"

"No, having their meetings and dancing and singing."

"People have no business working theirselves up crazy," Tom said. He turned away again.

"We can't know what's in other people's hearts," I said.

But he didn't answer. I saw he thought he'd talked enough. Tom saw words as commitments he did not want to make unless he had to. I think he felt any verbal commitment was over-commitment. I know he thought most talk was a mistake. "People get in trouble talking," he liked to say. "It's the tongue that destroys you."

I think he believed human honesty was in the arms and hands, in a strong back. That's why he was such a good lover. He had confidence in anything done with his body. "Nobody can talk for ten minutes without telling a lie," he would say. I don't know where he had heard that, but he would repeat it from time to time. Since Pa and me and Joe and Florrie and Locke all liked to talk, it was an accusation. But we didn't mind Tom setting there not saying much. He was a good listener when he wanted to be.

"Want me to read the paper?" I said. "There's another story here about Cuba."

"I don't care," he said. "It's almost bedtime."

After we got married I was surprised at who Tom got along with and who he didn't like. He did not often express his opinions about people, but I could tell how much he come to like Florrie. I think it was because Florrie teased him and was always telling jokes. And when she told a joke she would slap him on the arm or on the belly. If they was standing up she would almost certainly pat him on the tummy. It was a gesture she liked to make. Tom was such a strong feller, solid and compact, and it was like she couldn't hardly keep her hands off him.

Of course Florrie was always a flirt when she talked to men. She was a backslapper and nudger. Her husband David was even then getting sickly. He wanted to be a Baptist preacher and spent a lot of time indoors reading the Bible, and leaving most of the work to her. Tom was the opposite in every way.

I'd say every woman and every man are attracted to each other. It is the natural thing, and marriage is just a selection and guiding of that attraction. But Tom and Joe's Lily disliked each other from the beginning, or almost from the beginning. It was like they recognized each other from the first as somebody they couldn't hardly stand. And I never really understood it. I know it had something to do with religion, since Lily was always talking about a service her and Joe had been to, or some meeting out at Fletcher they was going to. Lily loved to talk about preachers they had heard and how they preached and how many people had been healed or led to the baptism of fire. Once she started she would talk nonstop. She would ask Joe to agree with her and then before he could answer she would go on.

It wasn't too long after Tom and me was married that Joe and Lily come down for Sunday dinner. Lily had a new lavender dress and a lavender hat. She liked clothes more than any woman I've ever knowed. She spent everything she could on new cloth or a new dress or a shawl. You would have thought she was rich to see the way she dressed, except her clothes was too colorful. She was always wearing yellows and pinks and lavenders, and I don't know if the rich would have dressed that way. She liked dresses with great flouncy sleeves. And sometimes she even carried an umbrella to match when she went to church or to a revival service. She said she liked to dress up out of respect to Jesus and the Holy Spirit. "It's a way of showing my faith," she said.

Lily knowed how to butter up Pa. She would hug him and kiss him on the cheek and bring him pieces of cake or pie. And he liked all the attention. What man don't? And by then he was old enough to be a little childish. She once begged him for a piece of land up on the road. She said, "Pa, I don't have a thing of my very own. If you give me a piece of ground I would have something that was just mine." And Pa went to town and had a deed drawed up and give her five acres there along the river road.

But strangely, Lily didn't bother me much. I'm not sure why, because she got on most people's nerves one way or another. I guess I just thought she was silly, and didn't pay much attention to her. Or maybe it was I only saw her Sundays, because she rarely come over to work with me, the way Florrie did.

That Sunday they come for dinner I fixed chicken and rice and a coconut cake. I had had to hurry to get things ready before church and never had a chance to put on a good blouse. What I wore was plain cotton, perfectly acceptable, but not fancy.

As we set down at the table Lily twisted herself in her lavender dress and patted her hat and said, "Oh Ginny, you always look so good in your clothes."

Now I was used to Lily and knowed she just wanted some-body to compliment her new outfit. I guess no one had thought to since she almost always wore a new dress on Sundays if she could.

"Thank you, Lily," I said. "And your dress just takes my breath away. Ain't it pretty, Tom?"

But she had made Tom mad. He had not made allowances for Lily, and her manner got to him more than I would have dreamed. His face turned red and he looked down at his plate. I guess he had not growed up with people like Lily around him.

"Well I had to have something to wear, if we're going to town to hear Preacher Carver," Lily said. "I told Joe I didn't have a rag to wear unless I could finish this dress in time."

"You look like a society lady," I said, pouring coffee for Pa.

"I think we should dress with respect for the Lord's work," Lily said. "Don't you agree, Pa? We should dress at least as nice as the devil's people."

"We should look the best we can," Pa said.

"Preacher Carver healed a goiter on a woman from Greenville," Lily said. "Before a thousand people he reached under her chin and jerked the goiter away."

"I hear he reached for their money to jerk away," Tom said.

Lily ignored him. Tom's face was flushed like he was sun-burned, and he wouldn't take his eyes off his plate.

"Preacher Carver has healed hundreds of people all over South Carolina," Lily said. "At his meetings the lame has walked and the blind has been able to see. He is a great man of God. Everywhere he goes the number of saved increases."

"I've heard everywhere he goes the population increases about nine months later," Tom said.

"Tom!" I said. But I had to laugh a little behind my hand too. I had never heard Tom talk so.

"Preacher Carver has blessings for them that will receive them," Lily said. She wiped her mouth with her handkerchief.

As soon as he finished eating Tom got up and went outside. He never liked to set around talking with my folks after dinner, especially if Lily was there.

She didn't like him any better than he liked her. She liked men that flirted and complimented her on her new dresses. And she hated men that argued with her. That's why Joe kept silent when she talked in her trembly voice. She had been raised an orphan after her papa died in the Confederate War, and she tried to act stylish and cultured I think to cover up how poor they had been.

Once before Jewel was born we went to pick huckleberries at the head of the river, the summer after Tom and me was married. Tom hitched up the wagon and put in three seats. We took buckets and a picnic basket, and left at daylight because it was ten miles. We stopped on the river road for Joe and Lily. David was sick and Florrie couldn't go. It was just us four with Pa.

Lily come out wearing a big white hat with a white veil. "I must protect my face from both sun and flies," she said. "I'll not come back with my skin all bit and blistered."

It was a fine summer morning and we got almost to the head of the river before the sun come over the mountains. I always loved that upper end of the valley where the river gets small as a branch and the ridges plunge to the water. The pines are straight and black and the cliffs jut like statues far above.

"Did you see the article in the paper about wrinkles?" Lily said, as the wagon rattled on rocks.

"I don't think I did," I said. I was watching the dapples of early light through the trees. The woods was spotted with coins and streaks of sunlight.

"It said the two ways to prevent wrinkles are to stay out of sun and wind, and to never wash your face with harsh soap."

Tom was guiding the horse around rocks and slowing the wagon over washed-out places. We started climbing, winding out of the river valley. We come into the bright sun.

"Did you read the article, Tom?" Lily said.

Tom did not answer. He kept looking at his shadow throwed over the horse in front of him.

"Oh I forgot," Lily said. "Tom don't read the paper."

"We need to get water," Pa said. "There's a spring ahead."

"There won't be any water on the ridge," I said. Anybody that went up to Long Rock to have a picnic or pick huckleberries had to take their own water.

Tom stopped the wagon a little further on and took the water bucket out of the wagon. I could tell how mad he was at Lily by how he banged the bucket on the wagon as he lifted it. Tom was usually too careful to bang anything. The spring was above the road in the laurel bushes. Tom disappeared into the thicket.

Pa took his glasses out of his pocket and saw a screw had fell out of a temple hinge. He searched in his pocket for the loose screw. "I can't pick berries without my glasses," he said.

But the screw was not in his pocket. He turned it inside out and found nothing but lint. "I have an extra screw in my purse," he said. He reached into his pocket and looked startled. "It ain't here," he said.

Pa patted his pockets, and then patted them again. He kept his pension money in his little leather purse, as well as a house key. "I had it this morning," Pa said.

"Maybe the man that can't read took it," Lily said. I looked at her and she turned away. I felt the blood rush to my face.

"I didn't mean that," she said behind her veil. "I didn't mean a thing."

Tom returned with the bucket of water and set it gently in the wagon. Cold water run down the sides of the pail onto the hay.

"Pa lost his purse," I said to him.

"Where?" Tom said.

"I don't know," Pa said. "I had it this morning."

"Where was the l-l-l-last place you saw it?" Joe said.

"When I left the house I put the key in the purse," Pa said.

Tom walked around the wagon and looked under the seats. "Here it is," he said, and picked the purse up from the straw.

"Glory be," I said.

When we reached the top we could look down on the river valley stretching blue and white in the summer haze. It was so wonderful to be out of the kitchen, away from the hot fields, up on the ridge where the breeze whitened the huckleberry bushes. To the north you could see the Pisgah Mountains climbing one on top of the other to the edge of the sky. "What a glorious day," I said.

It was that same summer before Jewel was born that Tom went fishing with Joe and David. Joe never invited anybody to go on his trapline, but more than once he had asked Tom if he wanted to go turkey hunting or deer hunting up in the Flat Woods. And every time Tom said he had work to do, had to split rails or clear brush, had to fix a fence. "And I don't have a gun," Tom said.

"You can borrow mine," Pa said. Pa had a muzzle loader, as well as a shotgun, but Tom claimed he didn't want to use them.

I don't think Pa and Joe believed Tom had never hunted or trapped. They thought he was just being modest or maybe trying to get some advantage. Maybe by working harder he was trying to show them up. Maybe by always working he was trying to show how he was in charge of the homeplace.

But late spring come and we had the awfullest rains. They must have lasted two weeks at least. Every day it rained again. And even though it might stop and the sun shine a few minutes and fog start rising on Cicero Mountain, the next thing you knowed it was raining again. When it finally stopped water stood in the plowed fields and the ground was too soggy in the garden to touch. The sun come out midmorning, and we could see the river high in its banks. The falls was roaring over at the mill.

Joe and David come by with their fishing poles and Joe carried a can of worms. David was too frail even then to do much hunting, or heavy work, but he liked to fish. Sometimes he set by a pool all day watching his line and studying some tract or magazine.

"Tom, g-g-get your pole," Joe called from the yard.

Tom was sewing up a hole in his overalls. He was the only man I ever saw who would sew. I guess he learned how when he was living on his own at the Lewis place. "I ain't hardly got time," Tom said when he come out on the porch.

"S-s-sure you've got time," Joe said. "Everyth-th-thing is wet and near about drowned except the trout."

"Come on," David said and coughed.

"I ain't even got a pole," Tom said.

"Pa's got plenty of poles under the eave of the smokehouse," I said. "One of them is mine. You take my pole."

"C-c-come on," Joe said, "while the fish are biting." Joe was like a little youngun he was so thrilled to be going fishing.

I saw that if Tom didn't go it would embarrass Joe and David. They had gone out of their way to be friendly to their brother-in-law. They might not ask him again.

"Let's go," I said to Tom. "I'll go too and we can get a mess of fish for supper."

I think that's what persuaded Tom, that there might be something useful to be gained. All our hog meat was gone and some fresh fish would be welcome.

"G-g-ginny used to love to fish," Joe said, "wh-wh-when she could take her nose out of a book."

I got the poles from the nails on the wall of the smokehouse and we followed Joe down the trail along the edge of the field.

When I was a girl, fishing was something we did in the spring and early summer. Pa would take us after a rain when the river was muddy and it was too wet to plant or hoe corn. Going down to the swollen river was so exciting my stomach would churn. Florrie and me learned to put worms on our hooks same as Pa and Joe did. Pa showed us how to throw the line into deep water and hold the pole with both hands, waiting to feel a trout jerk the line. He showed us how to fish the pools in the bends, and in the dark places behind rocks and under a log or overhanging bank. We got to know the Lemmons Hole and the Bee Gum Hole.

We followed Joe to the Bee Gum Hole where the creek joins the river at the bend. The river was a foot higher than usual. Muddy water lapped the sand where fishermen built their campfires.

"Th-th-throw your line over there into the deep water," Joe said, and pointed to the deepest part near the eddy. The fast current on the far side spun water backwards into the deep part.

Tom didn't say anything as he baited his hook.

"There's a grandpa trout in there so big and smart he'll never be caught," David said. "It eats the little trout. It must have been here since the Indians fished the river." He begun to cough.

"If you h-h-h-hooked it, it might pull you in," Joe said. "That f-f-f-fish is strong as a horse."

"We call him Plow Wing," David said. "Old Plow Wing."

Joe and David talked like little boys. I guess nothing makes men feel young again like fishing. Before Tom got his line in the water David had already caught a trout about eight inches long. The fish flashed its mirror sides as he pulled it to the bank.

"Now that's a m-m-monster," Joe said. David slipped the hook out of its mouth and threw the fish back in. "We don't need minners," he said.

I baited my hook and put an extra shot on the line for the strong current. I bit down on the sinker to tighten it and then spit out the taste of lead. It was something I hadn't done since ten or twelve. The lead was soft as candy between my teeth.

I saw Tom watching where he had throwed his line. There was little wrinkles and puffs in the eddies that took his line and worried it. Part of the mystery and thrill of fishing is you can't see what is happening. Everything is deep under the surface and all you can do is wait for the line to tighten, or the jolt to come through the pole. Fishing is like a lesson in patience and humility because you have so little power over what happens. Even if you hook a fish it may twist off before you pull it in. Trout are good at throwing the hook once they feel it in their lip. If they don't swallow the bait quick they will probably hurl theirselves off before you can land them.

Tom was being patient. He worked his pole to the left and then eased it a little to the right. He watched the swift current on the far side, and looked at a hawk circling the steep ridge above the river. Leaves was just coming out all different shades of yellows and greens up the side of the ridge. Spring colors are some of my favorite. The yellows and greens looked delicate as smoke. There was sarvis blooming and dogwoods starting to blossom. The woods shined like some new garden in the sun.

"If you w-w-worry, a fish won't bite," Joe said.

"You can think a fish to your hook," David said, "if you think only about good things."

"I'm thinking about how tired my arm is getting," Tom said.

Something tugged my line and I pulled it a little and the line jerked harder. The end of the pole tipped and I pulled up. The line throbbed and plucked at the pole. I pulled it all the way up and a fish flashed slapping at the surface. It was white and a kind of gold.

"Ain't nothing but a h-h-hornyhead," Joe said.

I raised the pole and took the jumping fish in my hand. It had thorns on its head and gulped air as I took it in my grasp.

"Throw it in the weeds," David said. "Nothing but trash."

I throwed the hornyhead into the laurels behind the clearing and heard it thrash in the leaves there from time to time. I rebaited my hook and tossed it back in.

The sky was clear now except for a few white clouds far above us. They was so bright it hurt to look at them. David stared at the clouds for a long time. "Just looking up there you can tell who made this world," he said. "Yes sir."

The clouds looked so bright they appeared to have lights inside them. The air was washed clean. It was good to glance away from the muddy river. The cloudtops was white as snowdrifts.

"S-s-s-signs and wonders right there," Joe said.

"How come this is called the Bee Gum Hole?" Tom said.

"Because a bee gum was found washed up here a long time ago," David said. "It was when white people first settled. Nobody knows where it come from."

"I guess the trout ain't hungry today," Joe said. "M-m-maybe they are fasting."

Just then Tom's pole whipped into the water. He jerked it and the line run taut through the muddy pool so fast it hissed. He swung the pole and then the line started upstream. I had never heard a fishing line sing that way through the water. It whistled and burned across the pool. The line went this way and that way.

"You've g-g-got one," Joe yelled.

The line shot to the end of the pool and come almost clear of the water, then started back, going z-z-z-z and zinging.

"It's a big one," David said. "Hold him." He started coughing. "That's old Plow Wing."

"That ain't no fish," Joe said. "That's a horse."

Tom run along the bank holding the pole clear of brush. There was no way he could let out more line from the coils at the end of the pole. I was afraid the line would break. He run to the edge and stepped off into the pool. The water was deeper than he expected and he stumbled up to his knees in the muddy river.

"Watch out," I yelled.

The line swung around and come right toward him. He lifted the pole as high as he could, but just barely kept it taut. The fish acted like it was going to attack him, but then swung back up the river. Tom run up on the bank to follow it.

This time when the trout reached the end of the line it jumped clear of the water. The fish looked a yard long. It was silver as a mirror and sprinkled with ink. Its sides flashed pink and gold and green. It was the prettiest fish I had ever seen, and looked untouched by the muddy water. It slapped its tail like a fan and danced across the pool before dropping back into the river.

"Don't you lose him," Joe said, his stammer gone.

When the trout headed downstream Tom went into the pool. He held the pole over his head and pulled the fish toward the sandbar. He was hoping to get the fish on the sand and grab him.

"Sweet Jesus," Joe said, when he saw the fish in the shallows.

"Please let him catch it," I prayed without thinking about it.

But the big rainbow recovered its strength and shot into the deep water. The line hissed and frothed like a hot wire dropped in the river. It went *zit* and then *zit* again. Tom waded into the pool up to his armpits, holding the pole as high as he could.

"Let him get tired," Joe called.

"Don't let him throw the hook," David said.

But the trout was far from exhausted. It pulled Tom along the side of the pool past the sandbar at the creek mouth. It run into the shallow water further down, and he followed, stumbling over the big rocks. He had lost his hat and he was wet to his neck.

Finally he turned the fish around and it headed upstream. I don't know who was more tired, the fish or Tom. He was out of breath and staggering in the mud. The trout must have thought it could escape up the creek for it turned toward the fan of mud from the creek mouth and run into the shallows. Tom jerked the pole and pulled it further onto the sand.

While the big trout thrashed in three or four inches of water Tom leapt on top of it and grabbed its gills with both hands. He wrestled it until the fish quit flopping. When Tom stood up I saw the fish was half as long as he was. Both him and the rainbow was covered with sand. Tom was out of breath, but he held the fish up into the sunlight like it was made of silver and rubies and emeralds.

CHAPTER EIGHT

Everything went smooth until our first baby was born. I mean Tom and me had our tiffs and sulks, same as any married couple will. Tom was usually so silent it was hard to tell at first when he was sulling. But I soon got to where I could tell. There was a stiffness about him when he was mad. It was like he pulled in all his feelings and interests. He might not talk less than usual, but he give off a kind of coldness. His eyes wouldn't meet mine, and he didn't answer if you asked him something.

But the sweetest thing about little quarrels is the making up. After ignoring each other, and saying hurtful things, and after maybe days of resentment and feeling sorry for yourself, you suddenly feel it's not important. It's like falling in love again. You notice the fine things about your husband. Everything he has done and said is forgivable. You want to touch him and be with him. Nothing makes loving so intense as a quarrel patched up. It's like the charge of anger gets in your blood and becomes pleasure and rediscovery. Something bigger than you takes over in the dark and you watch yourself in the thrill of strangeness.

Our first baby come the last summer of the century, and while she was still nursing the next spring Pa and me started attending the revival held in a tent over near Crossroads. I invited Tom to come with us. I hadn't been to a camp meeting since before we was married. It was a need I had coming back on me, now that Jewel was born. Tom knowed I had gone to the Holiness meetings before, but maybe he thought I never planned to go again. I don't know what he had thought. I just knowed I had to go. My reading was not enough, and my everyday life of marriage and work was not enough. I needed the fellowship of the meetings. There was a craving in me that nothing else could answer.

"That's a long way to go to church," Tom said. He had been burning stubble and brush by the branch and smelled like smoke.

"Ain't church," I said. "This is a revival meeting."

He didn't say anything else, but he agreed to go. He drove the wagon and tied the horse to a tree outside the tent. There was maybe a dozen horses hitched in the woods there. It was a warm night in spring and you could hear peepers down by the creek.

The preacher was Billy John Jarvis, and he was from the part of South Carolina called Dark Corner that had so many preachers as well as blockaders. Many had been blockaders in their youth, before they got right. I'd heard of Preacher Jarvis. He was fiery-faced with a bold roving eye. His gift was for speaking in tongues, interpreting the message of tongues as witness.

Joe and Lily come too, and there must have been near fifty in the little tent lighted by kerosene lanterns. It always seemed magic to me, that you could create a place of worship in the woods, just by throwing up a tent or brush arbor and building an altar. It showed that the Spirit was everywhere.

Billy John's voice was small and uncertain when he spoke at first. Like a lot of men he had to talk above and below his regular voice to have force. But he made up for the thinness with speed. It took me a few seconds to get used to his quick talk. I guess some of the old and hard-of-hearing had trouble understanding him at all. But I saw what a powerful preacher he was. He had the rhythm, and the right catch in his voice. Most important, he knowed when to pause and make people wait to hear what he had to say next. After a few sentences there was shouts and Amens, and everybody got pulled along.

"I sayuntoyoudoyouknow my Jesus? Isaydoyou come here tonight to learn of Him? I saydoyouknow salvation, friend? I come to you preaching the full gospel, uh. I say to you tonight have you seen my Jesus, uh? Have you looked upon his sweet face, uh? I say these are the times of Tribulation and trouble. I say, uh, to you it is within your choice to live a life of peace and joy, uh."

Sweat begun to stream from his red face. The glistening flush made his eyes look more searching. He raised his right hand as he spoke, not waving it and not exactly pointing to heaven either, but as if it was in contact with something invisible, like the arm of a streetcar in Greenville touching the wire above it, as he walked back and forth in front of his listeners.

"I say the Lord wants us to be joyous, uh, and to speak in tongues of joy, of men and angels. I say the Spirit is here with us tonight, uh."

There was a lot of "Amens" and "Yes, brothers." A large woman in white got up and started swaying where she stood. It was Tildy Tankersley. She wasn't jerking exactly, but her head swung around like she was swimming and she sung out with her eyes closed, like she was answering the preacher. In a few seconds I saw she was not saying words but sounds like "ari ai ari aiai ee."

The preacher stopped, then stretched out his arm over her and said, "My children we have a message tonight, a sign from our dear sister that the Lord is with us, uh. The Lord is not way off in some fine city. He is right here in this tent, uh. I interpret her message to say that the Lord will do great things right here in the community of Crossroads, uh, if we only believe him. That all you, and you, and you, have to do is cut loose from the ties of the flesh and praise him, uh. You stand at the threshold of a life of the spirit, of signs and wonders, and all you need to do is reach out and take, uh, what is offered to you tonight to step into the realms of joy. No one else can take that step for you any more than they can be born for you."

Among the shouting that followed another woman stood up and spoke in tongues. Her mouth made sounds but she stood like she was asleep. Her message was interpreted by the preacher as a warning to the old drunk Burt Jones that this was his last chance to get right before the Judgment. And there was a warning that somebody else present, unnamed, was living in danger of hellfire. Lily stood up in the shadows, and looking straight at the preacher begun to chatter also in a high-pitched voice. The preacher pushed through the crowd and stood in front of her.

"The Lord says somebody here tonight has, uh, stayed away from the Spirit too long and has been lukewarm. And she must rededicate her life, uh, or find the Spirit has turned away."

Preacher Jarvis looked straight at me and I knowed it was me that was meant. I felt like I was naked and my bones bleaching in his glare. My dirty sinful heart was visible to all. A pain went through me, and it was like my heart was tearing my chest. I had to move to get rid of the burden. I couldn't stand my blackness any longer. I saw I had been away from communion with the Spirit. I had tried to trade marriage and human things and reading and even hard work for the business of praise. I had ignored what was best about myself, most satisfying. I had lost something, and I had to get it back. I had to let go of myself to save myself.

Still holding little Jewel to my chest I begun to shout, and I moved among the crowd saying, "Jesus, I give you my life. Take it, it's yours." I guess I did a kind of dance, swaying among the people. I didn't notice I had moved across the sawdust to the front, still holding the baby. Jewel had woke up and screamed but I hardly noticed. Milk come out of my breasts and soaked down the front of my dress, but I didn't pay it any attention.

It was only when I got to the front of the tent and turned that I saw how Tom looked at me. I was feeling the sweet inner burning of the Spirit. I felt I was floating up above my life. But Tom looked shocked and scared. He come forward and took Jewel, and jerked me by the wrist out of the tent into the dark.

When we got to the wagon I never saw anybody as mad as Tom was. He pushed me up on the wagon seat, and stood on the ground holding the baby. He was so mad I don't think he could talk. He walked around the wagon and stomped the ground. We had to wait for Pa and Joe and Lily, and the preaching and shouting went on.

I was too dazed to know what to say. I had been feeling such a relief and glory when Tom grabbed Jewel and jerked me out into the dark. It was like my mind had gone empty with confusion.

"If you have to make a fool of yourself, and me," Tom finally said, "at least you don't need to scare the baby half to death."

Jewel was still screaming, but she slowed a little in the dark, the way a baby will when the worst of its fit is over. Tom rocked her and talked to her and walked among the horses. But I never thought men had a way with babies. Men like young children, but I never noticed they had a touch for quieting infants.

"It never hurt a baby to go to service," I said.

"This baby ain't going no more," Tom said.

"Be careful you don't commit the unpardonable sin," I said. I had been sweating, but the night air made me shiver.

"Ain't me that needs to take care," Tom said.

The horses was restless. They shuddered and whickered, and shook their harness. It sounded like the peepers down by the branch was answering the preacher.

When Pa come out he didn't say a thing to Tom. Even Joe and Lily was quiet when they got in the wagon. Jewel had finally gone to sleep, and Tom handed her to me before taking the reins. Nobody spoke as we drove in the dark. It was like a black curtain had descended around us. I could smell the milk souring on the front of my dress.

The next day we was both still mad. Our sulks and snits before had been little things. They didn't amount to more than bee stings that end up itching. What happened now was cold venom rushing in us and pouring over everything. I don't know where such poison could come from. I think it surprised

Tom as much as me. In our fighting we got fancy and cruel. It was like we become different people. What Tom had seen at the camp meeting made him doubt everything about me. His confidence in me was shattered. He acted like he thought I was crazy.

"Such goings-on is heathen," he said at dinner.

"Worship of the Lord is not heathen," I said.

"My folks never held with such," he said.

"Then I pity them," I said.

"Nobody needs your pity," he said.

I was putting on a pan of cornbread. I slammed the pan on the plate upsidedown and the cake fell out smoking and crisp.

"Such meetings take place only in the dark," Tom said. "They don't happen in the honest light of day." I tried to remember any Holiness services I had seen in the day. I was sure I had.

"People have to work in the daytime," I said. Because Tom was such an early-to-bedder he wouldn't approve of any meetings at night, I thought. He was drowsy by eight o'clock. His sleepiness seemed a simple-minded thing.

"You won't go again," he said.

"I'll go if I want to," I said.

"Then that shows the sin of this thing," he said.

"Only to them that are blinded."

"The Bible says a woman must honor and obey her husband."

"Not when the husband is blinded by worldliness and greed."

"Greed?"

I saw I had gone too far, but it was too late to take it back. It was something deep inside pushing me, something I couldn't see. "Yes, greed," I said. "For this place."

"Then keep your place, you religious fool," Tom said, his voice low and near breaking. He stood up from the table leaving his grits half finished. Grits and butter was just about his favorite thing. He walked out the back door without closing it.

Anger is among the sweetest feelings people know. That's why they cherish it and feed it and remember it so long. Anger is like a tightening and sharpening of sight. It is the brightest angle from which to look at things. Jewel started crying and I had to pick her up. I was so mad I didn't feel like nursing her. I told myself if Tom wanted to put his foot down I would show him I was more than his match. I was both scared and thrilled at the idea of a fight. I told myself he hadn't seen anything until he started matching wits and will with me. I was so excited it took me several minutes to calm down enough to nurse the baby.

All day I worked around the house and made up in my mind things I would say to Tom when he come from the field. Again and again I went back and forth about what I ought to tell him. Sometimes I thought I would say it was too bad we had quarreled over something good and sacred, and that we had agreed on things so far except the tent meeting. And I wanted to say I didn't think he was greedy and I was glad he had married me and had the place.

And then the anger swept through me again as I whisked around the hearth, and I wanted to shout in his face who did he think he was, telling me not to go to camp meeting? When he come back at suppertime I would tell him he could keep to his ditch-digging and rail-splitting and going to bed with the chickens. I had more things to do with my life than just grubbing for a little money.

But Tom never come in for supper. Pa and me eat our beans and taters and cornbread and the plate I set for Tom stayed empty. When I cleared the table I left it there for him. But he didn't return from the field till milking time, and then he got the buckets from the back porch and went right to the barn.

I left his plate on the table, and the beans and taters and bread in the stove, and dressed for meeting. Pa got dressed too. Tom still hadn't come and I wrapped Jewel in her warmest blanket.

Pa went out and hitched the horse to the wagon, and just as we was about to leave Tom come back from the barn. He set down the foaming buckets and walked to the wagon. "You're not taking the baby," he said. I held Jewel close in her clean bonnet.

"Give her to me," Tom said.

I hesitated a moment, and then handed the baby to him. I didn't want to scare her by arguing.

All the way to Crossroads I thought about the baby screaming after I had left. She would cry for at least half an hour. Tom would have to let her cry while he strained the milk into pitchers and carried them to the springhouse. She would bellow as he scalded the buckets and then got his supper from the stove.

I knowed that as he carried the squalling baby to quiet her he would consider his options. I understood Tom well enough to know he would think of shooting both Pa and me, and he would be both surprised and disgusted with hisself. He might ask the preacher at church to intervene, but that wouldn't do any good. I knowed exactly how Tom would think of going back to the Lewis place. And he was also thinking about going west, to Iowa, or Kansas, the wheatfields of Minnesota, or to California. But that was not his way, to leave what he'd started, pick up and run off among strangers. I knowed him better than he understood hisself.

The place and the child was all in the world he had to show for his almost forty years. He really had no choice but to stay and do his work and make a better place for hisself, as much as he hated it. I saw how he was thinking. He would compromise and make his decision. He would take a middle course.

Sure enough, when we got back late that night I saw he was not in bed. Jewel was in the cradle but Tom was not to be seen. I took the lantern and climbed up to the loft, and there he was. He had fixed a pallet of quilts and blankets and was sound asleep. I don't think he ever knowed when we come home.

Over the next few weeks Tom and me discovered new levels of hate and spite in ourselves. Outwardly we lived much the same as before. We did not sleep together and we did not touch each other. But we got more familiar in new and irritating ways. We each criticized everything the other did. There wasn't anything about Tom that looked right to me. If he got ready for church I kept him waiting until it was too late to get to Sunday school. I did my best to keep Jewel away from him, to have her asleep when he come in after milking. I warned him not to wake the baby.

"I had no intention of waking the baby," he said.

"Just walking in those heavy shoes will wake her," I said.

Tom put in longer hours than ever in the field. He worked by hisself most of the time. He started jobs at dawn and was done or mostly done before Pa ever joined him. He planted corn in the bottom on his own. He hoed and plowed, and planted a patch of watermelons in the loam by the river. He protected the melon vines against frost with sacks, and he put in an extra acre of cane and a garden twice as big as before. He hoed the corn three times before laying it by. I had never seen fields so clear of weeds. The madder he got the harder he worked. It was like he was trying to prove the land was his, that he had earned it.

But he knowed it was the best way to fight me, to work hard and prosper. I could read books, and I could go to meeting, and I could spite him, but I couldn't prevent him from prospering. He figured that out early. What he had to do was work and thrive. He growed big watermelons by the river. And he cut corn tops and pulled fodder so the fields was neat as flowerbeds.

From the extra cane he made more than two hundred gallons of molasses. By mid-November he had sawed and pulled in on the sled enough firewood for the winter. He sold molasses to neighbors, and he sold firewood. He sold watermelons, and he sold apples and cider. There was nothing I could do to stop him from working. It was his way of heaping coals on my head.

With the extra money Tom bought wire, the new kind with four barbs to the knot, and he begun to replace rails around the pastures. He started to clear ground at the upper end of the bottom. The Peaces hadn't cleared new ground since the war.

It made me mad to see him work so. Everybody noticed what he was doing. They said he was making the Peace place pay. They said he was making Pa's living for him. Tom didn't say anything at supper at night. Sometimes he went to sleep in his chair, and then climbed on up to the loft while Pa and me talked by the fire. He played with Jewel a little if she was still awake.

By the time the revival closed in the spring it was like there was a light over the countryside. The Spirit was there, and the mountains seemed to shine. It had been an awakening, and the churches had better attendance. I've heard that after a great revival people can't walk into a valley and not feel the Spirit there. It's like the hours and minutes are blessed. The mornings are changed, and dew is lit and pure. In spite of my quarrel with Tom I went through each day with a light heart, knowing I would go to a meeting that night. Didn't anything matter except the meeting to worship and praise. It was the purpose of everything, to praise. It was like falling in love with everybody, being married to the world. Nothing cleanses like shouting and speaking in tongues. You feel clear and free as a spring pool. Some mornings I walked along the river just for the joy of it.

When we was children Florrie and me would play down at the river. Sometimes we fixed a picnic basket and took it to the rocks at the shoals. We took boiled eggs and cookies and apples, and set on the rocks in the water to eat them. There was something thrilling about fast water, and the roar of the shoals was surprising, no matter how many times we had been there.

By myself I liked to walk along the still pools of the river beyond our fields, and into the woods up toward Cabin Creek. It soothed me to mosey on the banks where the water was slow and green. In fall leaves dropped in the river and appeared to float above water they was so dry. In places the bank was scratched by muskrat slides. The woods by the river looked dark as a cellar.

Pa said the Indians named Green River in their own tongue, and white people took the name from them. We lived so close to the head the river wasn't wider than a creek. It started as a spring eight miles to the west and swung through a long valley. At the shoals it poured through a slot between mountains.

Pa said the river run on almost a hundred miles to the east. He said it run fast through Green River Cove as it dropped out of the mountains into flat country. He said his great-great-grandpa that fought at Cowpens and Kings Mountain lived on Green River down there where it run into Broad River. When that end of the river was settled there was still Indians in the mountains.

Sometimes I would set by the river and watch the water. The pools had a shiny green skin. Around sticks there was lips of ripples. Rings and curls passed over deep pools. In clear shallows minnows sprinkled this way and that way.

I watched eddies where the river turned back on itself. Along the bank, water with lather and sticks on it was moving back upstream, going fast in places, then getting slow and coiling, and caught by the main current again. In places water got trapped in a pocket and turned and turned for hours.

When I walked the river trail I could feel the ground shook by current. Above the shoals the bank trembled with the roar,

like there was a furnace under it. The trail turned through laurels and climbed to a little bluff, and when you come down to
the rocks there was the water foaming. The sight made me
shudder.

The mountains rose straight up on either side of the shoals.
From below, the slopes looked black. There was pines and
hemlocks that stood by the water and pointed into the sky. And
pines rose up the sides of the mountains, among the rock cliffs.
The tops of the ridges was ragged and pointed with pine trees.

In summer there would be a long snake sunning itself on
the rocks. It was almost the color of water, and when you got
close the moccasin poured itself into a crevice.

The day I fell in love with the shoals I was standing with my
feet in water, below a big rock. It was like the water was talking, quoting scripture or muttering a poem. The river pulled at
my feet heavy and powerful. The surface appeared to sort and
resort a puzzle, scattering pieces and gathering them again.

But I was looking at the tall hemlocks pointing straight up
the side of the mountain. I looked through the tops of the
lower trees toward the pines further up, right to those on top
of the ridge. And then I saw a cloud moving. It was just a little
cloud in the clear sky, but white as snow. And it was like I was
standing and looking right up the ladder of trees into heaven.

That was when I thought of the words from the Bible about
the Ascension. "While they beheld, he was taken up; and a
cloud received him out of their sight. And while they looked
steadfastly toward heaven as he went up, behold two men
stood by them in white apparel, which said, Ye men of Gallilee
why stand ye gazing up into heaven?"

It was the words "while they beheld, he was taken up, and a cloud received him out of their sight" that struck me so deep. It was like I was looking up at that cloud. The cloud appeared at the top of the ridge, which was at the tip of the tall hemlock, which was rooted right in the river. It was almost like I could reach up and touch the cloud. All the trees pointed toward it. The sky around the cloud was blue, on and on, deeper and deeper.

The air felt haunted around and above me. And it was like there was many dimensions in the air. "He was taken up, and a cloud received him out of their sight," I said again. The words sparkled like the river. They shined and soared and lifted me past the hemlocks and pine trees, past the rock cliffs and trees on top of the ridge. I felt I was rising above the river, and everything below was just shadows. I felt lighter than a thought, and the mountains was nothing but shade, waves of shade. The cloud floated alone and blinding. It was white-hot and sweet as the light in sugar. The air was so bright it was almost black inside and behind. I felt took up in its shining breadth.

"A cloud received him out of their sight," I said. As I walked back up the river I repeated the words, and the woods along the bank felt different. The woods was brighter, and the river repeated the words over and over like a poem it couldn't forget.

When I was young I was always falling in love with a word, or phrase, with a particular image or sentence. Pa had a big dictionary he bought down in Augusta one time when he took honey and hams to trade. My favorite thing sometimes was to read in the fat Webster's, and make lists of words and facts. Sometimes I would read a passage and couldn't get it out of my mind. The color and strangeness of a word would trigger a feeling, and I would go through Pa's books for some mention of it. The name or phrase would have a sweetness that stayed with me. I couldn't stop saying it, and I couldn't get it off my mind. I looked through the catalogue of the American Book Company for more books about the subject. The sweetness stayed with me while I scrubbed and cooked, walked to the mailbox, or laid sleepless at night.

One time I fell in love with the description of the Transfiguration in the book of Mark, "And his raiment became shining, exceeding white as snow." The words kept coming back to me with a peculiar air, as if I was hearing them for the first time. Maybe it was the combination of "shining" and the purity of the snow. I repeated the words to myself for weeks, and studied the Gospels, finding other versions of the description. But no other pattern of words had the same effect. Gradually their power wore off, and I said the words less and less. But I still recall that sentence with pleasure, the way you remember something you have been in love with. The words had a soft blue glow. But how "white as snow" become blue in my mind I can't recall.

Another time I got interested in things about Egypt, after see-ing a picture of the pyramids in a magazine. I read everything I could find about that place and time. I read about the Sphinx and about mummies, and about hieroglyphs. Egypt seemed a vast and silent kingdom. I read about the river, about birds, and about the pharaoh's body embalmed in oils and spices. I thought about how they worshipped the sun, and thought the earth was a god that died and new crops and flowers growed out of his chest the next year. They thought the pharaoh and the sun and their country's law was the same thing. That Egypt was different from the one described in the Bible.

But everything quiets down eventually. A month after Billy John Jarvis went back to South Carolina we felt the need of another meeting. Joe called a service in his house. We gathered and sung hymns and prayed. But the spark wasn't there without a preacher. With just family and neighbors it never did take off. We needed a force from outside. Things went back to normal.

One night when we set down to supper I found myself looking at Tom more than I had in a long time. Usually we avoided noticing each other. I didn't say anything to him, but I kept looking at his strong shoulders and neck. And he seemed to be looking at me more than usual. Every time my eyes caught his he turned away, or I glanced away. We hadn't talked, except about things that didn't matter, for months. His face was reddened from the wind, and it seemed to get redder while he set at the table.

Later he set by the fire while Pa read the paper. Tom hardly ever looked at the newspaper hisself. Sometimes he would skim the headlines or study an article on farm prices in one of the papers we took. But after a day of work and a big supper it was hard for him to get concerned with what was happening far away.

"If they is anything important you-all will tell me," he once said. And I reckon it was true. If there was news about Cuba or the Philippines, we talked about it. When the president was shot Pa heard it at the store and come back and told us long before we saw it in the Greenville paper which always come a day late.

"Now if they was a paper that would tell what the weather is to be tomorrow . . ." he once said.

I saw Tom lift the shoes he had took off and place them by the hearth. He did that every night because he thought the last heat from the fire helped dry them out. Since the fire died down in the night they would be cold by morning, but I guess it was the natural place for him to put his shoes. They always smelled a little. Some nights I set them away while I rocked Jewel. But before I went to bed I put the shoes back on the hearth.

I took a lamp to the bedroom and started brushing my hair in front of the mirror. Jewel was asleep. I stood before the dresser and made slow strokes through my long hair. The door was partly open, and Tom had to pass the door to reach the ladder to the loft. I unbuttoned the top of my gown two or three buttons.

As Tom passed he paused to look in. He was usually not up that late. I did not turn but looked back at him. He is my husband, I thought. He is *my* husband. We are one flesh. It is our worship to be fruitful and multiply. All the harsh things built up between us begun to melt away. There was nothing to keep me from him. He started through the doorway and I went to him. He closed the door and started unbuttoning my gown. I dropped the brush and blowed out the lamp. It was like that night was our true honeymoon.

As I laid with Tom in the dark I kept thinking of passages from The Song of Solomon. I had been reading them in the

Bible the day before. As I rolled and turned I heard in my mind, "Awake, O north wind; and come, thou south; blow upon my garden, *that* the spices thereof may flow out. Let my beloved come into his garden, and eat his pleasant fruits."

And later as we loved I heard a voice say, "I *am* my beloved's, and his desire *is* toward me." And I felt I was right, and in the right place, even as I did at the revival services. And I thought how the thrill of loving was almost the same as communion with the Spirit and the thrill of solitude by the river, but I didn't understand how it could be. It was a mystery.

Our second child, a boy, was born in 1902. I named him Moody after the great evangelist. I was afraid Tom would protest, but he didn't. He was agreeable to most everything I suggested. It was like we had made a completely new beginning. It was as if we did everything for the first time, doing it right and better. We begun to discover what was really good about each other.

That year I was too busy with the children and with housework to go to revival meetings. And as I said earlier, the spirit of the meetings appeared to have left the community. Joe and Pa liked to talk about the Holiness services when they got together, and about the preachers whose books and pamphlets they was reading. And sometimes I joined in when Tom wasn't around. But as we worked or talked around the fire we sounded like elderly veterans of the spiritual awakening. We got sentimental about gone times and past glories. The last revival had been little more than a year before, but it felt like something in history.

"Preacher De Haan says if you're baptized with fire you can't fall from grace," Pa said. "At his meeting in Atlanta seven hundred people had the baptism of fire."

"That's the s-s-s-same as sanctified," Joe said.

"Them with the baptism are the same as saints, De Haan says."

"Nobody is a saint," I said. "At least I never met one."

Tom and me without saying it decided to let bygones be bygones. I reckon as long as we just talked about meetings it didn't matter. I didn't say anything to him about it. I felt a girl again, falling in love again, but wiser and more alert.

Through the late summer, while I was nursing the baby, and in the harvest months when we had extra dollars from the sale of cider and molasses, firewood and apples, our life together was better than it had ever been. I saw how ignorant I had been before. In our first year everything had been new and awkward. I didn't know how awkward I had been until I looked back on it.

That fall we reached a whole new stage in our loving. Our routines was at once habits and explorations. It was like we took long walks in bed while Jewel and the baby slept. Before, lovemaking had been something our flesh did, only slightly connected to us as people. Now we met, at least at times, as the people we truly was. Tom was strong and steady, his mind always on the goal, on the long work to be done. I was the distracted one, passionate and withdrawn by turns, you might say wild sometimes, too excited to think or remember later.

But more than the fullness of the new way we give ourselves, it was the alertness to moods and intentions of each other that made a difference. It was like we had been give an extra sense for knowing what the other felt. We knowed how to do the right things, even when we wouldn't have guessed it beforehand. It was as if we was in a new dispensation.

Christmas that year was the best I had ever seen. A week before Christmas we climbed up on the pasture hill, beyond the Sunset Rock, and gathered turkey's paw and holly to place over the mantel. Tom took Pa's gun and shot down mistletoe from a tree by the river. We cut a cedar along the fence above the spring and I trimmed it with chains of colored paper and popcorn. The house was filled with the smell of cedar and pine limbs on the mantel with the holly. Pine makes me think of the spices and perfumes of the Wise Men, of angels in the starry night. At Christmas it's like this troubled world becomes a part of eternity. Candles and carols and smells have a hush and thrill. The house smells of cinnamon and nutmeg. I won't forget that Christmas.

"We never did hardly celebrate Christmas at home," Tom said. "We didn't have no money and I reckon Ma didn't feel like celebrating after the war when Pa didn't come back." It was the most he ever talked about his family. If you asked, he would never answer questions.

CHAPTER NINE

The day after New Year's there was to be a pounding for the Brights down on the Turnpike. They was a large family that had moved into the community a few years before. They always seemed starved and sickly. They was the kind of people that just can't make a go of it. No matter what they try or who helps them their luck never gets any better. In the fall they had caught typhoid fever, three of the children, and the mother, who had died.

The preacher had told the congregation the straits the Brights was in. And it was agreed that one Sunday afternoon in January the members of the church would gather at their house for a pounding. Everybody was to bring a pound of something: coffee, sugar, tea, butter. Tom was going to bring a gallon of molasses. He was taking it hisself since he didn't want me and the children where they had had typhoid. But I told him if he was going I was going too, and taking three pints of foxgrape jelly also. He went out to hitch up without saying any more, and when he was done I come out with a basket on one arm and a box in the other.

"What's all that?" Tom said.

"These people are in need and I want to help," I said.

The basket held several jars of preserves and jelly, a cake, a canister of coffee, and two dozen eggs. In the box I had packed sheets and pillowcases, and some clothes I hadn't wore in a long time for the oldest girl. Tom glanced in the box.

"We can't give them everything," he said. "They're not kin."

"They need it more than we do," I said.

"It will look like we're putting on airs," he said.

"I'll take it in the back door so nobody will see," I said.

"I'm not going," Tom said. "I won't look like a rich fool."

He stomped into the house and never come out. I waited a few minutes, and went to get Pa to drive me. Tom set by the fire holding Jewel. He was so mad he just looked into the flames.

But that was only the beginning of his fury. Next day Florrie told him I had give fifteen dollars of his money to the Brights. It was like Florrie to tell him that. Though she was my sister she never had anything good to say about me. Sometimes we could be friendly and work together like we did as girls. But mostly she didn't approve of me. She didn't approve of going to revivals, and she didn't approve of Joe and Lily either.

But Florrie was wrong about the money. Ten of the dollars I give was mine, and five of it was Pa's. I had saved the dollars by selling eggs before I was married, and from selling a calf to Jimmy Jenkins. I kept my money in the bottom of my jewelry case and Tom didn't know a thing about it. And I decided I wouldn't tell him. If he wanted to act so stingy and listen to Florrie behind my back he didn't deserve to know the truth of it.

Now the strange thing was that Tom could be as generous as anybody if he was asked in the right way. There is a giving spirit in everybody if they will let it out. People enjoy helping others. There is nothing more thrilling than giving to another human being, because when we give we conquer our fear. To share makes us feel strong and part of the community.

What I mean is I saw Ida Jenkins come to Tom in the field. We was digging taters in October. Everybody knowed what a hard time Ida had after Jimmy died of smallpox. I was raking taters out and cleaning them, and Tom was loading baskets on the wagon.

Ida walked up on the rough clods, squinting in the sun. She always did have a kind of squint, and as she got older it seemed worse. "Tom," she said, "will you sell me a peck of taters?"

Tom was straining to lift a basket onto the wagon and his face was red. "No," he said. "I won't sell you a peck of taters."

I stood up to rebuke him. A smile broke out on his face.

"But I will give you a bushel," he said.

And I could tell how much Tom enjoyed that. He felt good about hisself. It made him feel happy and secure to give away taters to somebody that needed them.

The anger over what I give the Brights was only the beginning of Tom's fury. He made his pallet up in the loft, and he didn't hardly speak when he was in the house. Mostly he stayed away. Even in cold weather he worked in the barn or toolshed, or he gathered pine needles in the thickets for cowbedding. He acted like I had gone crazy and he couldn't trust me. He acted like I wanted to steal his money, to hurt him where he was most tender.

The first weeks of the new year was cold and silent, except for Moody's crying. Pa didn't talk much when Tom was around.

And Joe and Lily didn't come over often. When Florrie visited she talked a streak, but I didn't have much to say to her. Sometimes she stopped at the barn and talked to Tom a long time before she come in. By late February it was clear I was expecting again.

That spring Joe started holding small prayer meetings, and I attended those right up to the time of my laying-in. It was not a happy pregnancy. During the first two I was contented. It was like I had a mysterious joy. During the third one I thought mostly about spite. I thought if I could hurt Tom by giving, I might as well give away more. I couldn't seem to think about anything happy. I didn't even enjoy reading during those months.

A traveling preacher, a faith healer, come through and stayed with Joe and Lily. But because of the cold weather he was never able to hold services. I walked across the hill for the little prayer meetings they had. His name was Worley and he was from around Pickens. It was obvious he had little more than the clothes he wore, and they was threadbare. If he couldn't have services he had no way of collecting money. I made him two shirts, and some handkerchiefs. If I had had material I would have tailored him a suit. But I give him money instead. I handed him ten dollars from my savings under the jewelry. Pa had give it to me at Christmas, but I never let Tom know how much I had.

Of course Florrie went and told Tom, as I knowed she would. I don't reckon it was more than two days before he found out. Lily had told Florrie, and she must have come special to tattle to Tom. And that seemed like the worst insult to Tom. I can't say but what I meant it partly for an insult. With two children already, and a third one coming, I guess he was worried, as all men worry about their duty. It was winter and he had the place to look after, and who knowed what hard times might be ahead?

"You want to give what we have to any religious trash that comes through," he said. He spoke almost with his teeth together, hissing his words. "You will be the ruination of us," he said.

"You are already ruined by greed," I said.

We took to going to church separate. I went with Pa and the children almost till I was due. Tom had been sleeping on the pallet since the first of the year, and he got up long before I did. Weekdays he was in the fields before I even woke. Sundays he milked and got dressed and went to service on his own.

Tom had less and less to do with Pa, and Joe too. When we was first married him and his brother-in-law had always worked together at fodder-pulling time or when there was a shed to be built. Joe was the strongest man around, and though he stuttered when excited or among strangers, he was always a talker, just like Pa, with a loud voice, lots of laughing. He liked to read too, religious tracts and pamphlets, magazines and history books, and he talked about what he had read as he worked. He knowed the history of the community and the family better than anybody else.

The more Joe talked the harder he worked, and Tom never seemed to mind his talk. Joe went on and on about Darwin and evolution, while he dug holes for posts or sawed a pine log. Only somebody strong as Joe had the breath to work and talk at full speed.

"People don't come from no monkeys," he would say as he pulled the crosscut saw.

"No sir," Tom would say, and pull it back.

"If we are descended from monkeys how come we ain't got tails?" Joe said and pulled again.

Tom would grunt; he didn't need to answer.

"I heard Darwin caught a disease in the tropics," Joe said. "His mind was never right after that." He pulled again, working up a sweat and pulling faster. Tom had to strain to keep up.

"Now I've seen people that looked like monkeys," Joe said.

"Me too," Tom said.

"And I've seen them that acted like monkeys," Joe said, as he pulled the saw back. They was getting far down in the log and it was pinching. The saw was hard to pull.

"Put a block under it," Tom said.

Joe shoved a section of cut wood under the log to prop it up. "M-m-maybe apes is descended from people," he said. "Maybe they was people that didn't go to church or help other people out. They didn't b-b-believe in nothing, and eventually they just growed hair and tails and went to live in the trees. Maybe apes is d-d-descended from politicians." Joe busted out laughing just as the saw cut through and the end of the log rolled away.

Early on a Sunday morning I could sometimes hear Joe praying in the thicket on the hill. His voice would carry in the quiet, though you could only catch a word here and there. His voice would rise to a holler, then die away again. It was the way he prayed at church and at meetings. And he prayed so long the preacher almost never called on him. Joe had always wanted to preach, and he liked to take over prayer meetings and talk until it was time to go. Some said they didn't mind, that he knowed more and had more to say than other people. But Preacher Jolly didn't agree, and never called on him. Florrie said he talked so much at church and in the field because he never got a chance to say a word at home. Lily was a nonstop gossip. When Joe went out to pray or work all his bottled-up feelings and thoughts was ready to be let out, no matter where he was or who he was with.

But after Joe and Lily kept Preacher Worley, and I give the preacher money, Tom appeared to blame Joe. He didn't ask Joe to work with him anymore. I don't reckon they had words about it. But I rarely saw them working together. If Joe come over to help Pa, Tom was always busy someplace else. Tom had a way of disappearing, of just not being around when he didn't want to be.

One day in June I felt the pains start. Tom was thinning cane at the upper end of the bottom, and I sent Pa to tell him to go after Hilda Waters, the midwife. I had thought it would be at least another month. I kept walking around the kitchen because it helped a little if I was standing up.

It must have took Tom an hour to bring back Hilda. It seemed an eternity. I told myself I would not lay down till Hilda come. I thought if I could just stay on my feet the pain wouldn't get bad. I had heard Indian women walked up and down the river bank before they give birth, and they didn't need any help.

I kept thinking of the Sunset Rock, wishing I could walk there. I hadn't been on the west side of the hill in weeks. If I could go there and look up the valley to the cool mountains I would feel better. I got my bonnet and put on my shoes.

"Where you going?" Pa said. He was on the porch watching Jewel and Moody play in the sand.

"I'm going for a walk," I said.

"You stay here," he said. He almost never did give an order, but I guess he was scared.

"Tell Hilda and Tom I went out the trail above the barn."

"Can I come?" Jewel said. She run up and grabbed my hand.

"You stay here," I said.

The sun was so bright it blinded me. I reckon June sun is the brightest there is. It was like the air was full of lit white dust. Everything looked on fire. The weeds was green fires, and the air white clear flames. The mountains was far blue flames.

I walked the path through the lower edge of the orchard thinking if I could get to the rock I would feel better. My bones was so weak I felt something was about to go wrong. A little snake trickled like oil across the path and vanished in the weeds. The bright sun made me feel cold, and I shivered.

"Who are you?" somebody called from up on the hill. I stopped on the trail and shaded my eyes. There was pines looming way up on the hill but I couldn't see anybody. The trees was so dark they looked like standing shadows.

"Who are you?" they said again.

The pines was a bright black. It didn't make sense somebody way up in the trees was talking to me. I tried to see who it was, but there was just the trees up there, and the blazing sky beyond. The orchard tilted steep, and the pasture even steeper. Could it be Joe up there praying?

"Who are you?" they called again. And then a crow flapped out of the tallest pine. It was just a crow cawing, and it sounded like it was talking to me. I tried to laugh at myself. A June bug buzzed by my face and I could feel the faint wind off its wing.

The pain hit me again, a deep-down pain. And it felt like something burning, red hot, had been drove into me. I told myself I could get through this, for I had done it before.

But I had forgot how bad a pain can be. You can't really remember pain once it's over. A pain has a taste, but you forget it once it's gone. I thought if I could just get to the rock and rest I would be all right. The pain was loud and I couldn't get away from it. A million birds was screeching inside me and a train roared right between my ears.

As the pain begun to ease a little I looked up and saw this dog on the trail ahead. It was a dog I hadn't ever seen before. Wasn't exactly a cur, and wasn't exactly a bulldog, but it looked like part of both. It had short gray hair that appeared brushed the wrong way. I tried to think whose dog it might be.

I saw it wasn't walking right. A lot of dogs trot sideways, especially when they're young. But this dog walked sideways, weaving from one side of the trail to the other. I thought at first it was looking for something, since its head was down. Then I saw it wobbling with each step like it was about to fall.

When the dog got close it saw me for the first time, and stopped. A chill went through me, on top of the pain, when I saw the dog's eyes all wet and glazed over. They was fevered eyes with stuff crusted on the edges. And there was slobber hanging from the dog's mouth like a beard. It was a mad dog for sure. It looked at me like it was cross-eyed and couldn't hardly see me.

"Lord help me," I prayed. I knowed a pregnant woman wasn't supposed to look in a mad dog's eyes or it would mark her baby. It was the devil looking at you from those fever-crazed eyes. I tried to look away. I had heard of women that saw mad dogs and had babies that was blind and had fits. And I heard of one baby that had hair all over it like a dog, and moaned and barked.

The dog stopped like it was trying to figure out where I was. I knowed if I moved fast I would show it where I was. I stood still and the dog growled and groaned in terrible pain. Dogs that go mad burn up inside from fever because they can't drink water.

I thought I would take one tiny step back in the grass to see if it noticed. I eased my left foot so it didn't seem to move at all. The weeds twitched a little and I stopped. I moved my right foot back a little, so slow the grass and weeds didn't even shake. I tried to think what I would do if the dog jumped. Should I turn and try to run? If I was not carrying the baby I might be able to run faster than it. But that was a big risk.

The dog was confused. It tried to look and to sniff. It was in pain. I never heard anything more anguished. I figured if I could just back away far enough I would turn and run. But I had to keep my mind on the dog, and on each little step back. If I tripped on a rock or a weed I would be a goner, and the baby too.

There was a kick inside me, and I felt the pain again. It was like a red-hot wire pulled through me, a barbed wire that tore hunks off what it passed through. The pain made me want to bend over to ease it. I didn't dare put my hands on my back to cool the pressure. I had to balance the pain with the slow effort of stepping back. Every step seemed to make the pain worse.

Never have I had to work that hard. Sweat dripped in my eyes and run down my back. My neck was wet and my armpits streamed. My hair was damp around the temples, and it felt like the sun was hot enough to set my hair on fire.

One little step at a time I eased away. I got back a foot, two feet. The pain thundered in my ears. The dog swung its head side to side. Maybe it was trying to see where I had gone.

I took steps so slow it made me tremble. The heat come off the weeds in waves, like steam from a washpot. I wished I could sink into the blackness of the heat and go to sleep. Sleep would be a cool shade to slip into. Sleep would quiet the noise of pain.

It looked like the dog was pitching forward, about to leap. But it tumbled to the ground and begun twisting and growling. The dog was having a fit right on the trail. Its mouth foamed and it jerked and twitched. I backed a bigger step, and then another.

"Step to the side," somebody said.

I turned and backed into the weeds at the side of the trail. There was a flash and awful bang. It was as if the sky blowed away in smoke and my ears rung. It was Pa with his shotgun.

The dog jerked on the trail and then stopped. There was a wheeze coming out of the hole in its side, and blood wetter and shinier than any water soaked out. The dog laid still.

Pa had followed to see how I was, and seen the dog on the path. He went back to get his gun without making a sound. I was so startled by the shot I forgot my pain a few seconds. But it come flooding back. I didn't think I could stand up anymore.

"I'm going to fall," I said.

"Lean on me," Pa said.

Jewel run through the grass. "Mommy, Mommy," she said.

"Go back and watch Moody," I said, and stumbled on the trail. All I could smell was the burnt gunpowder from Pa's shotgun. The air was full of smoke, and heat made the smell worse.

"I've got to set down," I said. I thought if I could set down in the weeds the pain would go away.

"You've got to come to the house," Pa said. "Keep walking."

I held his arm and took slow steps. Pa wasn't that strong and I was afraid I'd pull him over.

"Mommy, Mommy, what's wrong?" Jewel said.

"Go back to Moody," I said. I couldn't stand anymore and had to walk bent over. The pain hit again, this time like it was coming from behind. A river of hot coals pouring into me wouldn't have hurt worse. I felt myself falling to the weeds, and was caught by Tom's strong hands. Hilda Waters stood behind him.

I don't even want to talk about what happened the rest of that day. I don't want to think about the pain of that labor. Whoever named it labor knowed what they was doing. I never worked so hard in my life, and I never hurt so much either.

When they got me to the house and put me to bed, Hilda started water to heating in all the kettles. I reckon they always boil water before a birth so they can wash the baby and mother. Every time you think of a birth you think of the kitchen steamed up.

I guess Pa took Jewel and Moody down to the river. Maybe he took some cookies for a picnic. I had just made sugar cookies the day before. I was too sick to notice much. Later he led them across the hill to Florrie's to stay the night.

Next time the pains hit Hilda looked at the clock. She wanted to know how close the pains was. "When did it start?" she said.

"Just then," I said.

"No, the first one this morning."

"About eight o'clock," I said.

Hilda was a big woman that had delivered more than a hundred babies. Her daddy was the blacksmith at the village, and he drove the mail every day from the depot to the post office. She had a manner like her daddy. She worked with strong hands like a man. There was a way she put her shoulder in her work that reminded me of a man. But at the same time she was gentle with her hands as a cat is with her kittens.

"Roll over," she said. "Roll on your side."

I turned and she rubbed my back. She rubbed slow and heavy and it helped some until the pain went away on its own.

"Is there anything I can do?" Tom said. He stood in the door.

"Stay out and keep the water hot," Hilda snapped.

It wasn't but a minute before the next pain wrenched through me. I didn't see how I could stand it, yet I knowed it was going to get worse. I didn't see how I had gone through it two times before. The room was awful dark after the bright sun. As my eyes got used to the dimness I saw the dresser by the bed. There was a tortoiseshell mirror that was Mama's, and a wire hairbrush. There was a powder bowl and puff, and a little green perfume bottle Pa had got me a long time ago on one of his trips to Greenville.

The pain rushed into my belly again and I tried to keep my eyes on the green bottle. I figured if I could think about the perfume it would keep my mind off the pain. Light hit half the bottle and it looked like an emerald with a fire inside. I had never seen such a bright green. It was like a liquor or extract of the deep pools on the river, rich as oil. I imagined the bottle held a soothing drug, some kind of green opiate.

"Push!" Hilda ordered. She pressed on my belly and I pushed from inside, and heard myself scream. "Push!" she thundered, and I pushed. But I tried to think of the green light in the bottle. The vessel was so little it held just a few drops. It must have been a sample give to Pa, a tight icicle holding the green oil.

"Push, more, more!" Hilda hollered. She pressed on my belly and she run around and looked between my legs. "A little more, a little more!" she said. "You've got to try a little harder."

I tried to think of the power of the green perfume, how when it was opened something pushed its smell into the air. I tried to think what made perfume so cool, and what made it flame out in the air so. Its fumes smelled like shadows and drying flowers.

"Harder, harder!" Hilda cried. I was crying that I couldn't stand any more.

"You can," she said. "Don't be silly."

It was a sick pain, like there was something turned wrong. It felt as if something was tangled up and tearing.

"I can't do any more," I said.

"I won't listen to such talk," she said.

There was a white wall of screaming, like a sheet that went on forever in front of me. I tried to turn from it. I looked at the bottle and it was some kind of green eye watching me. A tree moved beyond the window and the eye blinked.

"There, there!" Hilda said.

I didn't think I could stand the pain anymore. I wondered what was going to happen. Then I thought of the pigeon the Indian doctor had told me about years before. I thought of a pigeon high above the valley looking down on hot wilting weeds and conniptions of heat boiling the air. I said my secret name over and over. It sounded cool and green as the perfume bottle. And I thought of the little jug still in the bureau drawer.

"There, there!" Hilda said again.

The pain was the worst it had been, but it was a final strain. The hurt had gone into my eyes. They burned and stung. It was the pain of something straightening itself. "Jesus help me," I said.

Once more, once more!" Hilda said.

I was emptied and collapsing. Hilda carried the baby out of the room. I figured she was taking it to the kitchen to wash it. Tom hadn't brought any hot water into the bedroom. I listened for the baby to cry, but didn't hear anything. I was so tired I just floated back on the bed, relieved and cold. I shivered from one end of me to the other. The green bottle was so close I wanted to reach out and touch it like a piece of green Christmas candy. It was lit from inside and I wanted to taste it with my fingers.

Hilda come back into the room with a pan of warm water and started to wash me. It felt like she was pulling stuff out of me. "Oh!" I hollered.

"Hush," she said. "Got to clean you or you'll catch fever."

"Where's the baby?" I said. I was too tired to hardly think.

"You hush," she said. "You've got to rest."

She took the bloody sheets and put on fresh sheets. She took away the dirty water. I kept waiting for her to bring the baby.

"What's wrong with the baby?" I said.

"Shhhh," Hilda said. I could tell she wanted to finish and get gone. She was brisk and busy.

Tom come into the room with his head bent over, like he was trying to be humble. Hilda closed the door and left him alone with me. Tom knelt down on the floor beside the bed. "Ginny," he said, "the baby is dead. It died right after it was borned."

I was too tired to answer him. After a while he got up and patted me on the head. He stood there a long time before he left. I couldn't think of anything to say. When he was gone I looked at the bottle of perfume, but the sun had moved off it. It was the color of a very dark emerald, sleeping in the shadows.

That was the first death we had had in the family since Mama died. When I woke later that day I had this empty feeling. It was a feeling of slowness and calm. I reckon grief has a lot of dignity because mostly you don't know what to do. There is something awesome and sweet about the death of old people. There is nothing but a cold absence about the death of a child.

Tom had never knowed death in his family. His pa had died in the war, as a prisoner in far-off Illinois, when he was a baby. They only knowed what happened to his pa because a buddy who had been in the prison camp brought back his pa's gold watch, and a button from his uniform. The buddy said his pa died mostly of homesickness, though he had the fever too.

Funerals bring families together. That is a fact. Even people that are quarreling will patch things up at the time of a death. Brothers that don't speak serve as pallbearers and have to be civil. Funerals are a time for forgetting and remembering, of dressing up and feeling the honor and shortness of being alive.

People in the community will look forward to a funeral. They stop work and get together, even in the middle of the day. Everybody wants to see how the dead one looks in the laying out, the kind of coffin they have, to hear singing and sermons, to see how the family takes a bereavement. But I don't think anybody looks forward to a baby's funeral. There's not even any gossip, and not much a preacher can say.

I was too weak to go to the funeral anyway. I felt washed out and dirty at the same time. I laid in bed and listened to people come and go. Most brought something, a fried chicken, a cake, a basket of rolls. Some stayed and talked to Pa and Tom and Florrie. Some set longer in the living room with the family. I heard Tom out in the yard sawing and hammering. It took me a minute to think he was making a casket for the little girl. She was going to be buried and we didn't even have a name for her.

Some people come to the door of the room and asked how I was doing. Myrtle Goins asked if there was anything she could do.

"Thank you," I said. "You have been a friend."

"If they's anything I can do," she said.

"Bless you," I said.

And I heard her out in the kitchen talking to Florrie. "Did she work herself too hard?" Myrtle said. "Did she get too hot? I know Ginny works like they's a fire out. How is Tom taking it?"

"Tom don't say nothing," Florrie said.

"Are they getting along?" Myrtle said.

"I don't know," Florrie said. "Everybody has their troubles."

Of course people come to funerals because it makes them feel good to still be alive. It's the natural thing. I would be lying if I didn't admit I've felt it myself. And it's a good thing, because the quarrels and sickness and money worries and hate get pushed aside by the sad, sweet fact of a death.

But I knowed Tom didn't get any comfort from this death either. As I laid there I thought he was not one to weep and carry on and show his feelings. He would never empty out his grief to start again. Instead he would build the casket and say nothing, then take the buckets to the barn and milk. Afterwards he'd walk down to the cane patch where he was thinning earlier. The cut stalks would have wilted and looked bled and bleached.

I knowed Tom felt the sickening jolt as much as I did. The bond that held the world together had come loose a little, and you could see human life didn't mean much. The light was wrong, poisoned by the baby's death. The empty truth touched everything. I knowed that's how he would feel, and there wasn't anything I could do to make him talk about it or feel better. A baby's death shows you things about the world you need to forget.

As I laid there I saw why him and Florrie got on so well. Florrie had nothing to do with revivals, and she never cared much for church. She liked a good laugh above everything. I

had heard her laugh when her and Tom talked out on the porch
or in the yard. I never seemed to make Tom laugh and feel good.

I don't know if Tom ever went to bed that night. He might
have set up by the little casket, or he might have set on the
porch in the dark. About nine he come to the door and asked
if there was anything he could do. I saw what a change there
was in him. All the spite was gone, and he was humble to the
confusion and pain of what had happened. But I didn't say
anything. I still couldn't think of what was right to say. It was
the kind of situation he hated most, for crowds of people to be
around, and he hated to be polite and have to thank people.
He would slip out at the first chance, and spend hours around
the feed room and harness room.

The next day, before the funeral, Florrie come in and said
she was going to stay with me.

"No, you must go to the service," I said. "You can help look
after Jewel and Moody."

"But you will be alone," she said.

"I will be fine," I said.

It was the bleeding that had made me rest so easy. When
you lose blood you just feel sleepy. I had lost so much I must
have bled out the fever. I floated in the bed like it was a soft
raft. It was so quiet in the house after everybody was gone that
I could hear shingles crack in the heat. Nails growled in corners and up along the eaves. It was so still I could hear the air
threshing against itself, the way you can in a seashell.

It was too early in the summer for many flies, but I could
hear June bugs in the hot grass outside the window. And there
was bees humming from one clover to another. It sounded hot
out there. The house creaked like it was baking.

But inside was cool and dim. I felt at the bottom of a tall room, almost in a well shaft. The cool air fell around me and made me shiver. The air was chilled, like it was sinking from a mountaintop. I shuddered, because it seemed something moved in the air, though I couldn't see anything.

To warm myself, I thought of the funeral service and the walk to the cemetery. I knowed the church would be hot as the little casket was set on the table before the altar. The preacher would speak on the mystery of God's ways, and submission to His will. Everybody would be sweating, and women would fan theirselves.

As they carried the little casket up to the graveyard the sunlight would be harsh on the road gravel, and on the weeds and brush. The dirt piled by the grave would shine a brutal red. The clods and crumbs of dirt would be drying. The pine wood of the casket would sparkle like sugar in the blinding glare.

There would be crows in the trees above the cemetery. There was always crows on that mountain, in the pine trees and on the cliffs above. They would call and flap across the valley toward Cabin Creek and Buzzard Rock.

Something stirred in the air, but I couldn't see a thing. It's true the light was dim, but my eyes was used to it. It was breath stirring. Something moved in the air, but I couldn't see it.

"What is there?" I said.

It moved around the room and come close. I couldn't hear it, but knowed it was there. I could feel it, the way you sometimes know something is in the dark. But there wasn't anything to see.

"Who are you?" I said.

I wondered was it the spirit of the baby come back because she didn't have a name. She couldn't leave the earth without a name; she couldn't get to heaven unless she was called something.

"We will call you Alice," I said. But I was being silly. There wasn't anything in the air, and I was so tired I couldn't hardly hold my eyes open. I tried to think of them singing in the sunshine on the hill. They would stand by the grave and sing "Beautiful, beautiful Zion" and "By Jordan's Stormy Banks." Their voices would echo from trees on the curve of the hill. People would put flowers on the raw dirt, and stand in the sun talking before they started back down the hill. They would pat Tom on the back and touch his elbow. They would pick up Moody and pinch Jewel's cheeks.

Whatever it was crossed the room to the corner. It stayed there, like a bat hanging upsidedown, or a snake in a hole. I could feel it watching. Its eyes was on my mind. It was a hole in the air, a coldness. It was sucking everything to itself.

"What do you want?" I said. But of course it didn't answer.

"Go away," I said, because I saw it wasn't the spirit of the little baby. It didn't mean any good, whatever it was.

And then it moved again. I saw it stir a curtain, and cross the room to trouble the clothes in the wardrobe. It was a little wind that set things swinging.

"Don't knock things over," I said, and reached out for the dresser top. But it was too late. The perfume bottle fell over with a thump. I set it upright. The lid was still tight. It fell over again. I set it up again. My hand was shaking.

I tried to see what was there. It felt like a shadow inside the air, but you couldn't see a thing. It was like the breath of a snake, an emptiness that wanted to suck warmth to itself. It was a clear blackness that wanted to leach away color and heat, any feeling or thought.

"Get away!" I said, and slapped at it.

It swooped like a bat closer, and away. And then the room was quiet. I couldn't hear a thing in the whole house except the clock ticking in the next room. I figured it was time for Tom and Pa and the younguns to get back from the funeral. I listened for the sound of feet on the road. I knowed the kitchen table was piled with dishes neighbors had brought. I could smell the hams and chicken, the slaw and candied sweet taters. It made me sick at my stomach just to think of all the victuals.

The room was so still I thought whatever it was must have gone. The bugs was loud outside. And then something breathed right beside my ear. I jerked around and slapped the air to push it away, but it was like trying to stop wind with your fingers. The blackness lashed at my head with tongues and claws.

"No!" I hollered.

It was throwing a net of wires over me, pulling them tight. The wires was cold, sharp as razors. "No!" I yelled again.

"What is it?" Tom said. He was standing in the door. He looked sweaty and his face was red from walking in the sun. His collar was tight and damp with sweat.

"Come here," I said.

He walked over and stood by the bed and I took his hand. It was a big rough and callused hand. The knuckles was swelled from so much hard work. "I'm glad to see you," I said.

CHAPTER TEN

Like I said, my sister-in-law Lily never irritated me the way she did Tom and Florrie. I was not especially friendly with Lily, but at least I thought I understood her. And when you feel you understand somebody you tend to go the second mile with them. And maybe the fact that Florrie detested her and Tom disliked her made me prone to forgive. I don't know; families are strange. Maybe I was just doing the Christian thing and giving her the benefit of the doubt. I hope that's what I was doing. I'll be the first to admit Lily could act foolish and put on airs. It was just part of her disposition to be silly.

One time after Jewel was born Tom picked three bushels of peaches on the mountain. On Sunday Florrie told me she would come over the next day and help peel the peaches and put them up. Lily heard her and said, "I'll come over, Ginny, and help you too." She said it when Pa was listening. She never missed a chance to impress him with how pretty she was and how kind and loving.

"The old kitchen's too small for three to work in," Florrie said and smiled.

"Well, if my help's not needed," Lily said.

"It would be kind of you to help us," I said. Everybody in the churchyard was listening.

"I want to put up peaches for Pa to eat," Lily said, and took Pa by the arm.

The next morning Florrie walked over the hill and we had peeled half a bushel of the peaches and sliced them before Lily arrived. I had tied a bandage on my thumb to protect it from the knife and the rag was already soaked with streaming juice.

"Sorry to be late," Lily said, taking off her yellow bonnet. She patted her hair in place. "I was looking for my purse. I seem to have lost it walking back from church yesterday."

"How awful," Florrie said, and wiped the sweat off her forehead with the back of her wrist.

"I had the ten-dollar gold piece Pa give me in it," Lily said. "But it wasn't the money I minded losing so much. It was my earrings and my silver comb, and my picture of Mama."

"Certainly the money is a trifle," Florrie said.

"Do you have an apron?" Lily said. "This old frock is just a rag, but I'd rather not get peach juice on it. Ain't peach juice hard to get out, Florrie?"

"It is indeed," Florrie said. Both Florrie and me was wearing our oldest work dresses. Lily had on a white and yellow dress she liked to wear to prayer meetings.

I handed Lily an apron and she tied it on and set down by the basket. She took a peach and held it out from her lap to peel. She cut off a wide band which took with it a lot of sweet flesh.

"Better to peel a narrow strip," Florrie said. Florrie's hands spun a peach and lowered a coil of peel into the bucket.

"Oh, I forgot," Lily said and blushed.

"Did you find it?" I said to her.

"What, dear?"

"Did you find your purse?"

"When I found it gone I said to Joe we've got to go back up the road to look. He said somebody would already have found it."

"Did it have your name in it?" I said.

Lily finished the peach and sliced it into the dishpan, but dropped the stone into the pan. "Oh how clumsy," she said.

"Maybe a stone would flavor the peaches," Florrie said.

"No, my name was not in the purse," Lily said. "But anybody in the valley would know those earrings was mine."

"I'm sure they would," Florrie said.

Florrie and me finished the first bushel and started on the second while Lily was peeling her second peach. Lily had powder on her face and when she begun to sweat she patted at the drops with the back of her hand, trying not to disturb the makeup.

"I guess they don't teach peach peeling at finishing school," Florrie said.

"So you didn't find your purse?" I said.

Lily halved the second peach and dropped it into the dishpan. I got up to get another pan.

"Should I be washing some jars, Ginny?" Florrie said.

"I've already got most of them done," I said. The washed jars was waiting on the counter to be packed with peach halves. The rest would have to be carried up from the cellar and cleaned. I put another kettle on the stove to heat.

"I said to Joe," Lily said, "I said go out and look along the road where we walked back from church. He wanted to argue but I told him to go right ahead. If it was out there he still might find it before some peddler or stranger come along and got it."

"It's a good thing men do what they are told," Florrie said.

"Why don't you start packing?" I said to Florrie. I wanted to get her away from Lily, and I didn't trust Lily to pack them. Peach halves can be bruised. They have to be packed in jars before they brown, still firm and yellow. That's why canning peaches is such work. Everything has to be done almost at once.

"Have you got enough wood toted in?" Florrie said.

"Tom carried in the box full this morning," I said, and pointed to the stacked woodbox. When she got busy working Florrie always acted like the older sister. She tried to take charge even in my own house and kitchen.

"Have you got the syrup made?" she said.

"I'll make that while you're packing the jars," I said.

"Then who will do the peeling?" she said.

"We'll all peel after the first run is on the stove," I said.

Suddenly Jewel started crying in the bedroom. I wiped my hands and run to get her, then set down by the stove to let her nurse.

"Ginny, have you got the lids ready?" Florrie said.

"I have a box right over there." I nodded toward the table.

"I don't see any rubbers," Florrie said.

"They are in the drawer," I said. "Tom got them on Saturday."

"Tom is the kind of man that helps out," Florrie said.

"It's a good thing he is," I said.

"And whatever he does is done right," Florrie said.

While Jewel was suckling there wasn't much I could do to help. But I did reach to the drawer and take out the box of new canning rubbers. The kettle was beginning to steam.

"Have you got the boilers ready?" Florrie said.

"They're out on the porch," I said.

"And we're going to need water to fill them," Florrie said.

"Tom carried three buckets this morning," I said.

"Wouldn't hurt to have another bucket," Florrie said.

"I don't think we have another bucket," I said, "unless it's the milk bucket."

"I can always wash the chamberpot and use it," Florrie said.

"That's awful," Lily said. "I think I'm going to be sick."

"I think I am too," Florrie said.

Because of the heat Jewel went to sleep while still feeding. I put her on my shoulder until she belched and then took her to the bedroom. Soon as I got back I took a saucepan off the shelf and poured a pint of syrup in it, then mixed in water and half a cup of brown sugar and stirred them together over the stove.

"You mean you put brown sugar in peach syrup?" Lily said.

"It gives just a touch more flavor," I said.

"I use only white syrup," Lily said. "I want to keep the juice clear and light."

Florrie rolled her eyes as she went to get the boilers. There was two of them, big copper pots longer than they was wide that Pa had bought in Greenville after him and Mama got married. Florrie set one on the stove and lifted a bucket to pour into it.

"I can help with that," I said.

"If I break, it's only a back," Florrie said.

Steam from the kettle and from the syrup begun filling the room. It was already hot and the kitchen started to feel clammier. That's one thing I hate about canning, how hot it is. With fire in the stove and the air full of steam and peach juice over everything you feel you're going to drown in sweat. Peelings fall out of the pan and get stepped on. After a while the floor is covered with a peach mud that tracks everything and sticks to everything. At the end of the day you have to scrape off the floor and then mop the kitchen. It is so hot sweat gets mixed with the dirt, and the muck and trash is salty and oily. No wonder Florrie was happy to go to the springhouse for more water, then to the cellar for more jars.

"These are mighty pretty peaches," Lily said.

"The trees have done better since Tom pruned them," I said. "They had never been pruned before."

"Everybody has a talent," Lily said. "That's what the Bible says. Everybody has a talent and a duty to multiply it."

"If they know what it is," I said.

Florrie come in with the basket of jars and put them on the counter. She begun scrubbing them with a bottle brush.

"Some people have a talent for music, and some for preaching. And some that want to preach don't have a talent for it. But the Lord knows what he is doing," Lily said.

"Some people have a talent for talking," Florrie said. She emptied a jar with a gush and gurgle into the dishpan.

"Did David preach at Mount Olivet last week?" Lily said.

"He was too weak," Florrie said. "He had the cough in his chest."

"It's a shame he can't get a church," Lily said. "He is so good at visiting the sick and he studies so hard."

"Who says he can't get a church?" Florrie said. She begun to dry the row of jars with a towel.

"I'm only saying I wish he could," Lily said.

"He will find a church as soon as he gets over his cold."

"Did you find your purse?" I said to Lily. I put the rubbers and lids on the jars Florrie had already filled and begun stacking them in the boiler.

"Oh it was under some clothes," Lily said. "Soon as Joe was gone I started picking up clothes in the bedroom and there the purse was under my petticoat."

"Glory be," Florrie said.

I've noticed that when people work together they sooner or later get more friendly. It's natural that once you are sweating and straining together you begin to feel like a team. Even Lily and Florrie started to act agreeable as we worked that morning.

"I hear Bertha Lindsay is expecting again," Lily said when we put on the first boiler and set down to peel the second bushel. Lily had peeled and sliced maybe a dozen peaches on her own. Florrie and me took up our paring knives and got to work.

"What is this, her eighth?" I said.

"I don't know how she does it," Florrie said. "Even though I do know how she does it."

"I don't blame her, I blame Mr. Lindsay," Lily said.

"It takes two," Florrie said. "At least that's what I hear."

I busted out laughing at that, and so did Lily. Sometimes Florrie could be so funny you had to feel better.

"But what is a woman to do?" Lily said.

"There are ways not to have children," Florrie said, "if a woman don't want to."

"Florrie!" Lily said, "I'm surprised at you."

"She can sleep alone," I said, and reached for another peach.

"What woman wants to sleep alone?" Florrie said.

"One that has eight children already," Lily said.

"Some women want eight children," I said. "They want a big family to help out on the place."

"Be fruitful and multiply," Florrie said. "That's what the Bible says." Her hands flew as she slid the skin off a peach. Juice run off her fingers and the peel coiled into the pail.

"My grandma had so many children her insides come loose," Lily said. "She was tore up and her womb would fall out if she stood."

"I've heard of that," Florrie said. .

"Couldn't she have an operation?" I said.

"There wasn't anywhere to go for an operation back then," Lily said. "She just had to live with it. Maybe if she had gone to Baltimore or somewhere she could have had an operation. She just set in her chair by the fire all the time when I was a girl. That's all I ever saw her do, set by the fire and knit a little and smoke her pipe when there was no company."

"Women have to suffer the pains of childbirth," I said.

"And the pain of monthlies," Lily said.

"Those moody monthlies," Florrie said and laughed. I had to laugh too, though the old joke was aimed at me.

"A woman has to do what a man says," Lily said.

"No she don't," Florrie said.

"It says in the Bible she does," Lily said. It was amusing to hear Lily argue that, since she had been bossing Joe around since long before they was married. Florrie rolled her eyes again.

"The Bible says a woman has to satisfy a man," Lily said.

"That's different," Florrie said with a smirk. "That ain't nothing to worry her."

"What if it's unnatural?" Lily said.

"What is unnatural?" Florrie said. She wiped her brow with her forearm. Her dress was soaked under the arm.

"You know, if the man wants her to do something unnatural," Lily said.

"Depends on the people," Florrie said.

"Florrie!" I said.

"Ain't nothing men have thought of that women hadn't thought of too," Florrie said. "That's what I think."

"I suppose some people will do anything," Lily said.

"But everybody does pretty much the same things," Florrie said. "People are about the same, except some are skinny and some are fat, and some try to act superior."

"I wouldn't want to live like an animal," Lily said. She was blushing under her face powder. "Mama always wore gloves when she worked outside," Lily said then. "No matter how much work she done, she protected her hands."

I remembered hearing Pa say Lily's mama had to plow with the oxen after her husband died while the children was little. But I didn't mention that.

"A woman's skin is her greatest wealth," Lily said. "That's what Mama used to say. Take care of your skin and a man will always love you. And you will take pride in yourself."

"I'm thirsty," Florrie said. "I've near sweated myself dry." She stood and wiped her hands on the towel. But instead of going to the bucket on the porch she went to the corner where Pa kept herbs and tinctures. On the top shelf was the whiskey jug and she pulled it down. Florrie was the only woman I ever saw who drunk from the jug like a man. She pulled the stopper and raised the jug on her elbow for a swallow, then coughed and cleared her throat. When she turned around her dark skin was red a little.

"One drink deserves another," Florrie said, and strode out to the porch for a dipper of spring water. As she come back in she patted her chest. "That feels better," she said, "much better."

The smell of whiskey on her breath mingled with the fragrance of the peaches and the steam from the boiler.

"Ain't you thirsty?" Florrie said.

"Not much," I said. Florrie was always teasing me about drinking. I took a swallow from time to time, when I had a cold or couldn't get to sleep, when I was feeling the vapors. I never did drink the way she did, in the quantities she did. Sometimes David hid the bottle from her, but mostly he just ignored it.

"I ain't never been a hypocrite," Florrie said.

"Nobody said you was a hypocrite," I said.

"I take a drink from time to time and I don't care who knows it," Florrie said.

"It's disgusting to see a woman drunk," Lily said. "It's bad enough for a man, but worse for a woman."

"I don't think I've ever seen a woman drunk," Florrie said.

"It's not a pretty sight," Lily said. "I used to watch Alma Bright walk the road coming back from town and she was so drunk she staggered. Mama made me come inside so I couldn't see her."

"It's a good thing your mama saved you," Florrie said.

"I've heard Alma done worse than drink," I said.

"She had to pay for her liquor some way," Lily said.

"There's not many ways a woman can earn money," Florrie said.

The smell of peaches and the smell of the whiskey and all

the sweating was making me thirsty too. I wished Florrie and Lily wasn't there so I could get a drink from the jug and nobody would be bothered. It ruins the fun of drinking if people are disapproving of you. I got up and went to the porch for a dipper of water. "Would you like a drink of water?" I said to Lily.

"That would be lovely," she said. I brought her a dipper from the bucket and she wiped her hand on the apron before taking it.

"We need a new towel," I said. "I'll get one from the closet."

My linen was stored in the closet at the end of the hall, and my bottle was under the sheets. I felt for it among the cool folded cloth. The bottle was cooler than the linen. I unscrewed the cap and took a drink. The whiskey sunk to my stomach with force and strength. I got a towel and hurried to the kitchen.

"Whiskey is good to fight off sickness," Florrie said. "That's why it's called medicine."

"I'm sure it's helpful, as medicine," Lily said. "Though not this awful moonshine around here."

"We should order some fine brandy," Florrie said.

"I've heard whiskey will fight off typhoid," Lily said.

"I've never heard that," I said.

"Whiskey won't cure somebody that has typhoid," Florrie said. "But it will help fight off catching the fever."

"How do you know?" I said. Florrie always did have the habit of creating history as she went along. She would make up a story and tell it with such conviction you'd believe it was gospel.

"Have you ever knowed anybody that drunk a lot that got typhoid?" she said.

I tried to think. Many that had died of typhoid was children and women. I couldn't recall any that was known to drink.

The drink had made me feel better. I could hear the hens clucking out in the henhouse as they will midmorning after laying their eggs. They fussed in a regular chorus.

"We sound like a bunch of hens," I said.

"What a thing to say," Florrie said and laughed.

"I don't feel like no hen," Lily said. I started laughing, but just then I heard Jewel crying and wiped my hands on the towel before running to the bedroom.

By the time I got Jewel to sleep and they had the second bushel peeled, Lily was getting warmed up in her talking. She was the talkingest woman I ever met, and when she worked her tongue was busier than her hands. "I like a man that has something to say," she said as we started on the last bushel, after loading the second boiler and lifting the first one off to cool. "I like a man that has refinement and reads books and talks about them."

"Ain't just talk that makes a man interesting," Florrie said.

"It's hard to like a man with nothing to say," Lily said.

"Every man is different," I said.

"Every woman is different too," Florrie said.

"Give me a man with some culture," Lily said.

I was embarrassed, because I knowed Lily was talking about Tom. I didn't think Tom needed any defending, but my blood was beginning to spin a little. Yet we had to get through the peach canning without fussing. I told myself it wouldn't do to quarrel with Lily, silly as she was. "I like a man that knows what he's doing, and what he wants to do," I said.

"Nothing means as much as worship, and being married to a man who will worship with you," Lily said.

"There's all kinds of worship," Florrie said.

"Why, what do you mean?" Lily said. "I'm talking about the worship and fellowship with the Lord and you know what I mean."

"Worship for some people might be just staying home and watching the sunset," Florrie said.

"That's not the same as going to service," Lily said.

"Why not?" Florrie said. "What's the difference between a briar thicket and a brush arbor?" She went to the shelf for Pa's jug again. This time she held it to her lips longer, and didn't bother to go to the porch for a dipper of water.

"How you do talk, Sister Florrie," Lily said. "If I didn't know you better I'd think you was a heathen."

"I am a heathen," Florrie said, and laughed.

Lily screamed. She was looking at her hands. "They're all wrinkled and watersobbed," she said. "Look at that. They're ruined. I'll have to put lotion on them as soon as I get home."

"Peach juice won't hurt your hands," Florrie said.

"I'm shocked at you," Lily said to Florrie, "comparing the beauty of nature to the worship of the Lord."

"Praise was the purpose people was put here for," I said.

"How do you know that, Ginny?" Florrie said.

"Because it says so in the Bible," I said. But I couldn't think of any special place where it was quoted.

"It says a lot of things in the Bible," Florrie said.

"I'm surprised to hear you talk so," Lily said. "You sound like you don't believe nothing. You sound indeed like a heathen."

"It might be more interesting to be a heathen," Florrie said. "I don't see any use in getting together like it was a party and having a good old time and then calling it something else."

"I am horrified," Lily said. She had stopped peeling and held the peach in her left hand and the knife in the right. I wished I had never agreed for her to help with the canning.

"Why can't people just be good on their own, without all this rigamarole?" Florrie said.

"We need each other's support," I said. "We learn from each other, and remind each other of things we forget on our own."

"I don't see what anybody learns from rolling on the ground speaking gibberish," Florrie said. "Now rolling in the hay with a man . . ." Florrie peeled faster than me and Lily together. She dropped a peach in the pan and picked up another without a pause.

"I've heard that in the old days young couples went out to the plowed fields in spring and took their clothes off," Florrie said. "They rolled through the fresh dirt to make it fertile. When they had crossed the field and got all dirty the field was blessed and would grow a big crop."

"I've never heard of such a thing," Lily said.

"If they rolled together enough I guess they was blessed with another crop," Florrie said.

"I can't believe people was ever that common," Lily said.

"People won't stop being common," Florrie said. "At least I hope not."

"Oh no!" Lily screamed. She held out her left hand and I saw blood on her finger. "I have cut myself," she said. "I have ruined my hand."

"Let me see," I said. A drop of blood fell into the peaches.

"Can't breathe," Lily said. "The sight of blood makes me faint."

"Hold it out," I said.

She shook her hand like there was a spider on it. "It stings," she said. "The peach juice has got into it."

I wiped my hands and run to get a towel. I stepped on the peach Lily had dropped, crushing the peach to juice.

"It's bleeding," Lily said. "It takes my breath away."

I grabbed her hand to hold it still. A drop of blood fell on her dress. "Look at that," she said. "This dress is ruined."

When I finally got a look I saw it was just a little cut, maybe half an inch long and not very deep. I wiped the blood off.

"Better put something on it," Florrie said. "You wouldn't want to get lockjaw."

"I could put some whiskey on it," I said.

Lily stomped her foot into the tub of peelings, but whether from anger or pain I couldn't tell.

"Here," Florrie said, and poured a drop of whiskey on the cut. Lily screamed, and stomped her foot like a little girl.

"Does it hurt bad?" I said. "I don't think the cut is deep."

"This dress is completely ruined," she said. "And I don't have another in this shade or this pattern."

"The blood stains will come out," Florrie said. "Just sponge them with cold water." Florrie took another drink from the jug.

I tied the tip of Lily's finger in a strip of linen. The bleeding had stopped and the little bandage looked like a scarf on someone's head. "It's almost time to fix dinner," I said. "Tom and Pa and Joe will be back from the field in an hour."

When that day was over I was wore out from trying to keep Florrie and Lily apart. I promised myself I never would let Lily help us can peaches again, and I didn't.

CHAPTER ELEVEN

In the summer of 1904 we made our biggest garden ever. I could tell Tom felt bad for not showing more sympathy to me. The truth is that only concern for other people eases our own grief, and Tom had not showed much concern until he set down on the bed after the funeral. Soon as he took my hand and cared that my heart was broke I think he started to feel a little better. I could tell he saw in me then the girl he had married. At that moment the emptiness we both felt started to go away.

By July I was pretty much well again, and figured the best way to show my friendship with Tom was to help in the fields. I went out with him every day and left Jewel and Moody at the house with Pa. I had always done my share of work outside, but that hot summer I pitched in like a field hand. It was what needed to be done, and it was what I needed to do. If you sweat enough it will cleanse you. If you have a cold or feel you're taking sick sometimes a good sweat will heal you. As I worked in the dirt by Tom I felt I was being cleansed from inside.

And nothing makes a woman feel better than to pitch in and work alongside her husband. I didn't wear shoes, and it felt like the dirt itself healed me. The hot ground drawed the poisons and ill will through the soles of my feet.

The dirt by the river was moist, even in the hot dry weeks. Working in the loam you could feel the cool of the river way down under the topsoil, and at times you could even feel the movement of the river like a pulse, and hear the whisper and swallow of the stream going over rocks and riffles.

Tom had planted more corn and beans and peas and taters and watermelons than ever before. He had planted the new ground at the upper end of the bottom and he planted the terraces in the orchard above the barn. It seemed like he had put every foot of available land in crops of one sort or another. There was butter beans and crowder peas, squash and pumpkins, tomatoes and onions. He planted twice as much cane as he had the year before.

Every morning after breakfast we went out to pull weeds and hoe dirt around the stalks and vines. There is a thrill to cleaning a row, getting rid of ragweeds and bull nettles. The hardest thing is to take morning glories out of corn, for they wind up the stalks and wrap theirselves tight on the leaves. You have to find the bottom of the vine and cut it, or pull it out. When you weed a row it feels like things has been sorted out and clarified. You have made sense of something.

A small lake and cottonmill had been built down the river on the other side of the Turnpike, and they was putting up more houses there. They built a powerhouse below the lake to run the mill, and the new houses would have electricity and running water, it was said. But folks working in the mill didn't have time or land for gardens. And they couldn't keep cows and chickens. Tom had found a market there for cider and firewood. He guessed the hands from the flatlands would need vegetables too.

One day in July Tom loaded the Studebaker wagon with sweet peas, fresh corn and beans, tomatoes and squash. He had taters and lima beans we had picked after daylight. He had done a half day's work before milking time. By the middle of the morning he was ready to peddle door to door among the new two-room houses.

All day I did the washing and hung it out in the hot wind. That evening it come up a thunderstorm, as it will in July, and I just barely had time to run and get my clothes in. Tom come back later, completely soaked. He had tried to stop Old Dan under a tree, but the wind swept the rain right on him. He come dripping to the house and set by the hearth. He looked wet as a dog. But he reached into his pocket and pulled out dimes and quarters give him by the mill people. I thought he was mad at first, he looked so bedraggled by rain. I had started a fire in the fireplace to dry some of the towels. Tom bent before the fire and counted coins on the hearth. He put quarters in one pile and dimes in another. He had a few half-dollars and nickels, and one silver dollar. He counted it up in the firelight. There was almost ten dollars. I never saw such a happy look on his face. Tom was not one to show much pleasure. But he couldn't cover the smile as he added up the earnings for the day.

"Take off them wet clothes before you get sick," I said.

"A good soaking makes you feel clean," he said. He put the money in the cigar box he used for a bank.

I had always been a worker by fits and spells. But that summer I found I could work steady. We got up at four or five, and Pa was already up and reading his Bible at the table. By the time

Tom had milked I had breakfast ready. We drunk several cups of Pa's coffee before going to the fields in early light. Every bit of work was precious. I found myself thinking like Tom that summer. A woman naturally comes to think like her husband sometimes. I thought of every squash as so many pennies, and every row as so many quarters. I saw green leaves turning into dimes, and gold roots and veins in leaves turning into silver dollars. Every bit of soil come to promise its secret of money.

In the early morning cucumbers was cool as jars of ice water. I reached into wet leaves and plucked the firm beans. The crust on the soil was breaking as new taters swelled under it. Every tater we got out was that much more wealth. Tom had always sold eggs down at the store. But the vegetables was something extra. It was his idea, beyond anything Pa had ever made on the place.

My face and arms turned dark as an Indian's that summer. I always did tan easy, but that summer I didn't even wear a straw hat. Florrie teased me for getting so dark. "You will look like a field hand," she said. "Lily may not speak to you."

My arms and shoulders got strong again, and I helped Tom pull fodder and stack it in the barnloft. In September I helped strip the cane, while Jewel and Moody played at the end of the rows.

Fodder pulling is supposed to be the worst job there is. The fields are hot and dusty by late August, and you strip the leaves off corn below the ears, after the tops have been cut and stacked in shocks to dry. The heat and the dust, rough rasping leaves, will give you a rash. And you can easy put a hand on a packsaddle worm that will sting you in ten places. If a pack-saddle nails you nothing will put out the fire on your hand for days. It is worse than ten hornet stings.

After both hands tear off leaves and are full, you put the bunches together and tie them, wrapping one leaf around and through the middle. You stick that hand on a stalk until you have enough to tie into a bundle. When the bundles are carried to the barnloft to cure, they fill the barn with a scent sweeter than tobacco or tea. Fodder is too rich and tender to give to cows. The sugary lower leaves of the corn are saved for the horse.

The work in the sun and the sunburn acted like a spur to our lovemaking. It was as if the heat of July and August stored up in our veins and skin as a fever to be quenched by love in the hours of darkness. Never had I seemed to need less sleep. After he got home each evening, milked and washed and had supper, Tom counted the money he had made. The coins shined like little flames and faces on the hearth. The bills crackled as he smoothed them in booklets. Afterwards he put the money in the cigar box.

As he counted the money, we talked about what we needed to buy for winter, for the children and for the place. Jewel would start school that fall, and needed new clothes. "You have to dress your girls nicer than boys," Tom said.

As soon as the children was asleep Tom and me went to bed ourselves. Pa was reading in the kitchen, and we tried not to disturb him. When Locke come on furlough for a week he slept on the couch and we tried to be careful not to bother him as we giggled in the dark and tried to keep the bed from creaking.

It was as if we was not ourselves some nights, but bigger and more powerful, more perfect, as we would want to be. The day had been a long delay and build-up of fever toward the summer night. And it felt like we couldn't do anything wrong. Every place we touched was right, and every pause was right. Everything we did in the dark led to something new and better.

As a girl I would not have thought a man of forty was capable of such exertions, or a woman of thirty-four for that matter. At moments of joy I felt this was what all the feeling of my life had been tending toward, including my shouting and dancing at meetings. It was all just a preparation for this.

But I put such thoughts out of mind for they was blasphemous. I may have felt them, but I didn't want to think them, least of all to say them. Long as I didn't put my feelings in words they was innocent. Kept at the edge of thought they couldn't hurt.

And I told myself lovemaking was also worship and praise. I told myself it was through love we take part in God's creation.

I remember one night in August special. We had picked beans in the far end of the bottom and Tom sold them by the bushel to women in the village. I reckon he had made more than ten dollars. But on the way home the axle of the wagon broke. I don't know why it broke. Maybe the extra hauling had wore it out. Tom had stuck in a sapling to hold up the wheel till he got home. The new axle would cost ten dollars, so the day had been wasted, he felt.

Now I have noticed that loving is best when you're feeling real good, or sometimes when you're feeling a little bad. If you're feeling a mite low you resist lovemaking at first, and then it comes like a blessing. And your body takes over and reminds you of things you had forgot. The body has its own wisdom and its own will, and sometimes it knows what you need most.

That night I saw Tom needed to be cheered up. I took a full bath in the tub in the bedroom, and made myself rosy and soft. I put on powder and rubbed on cologne. By the time I had finished Tom had already gone to bed. I knowed he was tired, and when you want to forget some loss or bad news nothing is as comforting as sleep. In fact, I think he might already have been asleep when I put out the lamp and got in bed.

But as I slipped under the covers I could feel him waking. First, it was the way he stirred and was quiet in his breathing. Then he pushed against me a little, just enough to show it was intended. It's strange how much a little pressure tells you.

Well I won't go into detail. Folks got no right to hear what married couples do. But it was a time I never forgot. The katydids was out, loud in the woods beyond the orchard. And there was crickets in the yard, meadow moles with their mellow note. After the heat of the day the house was cracking and knocking.

But I soon forgot the sounds in the dark. Time got big and magnified. The dark was lit with purple fires. I could feel colors through my fingertips and through every place I touched.

And we had so much time. Every instant was stretched out, and stretched further. Our bodies was big as landscapes and mountains and we had all the time in the world to climb and cross them. There was no hurry, never had been. There was years for a kiss.

It was also like a patient waiting. We was in no hurry because we knowed something would be give to us. I thought about the beans we had picked that day, and how beans get hard when they are ready to pick. You could pick beans just by the feel of them. With your fingers you could tell the pulses in a bean, and then count the beans into a basket.

I thought of Solomon again. "I *am* my beloved's, and his desire *is* toward me," I whispered. The words seemed perfect in the dark. "I *am* a wall, and my breasts are like towers: then was I in his eyes as one that found favor," I said.

We did some things new that night. Don't matter exactly what, but they was new to us. It was like we found out more things about each other. I guess it was like climbing way up a beautiful mountain past ridges and hollers. Laboring up a slope you think you are almost at the top, but when you get there see it is a false peak, and the real summit is higher and further.

The smells of the body are thrilling, the scent of armpits and sweat on skin. The skin has its own savors and salts. It is the salt of memory and wit and laughter. There is the salt that wakes you up, and salt like the taste of rocks deep in the ground.

"Tom," I said. I had never been one to talk much while making love. Before, it had felt better to be hushed. "Tom," I said again, "this is the best thing, ain't it?"

He didn't say anything. He was waiting for me to say more.

"Tom," I said, "we won't never know anything this real."

It was like the dark was smoothing out in contours of pasture hills and deep valleys lined with fur and velvet.

"I can see where the sky touches the ground," I said, "and it's smooth as milk."

There was rivers of sparks in the soil and they swirled through the dark and spread in wind to the end of the earth. It was a warm Nile flooding out of soil, lifting higher and higher.

"This is the place," I said, "ain't it?"

Tom still didn't say anything. He was waiting for me to go on. He never liked to waste a single word. It was for me to say things to him.

"This is the place it all starts," I said. "This is the place of creation."

And then in the dark I could see Tom's face. I don't know how I did in the pitch dark. Maybe there was heat lightning, or maybe a meteor outside. But I saw Tom's face, and his eyes was looking right into mine, like he saw what I was thinking and feeling. He could see and feel any part of me. Even if he laid still he could feel every inch of me that was moving.

"Tom!" I said. And then I knowed my talking made another kind of sense. It wasn't daylight talk with its words and sentences. It was a higher kind of talk. And it come to me I was speaking in tongues. It was the first time I had spoke in tongues outside a service. I didn't know what I was saying, but I saw what was visited upon me was a gift. "Tom!" I said, and my mouth flew like a bird and my tongue soared. I gripped and sung out and didn't hardly know what I was doing. I was on a long journey that went on and on over banks and gullies, valleys and mountains of flowers. The whole world was coming to us in the dark.

And then I saw what we had been going toward. Everything swung around like compass needles pointing in the same direction. It was in the eye of a pigeon setting high on a tree at the mountaintop. The eye was still as a puddle with no wind. It was still at the center of the whirl and clutter of things.

"This is what was meant," I said.

Tom still didn't say anything.

"This is really the place," I said. "Ain't it?"

"Yeah," Tom said. It was all he said, but it was enough.

Sometimes in the evenings, after Tom counted his money, I read to him. As the nights got cooler we set by the fire and I read from the paper or a magazine. Sometimes I even read poems, or the Bible. Though he never would say much about what I read I thought he enjoyed it. Keeping up with the news is as much a habit as anything else, and the more you know about what's going on in the world the more you want to know. You start following out the threads of events and you want to know what happens next.

The Russians was fighting the Japanese off in the Pacific, and the Japanese had attacked one of their seaports. I couldn't say the name of the place, so I spelled it, V-l-a-d-i-v-o-s-t-o-k.

"What kind of name is that?" Tom said.

"Russian, I reckon."

"And what happened?" Tom put the coins in the cigar box and took off his shoes. On cool evenings he liked to warm his feet in front of the fire.

"'The Japanese warships bombarded the port city for most of a day,'" I read from the paper. "'Before nightfall the Russians surrendered and the city was occupied by Japanese troops. All inhabitants, including American citizens, were taken prisoner.'"

Tom listened to every word I read. Jewel come and set in his lap. "What is a citizen?" she said.

When I read Longfellow to Tom I think he was a little embarrassed. I would read from "Hiawatha" for several min-

utes and he listened close. I think he liked the song of the
words, the rhythm and repetition. I read on and it looked as
though he was listening, but then his head would begin to
nod. I stopped.

"Don't stop," he said, and straightened up.

"You want me to go on?" I said.

"Sure," he said.

I read a few lines more and his head started to nod again. His
chin touched his chest and his eyes closed. I stopped reading.

"No, go on," he said, stirring hisself.

"No use to read if you're just going to sleep," I said. "I can
read something else."

"No, that's fine," he said.

I started reading again, and the next thing I knowed his eyes
was closed and his head tilted over. I closed the book. "Tomorrow
I'll read something else," I said.

"No need to," he said, pulling hisself up.

"I don't think you're interested in Indians," I said.

"Them ain't Indians," Tom said.

"How do you know?"

"Indians don't talk like that," he said.

"How do you know how Indians talk?" I said.

"They don't talk like that," Tom said. "I know that much."

That winter I was expecting again. It was the fourth time,
but I reckon I was scared by what happened to the last
baby. I couldn't get it out my mind that I had done something
wrong, though I didn't know what it was. It come to me I had
worked too hard in the heat, or eat the wrong things, or bent

over the washpot the wrong way. They say drinking liquor before a baby is born will hurt the youngun, but I had just took a drink from time to time to calm myself. I done that more after Moody was born, but I never did it much. Pa kept a jug of whiskey in his cabinet, along with herbs and powders. Sometimes I bought a bottle myself and kept it in the linen closet. It was something I did to soothe myself when I got too worked up.

As winter went on and spring was near I was irritated by little things. I couldn't stand for the younguns to make noise or fight. If one started to cry it bothered me. If I looked at the mess in the house, or washing to be done, it made me mad. I lost my temper and snapped at Pa and Tom. I couldn't take the sight of the younguns getting dirty in the yard. As Moody got bigger I saw how much more trouble boys was than girls. He was always climbing, or pushing something over. He would fight with Jewel, and lash out in fits of temper. From the time he was two he liked to play shooting a gun. I thought how different he was from Tom. "Bang, bang," Moody would yell, as though he had shot me.

When I couldn't stand it anymore I went to the outhouse under the big hemlocks down the hill. A woman that's expecting has to go more often anyhow, because she don't have much room inside her. But I found it was such a relief to be out of the house and away from the bother I stayed for several minutes. Nobody could pester me in the toilet. I would set there longer and longer, and put off going back to the kitchen.

Even the cold wood of the seat felt good on my bare skin. The wood had been polished by more than twenty years of wear, and it had the shine of a waxed floor. The cold wood made me shiver, but it felt soothing. Soon the wood I touched warmed up.

There was something about the dim light that made me feel sincere, prayerful. It was shadowy as a chapel or closet. The hemlocks brushed the sides and the roof when there was wind. Needles seeped through the cracks and gathered on the floor.

I thought how this was a place where earth was brought back to earth, an offering made for what we received from soil. It was a place of return and payment. I thought how important it was to have a place of quiet, of asylum. In our head we hide and look out from a secret place. But sometimes the eyes see too much and we hear too much. It was good to have a second shelter to go to.

It felt like I could almost get outside of time setting there. I could let the stream of seconds go past, while I stayed in that still pocket. The space was a gray crystal I climbed into. I could hear the younguns shouting and the cows bawling, and crows in the hill pines. I could even hear the river mutter after a big rain. But mostly I heard what I was thinking.

And I thought how that calm was the farthest thing from the rapture of a service, and yet it was almost the same too. To get off to the side of time and think and remember was a special privilege that had its own sacredness.

Sometimes I felt like a little girl again, and it seemed I didn't have any work that had to be done. I imagined I didn't have a husband to worry about, and I had all the time I needed to read and go to meetings or do whatever I wanted. I could play in the woods if I felt like it, or go down to the river and wade in the shallows looking for crawfish or periwinkles.

Setting in the gloom I felt closer to Mama that died when I was a girl. I could remember how she taught us Bible verses. She hated the Holiness meetings as much as Tom did. I thought how the generations was linked and kept doing the same things even when they didn't know it. I saw how we was like our mamas and daddies in spite of ourselves, and how our younguns would be like us. And there wasn't much we could do about it, even if we wanted to.

Then I heard Moody bawling, screaming at the top of his lungs. It sounded like he was down the bank by the chickenhouse.

"Mama, Mama," Jewel yelled. She run to the house thinking I was in the kitchen. Through a crack I saw her go up the steps.

By the time I got outside and up the bank Jewel had run back out on the porch. "Come quick," she said. "Moody has fell over."

"Fell over what?"

"He fell over the bank."

I run by the house and looked over the edge of the yard, and sure enough, Moody was in the weeds at the bottom. He was upside down, like he had tried to do a somerset and stopped halfway. Sticks and leaves stuck to his jacket. I don't know if he had got the breath knocked out, or if he was too scared to get up. It was clear he had rolled down and stopped on his head.

When I picked him up his eyes bulged out. It looked like he was too scared to cry. Dirt and trash stuck all over his face.

"Are you hurt?" I said.

He started jerking like he was beginning to cry again. I felt him to see if any bones was broke. Then he started bellowing again and I knowed he was all right.

The baby born in June was a boy. Tom named him Muir Ray, after his boss at the Lewis place. He said since I had named Moody after my favorite preacher he would name this boy after somebody he liked. I didn't make any protest for I figured it was fair. But I never much liked the name. It sounded dark and hard. I knowed it was Scotch, and it sounded stingy and unfriendly.

After the wonderful nights of the summer and fall, and the hard work of the fields, you would have thought the new baby would have brought us closer together. You would have thought Tom's pleasure in a second son would have spilled over into his feelings toward me. But nothing works out the way you expect.

At first, after the birth of Muir, Tom just got quiet. He come around me less, and he didn't touch me as much when we was together. We had slept together until I was six or seven months along, and then Tom had fixed his pallet up in the loft again. He forced hisself to move, he said, for the sake of the baby. There is always the danger of injury, both to the mother and the baby, Dr. Johns had said. But we found again that when a man and woman ain't sleeping together they don't feel the same toward each other. No matter how careful they are not to quarrel it's not the same. I reckon the sex thing is a lot of the glue that holds people together. That's the way the Lord made them. But I wasn't sure I believed the doctor. Sometimes I found myself looking at Tom, before he climbed into the loft. But he was a man awful strong and strict in his ways. Though I couldn't hardly see it when I was mad at him, I knowed he was a man with his own honor.

The Waters family had typhoid fever that summer of 1905 after Muir was born. I told Hilda to let the children that wasn't sick stay with us. I knowed people with typhoid needed absolute quiet. They had to lay in a still dark room until the fever broke. It was hard to nurse them with other children running around.

I said that to Hilda on a Saturday, not having mentioned it to Tom. She had helped birth all my babies, and it seemed like the least I could do. If folks don't help each other, then nothing good will ever happen. If women didn't help each other out I don't know how the world would ever get its children raised.

Since we didn't have any extra beds it meant having two of the Waters children sleep with Jewel, and two on the floor on a pallet. But I saw quick that Tom was angry when I brought the Waters younguns back with me. I reckon I should have asked him first, but it was too late. I got angry too. When you think you might be a little wrong it always makes you madder.

"I didn't know we was taking in boarders," Tom said.

"I had to help Hilda," I said.

"And now our younguns will catch typhoid," he said.

"That's not the way you catch typhoid," I said.

"And how do you know, Dr. Powell?" Tom said.

I had read that folks catch typhoid from water, from tainted water in wells and springs. But I didn't know for sure. It was a return of the old anger. That at least was contagious. Once one of us got mad the other one caught it. It was a fever that come on us, and seemed as familiar as a cold.

"You don't need to get mad," I said, trying to think of some way to stall our argument. "They will be here only a few days. The doctor said they had to be out of the way."

"Then why does it have to be my house?" he said.

"It's not your house, yet," I said. It come out before I thought. Once it was said it could not be took back. "I mean it's my house too, and Pa's," I said.

Tom was too mad to answer. He walked out and didn't come back for supper. When he milked he set the buckets on the porch for me to strain and went back to the fields. When he did come in that night he went to the ladder and climbed to the loft to bed.

By the time Muir was two months we was no longer speaking. Tom kept his schedule in the fields and garden, but this year I was not helping. Every day he wagoned produce to the village, and made more money than ever. But he didn't count it on the hearth. He put the coins in the cigar box he kept in the attic.

Though I had never seen inside the cotton mill, it ordered our lives. Almost all Tom's farming was done for the village trade. He cut wood in winter to sell there, and made extra molasses and raised hogs to sell to mill hands. The mill had a whistle that blowed every morning at seven, and by then Tom was out at the barn or in the fields. It blowed again at dinnertime and I come to depend on the long note to tell me when it was noon. And it sounded again in the middle of the evening, like a hawk calling across the mountain, and the sound washed up the river valley. Soon it come to seem like something we had heard all our lives.

CHAPTER TWELVE

Because he was so busy in the fields, and because I was taking care of the baby, and since he had the extra money, Tom hired Florrie to come over the hill and help with washing and cleaning. Florrie had helped me in the past from time to time, and I reckon she would have again for nothing. It seemed strange to pay your own sister for work. But I guess Tom thought he couldn't ask her unless he paid her. After all, Florrie had her own house, and David was sick more than he was well.

But I resented that Tom was paying Florrie, and that he had asked her to work with me. I know I shouldn't have, but I did. "I have helped Florrie for nothing," I said. It didn't seem fair, and I reckon I didn't show as much appreciation for Florrie's work as I might. I felt slighted, like I had been accused of laziness, and never recovered from my laying in.

The whole thing looked odd, because Florrie, everybody said, was a terrible housekeeper. "You could grow a garden on her kitchen floor," women would say. She liked to gossip and read magazines, and she liked to drink. She kept a bottle in her kitchen cupboard, for making cakes and puddings, she would say. To be honest, she worked harder away from home. Helping me, she was quick and thorough, though I hated to admit it.

Tom give Florrie a dollar a day to scrub and clean, to wash the clothes and diapers out by the springhouse. I think he hired her just to spite me, and because he liked to listen to her talk. Florrie was always ready for a good laugh. And she was happy to gossip about the revival meetings. I heard her one day at the clothesline talking to Tom. She was hanging out shirts and Tom had stopped on his way to the pasture to catch the horse.

"I'll tell you the truth, Tom," she said, "I don't confidence these Holiness goings on. I was setting there pretty as you please at meeting and Sister Lily stood up to shout and testify. She was going on to beat the band and accusing everybody else of not being in the Spirit. So I says to myself, I'll just test her spirit. I up and smiled at her this pretty smile when she turned toward me. And she said to everybody, 'Now Sister Florrie is in the true spirit.' But actually I was setting there thinking what a hypocrite she was and how I didn't confidence her at all."

Here is my own sister talking to my husband about our meetings behind my back, I thought. How would any woman feel? I figured Tom wanted me to get mad and tell Florrie to leave, and then he would have won by seeming so kind toward Florrie and me so mean. She knowed how to be sweet as pie to Tom, and she stabbed me in the back right there in my own house. But I saw if I throwed it up to her and Tom it would only make me look bad. And she would have another story to tell people.

That fall after Muir Ray was born there was a meeting in a brush arbor up in Mountain Valley. That was a little community near the head of Cabin Creek. About a mile above where it reached the river the creek plunged through a gorge of rocks and hemlocks and turned the biggest mill in our end of the county. And above the gorge was the prettiest valley you ever saw, setting like a cradle on the ridge tops. Most of the people that lived there was Raeburns, and they had lived there since it was Indian land.

It was a Raeburn converted by a preacher from South Carolina that built the brush arbor. He could have held the service in his house, except his wife was a strict Baptist and threatened to shoot anybody that come near with the "Holiness sickness." But meetings always went better in the woods anyway, among the trees and elements. It was like houses and too much light killed the Spirit. There was a secret and a mystery to meeting in the woods. In the lanternlight you could feel the Spirit moving. It was good to get away from the greed and spite of everyday life.

I took the baby with me to the first meeting. Pa and me rode in the wagon up the valley with Joe and Lily. It had been almost two years since I had gone to a revival. There was a hunger in me I had noticed more and more. It was a craving for joy, for praise and thanksgiving. The purpose of life was to praise. Whether Tom understood or not, it was a need that was real. As we creaked up the road just before dark I said to myself, Human life is too short for us to put off doing what we was meant to do.

The brush arbor was built at the edge of a pine thicket, across a field from the road. Among those standing outside was the Gibson boys from up on the mountain. Some carried rifles and some had pistols in their belts. I'd never heard of the

Gibsons coming to service before. During Pa's boundary dispute with the Johnsons when I was a girl the Gibsons had sided with the Johnsons. It was said they was blockaders and horse thieves. During the Confederate War the Gibsons had been outliers with the Johnsons, running in bands at night and robbing folks. I wondered if they had been converted.

But many others was regular Pentecostals. There was old Jim Wheeler who was a whirler. When he got full of the Spirit he stood up and swung his arm around like it was a windmill. He would stand there sweating and his arm went round and round in a blur. And there was little Ronnie Cartee that was known as a barker. After the Spirit touched him he run out to a tree and grabbed it with both hands. Looking up the tree he howled like a dog at the moon. Nobody knowed why he did it. It was his way of showing joy. Everybody has their own way of being happy.

At the back of the brush arbor was lanky George Leland. He was knowed among the people as "leaping George" because when he got happy he started jumping over things. He would jump over stumps and chairs. He leapfrogged people praying, and once at Crossroads he jumped all the way over the pulpit. To watch him slouch before a service you wouldn't think he had so much life in him.

I wish I could tell you what the preacher preached that night, but I can't recall. I just know he kept us waiting a long time as we set on the benches, and the air was tight. The boys outside kept muttering and laughing, and that sounded wrong. It was like they had come to a fair or circus show. I was scared a little.

Finally Allen Raeburn and Ben MacBane come out of the woods carrying a lantern. The preacher was behind them. He was a little red-faced man in a gray suit. Ben hung the lantern on a pole and stood in front of us. I looked to see what had happened to the preacher. He had dropped to his knees just at the entrance to the arbor, and he stayed there with his eyes closed.

"We will raise a hymn," Ben said. Now it was always a joy to hear Ben sing. He had a voice so pure it seemed to come from clear back in time. When you heard him you thought, That's what music was meant to be. Other voices was just echoes of his.

"'Revive Us Again,'" Ben called out. And we sung that old revival number, as Ben lined out each verse beforehand. I felt this sweetness raising in me. It was a taste from deep down. I believe people have a taste for food, and for loving, but those are just echoes of the taste for divine love. Humans was put here to experience that love, and to praise. Now that I was beginning to find joy, I saw how hungry I had been for the last two years.

After "Revive Us Again" we sung "Work for the Night Is Coming." The Reece woman from the village and Tildy Tankersley was already shouting. But when the song was over they stopped. Everybody looked at the preacher. He stayed on his knees with his eyes closed. It appeared he was in some kind of spell.

"Wake him up," one of the boys out in the dark muttered, and there was giggles among the trees.

Slowly the preacher got to his feet. He walked to the front and stood by the lantern. He stretched out his arms and looked side to side. "I don't believe we have to settle for less than joy," he said. "We was put on earth to praise and feel joy."

"Amen," Joe said.

"I believe we can know the Savior and feel joy," the preacher said. "I don't think we was put here to mourn. I don't think we was put here to whine and complain, to backbite and prevaricate. I believe we was put here to see the light and to be the light."

"Amen," Joe said. Other men joined in.

I felt a burning in me. It was as if a flame of sweetness went through my bones, up and down my spine. It was a wine flame flushing through me in many colors a message I needed to hear.

"Only thing keeping you from the joy of the Spirit is selfishness and timidity. Only thing stopping you is yourself. The Devil wants you to fall back into fear and self-pity. The Devil wants you to feel miserable and alone."

"Amen," Joe and other men said. Women never said amen to the preacher.

"All you have to do is accept the baptism in your heart," the preacher said. "It is a gift, and all you need to do is take it."

Somebody belched loud in the dark. There was snickers out in the trees. The preacher stopped and looked around. He looked out in the dark, and he looked from side to side of the brush arbor. He waited a long time to speak again. "Woe unto them that try to mock the Spirit," he said. "God will not be mocked."

"Amen," Joe said.

"He that mocks the Spirit is in danger of hellfire."

"Hellfire!" somebody said out in the dark.

"Woe unto the doubters and mockers, and them that would test the Spirit," the preacher said.

"Amen, b-b-brother," Joe said.

"Someone is here tonight who may have lost her way," the preacher said. "Someone is here tonight that has lost her joy and assurance." The preacher paused and looked at me. It was like he saw right into my head. I felt a shudder go through my bones.

"I'm here to tell you it's not too late," he said. "The baptism is here for whoever will accept it."

I felt myself lifted up. It was like a wave went through me to bear me away. I looked right into the preacher's eyes and a wind roared through my head. I didn't know what I was doing, and at the same time I did know, because it had happened before. I was watching myself soar in a high black wind. I knowed I was tasting a drop of the glory that was meant for everybody. I was riding in the flood of words white as mountains of dogwood blossoms. It was white-hot at the center of everything.

"Bless you, sister, bless you," the preacher said. He was standing in front of me and I could feel my feet again. "Bless you," he said. "You have received a message meant for us all."

I was holding the baby to my chest and once again the front of my dress was wet with milk. I felt I had woke from a long fever unsteady on my feet. It was like I had been give a new life and was weak as a newborn. Pa held me at the elbow and shoulder.

Just then there was a noise, like the sky had cracked open. My first thought was the Rapture had come and Jesus was breaking through the top of the sky. "Lord help us," somebody hollered.

Then there was another crack, and I knowed it was a rifle shot. Somebody on the ridge or in the thicket was shooting over the brush arbor. The bullets hummed like guitar strings.

"Don't be afraid," the preacher said.

There was another shot, and this time the bullet hit the brush above our heads. Pine needles and bits of bark and trash sifted down on us. I held Muir tight to my chest and bent over to protect him. People had dropped to the sawdust and others crawled to the door. "Keep low," Pa said.

A lot of the men inside had pistols in their pockets. They must have knowed there was going to be trouble. They waved the guns around like they didn't know where to point them.

"Who is out there?" the preacher hollered.

"Stop shooting," Ben MacBane called.

There was shots from all directions. Bullets buzzed like hornets in the brush. The lantern was shot out, but guns went right on banging. The night was exploding in booms and squirts of fire. You could smell burnt powder. Muir started bellowing.

"Let's go," Pa said. We stooped over low as we could walk and worked our way to the door. There didn't seem to be anybody blocking the door, but everywhere there was flashes and bangs in the woods. We bent low as we could and kept going toward the wagon in the field. Joe and Lily stayed right behind us.

When Tom heard about the shoot-out at Mountain Valley he was madder than ever. "You're not taking the baby again," he said.

"A baby belongs with its mother," I said.

"A mother belongs at home with her husband," Tom said.

The second night, as we prepared to leave, Tom come in from the field and picked up Muir. I run over and held out my hands to take him back. I stood there a few seconds looking Tom hard in the eyes, and then I turned around and left with Pa.

"You'll come back when your breasts get full," Tom said.

After that second night Tom had a new attitude. Maybe it was the fact that he was getting older, or was long familiar with the bitterness between us. It was like he turned away and shut me out that summer. I know he hated me for shouting in front of other people, dancing in front of other men. I know he felt betrayed in some intimate way. Through the long days of summer and fall he worked hard as ever pulling fodder and cutting tops, selling corn and tomatoes in the village, making molasses. It was the money that he used to spite me. He made more than he ever had. He paid Florrie to come over and clean, and he paid Joe and David and the oldest Waters boy to help in the cane patch. I had never seen him work so hard or ignore me so completely.

Tom come from the field dirty and tired just as Pa and me was leaving for Mountain Valley. He kept Jewel and Moody on the porch with him, and he held the baby. Sometimes he made a cutting remark, but mostly he just watched. His silence was sharper than words. I believe Tom had come to some rage beyond rage that looked like patience and cunning. But it might also have been indifference. It was a virtue he had, for hard work and waiting, but tempered with hate. He was showing the world how patient and frugal he could be, while his wife was shaming herself at meetings and giving his money away to preachers.

I know Florrie must have told him that's the way she saw it too, and that's the way the rest of the community saw him.

That was his new satisfaction, that he had an ally in Florrie, and that he could endure. His hard work was itself a revenge.

All that summer and fall Florrie worked at the house. She come almost every day. Since she never did any work in her own house, and didn't have children of her own, there was nothing to keep her from coming to mine. I know she enjoyed taking Tom's side against me. Since we had been little girls she was always teasing me about my reading, and about religious things. She said the revival meetings caused more trouble than any good they did. Our mama had taught her that when we was little girls.

I tried not to show my resentment of Florrie. I would be playing right into her trap if I did. And after all, she was my sister, coming over every day to help out. It would look bad if I quarreled. David's cough kept getting worse, and she needed the money Tom paid. David had bad lungs, and had to be careful not to strain hisself. People said he had TB, but him and Florrie would not admit he was suffering from anything but a cold.

I said to myself it didn't mean a thing that Florrie talked and laughed with Tom whenever she got the chance. They was brother and sister by marriage. They was close in age, and in the same family. And Florrie was a lively person. She had the same spirit I had in me, except she didn't spend it reading and going to meetings. There was certain things her and me didn't talk about and that was how we managed to get along. She never did tell me many jokes and we almost never talked about religion. That's what I had to do to keep the peace.

But I noticed Tom and Florrie was always aware of where the other was. Florrie had begun to dress better and to fix her hair. She had not lost her figure. There was color in her cheeks. At dinnertime, if you glanced around, you might see she was looking at Tom. Her skin was darker than mine, and she didn't have any wrinkles, even though she was older than me.

I heard her talking to Tom out on the porch. They thought I was still in the bedroom, putting Muir down for a nap.

"What's round and swells with pleasure?" Florrie said.

"Don't know," Tom said.

"An eyeball," Florrie said, and slapped her apron as she laughed.

One day when I had gone out to the springhouse for a jar of buttermilk, I lingered by the branch to pick some cardinal flowers. Tom had come from the field to wash and eat dinner before driving to the village. Florrie was hanging clothes on the line between the smokehouse and the springhouse. While I was in the springhouse she finished and went back to the house.

For some reason I decided to walk up the hill behind the springhouse to see if there was more cardinal flowers under the hemlocks there. And then I went on around the junipers and come back to the house from the other side. As I stepped on the porch I could hear their voices in the kitchen. I stopped without opening the door, and saw them through the west kitchen window.

Tom stood before a pan on the table sponging hisself off. His shirt was open and he had loosened his pants. It looked like he had lathered his face to shave and Florrie had come in on him.

"Where does Ginny keep her blueing?" Florrie said, giggling.

"In the cupboard there," Tom said.

He turned to hand her the blueing, and grabbed at his pants that was unbuttoned.

Florrie looked at him as though she was studying. "Some women like hairy men," she said. "But I always preferred ones that was strong, however much wool they have on them." And then she slapped his belly right over the navel. It was something she used to do to David when they was courting.

I felt like I had been hit by lightning, and waited to see what happened next. My skin prickled and stung with heat, as if sweat was hurting to get out through my pores. I didn't want to see any more, but I couldn't move.

Tom reached out like he was going to touch Florrie's neck with his left hand, and then he stopped. "I'll just finish washing up," he said with a laugh.

Florrie laughed too, and hurried back outside.

I waited at the front door for a few seconds before going in.

Since Tom and me wasn't speaking then I never said anything to him. And later I tried to see it was an accident—which it was—her coming in on him in the kitchen. I told myself it didn't amount to a thing. When people are living and working close such embarrassments are bound to happen. I tried to let the sweetness of the meetings touch the rest of my life. Wouldn't make sense, if everyday life was bitter. What good was the revival Spirit if it couldn't soak out through the rest of my life too?

After the molasses was made that fall Tom started working to improve the place again. Even before the corn was gathered he started widening the road. He kept working just as hard as he had in the garden and in the fields. He took a shovel and dug into the bank of the road in the steep places, and he piled the dirt on the outside shoulder. After years of hauling and bumping on the rocks and puddles the road was nothing but ruts. In places rain had washed right across the tracks.

The first third of the road followed the old wagon trace right down to the original homestead where Pa was raised. It had been cut almost a hundred years before through mealy yellow dirt with plows and dragpans. Runoff from the draw above sliced through its soft ruts. Tom dug a ditch from there down to the bend.

When Pa had built the house by the river he plowed and shoveled a road around the hill above the spring. The ledge he cut was just wide enough for a wagon. One wrong step and the horse would stumble over the edge. That was where the most widening had to be done, above the spring.

After the road swung out of the woods beyond the spring it followed the curving hill to the turning yard above the house. It passed the strawberry beds and Joe's Poplar then forked, and one set of tracks run through the gate past the junipers to the wagon shed by the crib. The other followed the fence out to the log barn. Both tracks continued to the bottomland fields, the first dropping down the bank past the hogpen, the other sloping along the upper edge of the fields toward the river.

Tom made a new gate where our road entered the Green River Road. We had always had a pole gap there, and every time we drove out or in the poles had to be took down and then put back in place. It was a job I hated, especially in wet weather when the poles got wet and slippery. Tom dug out space at the entrance to turn a wagon around in. It looked like the entrance to a fine estate. He never said a thing to me or Pa about his plans. He just went ahead and did it.

He built the gate itself out of oak slats. It was at least ten feet wide and strengthened with crossbraces. The gate swung on a locust post in iron loops that Tom greased with wagon grease. A blacksmith in town made a latch that could be worked from either side. There was no lock, but a chain could be padlocked around the latch. A guy wire from the top of the post held it level and light. The gate could be pushed by your little finger. He painted the whole thing dark green.

I didn't speak to Tom in those weeks, and I was busy with the baby. But I took an interest in what he did. Hadn't anybody worked on the road in my lifetime, except for stopgap digging and filling in puddles. It was amazing to see the difference the work made. The old section of the road must have been the easiest to rework. All he had to do was dig out the ditch on both sides and throw dirt to crown the middle. The ground of the first fifty feet was hard red clay, but after the road turned at the hill and passed a big poplar it run through loose yellow soil and rotten rock. The ground was shiny with pieces of isinglass and sparkled as if a mirror had been crushed and scattered. The ground crunched on the shovel. Where the tracks had washed in summer rains Tom dumped rock gathered from the pasture. He didn't want to buy pipe for culverts, and I guess he figured the rock would do the trick if he reworked the road every four or five years.

Below the big poplar, sycamores growed down the wash of the gully. The road there was covered with their seed balls which got crushed to a golden mat by wagon wheels. Sycamores will plant theirselves all down a valley, they drop so many seeds.

The curve above the old homestead had a wet-weather spring, and after the least rain the place got muddy with seepage. I reckon Tom hauled more loads of gravel to pack there than anyplace else. He shoveled gravel and sand out of the edge of the river and carried them in the wagon to the road. He broke rocks in the pasture with a sledgehammer and pounded the pieces into the roadbed. I think he figured how to do it as he went along.

I walked up the road and saw what he was doing when I took Jewel to school the first day of the term. I put on her new blue coat and carried the baby. Moody stayed with Pa. Where Tom had cleared the brush and leveled and widened the road so much I hardly recognized it. You could look out over the branch valley and the pastures to the church and schoolhouse. I could see down to the school spring where boys was already fighting.

Beyond the spring the tracks run through solid clay above the strawberry beds, except for one spot where the hill seemed made of gravel. I thought the Indians had chipped arrowheads there. The ground was sharp with bits of quartz and flint. They must have worked on that very spot. Many of the rocks Tom dug he spread on lower sections of the road and in the turning ground near the house. Digging in the clay was like carving cold butter, always chilled, melting at the top in rain. He leveled out a place wide as two horses and wagons end to end. And then he built another gate above the house and painted it the same dark green. I didn't say anything to him, but I thought it looked like the entrance to a rich man's estate. Tom had an eye for making things look right, not fancy, but solid and prosperous.

CHAPTER THIRTEEN

The winter of 1905–06 was one of the coldest and snowiest I ever saw. Usually in the mountains we have some hard freezing weather and a few snows, but they don't last long. A whole night of snow will melt by the middle of next day. The white frosty world of morning will be a muddy thaw by evening, on the southside of any bank or hill. Old-timers used to talk about seeing the river freeze over when they was young, and driving wagons to mill on the ice. But I had never seen such. You know how old-timers like to brag to the young about the awful times of their youth. They like to say they've seen snow over the fence rails for weeks, and freeze so deep it got taters in pits, and now they said there was signs those times was coming again.

All my life I heard Pa talk about Cold Friday when the sun never did come up and chickens didn't leave the roost. He said the mill froze to the creek by a beard of ice, and the fireplace wouldn't hardly give any heat.

That winter there was snow in December while Tom was working on the road, but it disappeared by the next day and didn't stop his work more than a few hours. But in early January, after he had finished the gates, it snowed again, two or three inches, and a bitter freeze turned everything to ice. The snow sealed over the ground, and the top of the snow crumbled like stale bread when you walked on it. The cows in the pasture had to step careful on the crust to keep from sliding, and they cropped the tufts of grass sticking through. Tom went out and spread tops for them at the edge of the pasture. The stack of corn tops was so weighted with ice and snow it was hard to pull stalks from it.

After a day or two of setting inside Tom went back to work as usual. He never could stand to stay in where I was working. He called daytime "the cook's time," meaning it was the time only the cook was supposed to be in the house. I reckon he figured it was wise to bring in more firewood, in case it snowed again.

Joe come by and said he was having trouble reaching his traps because of ice along the river. Pa put an extra sweater under his coat when he walked to the road to get the mail. Every time the younguns went out in the snow they got wet and started coughing. I had to make them stay inside. Moody was playing cowboys and Indians and he kept saying there was outlaws outside. "Look Mama, they're hiding behind the smokehouse," he would say. "I'm going out to kill them."

"You stay here," I would say. "You don't want to kill anybody, and besides it's too cold."

"What if they shoot us?" Moody said.

"Maybe the outlaws will freeze," I said.

Exactly a week after the first snow I got up early and went to the kitchen. Pa was reading his Bible at the table. Tom had took the buckets to the barn to milk. I stepped on the back porch to grind more coffee and saw this glow in the sky, a faint, almost blue haze, as if from a lighted city just beyond the mountains.

"There's a light in the sky," I said to Pa back inside.

"Snowlight," Pa said.

"What does it mean?" I said.

"It means there's some condition in the air that shines like the northern lights and makes snow."

I had heard Pa talk about snowlight all my life, but I never believed in it. Didn't make sense a light coming from somewhere else could tell you it was going to snow. It wasn't daylight yet, and it wasn't dark either. The glow outside made me shiver as I fixed oatmeal. When Tom come in from milking and feeding the stock I saw the first flakes brush against the window. I was nursing Muir at the table. "This is wash day," I said. There was a basket of diapers on the porch that needed to be washed.

"If it snows I'll go get Florrie to do the wash," Tom said.

"I'll do the wash myself," I said.

"No, I will," Tom said. But he didn't look at me. I didn't say anything else. I knowed that soon as he finished eating he would turn the horse out to pasture. While he was gone I put Muir in the cradle and got on my shawl and tied a scarf around my head.

"Can I go?" Moody said.

"You stay here by the fire," I said.

"I want to fight the outlaws," he said.

"You stay here and fight the cold," I said.

"Moody told a big fat lie," Jewel said.

"I did not," Moody said and hit her on the arm.

I took matches and cobs and kindling out to the washpot. To start the fire I had to protect the match from falling snow. Even so, the first match got hit by a flake and hissed out. I cupped my hands around the next flame. Soon as the kindling caught I throwed on cobs and run to the woodshed for wood. I carried a big pile to the washpot and got a crackling fire going.

By the time I had carried a third bucket of water from the springhouse Tom come back from the barn. When he saw me filling the washpot he hollered, "I said I will do the wash."

"No, I will," I said, and started back to the spring for another bucket. The trail was slick with new snow already.

"Then I'll go after Florrie," he said.

"No you won't," I said. "I'm doing the wash."

"You'll kill yourself, Ginny," he said.

"If it's so dangerous, why ask Florrie to do it?" I said. "Don't you care if she kills herself?"

"You are a fool, Ginny," he said. He followed me to the springhouse and grabbed one of the buckets of water out of my hand. Some of it splashed on me. "Now you will freeze," he said.

We walked back to the fire and dumped our buckets in the pot. It was beginning to steam, and steam mixed with smoke made a column that rose straight into the falling flakes. I had never seen it snow so hard. The air was full of white blossoms and you felt you was rising into the fizz of flakes. I couldn't hardly see the house across the yard. I throwed more sticks on the fire.

"It's too cold for you to be out here," Tom said.

"But it's not too cold for Florrie?" I said. I had learned a trick in arguing with Tom that always worked. Instead of acting mad I would be calm and cheerful. He couldn't stand to see me smile when he was mad. He depended on me getting angry too.

"I'd be ashamed," he said. "A woman with a nursing baby has to take care of herself."

"But you don't mind if Florrie gets sick?" I said, and smiled.

"I'd be ashamed," he said.

"I'll be fine," I said with as much cheer as I could muster.

I was going back to the porch for the diapers, but he stalked ahead and grabbed the basket. I thought at first he was going to take them out of my reach, but he hurried with the load to the wash table. He dropped the basket on the planks and walked away without another word. The snow was coming so fast it fell in my eyes like gnats, and I had to keep brushing snow off my cheeks.

All morning the sky fell like pollen and big crumbs of sugar. I fed the fire under the washpot and smoke pushed its way up through the snow. Sometimes a breeze would sway the smoke into my face and then jerk it away again. I scrubbed diapers and clothes in the steaming tubs until my hands and arms was pink. I figured if I worked hard enough I would stay warm.

The snow come straight down, not reaching under the hemlocks. But the clothes I had hung on the line was beginning to freeze. First they got stiff like they had a lot of starch, then they got hard as boards. Fins of snow built up on top of the clothesline.

I dumped another basket of stinking diapers into the hot water, and thought, This is one load Florrie won't touch. She has got into my house, into my kitchen, into my clothes, but this is one day she won't need to cross the hill. As I stirred the boiling diapers with the troubling stick I felt a child's delight in getting my way. And I guess I was thrilled by the snow too, and the feeling of closed-in-ness inside the falling snow.

With the white world descending over me it seemed my troubles was being buried and smoothed over, just like gullies and stubble and muddy roads and the manure pile in front of the barn got covered and made clean by new flakes. After hanging most of the diapers on the line I took a few inside to stretch by the fire. If it kept snowing all would have to be brought in to thaw and dry, a dozen at a time, by the fireplace and kitchen stove.

It felt too hot in the house. After the flush of the morning's work the house was smoky and dark. I needed to nurse Muir soon, but I was happy to get back outside after a few minutes, into the pure whiteness of the storm.

At sundown I went out again to get more clothes. The sky was clear and wind off the hill was smoking cold. Snow tossed around devils and tall sails in the pasture. The air was filled with crystals that glittered and swirled in the late sun. Everything in sight was turning gold. I felt giddy in the light and wind.

Soon as I put the clothes inside I went out to gather eggs. The ground from barn to chickenhouse was pure untracked snow. The manure pile steamed with inner heat, and in a day would melt away the snow on its sides. The low roof of the chickenhouse was piled like a layer cake with last week's snow and the new snow.

It was awful dark in the crib as I shelled corn into a basket. The smell of shucks and cobs was sweet in the air that cut through cracks. I felt weakness in my bones, and tightness in my throat. I hurried to the chickenhouse with the corn.

I scattered corn on the floor and gathered eggs into the basket. Reaching into the nests was like searching for secrets. Where a hen was setting you had to reach under her and feel which of the warm eggs was just a china egg. Real eggs was heavy.

Suddenly I sneezed and the hens started cackling and flapping. There was dust in the air, and the more they fluttered the worse the dust would be. I tried to hold my breath, but found it was short. I imagined mites and lice in the air that got stirred up. A chickenhouse smells so sweet it makes you sick. And chickens are so hot-blooded they warm it up in all but the coldest weather. I gathered nineteen eggs in the basket and hurried out.

As I walked to the house I was suddenly dizzy and my legs and arms hurt. It's the low temperature, I told myself. When it gets this cold strength drains away. I held a sleeve to my mouth, but couldn't see that way and had to inhale the ether-cold wind. I almost slipped on the snow, and kept losing my balance.

Even while I put on supper I felt hot and flustered. The cold had tired me more than I realized. I would start to do something and then forget what I meant to do. I would begin to speak, then wonder later if I really said it. Halfway through the meal there was an ache in my bones and I wished I could go to bed.

I tried to feed Muir some mashed potatoes, but my hand trembled as I held the little spoon.

"Are you sick?" Pa said.

"Mama, your face is red," Jewel said.

Moody come over and pulled my sleeve. "Are you sick, Mama?"

"No, I ain't sick," I said.

"You look like the outlaws shot you," Moody said.

But things was spinning around, and I couldn't even clear up the dishes. It was as though things started swelling and shrinking wherever I looked. The lamplight got brighter, then dim. At some point Tom led me to the bed.

I can't remember any more about that night except the sound of wind pushing the side of the house. It was like the storm was grabbing the walls and squeezing them. The soreness in my breath got all mixed up with the wind pressing on the house and wheezing in the eaves. The wind was crushing my chest. The air was dark red, and burned when I breathed it in.

Early next morning I knowed what was going on, even though I was far away from it all. "You go over and get Florrie," Pa said to Tom. "You're going to need help."

The younguns had gathered around the fireplace. I could hear Muir crying in the kitchen. "Bang, bang," Moody shouted. I wanted to get up, but I couldn't. It was all too far away. The air I breathed was full of broke glass and razor blades.

"Drink this," somebody said. It was Tom bent over me. I could smell the whiskey in the cup. Much as I wanted a sip I moved my lips away. It was too hard to breathe to drink anything. And yet I was all dried out. I was thirsty.

"It's sugar and whiskey in water," Florrie said. Maybe it was later when she said it. "You always liked whiskey didn't you?"

"She needs whiskey to give her strength," Pa said.

I saw Jewel and Moody standing at the door of the room looking in. They had been sleeping on pallets on the floor.

"Where is the baby?" I said.

"The baby is fine," Florrie said.

Dr. Johns come by when it felt like the middle of the night. He took the bottle of whiskey and drunk some. As usual he was testing medicine whiskey to see if it was any good.

"Drink this, Ginny," he said.

I took a swallow and it felt like my throat and chest was scalded, and I was sinking into a hot bath.

"You're doing all that can be done," Dr. Johns said.

Muir was crying in the kitchen. The house popped with cold, timbers shrinking on the north side. I knowed there was a big fire in the fireplace for I could hear the flames crackle.

"Put hot bricks in the bed to warm her feet," the doctor said. "And keep her wrapped up, even if she is sweating."

The doctor took another drink before he left. I didn't know if it was day or night. It seemed the middle of the night. There was a light at the window, but it could have been moonlight. It was brighter than lamplight. It was like somebody was watching me from the window, even though the light come from way off.

I knowed Tom and Pa and sometimes Florrie was keeping the fire going through cold days and nights. They took turns setting by the bed, putting damp cloths on my forehead, and changing the flannel on my chest.

"Where is the baby?" I said.

"The baby is fine," Florrie said. "I fed him grits and he's full as a tick."

The bedclothes got all soaked with sweat and she changed them, rolling me one way, and then the other, to take off the wet sheet and spread a fresh one under me. I could smell the clean sheet I had washed and dried by the fire. But mostly I smelled the fever. It was the smell of soreness and inflammation. It was the way an infected sore on your finger smells, except it was coming from inside me. The smell was in my breath.

I don't know how many days passed. It might have been five or six. My chest felt like it was full of dumplings and pie crusts when I breathed. My lungs whistled and gurgled. I wondered where the wheeze was coming from. There was kettles boiling somewhere.

A cloth was throwed over my head. It was as if a sheet had been pulled across my face. Had I gone and died without knowing it? But it was a rough sheet with grains on it. It was a towel.

"Breathe this," Tom said. He put a bowl under my chin. It was full of steam, and under the towel there was nothing but steam. He had put salve in the hot water, from the can on the mantel that I rubbed on the younguns' chests when they had colds. It was the smell of spruce resin and the far edge of the sky. There was something silver and spiritual in the scent that went up into my head and throat. But I couldn't breathe it down into my chest.

"Breathe deep," Tom said.

I tried to breathe, but it was too hard. My chest was sore and full. It was all I could do to take short little gasps.

"Breathe deep," he said. But I couldn't inhale any deeper.

The strangest thoughts come to me in the wet dark under the towel. It was like I was in a tent. I thought how it was only rubbing things together that made them work. If men and women touched each other that was one thing, but if the touch become a caress that was another. It was the rubbing that made the spark of desire. The roughness was important as the smoothness. It was the caress, and resistance to the caress, and resistance overcome, that made the pleasure. I had never thought of that before. In the muggy dark it seemed like the secret of things.

"The road is buried," I said to Tom.

"What did you say?" He lifted the towel and I felt cold air.

"The new road is buried," I said. But he couldn't hear. It was like I was trying to talk in water instead of air. Nothing I said come out right. But I was thinking about how wind and snow was burying his work. The wind was rubbing on snow; snow was rubbing on the ground. Everything was resisting everything else.

When he took the towel off my face sweat stood on my forehead big as berries. It rolled into my eyes and down my temples. I was still breathing in little gasps. There wasn't any air to breathe.

"It will take onions," Pa said somewhere way off.

"Onions?" Tom said.

"I saw it when I was a boy," Pa said. "Only thing that will break pneumonia fever is an onion pack."

Later I could smell the frying onions. I wondered if Florrie was fixing liver and onions. It was something Pa liked, but I never fixed because it stunk up the house. It smelled like they was burning. I thought I could hear the crackle and snap of the grease in the pan, but it was the rasp of my breath. The whole house was full of the smell of greasy fried onions.

"Put this on," Tom said. He pulled back the covers and lifted my gown. What he put on my chest was like a bag heavy with hot applesauce. It was flattened out, steaming, and looked wet and greasy. It was so hot it scalded me. I shivered like you do in a hot bath. I guess bad cold and heat are almost the same thing. They make you jerk and shudder the way the Spirit does.

And then the smell hit my face. It was as if a bushel of crawling slivers of onions had been put under my nose. I've heard they once used onions to scare away the Devil. I don't think any demon could stand the smell of greasy half-cooked onions. The stink of the grease, and the feel of the grease on my chest, was worse than the smell of the onions itself.

"Drink some of this," Florrie said. It was whiskey and warm lemon juice in a cup. I drunk some just to take away the smell of the onions for a little. And then I drunk some more.

I could feel the grease in the poultice sink into my chest. My skin was opening and soaking up the taste of the onions. It felt my chest was melting in the heat and foul stench.

Suddenly the room was stretching out to ten times its size. The air was like rubber, stretching and rushing back. "Hold the bed still," I said.

The room was rocking back and forth, not just from side to side, but whirling and rocking at the same time. The walls spun and squeezed, then bulged away. It felt as if the bed was falling down a mountain. There was a roar and a gray flame in the air.

"Hold the bed still," I said. The bed was on rollers and shooting down a tilted floor. The room got long as a hallway, and I was flying toward the end of it.

Then something exploded. My chest and throat busted open and whiskey shot into my mouth and nose. I could taste lemon juice, sourer than before. My nose burned like I had been slapped and pushed underwater. My mouth was full of water and sour whiskey.

Before I knowed what was happening my mouth opened and I spewed over my chin and on the pillows. The hot clabber sprayed on the sheets and quilts. I retched over the poultice and on myself. The stuff come out so hard it shot up in the air and splashed my face before I could turn sideways. The puke burned my nose and eyes like lemon juice.

Suddenly it stopped and I felt cold sweat over me. I was so weak I couldn't hold my head up. I was wet all over my front with fried onions and throw-up.

"Let me change your sheets," Florrie said.

"Oh," I said. And then it started again. The seizure hit like a crushing weight that pushed from below. It was like I was being squeezed to death. I had read they killed witches in the old days by crushing them with rocks, "pressing" it was called. That's what I felt, that I was being pressed to death.

There was nothing else to throw up, but I kept heaving and gagging on little bits of sour water, strings and yellow gobs of bile. It felt like the marrow of my bones was trying to come up.

Florrie put a cool hand on my forehead. It was what Mama used to do when I was a girl. It's what I did for my younguns when they was sick. It was the only thing that made me feel better. Her hand on my forehead steadied me and quieted my heaving.

That's when I saw what I had throwed up. It wasn't just bile and juice, whiskey and lemon juice mixed with spit. There was clots and chunks of mucous, yellow and hard, throwed from my chest. There was strings, and big drops of congestion and corruption. Tom and Florrie took away the poultice and changed the sheets, but I was dropping into a cool dead sleep.

I don't recall much of the next few days. All my memories of the week are vague and out of order. But everything I do remember has to do with the light at the window. It come in and stood at the foot of the bed tall as a man. It stood there hours and went away. It was gone for a while and then returned and stood a long time in front of me. It was so close I could almost touch it with my foot, and then it backed to the window. I watched it by the window for hours, and then I saw it had slipped behind the snow drifted on the sash and the ferns of frost on the glass. The light was watching me, but further away. And I thought it was an angel guarding over me. It was a messenger from the Spirit telling me I would be well. The angel was looking right at me and I felt as though I was speaking in tongues. I knowed it would be there whether I saw it or not. And I felt guilty that I had not prayed once while I was sick. I had not called on the Lord even when I was out of my head. I whispered a prayer of thanksgiving.

One day I felt an itch all over. It was not like the itch when your foot is asleep and begins to wake, twinkling and seething.

It was more like the itch where a bee sting or cut begins to heal. My whole body had been sore with fever and was beginning to get well. Feeling was coming back and my skin was itching.

But there was a deep weakness in me too, like I had been froze and was thawing out. I was attracted to warmth, to the fit of quilts and blankets around me. The heat had gone out of me, and I was pulling together to recover what warmth was left. I thought if I had somebody to lay against maybe I would feel better. The warmth had seeped out of the world. There was just a tiny flame somewhere in me, like a candle that had not gone out.

One morning I saw the white at the window was ice, and I remembered the snow and extreme cold. I wondered about the washing, and about the cows in the pasture. What about the wood supply? And how had the chickens fared? I wondered, and yet it was no real concern to me. I was curious about what was happening outside, and I could feel the wind shove against the house from time to time. But I was too weak to worry, and too cold to care.

There was a smell about me of fever and sickness, a sweet smell of flesh slightly cooked and drying on the skin. I brought a hand to my nose and sniffed. It was the scent of dead skin. But I couldn't be sure I wasn't smelling my breath. For my lungs was full of loose matter that rattled around like dumplings floating and bumping when I breathed. I started to cough. My chest was still sore, but not tight as it was before.

Tom got a handkerchief and said, "Here, cough in this." I spit clots and gobs in the cloth. Some was hard as crumbs of bread.

Jewel and Moody stood in the door watching.

"Jewel pushed me," Moody said.

"I did not," Jewel said.

I was going to speak to them, but I started coughing again. When I stopped they had gone.

You was in a fever five days," Florrie said when I got my strength back a little. "It was only when you throwed up the bile and congestion that it broke." She brought me warm broth.

"Where is Muir?" I said.

"That baby is fine," Florrie said. "He's eating like a hog."

"He ain't nursed," I said. My breasts was sore and shrunk.

"He's been weaned since Thursday," Florrie said. It seemed she was bragging, pleased that Muir had been weaned. I turned away on the pillow. I told myself I should be grateful for all her help.

"This is the coldest spell on record," Pa said when he come in later. "This country has never seen such a winter."

"How cold did it get?" I said.

"Twenty-two below for three mornings, below zero for a week."

They had kept the fire going day and night, and put heated rocks in pans under my bed. It had been too cold to snow, but when it warmed up a little after a week it snowed again. The river had froze, and even the pools in the branch. The spring smoked like it was on fire, Pa said. Where snow melted a little the thaw turned to a sheet of ice and sealed the snow under it. Joe had walked across the hill twice to help bring in wood. Tom and the children had been sleeping in the living room by the fire, Jewel and Moody on a pallet, Muir in his cradle.

"I want to see him," I said. Tom come back with the baby and put him in my arms. Muir had been growing. He was heavier than I expected. Weaning hadn't made him lose weight, but he smelled different. I guess a baby that's not nursing does smell different. A mother smells her own milk on the baby's breath.

I held him to me and he went right for my breast. I guess he wasn't completely weaned. But there wasn't any milk for him and I pulled him up to my chin and he only whimpered a little.

Now while I was holding Muir I saw the strangest thing. I was thrilled and warmed to have his body against me. It was like a pleasure and a touch I had forgot in my fever. When you're sick you become a child again yourself. And now I felt like a mother again. Thankfulness flooded through me. I rubbed Muir's little bottom through his gown and it was round as two apples. I felt I was holding all of humanity and the world in his little form. I could feel his heart fluttering like a tiny animal, and his breath was sweet against my neck. He had been eating grits.

"Thank you, Jesus," I said. And I thought again how in my fever I had not prayed, or if I did I couldn't remember it. But now that I was cool I felt gratefulness pour through me. Gratitude rose and brought tears to my eyes. "Thank you, Jesus," I said again. It come to me that the light at the window while I had the fever, and at the foot of my bed, had indeed been the Spirit watching over me. I had never been deserted, however thoughtless and forgetful I had been. The love had been there, and the grace had been there, all the time. I held Muir closer to my chin.

While I was holding him I could see through the door down the hall to the living room and a little bit into the kitchen. Tom and Florrie stood talking. They was just out of sight of the fireplace where Pa set. What I noticed was how close they stood. Wasn't any need for grownup people to stand that close. There's a distance people keep when they are talking. But they looked just a few inches apart. They wasn't touching far as I could see, just standing close. And then I saw Florrie's hand come up and touch Tom on the arm. It lingered there for several seconds.

It don't mean a thing, I said to myself. They've worked hard together while I was sick. They've set up nights and Florrie has changed my bed. They've had a hard time looking after me.

I held the baby closer. I have always hated the sin of jealousy. I've seen it make people crazy. It will begin with a little hurt vanity, when somebody else gets more attention, or somebody is a little prettier, and next thing you know it turns to hate and sinful spite. I had always thought I would not be jealous. After the way Tom and me had quarreled it didn't seem possible I could be jealous of a look, a touch.

But the fact was I was suddenly stiff with anger. I couldn't help myself. Maybe I was too weak to get hold of myself. If I had been well I would have seen what to do. I think now I had always been jealous of Florrie, that she was prettier than me, and littler than me, that boys liked her more, and that she drunk a lot of liquor on the sly and got away with it.

I told myself again it didn't mean a thing. After all, two people working in the same house are bound to stand close and talk. But in my heart I felt Florrie was taking advantage. She was profiting from my quarrel with Tom, from our differences over religion. While I was sick she had took charge of the children and the house.

It was twenty minutes later Florrie come busting into the bedroom. "Well, Mrs. Powell, are you feeling fit?" she said. She opened the curtains a little and sunlight leapt into the room. I did not answer, but kept playing with the baby.

"We thought you was going to leave us," Florrie said, picking up cups and dishes on the nightstand. She stopped at the bed.

"I know what you're doing," I said. It come out; it was too late to not say it.

"What do you mean?" she said. She cradled the dirty cups and saucers in her apron. She was always great at playing innocent.

"I've seen you buttering up Tom," I said. She looked down at me like I was a little kid that needed a diaper changed.

"You are still sick," she said. "You are out of your head."

Just then Muir started to cry. I guess he felt the anger and it scared him. Babies can tell when their mothers get mad.

My throat was suddenly tight, and I started coughing. It was a cough that seemed to come from deep in a well. The rattle in my throat was way down and heavy.

Florrie took the cups and saucers out of her apron and put them back on the nightstand. "I'll take Muir," she said.

"No!" I said. But my voice turned into another cough. I was too weak to cough and yet I had to. The cough come from deep in my guts and heaved through me in a wave. I was so weak I couldn't hold on to Muir, and Florrie lifted him out of my hands.

After I had coughed a few minutes I spit up more hard clots on the handkerchief. It was like everything I spit up left holes in my chest. When I stopped coughing I felt emptied out and ready to sink back into myself.

"Here, drink this," Florrie said. She held a cup to my chin.

"No!" I said. It was the same concoction of whiskey and lemon juice and warm honey they had give me before. The spirits smelled up the room and spread right into my chest.

"You need this," Florrie said.

I took a sip and it felt as if a hot wire run across my tongue and down my throat. But the warmth soaked out in my belly and chest and made me feel a little stronger. I took another sip.

"You always was a fool, Ginny," Florrie said.

I didn't say anything else. I didn't want to talk anymore until I had time to think. I drunk all the whiskey and honey. It seemed to loosen up my chest more than anything else had. Nothing else made as much sense as the whiskey, and I drunk it all.

"Do you want some mush sweetened with sugar?" Florrie said when the cup was empty.

"No," I said, and turned my face away on the pillow.

CHAPTER FOURTEEN

Late that night after the house was quiet Tom come into the bedroom carrying a lamp. "It's snowing again," he said. "I seen the snowlight this morning and Pa said it was coming again."

I listened and could hear the tinkle of flakes on the window. It sounded like somebody was throwing fine sand at the glass. Tom stood by the bed holding the lamp, as though waiting for something. He had brought the heated rocks in earlier and put them in pans under the bed. The room was warming up a little. "Are you warm enough?" he said. He had his red plaid shirt on, the one I had ordered from St. Louis. It was open at the throat and his flannel underwear looked orange in the lamplight.

"Is Florrie gone?" I said.

"Florrie went a long time ago, before dark," he said.

I had forgot how strong his neck was. His shoulders looked wider than before. He had been using the ax a lot lately and pulling the crosscut saw with Joe. In the lamplight he stood thick and powerful. The lamp throwed shadows behind him. The flame stroked like a tongue in the glass chimney.

"Close the door," I said. "Don't want to wake the house." Tom shut the door slowly. He looked at the floor solemn as somebody does at a funeral.

There was a spark in me. I had been cold so long it didn't seem like there could be any life in my body. I had forgot what it felt like to be warm. It was like a match struck somewhere far inside me. "Are we out of wood?" I said.

"We cut a tree today," Tom said, "on the pasture hill."

Snow tinkled and brushed on the window. I couldn't see anything there but blackness and the reflection of the lamp. The house was so quiet I heard the fire snap in the next room.

"Is the baby asleep?" I said.

"He's been asleep since supper," Tom said.

"Then you might as well come to bed yourself," I said.

He stood like he was trying to make up his mind. Tom was never one to do anything in a rush.

"Are you well enough?" he said.

"I'm almost well," I said.

Tom put the lamp down on the stand. Then he cupped his hand over the top of the chimney and blowed it out.

The spark that had been lit in me traveled along my bones and veins. It was a little flame that tried to search every corner of my fingers and elbows, toes and knees. The light worked its way closer, up my legs and through my arms. It was as if I was waking from a deep cold sleep in joints and places I had forgot about.

When Tom laid down the bed tilted and quaked. I had been sleeping by myself since before Muir was born. The bed trembled and shook on its springs like we was sliding out on a current.

"What are we going to do if it keeps snowing?" I said.

"Keep cutting more wood, I guess," Tom said.

"A fireplace takes a lot of wood," I said.

Snow sprinkled on the window like little feet running in the dark. The snow sounded blue to me, the blue of a star. I was so weak I couldn't hardly move, and at the same time it felt like I was waking up from a long dream and seeing it was just a dream. There was voices in my toes and hands and echoes running back and forth through me. One part of me was speaking to another.

"Is the branch froze over?" I said.

"Most places," Tom said. "In the fast spots you can still see water."

There was a sweetness approaching from way off. It was like the minutes on the Sunset Rock when the sky shone side to side. The seconds was flavored in a way I had forgot. I remembered how mad I had been at Tom, but couldn't exactly recall the feeling.

"How long is it going to snow?" I said.

"It ain't never going to stop," Tom said. But he said it like he didn't care, and we was safe and warm in the house and it could snow all winter and not hurt us.

"Has the newspaper come?" I said.

"Two has come," he said. "I saved them for you on the mantel."

Wind hit the house with a jolt. I closed my eyes and imagined us sailing on a wide river. Wind pushed us over the top of a great wave. The house soared into the storm on deep blue light.

"Can you breathe?" Tom said.

"My breath is a little short," I said.

"You've been sick a long time," Tom said.

"I will feel better soon as I get my strength back," I said. My breath was so short I could barely whisper.

Now the bed felt long as a ship, and my feet went way down under the cover for miles and miles. The room was stretched out like a hallway or tunnel. The feeling in my toes and legs lighted the way. They reached all the way to the end of the dark.

I wondered if my fever was coming back. I wondered if the bed was going to stream away into the tunnel through the mountains and beyond. The bed was so long it touched the sky. As I breathed I imagined stars swirling through my head and pouring out of my mouth. I had a mouthful of light and was breathing it out.

Never have I felt so relaxed as later that night. There was still a trickle of milk in my breasts, even after all the fever, and it wet the sheets. I was flowing with milk, and in milk. I remembered the talk in the Bible about a land of milk and honey. I was in a river of milk and honey whipped to a foam. Sweet bubbles broke on my skin as the river poured through and over me.

The next day I got up and set by the fire for an hour. I held Muir, and Moody come cautious up to me. "You was sick," he said.

"I was bad sick," I said.

"You ain't going to die?" he said.

"No, I ain't going to die," I said. I took him on my knee and held both him and Muir. Jewel come and leaned on my shoulder. I was too weak to do more than just set there. But it was like I had been washed in boiling water and was clean. I felt stiff as a rag that had been boiled and dried by the fire.

After an hour of setting I was so tired I had to go back to bed. My arms was trembly and my legs sore. I put Muir down, and just as I started to stand up Florrie come in the door. The cold air that entered with her reached me across the room.

"Let me help you, Ginny," she said.

"Don't need any help," I said. I stood so she wouldn't see me tremble. The blood run from my head and the room got white.

"It's snowing again," Florrie said. There was flakes on her scarf and she shook them off in the fire. "It's snowed every Thursday for the past month."

I started toward the bedroom, taking short steps so I wouldn't stumble.

"Here, let me help you," Florrie said.

"No," I said. I turned toward her and was going to say more. But I stopped myself. I knowed if I said anything it would be the wrong thing. "Thank you for all your help," I said.

"It's good to see you up," she said.

By the time I got to the bedroom I was so tired I dropped on the bed and got under the covers without taking my shawl off. I was shivering and just wanted to wrap up in the quilts and lay still as long as I could. When I quit shaking I went to sleep.

That night Tom come into the bedroom again. By then I was rested and warm. He brought me some canned peaches and blackberry juice. "It snowed five more inches today," he said. "It's wet mush that stands tall on stalks and fence wire."

He said the snow was so heavy it had broke down the pines and hemlocks. He said the Lindsays' barn had fell under the weight of snow. Joe's traps was froze under ice and he hadn't got to them for a month. Snow was so deep in the woods it was hard to walk to the traps anyway. Joe's trapline went way to the head of the river and through the Flat Woods into Transylvania County, then swung around to South Carolina and Dark Corner. It took him a full day to walk it when the ground was clear.

"I seen the snowlight again this morning," Tom said.

Night was my favorite time over the next few weeks. To be in bed with Tom warmed me up the way nothing else did. As he laid in bed he told what he had done that day, how he had got up on the barn roof to clear the snow away, how he had run out of leaves and pine needles for cow stalls. The wood on the porch and in the shed was gone, and he had cut two more trees on the hill. He was always better at talking in the dark than in daylight.

As I laid with Tom in those nights I thought how precious it was to be married. It was like we was new to each other, yet knowed better how to please each other. Sometimes I drawed him to my breast like he was one of the children. He was surprised at the pleasure I took as I laid soaring on the bed. I had heard women say you wasn't supposed to show pleasure, or a man would take advantage. But I didn't care. I was thirty-six and felt like a girl. When I was a girl I wouldn't have believed middle-aged people could act so. I didn't care how much pleasure I showed.

The next week it snowed again, and the next. We heard of houses in Saluda that caved in under snow. The worst danger was fire I reckon. Chimneys overheated; they got clogged with soot in the long nights and caught fire. At least three houses at the lower end of the county burned, including the McCalls' at Cedar Springs. Chimneys caught fire and roared like trains into the night sky. The masonry cracked and spilled flames into attics.

When I was well enough to set up I watched the flames in the fireplace. I felt they might have a message for me, but I couldn't tell what it was.

The fifth snow come when it was almost warm enough to thaw, and big wet flakes fell until there was eighteen new inches. Everything I could see out the window was hid by white. The hemlocks was piled and stooped, slumped and twisted under their loads. Their tops tilted like they had broke. Tom said the drifts now reached to the eaves of the springhouse.

The second day of that snow Florrie come over to do washing on the kitchen stove. The boiling pot filled the house with steam. She hung wet clothes on strings over the stove and made the air even damper. The wetness made me irritable.

Jewel and Moody got bundled up and went out to play on the bank behind the house. I watched them through the window. They tried sliding down on a board from the shed, but the snow was so deep the board just sunk and stuck. Then they laid on their backs and made angels in the yard. They rolled down the slope and the snow caked in layers on their clothes. That give them the idea of making a snowman, and Jewel begun to roll up a big ball. But she would not let Moody help, and that made him mad. He run away and sulked, until Jewel almost had the snowman made. But after she set the head on top, and while she was looking for sticks or rocks to make its eyes, he knocked the top two balls off.

When Jewel saw what he had done she took a handful of snow and rubbed it in his face. Moody tried to kick at her, but she threw more snow in his eyes, and backed out of his reach. He started kicking the balls she had rolled up until they was just mush and trampled snow. She pushed him down the bank and kicked him. Moody never had a chance, and come running to the house, caked with snow and dripping, his face red with cold and anger.

"Moody, look what you have done," Florrie said, and pointed to the snow dropped on the floor. She had swept the floor before she started washing. He threw down his wet cap on the floor.

"No!" she said, and smacked him on the behind.

"You can't hit my younguns," I said.

"I will if I have to clean this filthy house," Florrie said.

"You ain't looking after this house," I said.

Florrie stopped in the middle of the room. She had a wet rag in her hand and she put both hands on her hips. Moody was howling. I reached out for him. He was covered with melting snow.

"That's a fine kiss-my-ass," Florrie said. "I come here for a month to do the washing and cleaning and that's the thanks."

"Nobody asked you," I said, though I knowed that wasn't strictly true.

"Tom asked me," Florrie said.

"I didn't ask you," I said.

Florrie tossed the rag into the kitchen and went to get her coat. I think she expected me to ask her to stay, but I didn't. She went out just as Jewel come in all flushed and covered with snow. Florrie slammed the door.

"Where is Aunt Florrie going?" Jewel said.

"She's going home," I said.

The children made a mess with their snowy things by the hearth. The drying frames was loaded with washing, and diapers and underwear hung on strings in the kitchen. The house felt damp and dark. Water was boiling on the stove, and wet diapers, wrung out and twisted, laid on the table. The windows was fogged over.

When Tom come in from the barn he looked around and saw the pot still bubbling on the stove. "Where is Florrie?" he said.

"She went home," I said. He looked at me like he saw what had happened.

"Who's going to do the washing?" he said.

"I will," I said.

"You'll have a set back," he said.

"Who cares?" I said.

It took me all day to finish the wash. I had to stop and rest every few minutes. Pa and Jewel helped me lift the water to pour in the pot. It was hard to wring out sheets, and scrub underwear on the washboard, but I did a little at a time. By supper I had the washing hung on strings, and on the frame by the fire.

As we worked, Moody run around the house shooting Indians or outlaws. "Bang, bang, you're dead," he shouted.

"Shut up," Jewel said, and pushed him away.

"You're dead," Moody said.

"Stay out of the way," I said.

I don't think Tom ever forgive me for running Florrie off that day. We did not quarrel about it anymore, and I never said any of the things I thought of, like "Do you wish you was sleeping with Florrie?" or "Did you marry the wrong sister?" But I was thinking them. And Tom knowed I was thinking them.

There come a day of thaw, and I walked out and stood on the porch for several minutes, watching the drip from the eaves and scabs of ice tear one at a time from the hemlocks. A chunk would begin to slide with a whoosh into the heaps on the ground, leaving the limb it had stuck to twitching and dark. The chunks reminded me of the lumps I had been spitting up. My chest was almost clear, but when I breathed deep there was a rattle down there, and when I coughed something always come loose.

I wanted to walk out in the mushy mess and see how the stock was doing, and I wanted to see the branch covered with snow. There was rabbit tracks in the yard, and the thousands of rabbit trails around the hill would lead to sinkholes along the branch. There was all kinds of tracks in the snow, bird and possum, coon tracks. Way across the river I saw somebody walking the road with a sack on their back. The mill must have been running again.

Just then I started to cough, and the thaw air cut into my lungs. With a shiver I went back inside. I set by the fire the rest of the evening, holding Muir in my lap.

That night it snowed again, and cold returned. The slush set in a seal and made travel impossible. It was the week of that last snow that people suffered most, from lack of wood and coal oil and staples. Nobody could have been ready for such a winter.

"I ain't never seen nothing like it," Pa said, "since the winter of '65, when I was a prisoner at Elmira." He stood in front of the window and looked out for hours at a time.

Some people in a cabin beyond Pinnacle froze. They was found weeks later still huddled to their fireplace, a jug of liquor on the floor beside them. The cabin was almost covered with snow and the door was in ice. The bodies had froze and hadn't even started to rot, though it looked like mice had been gnawing their hands.

Because I had been sick so long it was like I had dreamed the bad weather. If I hadn't seen the last two snows myself I'm not sure I would have believed the others happened. The quarrel with Florrie, the sight of her and Tom standing close, the irritation of not being able to work, at the mercy of others, all blended in memory to a special mixture I would not forget, reminding me of the light at the window and the smell of congestion in my breath. There was some kind of bookkeeping going on and all accounts balanced each other. As the final thaw set in I thought how everything always come out even, or maybe only a little behind.

The effects of the pneumonia lasted longer than I would have dreamed. Even after it was spring I still wasn't able to work like I used to. I tired quick, and needed long spells of rest. I felt a lot older, and by May I knowed I was expecting again.

Tom got Joe to help him put in a garden that year, because I wasn't much use. He said there was some advantage from the long hard winter: the cold had killed a lot of bugs, and rabbits, and the soil was loose and airy from all the freezing and thawing.

"Snow will fertilize the ground," Pa said.

"Snow ain't nothing but water," Tom said.

They had took to disagreeing more than they used to. Tom tended to argue with everything Pa said.

"It's the air in snow that makes the ground fertile," Pa said.

"Air ain't no fertilizer," Tom said.

"After a snowy winter crops is bigger," Pa said.

There was a preacher from Memphis that come in September and put up a tent in Joe's pasture. He was a Greek everybody said. It's true his hair was dark and curly. His name was Preacher Stratis and he stayed with Joe and Lily while he was running the meeting. He was a faith healer, and Joe said he had healed people of cancer and dropsy. Folks had come to him on crutches and left running and shouting. He had healed women of goiters.

"You ain't going in your condition," Tom said.

I was sick at my stomach and stayed home, but didn't tell Tom that was why. I guess he thought I was minding his warning.

It was a hot evening in fodder-pulling time. After supper I set on the porch breaking beans, and Jewel helped. I wanted to break a bushel before bedtime and put them under a damp cloth overnight to can in the morning. Pa had gone to the service. Across the hill you could hear the music from the tent meeting. There was the sounds of a tambourine and cymbals, and voices singing. Suddenly a shout cut through the air. It was like somebody calling from the center of the sky.

"What heathens," Tom said. He was standing by the door. I had not noticed him there.

"What is heathens?" Jewel said.

"Heathens is people that don't have self-respect," Tom said.

"Be careful you don't mock the Spirit," I said, and kept breaking beans.

"That ain't the Spirit," Tom said. "That is Devil worship."

I didn't say any more. I didn't want to upset my stomach and have to throw up again.

But the next night I was feeling better. After cleaning up the supper dishes I went to the bedroom to put on fresh clothes. I washed my face at the basin and put my hair in a bun. And then I slipped on my shiny white blouse that I hadn't wore in almost a year. And I put on my black skirt that had buttons down the side. It was the last time I'd be able to wear it for months.

Pa was already gone. He had eat supper with Joe and Lily and the preacher from Memphis.

When I come out of the bedroom Tom was setting on the porch with Moody in his lap. He looked surprised to see me in the good clothes. "You ain't in no condition . . . ," he said. His face turned redder than before. He had been pulling fodder and was sunburned on his face and arms.

"I am in fine condition," I said.

Tom put Moody on the floor and stood up. I think it was partly the surprise that made him so mad. He stomped across the porch and hollered, "You fool!"

"The Bible warns about calling others fools," I said.

"You ain't going," he said. He grabbed at my arm and I jerked away. He had never touched me before when he was mad. I was suddenly afraid. He stood in my way to the steps. I could smell the sweat of work on him. His face had broke out in new sweat.

"Let me pass," I said.

"You will mark the baby," he said. "The baby won't have a bit of sense."

"The other children have plenty of sense," I said. I could hear the music starting across the hill. The beat of the tambourine and cymbals rung through the evening air. And there was voices raising a hymn. I felt so dried out and in need of music and fellowship. I was heavy with boredom and needed emptying out. It had been a long time since I had worshipped and fellowshipped in the Spirit. It was a need, a craving. Ordinary things, and knowledge from books wasn't enough. It was a spiritual hunger. I think Tom could tell the dullness I felt.

"You ain't going," he said. He stood right in front of me. He had never looked at me hard in the face like that before. It come to me he thought he was dealing with a drunkard. He was trying to keep a drunk from her bottle.

"Leave me alone," I said.

"I'd be happy to," he said, "except for the baby."

"The baby is fine," I said.

"The baby will be marked by your crazy doings," he said.

I felt like I did when I faced the mad dog. I had to think what to do. I started to go around him and he grabbed my wrist.

"Leave me alone," I said, and flung his hand away.

"Mommy!" Moody hollered.

"You're scaring the children," I said.

"*I* ain't doing nothing," Tom said.

"It's all right," I said. "Mommy's just going to camp meeting."

Jewel was standing by the door holding Muir. Suddenly I saw what to do. I spun around and opened the door and walked right through the living room and kitchen to the back door. I heard Tom behind, but he didn't touch me. I opened the door and went down the steps and kept going out the trail to the springhouse.

The door slammed behind and there was this explosion that went out level with my ears, stretching the air toward the pasture. I looked around and Tom stood at the steps holding Pa's shotgun pointed up. Smoke floated above the end of the barrel.

"Put that thing up," I said.

"You ain't going," he said. He stepped forward. "Stay home, Ginny," he said quietly.

"I can't do that," I said.

Bats was swooping between hemlocks and the house. They whispered in the air like bullets and tight strings. Tom had gone farther than he ever had before. I wondered how much farther would he go. I don't think he knowed hisself.

"Put that thing up," I said.

I turned around and started down the path. I didn't have any choice but to show I meant to go where I had started. Another explosion rung past my ears and echoed off the springhouse and pasture hill, and finally off the mountains. I smelled burnt gunpowder. I turned around to face Tom. "You're crazy," I said.

He was taking more shells out of his pocket and putting them in the double-barreled gun. He was so mad his hands shook.

"Shoot me if you want to," I said, and started down the path again. With every step I could feel something hit me in the back. I imagined the tickle of little pebbles or sand on my spine.

When I got to the fence I could hear the music again from the camp meeting. There was shouting above the singing, and I could hear the preacher's voice fast as an auctioneer's.

Tom shot the gun again behind me, and then again. I listened for the sound of pellets, but didn't hear any. There was crickets in the pasture, and katydids in the trees across the branch. All the way across the pasture I listened to the singing from the tent and the katydids that answered it. And then Tom's gun boomed again. Even after I got to the meeting I heard him fire several times. It sounded like a war going on across the hill.

CHAPTER FIFTEEN

March 4, 1907

Dear Locke,

I 've been meaning to write to you for weeks to thank you for the fan and the little Chinese doll for Jewel. It made Christmas truly special to have something under the tree sent all the way from the Orient. Jewel has played with the doll every day since and I have hung the fan by the mirror in the bedroom so I can see the designs on both the back and front.

I had planned to write you in January, but I caught a cold in my chest and had to stay in bed more than a week, but I've wanted to write you for some time because I think it's easier to talk in a letter than face to face. Don't you think? Everybody has gone to bed here and I'm setting up by the window with just one lamp and can see the full moon over the snow. You wouldn't recognize the world out there. It looks like something you might dream of, with the Cicero Mountain going up to the stars and the moon high above everything, but down on the river too. Looking out over the river valley tonight you feel already dead and in eternity.

But, Locke, what I wanted to ask you in this letter was about Mama. Even though you are younger than me you was closest to her of any of us. She always said you was just like a Johns and not a Peace. She said you took after our uncle the doctor.

I have been thinking lately about Mama and wondering why she was so set against the revivals, and why it made her so mad for Pa to attend. Tom feels the same way, and if I could understand Mama's feelings I might understand Tom and know what to do.

Locke, you have come to a bad way when you quarrel day after day with a spouse. You don't know this yet because you're not married, but you will find it out. It wears you down and wearies the spirit to live day after day with somebody that disapproves of you. I don't think the Lord meant marriages to be that way.

Now the thing is I'm not bothered that Tom don't read books and talk a lot and lead in prayer at church. He has his way and I can see that. But he can't accept me going to the Pentecostal services, no more than Mama could accept Pa's going to the Holiness revivals. And I'm trying to study out what to say to him.

Do you remember what Mama had to say about the subject? I know she claimed to be a Hardshell. She was brought up in the Old Regular church at Upward and that's what she was in her heart. Even when dying that's what she claimed, pointing up toward heaven at the last minute as she passed away. And I was proud of that. Except I never really knowed what she meant. As I got older I understood it less. The Old Regulars don't approve of music instruments in church, and they believe in predestination. They think once you are baptized you're sure to go to heaven. They sing hymns in their mournful way. I remember when Mama took us to church at Upward the preacher preached in this dry harsh voice for three hours.

And the service seemed like a funeral in August heat with wasps buzzing around. Mama wanted to be buried out there. She is laying in the ground at Upward right now.

Do you recall what she said to Pa about the Holiness revivals, Locke? Was she afraid Pa would go to hell if he wasn't baptized in the Hardshell church? Was she afraid of any display of joy? Because her papa drunk so much and her brother drunk so much, was she afraid of any sort of intoxication? Or did she dislike the people that organized the brush arbor revivals?

I have trouble remembering what she said. All I can recall is her anger. And when her and Pa quarreled I felt awful and sorry for myself the way children do when grownups fuss. There was a bad feeling in the house. We would all act cheerful if visitors come and set on the porch talking, but still feel sick inside.

What I don't understand is why something of joy, a service of praise, can make people angry. Are they afraid of going out of control, going crazy? I can ask you these things, Locke, because you are far away, and because you must have studied about them. I know you tend to joke about things, but I think you're serious inside. That's why it don't bother me if you study strange things and consider all kinds of new thoughts. Because I believe you will always come back to the truth. I know you don't like the brush arbor meetings, but they don't seem to make you angry. Do you know why people like Tom feel so threatened?

I'm taking this up two days later because the baby woke me and I had to get him. Let's see if I can find my thread of thought.

Remember the Sunday we all dressed to go to the home-coming at Cedar Springs? Mama and Florrie had packed chicken and taters and a jug of lemonade in a basket. We had all put on our Sunday clothes and was climbing into the wagon when Mama asked who was leading the singing. And Pa said it was Ben MacBane.

And just like that Mama said she wasn't going, and climbed down. I felt sick all day knowing Mama was that angry at us.

There was another time in the fall right at molasses-making when we had been cutting cane and pressing it in the mill. Pa was going to sell some to the Lewises. This traveling preacher come by that had been holding services down at Chestnut Springs and was on his way to Buncombe. Pa give him a gallon of sorghum and invited him to stay for dinner. Mama was so mad she went to the house without a word. And she didn't speak at the dinner table either. She even banged the bowls and plates on the table.

I'm asking you, Locke, because you always took Mama's side on things. So I think you may have some idea how Mama felt.

When you get married, Locke, you will find it's mostly a matter of work. I don't mean there's no joy, for there is. There's great pleasure in loving, just like the poets said. But what keeps you going day after day through spurts and quirks, fits of temper and irritations, is the steady work. I don't know of anything else that would get you through it.

Now I know that Pa had him another woman that he met at a service near Mountain Page. Don't pretend you don't know about it, and are shocked that I have heard. I have knowed a long time we have a half-brother over that way. But it was after

Mama and Pa had been quarreling a long time that that woman had a youngun, and that wasn't the reason Mama hated him for going to the services. I reckon it was just a happen.

But Tom has no cause to think I go to services to see another man. I've never once liked Holiness preachers and men that way.

It's taking me forever to write this letter. It's already the longest letter I ever wrote. A whole week has passed now before I was able to get back to it.

Locke, I want you to think about what I'm saying and see if you can help me out. I just know there's something useful about Mama's feelings that you know and I have forgot.

Now what I think I can say to you in writing that I can't in person is how I feel when I go to meeting. I don't know if people are alike or not, and I don't know if people ever really understand each other. But I still think we're all akin inside, at the place where we feel things and know things. And I think we have to help each other out; otherwise there's no hope at all.

I'm the kind of person that has to do things with enthusiasm, or I get dragged down in a terrible study and confusion. I have to be doing, planning, or I get to feeling nothing is right.

When I'm not doing something I care about I feel everything is lost and drifting toward doom. I just can't help it. Would you say this is my fault? Would you say I just need more willpower to meet obstacles? Sometimes it seems beyond my control to take things in hand and cheer myself up. But before I was married I somehow did get through by rushing from one project to another. Remember when I ordered all the books on herbs and planted the garden by the house in a circle of rocks? I was near beside myself to know their names and uses, leaf patterns and places the plants had come from. I wanted to study what they call the signs or signatures of herbs, like the leaf shape showing they was heart medicine or a big root showing they could make men potent. The curiosity lifted me up above the weakness of my life.

And then there was the time I got interested in sewing. I never had took to making clothes as other girls do. People said I didn't take care of myself, because I didn't have anybody to teach me. But one time I just fell in love with making white blouses. I never had had any fine clothes. But that time I must have made a dozen blouses, each one with a different pattern of lace and ruffles, some with mother-of-pearl buttons. I made ivory-colored blouses, and sparkling silk blouses, white as snow.

When my interest in something fades it's like my temperature drops, and I am normal again. I'm not hardly aware when it happens, until one day I realize I'm going about my work and not feeling the sweetness and pain of a passion. But it is the time just before I fell in love with something that I look back on with such feeling. It is a kind of homesickness. I try to recall the time just before I discovered herbs and white blouses. It is the rush of discovery I try to remember and relive.

I'm asking you because you have studied doctoring and books on the mind. Do you understand this? Why when I was intense and in love with the study of herbs and growing and drying them for tinctures and concoctions, was I calm and happy? I was so happy I even wept for the ignorance that led to the joy of learning.

Then comes periods when nothing makes sense. It is like nothing I do fits with anything. Everybody is going about their lives and don't seem to realize how awful things have got. I see nothing but desolation because nobody cares for me. Pa and Joe and Florrie are all going ahead with things. You have your work and friends. That's when I see I don't have any friends. I have gone so long without caring for anyone they have forgot me.

When I'm confused I feel too weak to work. And nothing seems worth the effort. The next moment, the next hour, is like some mountain to scale. I can't see where to put my foot for the next step. When you feel bad it's like you are blinded and can't see where to go. Knowledge won't help, and no book will help you.

That's when I need the fellowship of the Spirit. That's when only the meetings can make me feel better.

Does this make sense to you, Locke?

I found that by thinking of others I could help get myself through. By helping out, or giving to someone that needed it, I could make myself feel better. When the Short younguns all had smallpox I sent dinner every day for near two weeks. And I did washing to help Shirley MacBane and her husband that had dropsy.

But the thing that lifted me most out of the dumps and blues and vapors, more than work or new discoveries, or charities, was the revivals. Once Pa took me to the first one it was like I had found a new part of myself. When I spoke in tongues or danced and shouted it was like a force greater than me lifted and filled me. I was freed from the tangles and shambles of life. There is no other way to describe the feeling of being cleansed through and through when the Spirit takes hold. You are carried away, lifted up, and something greater than you has you in its grip.

And afterwards you feel this great love of ordinary things.

What I feel after a service is greater than any pleasure I ever had watching the stars at night, or sunset over the valley, or the first greens in spring on the ridge across the river, or reading any book. Only thing that even comes close to the joy of Holiness is the joy of loving, and I've come to think they are really much the same. I don't know how the pleasure of the flesh could be so similar to the pleasure of the Spirit. But it is.

I'm not sure what I'm asking you to do, Locke. I'm not asking you to explain me to myself, and I'm not asking you to talk with Florrie and certainly not to talk to Tom when you are home. He wouldn't understand.

This is turning out to be the longest letter in the world. It's been four days since I wrote the above, and I'm taking up my pencil at night, after the younguns are asleep.

Sometimes I wonder if Tom don't have his own black studies and confusions, and he just never talks about them, or even knows how to talk about them. I wonder if he don't get just as tired and weak as anybody, but covers it up with hard steady work.

But the thing I worry most about with Tom is what he really believes. Sometimes I don't think he believes anything at all. I think he is trying to stuff all the wealth of the fields and weather into a bag of money. He is wringing the fat and sugar from the dirt the way a druggist gets the extract and essence from a leaf or root. But I know that's not really so, for he loves the place itself too, and the work itself.

Those we know best we know the least. They are so close we can't see them. I feel married to a foreign being, and I don't know what he means or wants. I don't know what we have to tie us together. Sometimes I can't remember why I married him.

I wish I knowed how our people back in old times thought about religion. Did they believe as we do? Did they have churches at the beginning? Revivals are something recent in the mountains, since Pa come back from the War. But it's hard to believe they did not have brush arbors back yonder. Maybe they worked too hard in those days clearing land to have time for the joy of meetings.

I think about this because I wonder how steady over the long time our beliefs are. I feel part of something that goes on forever, but I can't be sure it's what others have felt.

It worries me that others have not heard the gospel, that most people in the world have not heard the plan of salvation. But I can't think as some preachers say, that everybody that's not been baptized is going to hell whether they ever had a chance to know better or not. That would not make sense, that people would be lost that never had a chance to believe.

But that brings me to another of my worries. If people in ignorance are not going to be lost, then what is the purpose of sending all these missionaries to convert them? Do you see my point? It can't work both ways. Either they are not damned in their ignorance, or they are. So I can't make sense of it. I've asked Pa and he can't explain it. As you can see, Locke, I'm saying things I've never told to anybody.

Locke, I envy you men, able to go where you want, to join the army and find an occupation, to travel and buy up a homestead in Arkansas or Texas if you want to and start all over. Maybe that's my favorite dream, of going away and starting all over.

But I don't think I really want to go either. I don't think I could leave here, or that there is another place I could be happy, much as I want to believe it. When I've gone to Greenville or to Asheville with Pa I ain't seen any other place I'd like to live. I wouldn't mind going for a few days, to that hotel in Asheville where honeymoon couples stay, where you can look all the way to Pisgah from your window. But it would be for just a few days, to get away from the kitchen and hot stove.

One of the things I love about Tom is the way he is drawed to this land. That attracted me from the first, how he was attached to this place. We have felt the land was almost a burden. But through Tom's eyes I saw what a beautiful piece of ground it is.

Sometimes I feel such love of the place I just stand and look at the yard running down to the fields, and the fields down to the hazelnuts on the river. I stare at the trellis Tom made for roses and the sandbox he built for Jewel and Moody by the chimney and filled with river sand. Even the flowerbed that needs weeding seems intimate and perfect. The shed Joe made beside the crib for Pa's wagon shines silver with weathering. I think the room I set in is like a pyramid, and has the power and focus of a crystal. It is my room and everything is located around it.

When I look at the yard, even under the moonlight, I feel close to Great-grandpa Peace who cleared the place up long ago and set out arborvitaes and hemlocks, magnolias and junipers. And I see where Tom has trimmed the boxwoods and pruned the cherry tree by the chickenhouse. And I feel how people work together across time, just as sure as if we was all together. Even you, way out in the Pacific, doing your nursing, are working with us.

It don't bother me, Locke, that you talk about Darwin and Ingersoll and Emerson and other agnostics and infidels. I don't worry about what you read and study about. What does worry me is that you are so far from home out of reach of our affection. I hate to think what being alone might make you think and feel. That is one reason I have been writing this long letter, to let you know you are not so alone way out in that army hospital on the other side of the world. You are right here in my thoughts just like you was setting on the sofa and telling funny stories.

If you have any ideas that can help me, let me know.

With love through Christ, your sister
Ginny

CHAPTER SIXTEEN

Somebody has been cutting timber on the ridge," Tom said. It was early November and he had gone up to the summit orchard to pick the last apples before a freeze ruined them.

"Where on the ridge?" I said.

"Just beyond the orchard, out along the ridge and just under the ridge," Tom said.

"You mean on the other side of the summit," Pa said. "Our line runs right along the top."

A sick feeling soaked through my back and down into my legs.

"The timber is cut on this side of the ridge," Tom said.

"Surely not," Pa said. "Do you know where the line is?"

"I know where the top of the ridge is," Tom said.

"I should have showed you just where the line is," Pa said.

"Maybe somebody made a mistake," I said.

"Sounds like it," Pa said.

They agreed to go look first thing in the morning. As I put supper on I felt all hot and rushed. Pa didn't say any more, but I could tell how bothered he was. There had been a boundary dispute with the Johnsons years before and it had come to a trial finally. Pa never liked to talk about it. The Johnsons owned the other side of the mountain, and they had quarreled with their neighbors on every side. Old man Thurman Johnson believed that somehow he had been cheated by surveyors and had never got the land called for in his deed, so every few years him and his sons would claim a few more feet on one side or the other. One of his sons had been killed years back when they disputed with the MacBanes about their western boundary. Nobody ever proved who did the killing. But it had been twenty years since the Johnsons had give anybody trouble over property lines.

"You'd think people would respect boundaries that have been here so long," I said. "The line is where it always was."

"What is a line?" Moody said.

"It's where our land ends and theirs begins," I said.

"Are you going to shoot them?" Jewel said to Tom. Recently she had tried to avoid talking to me.

"Nobody's going to shoot anybody," I said. "We don't even know what's been done yet."

I've always cringed at talk of boundary feuds because they never really get settled. If somebody believes he don't have all the land he should there is no way to persuade him otherwise. Even good Christian people get filled with hate. So the fussing and lawsuits go on and on. There was neighbors in the valley that hadn't spoke for thirty years. They carried boundary quarrels into church work and politics. Their children got in fights at school. They took shots at each other out squirrel hunting, and stole timber off each other's land. People otherwise accommodating, deacons and pillars of the church, dumped trash and run cattle on each other's corn patches. Women had got in fights down at the store over a few feet of scrubland.

I had always told myself I would never be involved in a boundary fight. It was too simple-minded. Better to give away a few feet of dirt than ruin your life feuding with a neighbor.

"How much timber have they cut?" I said to Tom.

"It's hard to tell. I saw maybe twenty stumps, and the laps and sawdust where they had sawed up the logs."

"We have oaks on that ridge," Pa said, "never been cut."

"They have now," Jewel said.

"Be quiet," I said. "We don't know that for sure."

But while Jewel and me cleaned up the table, and while I set by the fire reading, I couldn't think of anything but the line on the mountain. I told myself to be calm, but anger rose in me like vapors off vinegar. I told myself to wait and see and not get riled before it was clear what had happened. The Christian thing was to give the benefit of the doubt, love your enemies. But my words didn't have any effect on the anger growing in me.

What could you do if somebody took part of your land? Even if it had been in your family a hundred years, it appeared they could just step across the line and take it. The Johnsons had give trouble to my grandpa, and great-grandpa. Surely there was a way to put a stop to their wickedness. They had the advantage that the mountain was so far from our house. It was almost an accident Tom had been up there to see where they cut the timber. My anger rose till I was astonished. I couldn't have explained the fury that roared in me. I felt betrayed. My deepest privacy had been invaded. I was as mad as if my children had been harmed, or my trust took advantage of.

"The Johnsons have done this one time too many," I said to Pa.

"Tom and me will go up and see what has been done," Pa said.

"We'll all go," I said.

"No, Tom and me will go," Pa said.

That night I laid in bed thinking about the land on the mountain. I almost never went there except to pick apples. I wasn't even sure myself where the line was. It run along the top, but a ridge is not as sharp as the comb of a roof. And I wasn't sure I had ever seen where the corners was. Tom kept the road up to the orchard, and the field around the orchard, mowed. But there was woods up there he had never been in. Pa used to hunt squirrels on the mountain, and Joe had trapped foxes there. I knowed there was a holler with a spring at its head, and a cliff called Buzzard Rock further out the ridge. And there was another cliff called Hog Rock where hogs used to gather out of rain. It had been years since I had seen those places. We once climbed up there as children for a picnic on top of Buzzard Rock. There was a cave under the rock blackened by fires of hunters and maybe Indians. Joe found a tomahawk in the leaves below the rock.

That night I dreamed I took Pa's gun and climbed the mountain by myself. I found Thurman Johnson and his sons and daughters and daughters-in-law chopping trees, clearing the mountaintop.

"In the name of Jesus stop," I shouted.

"We're all working for Jesus," Thurman said. "We're building a church to keep out screamers and blasphemers." Tobacco juice run from the corner of his grin. All his kin was looking at me. They had chopped down peach trees and apple trees too.

I raised the gun at Thurman, but just as I pulled the trigger I woke up. My heart was racing and I trembled in the bed.

The next morning Tom hitched the horse and wagon as soon as we had finished breakfast. I was glad Pa wasn't going to walk to the top of the mountain. Tom brought the wagon around to the gate and Pa carried his shotgun and his musket out of the bedroom.

"You won't need those," I said, remembering my awful dream.

"You never know," Pa said.

"I don't want you to get excited," I said. "It won't do your heart any good."

"I won't," Pa said. "We've got to see what has been done."

I walked out to the wagon with him, and Jewel and Moody and Muir followed me. "You all go back inside," I said. They stopped on the porch. "You be careful," I said to Tom.

I watched them drive out of the yard toward the pasture gate.

"Is Grandpa going to shoot Johnson?" Moody said.

"Nobody is going to shoot anybody," I said.

Pa and Tom come back just before dinnertime. They looked tired, like they had been working all day. Pa had a gray look, the way people do after a heart attack or major disappointment. He climbed from the wagon and carried the guns into the house.

"What happened?" I said. But Tom drove to the shed to unhitch.

"Did Grandpa shoot them?" Moody said.

"Be quiet," I said.

I put cornbread and beans and squirrel pie on the table, but I wasn't hungry. Moody set down and I told Muir to quit picking his nose. Pa come out of his room and set down as Tom returned from the barn. Pa said grace and the children started eating.

"Is nobody going to tell me what happened?" I said. I looked from Pa to Tom and back. "Has the cat got you-all's tongue?"

"He took up the stakes," Tom said.

"Who did, Johnson?"

"He had pulled up the corner pins," Pa said. "Every marker up there has disappeared."

"That's illegal," I said. "He can't do that." But even as I said it I had the awful insight that people will do anything they think they can get away with. And the bolder the act the more apt they are to get away with it. My bones felt rotten with dread.

"How do you know it was Thurman?" I said, just for the sake of trying to sound reasonable.

"We seen him," Tom said.

"He was up there?" I said.

"Him and his boys was right there cutting timber," Pa said.

"And you didn't run him off?" I said.

"I said, 'Thurman, what are you doing on my land?'" Pa said. "And he said, 'Ben Peace, what are you doing on mine?'"

"The lowdown scoundrel," I said.

"I said, 'Thurman, you know we settled this line long ago.'"

"'No we didn't,' says he. 'You've been using Johnson land for nigh a hundred years and I'm putting a stop to it.'"

"And what did you do?" I said.

"I said, 'Thurman, you know the markers are where they've always been.' 'What markers?' he says. 'Can't find no markers.'"

When Thurman said that, Tom and Pa went looking for the corner pins, and they saw all the markers had been pulled up and hid.

"What have you done with the stakes?" Pa said to Thurman.

"I ain't seen no stakes," Thurman said. "But come next summer I'm going to harvest my apples and peaches on this ridge."

"That's when I knowed I'd better get away," Pa said. "I didn't want to end my life killing somebody. Last man I shot at was a Yankee sharpshooter at Petersburg. Last thing I said to Thurman was, 'I'll see you in court.'"

Both Pa and Tom looked defeated.

"Mama, what is going to happen?" Jewel said, with tears in her eyes.

"Nothing is going to happen," I said, "except Thurman is going to be taught a lesson."

"Thurman has been coveting our land all his life," Pa said. "And he figures this is his last chance to get it."

"Well, he will die disappointed," I said.

"What are you going to do, Mama?" Moody said.

"I'm going to swear out a warrant for trespass," I said.

"He is depending on us doing that," Pa said.

"He is depending on us not doing that," I said. "He thinks we won't take the trouble."

"It won't do any good," Pa said. "The court will appoint a surveyor, and Johnson will hire a lawyer to bribe the surveyor or he will lie to the surveyor about the corners."

"Do you have a better idea?" I said. Neither Tom nor Pa answered. "Then we'll go to town tomorrow," I said.

Word of the dispute traveled fast. Florrie come that afternoon and said David had heard it at the store. She said Thurman bragged that he had run Tom and Pa off his property.

"The Johnsons have always been trash," Florrie said. "During the Confederate War they was just outlaws and thieves robbing from widows and children."

"The Devil protects his own," I said.

"Everybody lets a skunk have its way," Florrie said.

Tom's silence worried me. I was angry and I knowed Pa was terrible upset. But Tom didn't say anything all through supper that night. And later while we set by the fire he just stared into the flames. He set like he was studying on something. I knowed how much the land meant to him, and his silence scared me.

"Now don't you even think of doing anything," I said as we was going to bed.

"Somebody's got to do something," he said.

"I'll do something," I said. "I'm going to see the lawyer."

"A lawyer won't help," he said.

"A court order will help," I said. "A court order will put some fear into Thurman."

"These cases get dragged on for years. Only ones to profit are lawyers. People lose their places just to pay the fees."

He was right about that. But it didn't do any good to study on it. The time for settling disputes with guns and fistfights was over. Both Pa and Thurman was old men. Maybe Thurman didn't care if he got shot. I had heard he was ailing, getting feeble. That made it all the more surprising he had chose this time to claim our land. That night I kept thinking about what I'd say to Lawyer Gibbs. I rehearsed the facts and the story of the dispute with the Johnsons. I decided removal of the boundary markers was the most important point, more than cutting of the timber. Johnson could claim the line was further down the mountain, but there was no excuse for disturbing the corner pins without a court order. The destruction of the markers had to be the center of my case.

The following day was cold and overcast. In the early gray November morning Tom drove Pa and me to the depot.

"Can't I come?" Jewel said. "I want to go to the cloth store."

"You have to stay with the younguns," I said.

"I want to come," Moody said.

"Me too," Muir said.

"I'll bring you a poke of candy," I called back to them.

It had been a year since I had gone to town. I shivered with excitement and fear. I had put twenty dollars in my purse to pay the lawyer and get something for the children. I took another ten from my jewelry box. I hated to go to town for it made me feel dizzy and lost to be among so many people.

We drove through the mill village just as people was going to work. The mill hands carried lunch pails with them. They looked like prisoners lined up to go through the bars. At the same time the night shift was leaving. The lint on their shoulders and hair looked like frost. They slumped in the cold morning.

The depot was on the hill past the village. We drove by the lake and Crossroads Church. Tom stopped at the platform and give me a twenty-dollar gold piece. "Pay what the lawyer asks," he said. "I'll be here when the train comes at five-thirty."

I saw I had to do this for Tom, as well as for Pa and the children. The place meant more to Tom maybe than anybody else. I had never gone to talk to a lawyer before, but I was going to make this trip count, whatever had to be done.

There was half a dozen people waiting on the platform. One of the Jenkins boys had a crate of chickens he was taking to market. Tildy Tankersley stood there with a bandage around her jaw. I guess she was going to the dentist. "I hear you're having some trouble," she said, talking from the side of her mouth.

"If it's not one thing it's another," I said.

"The Lord lets his own be tested," she said. She talked slow, as though in terrible pain.

Everybody was watching Pa and me, and I felt like they knowed exactly why we was going to town. Bad luck is made even worse when everybody knows about it.

I was glad when the train come grunting and groaning up the mountain. There was a steep grade above Saluda, and every time the train arrived at the depot it looked tired-out and covered with sweat. The pant of the locomotive was fast as a dog on a hot day. When the cars come to a stop I started to climb up but the conductor stood on the steps and yelled, "Stand aside. I say stand aside!" I jumped back and he handed a mailbag to Wiley Waters. I had forgot how rude conductors would talk to you.

When we finally got on and set down I was shaky with anger. The seats looked smaller and dirtier than I remembered. Maybe it was an old car. "We could have drove the wagon," I said to Pa.

"That would have took half a day just to get there," Pa said.

Once the train started I felt better. It always lifts my spirits to move. The train creaked and squealed at first and then begun to pick up speed. I could hear the thud of the puffing engine. We pulled through the big cut beyond the depot where the tracks curve across the divide and down into the valley of the French Broad. There was houses above the cut, and a few hickories that still had yellow leaves. As we come out above Flat Rock I saw men butchering a hog hoisted on a walnut limb. The scalding water boiled up to the clouds.

The fields along Mud Creek was level as an ironing board. Water from October rain stood in low spots. The soil looked sooty.

"This land never was no count," Pa said. "Just fit for a town."

Beyond the creek we passed sheds and shacks and lots covered with scrap metal. There was a sawmill, lumberyard, brickyard. Warehouses echoed each other across the tracks. A gravel heap was held by pilings. As we come alongside the platform men with hand trucks and pushcarts moved toward the back of the train.

Women in fine dresses and velvet hats, and men in fancy coats, was getting off the forward cars. Carriages lined up to meet them. I saw a woman in a lavender coat and hat that could have been Mrs. Vanderbilt. She looked slim and beautiful.

The main part of the town was on the hill above the depot. I took Pa's arm and we hurried up Seventh Avenue toward

Main. There was pawnshops and secondhand stores along the avenue.

"Do you want to see my new shipment of cloth?" a man shouted from the doorway of a dry goods store.

"Let's go right to the lawyer's office," I said.

Most of the lawyers in town had offices at the south end near the courthouse. We walked almost the length of town to get there. A trolley clanged down the middle of Main, and there was horses going every which way. My head buzzed with all the movement. It was hard to remember what I was doing among the confusion.

Lawyer Gibbs's office was on the second floor of a building just beyond Drake's Store. We climbed the dark carpeted stairs to a waiting room. A young man set at a desk piled with papers and bundles tied in red ribbons. "How may I serve you?" he said. He had garters above his elbows.

"We want to see Lawyer Gibbs," I said.

"And what is the nature of your business?" the clerk said.

"It's about our boundary line," I said.

"I see, a land dispute," he said, and raised his eyebrows.

"Tell the lawyer Ben Peace wants to see him," Pa said.

But we had to set in that dark room near an hour before talking to Lawyer Gibbs. I don't know if he was at court and come in a back way, or if he was just working with his papers. It was almost dinnertime when the young man admitted us to see him.

"Good to see you, Ben," the lawyer said when we finally walked in. He rose and shook hands vigorously with Pa. "And this is Ginny? Why I've not seen Ginny since she was a button."

Gibbs's desk was also covered with folders and bundles of papers in red tape. It was hard to believe people had wrote so many thousands of pages. There was stacks of papers on the floor, and books piled in corners and spilling out of bookcases. The room smelled of paper and dust and some kind of cologne.

I explained to Mr. Gibbs why we had come, and he listened, turned in his chair toward the window. I described the boundary line and how long it had been where it was.

"Have you had the line surveyed?" the lawyer said.

"The line was run about thirty years ago," Pa said, "the last time Johnson made trouble."

"And the boundary was marked?" Gibbs said.

"It was marked," I said. "But Johnson took up the markers."

"How was it marked?"

"With iron pins at the corners and a right-of-way cut along the line," Pa said.

"And the pins are gone now?" Gibbs said.

"Every one of them."

"And I suppose the right-of-way has grown up?"

"It had till Johnson started cutting timber there," Pa said.

The window of Gibbs's office looked out over rooftops. There was false fronts and walls of brick and sooty chimneys. A clothesline stretched from poles. Birds set on telephone wires and a cat crouched on the edge of a wall watching them. It seemed strange to be looking over people's roofs. Some roofs was covered with tar paper and had puddles on them. Smoke leaned from chimneys. It was the drabbest thing I had ever seen. But way beyond the smoke and wires I could see the line of mountains. Overcast covered the tops of ridges, but the blue slopes looked clear and fresh compared to the clutter and soot of rooftops.

"Do you have a deed?" Lawyer Gibbs said.

"We sure do," I said. I got the paper from my purse. I had took it from Pa's trunk that morning. It was yellow with age.

"This is not a deed," Gibbs said as he turned the document over and read it on both sides. "This is just a bill of sale."

"It specifies where the land is," I said, and how much there is. It has always served as a deed before."

"This is not a legal document," Gibbs said.

"It says the tract corners at the mouth of Cabin Creek and at the mouth of Schoolhouse Branch," I said. "And it runs straight to the top of Olivet Ridge. It has the compass readings on it."

"Readings that old don't mean a thing," the lawyer said.

"What are you saying?" Pa said.

"I'm saying it don't look like you have a valid documenta- tion of boundaries," Gibbs said.

"This land has been in the family almost a century," I said. I felt my face getting hot. "And it's registered in the courthouse. And besides, everybody knows where our land is."

"Except Johnson?" Gibbs said.

"Johnson knows too," Pa said. "He's trying to get back at me."

"For what?" Lawyer Gibbs said.

"Don't know," Pa said. "I just know he wants to get back at me."

"So you're not going to help us?" I said. A flock of pigeons flew by the windows. They looked like flakes of paint that had peeled off the gray sky.

"It's hard to make a case without a valid deed," Gibbs said.

"Our deed has always been valid before," I said. I wanted to get up and leave that office. And I wanted to get away from town. But if I up and left our trip would be wasted.

"Times are different now," Gibbs said. "The courts have got tougher and the laws are tighter."

"We can pay you," I said, and lifted the purse from my lap.

Gibbs paused, then turned toward Pa, like he wasn't talking to me. "I'd like to help you, Ben. Maybe if I check to see what they have at the courthouse I can have a deed made as the basis of a suit. At least you would have a valid document then."

"I'd be mighty obliged," Pa said.

"Of course that won't solve your problem with Johnson," Gibbs said. "After getting a solid deed you will have to charge him with trespass and ask the court for an injunction against him. The court would then authorize a survey before it would listen to arguments or go to trial. That could take months, even longer."

"I know that," Pa said.

"Is there no way to hurry it up?" I said. "Johnson has cut a lot of timber on us."

"No legal way," Gibbs said.

"Johnson has to be stopped," I said.

"I will need a retaining fee for my services," Gibbs said.

"How much?" I said.

"Say a hundred dollars," Gibbs said. "But it may require more as the case proceeds. This kind of suit can take time."

"I have only fifty," I said.

"I have fifty," Pa said.

We counted out the money in gold pieces and silver dollars. It was more than I had ever paid for anything. "Ain't there nothing we can do now to stop Johnson?" I said.

"I can send him a letter saying proceedings will be instituted against him unless he desists," Gibbs said. "Sometimes such a letter will have the desired effect."

"Then please send it," I said.

By the time we left Gibbs's office I was exhausted. The air outside was cold but refreshing. I wanted to hurry out of town.

"Do you need to do some shopping?" Pa said.

"I have spent all my money except for change," I said. "Let's buy something for the kids and go back to the depot."

It was exactly a week later that we got the letter from Johnson's lawyer, answering the one Gibbs had sent to Johnson. It was a long letter on crisp paper and Pa read it on the way back from the mailbox. He handed it to me without saying a thing. I wiped my hands and set down to skim the shiny pages.

Insofar as you have trespassed for decades on Johnson land and had the use of the mountaintop property where the peach and apple orchard is located, and have cut firewood and timber inside the said Johnson boundary, you are hereby asked to cease and desist from further intrusion. Unless my clients are satisfied your trespass and usurpation are at an end they will have no recourse but to institute proceedings in court to restrain and punish the infringement.

"What does it really mean?" I said.

"It means Thurman is answering Gibbs's letter with his own threatening letter," Pa said.

"That's all it is?" I said.

"Just a bluff," Pa said. "I've gone through this before."

The letter made me feel dirty. I went to wash my hands. It was a terrible thing to touch, some lawyer's fancy words of warning about our own property. We almost never got an official type letter. The talk of lawyers was calculated to make you feel stupid and guilty. Just reading those sentences made you feel hopeless. The letter laid on the table like a sentence of doom.

When Tom come back to the house for supper I read the letter to him. He listened with his head down looking at the floor. It was the way he always set when he was worried. His cheeks reddened as I quoted the lawyer's bleak words. Once he started to slam the table with his fist, but stopped hisself.

"Ain't this a pretty come-off?" Pa said. "After all the work you've done to improve that orchard."

"Are you going to shoot Johnson?" Moody said.

"Be quiet," I said.

Tom studied for a while without touching his supper. "I don't even know where the lines are myself," he said. "The first thing to do is find all the boundary lines and mark them again."

"Nobody but Pa knows where all the lines are," I said.

"Then we'll walk the lines and mark them," Tom said. "It's the first thing to do."

I couldn't see that just walking the boundaries and driving stakes and trimming brush would solve the dispute with Johnson, but at least it was something to do. If Pa showed where the lines was we could mark them for the future. Tom and me needed to know. Iron pins would have to be drove into the corners again.

"Can I come?" Moody said.

"Me too," Muir said.

"You will stay here with Jewel," I said.

"Oh goody," Jewel said.

Next morning was clear and cool. I put on a coat and scarf. Tom got an ax and four pipes from the shed. He cut stakes from sourwood saplings. Pa carried an ax also, and his walking stick.

I took my little notebook and a pencil from the mantel. I wanted to record all the boundaries Pa showed us. Putting it down in writing would make the effort more worthwhile.

"What are you going to do with that?" Tom said.

"I'm going to write down everything Pa points out," I said. "That way we will have a document of what he knows."

We walked through the cornfield down to the river. Tom had already picked the corn, and stalks rattled their dry leaves.

"The river is high," Pa said. Rains had kept the water murky and sloshing into the bushes on the bank. The current was faster than I expected, as though hurried by the sunlight and wind.

"There goes a muskrat," Pa said.

A whiskered head swum and disappeared under the far bank.

"There'll be no traps set in water this high," Pa said.

We crossed the pasture branch on the foot log. Minnows playing in the shallows shined like seeds. Sand had pushed up in cushions and fans where the branch entered the river. We had not tended all the lower bottom that year and goldenrod there was singed by frost and smoked thistledown across the blackened weeds.

"I cleared up this land when I married your mama," Pa said. "It was nothing but a maple swamp, and still floods in a wet year." Big puddles stretched under the weeds in places. The water was stained by leaves and dead stalks. A rabbit darted through the briars. It was an ugliness I loved.

When we reached the mouth of Schoolhouse Branch I saw the water was high over the foot log. Or maybe the foot log had been washed away. "Where does the marker go?" I asked Pa.

"The deed says the corner is the mouth of the branch," Pa said. "But the branch has moved downriver a little in the past sixty years. The pin Johnson removed was right here."

There was no dent where the pin had stuck for so long. Whoever pulled it out had smoothed the place over and piled leaves and trash on it. Tom drove a pipe so deep you wouldn't notice unless you was looking for it. I wrote a sentence about the place in the notebook. It was odd to be writing outdoors, to put the mouth of the branch and the sand and trees into sentences.

As I watched Tom work I thought how the place meant more to me because it meant so much to him. I wished I could write down how I felt about him in the notebook, just like I was describing the corners and boundaries. I wished I could put down once and for all how he really was.

"If we had a compass we could run the line from here just by sighting to the top of the mountain," Pa said.

"But we don't have a compass," I said.

"It's best to set a transit by the North Star," Tom said.

"That's true," Pa said. "But it's daytime, and we don't have a transit." He chuckled, but I knowed he was as worried as I was.

The woods across the branch had overgrowed the bank. There was hazelnuts and shoemake bushes crowding there too.

"The line runs up this side of the bank," Pa said, "right to the ridge yonder." He pointed to the mountain with his cane. It was easy to look up there, but between the river and the corner on the ridge we had a mile of muddy branch and sinkholes, thickets and barbed wire, briar and rocks to get through.

"Can you walk that far?" I said to Pa.

"Huh!" he said with a snort. "I've walked fifty miles a day in my time, with a full pack on my back and a rifle in my hand."

As we worked our way up the branch through pines Tom drove stakes and blazed trees. We passed a pit where Joe and Locke had dug for zircons years ago, filled with leaves and sticks. Pa showed us a rock below the schoolhouse two feet from the line. Florrie and me had played house there as girls. I hadn't seen it for years. The rock was hid by ivies and there was still broke cups and saucers in leaves. The rock was white quartz with moss on its sides. Florrie and me had called it the Ice Cream Rock.

Children was playing in the yard of the school, even though the new term hadn't started. "Hey, what are you doing?" one of the Waters boys called.

"We're looking for something," I called back.

The new session wouldn't begin till after Christmas. I reckon the kids had just met there to play.

"Are you going to fight the Johnsons?" the Waters boy called.

"Nobody is going to fight," I shouted back.

As we started climbing we slowed down for Pa's sake. He showed us where the line crossed the road and run right up the holler adjoining the Jenkins yard. There was a pin on the roadbank under brush that Johnson had missed. It was right where Pa said the line was. I wrote down the place by the road.

I stayed with Pa on the higher ground while Tom went through the holler blazing trees and driving a stake every few yards. The trees there was strung with grapevines that looked like big cobwebs. It was a good place to pick foxgrapes in September. Pa used to gather enough there for Mama to make fifty jars of jelly.

It was midmorning before we reached the top. I was out of breath from climbing and from excitement. All the way up I had wondered what we would do if the Johnsons was up there. But I saw no sign of them around the orchard. A breeze over the top from the north made me shiver. The orchard was deserted except for bluejays and other birds pecking rotten apples.

Pa showed us where the corner was beyond the east end of the orchard, and Tom drove a pipe there. He hammered the pipe until it was just under the leaves. "If Johnson pulls this up I'll dig a hole and bury the next pipe in cement," Tom said. "We'll see how fast he digs that up." I put the corner in the notebook.

From the orchard we could look down on the church and school and whole river valley. Some people had done their winter plowing and the fields sparkled red. Broomsedge shined on hillsides. I could see the roof of our house by the hemlocks. From up there it looked as if the house was right by the river. The mountain beyond was brown and gray at the foot, then lavender further up. The distant mountains was blue and smoky. The MacBanes up the river was killing hogs. I could see the smoke of their scalding fire and the bright carcasses hauled up on a pole.

If only we could get over this quarrel and return to everyday life, I thought. Nothing is as sweet as ordinary work and freedom from worry. The fuss had poisoned everything, including sleep and worship and trust of neighbors. It was normal peacefulness that was most beautiful. I wouldn't mind work dirty as rendering lard if I could do it without strife. Time free of anger and fear was the dearest thing I could think of.

A bullet stung the air nearby and a shot rung in the woods.

"Who is there?" Pa called. The woods echoed his words.

We looked toward the oaks at the end of the orchard, but nobody was in sight. There was a clump of shoemake bushes where Tom had piled stumps, and something moved a branch. "There," I said and pointed. But it was only a bird pecking the red seeds.

"Hey!" I called to the woods. But there was just the breeze.

"Maybe it was somebody squirrel hunting," Tom said.

"We didn't even bring a gun," Pa said.

"Hey!" I hollered again. There was no answer from the woods.

"Never thought Thurman would shoot unarmed people," Pa said.

"He was an outlier," I said. "No telling what he or one of his boys is liable to do."

The breeze stiffened the orchard grass and jays quarreled and pecked among the spoiled apples. It was the most beautiful orchard I had ever seen. I understood why Tom had spent so much time up there against the blue sky, pruning and mowing, plowing around the trees and setting out more peaches and apples. It had to be the best view in the whole valley. There was two or three white clouds hanging to the east. If we got the dispute settled I planned to spend more time up there working with the trees.

A boom washed out through the trees, but it was from way down the ridge. Somebody was hunting beyond Cabin Creek.

"We might as well move on," Tom said.

"Hey!" I called again to the woods, but the only answer was an echo from the big oaks.

Tom drove a stake by the orchard where Pa showed him. Beyond the peach trees I saw the stumps and laps where the Johnsons had cut timber. It made my throat hurt to look at the piled brush and clutter of limbs. We walked through the mess to the corner. The ground felt hot, as though I was trespassing. There was sawdust souring in the leaves and more than two dozen stumps. I expected to see a Johnson appear from behind every bush.

"I don't think they've cut any more trees," Tom said.

"Maybe not," Pa said, "but it's hard to tell. I didn't count the stumps careful before."

There was something red laying in the leaves. When I got closer I saw it was a bandanna, tore and stained with something dark. I didn't pick it up. There was stains in the leaves. Perhaps a squirrel had been shot there, or maybe a deer.

"The corner is right over yonder," Pa said and pointed down the ridge. "It is in that clump of laurel bushes."

Tom and me crawled into the rhododendrons and found where the pin had been pulled out. Thurman had not even filled the hole. Tom drove a pipe into the hole so deep only half an inch stuck above ground. I wrote a sentence describing the laurel bushes.

I could tell Pa was getting tired. He leaned on his walking stick and was short of breath.

"Here, I'll take the ax," I said.

"It's all downhill from here," Tom said.

"Climbing down is harder than climbing up," Pa said.

I went slow down to Buzzard Rock and walked out on the cliff. The holler below was so deep I felt I was soaring up just by looking into it.

"That's where I killed my first deer," Pa said, and pointed to a spring holler. "It was a cold January day and the buck must have come down for a drink."

"When was that?" I said.

"Oh that was before the war," Pa said. "I must have been twelve or thirteen."

Going down we passed several more pits Locke and Joe had dug. They had hoped to find zircons to sell to Thomas Edison. Dr. Johns had opened a mine above the depot and sold several tons to the inventor to make filaments, and got in a terrible dispute with Lawyer Gibbs's father who claimed the mineral rights to the mountain. Locke and Joe must have dug a hundred holes on our property hoping to get rich. But far as I know they never found a single zircon, and before Dr. Johns and Gibbs settled their conflict Edison quit using zircons to make filaments.

The roughest going was through the swamps by Cabin Creek. There was places I had never seen. Tom had to chop limbs and brush just to get through. "Watch out for poison oak," he said.

Many poplars and sweet gums was wound with fuzzy cables of poison oak. There was sinkholes and puddles. The leaves and sticks smelled musty. Logs glowed green with moss. I avoided anything spotted like poison ash.

"This is the way the whole bottom looked before it was cleared and drained," Pa said.

We had to stoop under vines and low limbs. It was dark in the thicket. Everything I touched left soot on my hand. There was groundhog holes and snake holes. I don't know how Pa and Tom kept to a straight line. But Tom drove stakes and cut limbs right through the swamp, and slashed maples and birch trees. At the mouth of Cabin Creek he drove a pipe deep into the sandy bank.

The new ground Tom had cleared along the river was so open the light hurt my eyes after the dark swamp. I could see all the way to the barn and the hemlocks around the house. Smoke jumped from the chimney in spurts. Chickens pecked the bank below the chickenhouse, but none of the children was outside.

"That is the prettiest place in the whole valley," I said.

The house above the fields looked peaceful and timeless. Never had freedom from conflict and hate seemed so precious. When we got to the house I picked up Muir and hugged him. And I pulled Moody to my apron. The children had been playing by the fire and left spools and sticks and newspapers scattered. But for once I didn't scold them. I didn't want to feel any more anger.

Our work marking the boundary may have been useless in a legal sense, but it did make us feel better. There was nothing to keep Johnson and his boys from pulling up the stakes and pipes, but he would have to go to the trouble. At least we had done something. And I had wrote down Pa's directions and the location of the lines. It was satisfying just to walk the boundaries all around the place, and now Tom and me knowed better where they was.

But nothing turns out the way you expect. Just when I had made up my mind to fight the Johnsons to the end and pay Lawyer Gibbs whatever it took, the whole situation changed. Three days after we walked the boundaries with Pa and marked the corners we heard from Joe that Thurman Johnson had died.

"H-h-he had a stroke," Joe said.

"When?" Pa said.

"H-h-he had a stroke last Monday," Joe said.

"Where?" I said.

"He was ch-ch-chopping and fell on his ax. He c-c-cut hisself, but it was that stroke and then another one yesterday that killed him." I remembered the stained bandanna on the mountaintop.

"Now what do we do?" Tom said.

"We don't do nothing," Pa said. "We wait and see what Thurman's boys do."

"It was them that cut the trees," I said. "They may be just as mean and crazy as their daddy."

"We'll wait and see," Pa said.

The day after Thurman's funeral we got a note from Morris Johnson. It was left in our mailbox up at the river road. It was made in pencil on a scrap of lined school paper. It said:

> Now that pappy is gone we don't wont no argment and no trouble with nobody. They must be some land on that mountain that don't rightly belong to anybody. But we don't care atall. We wont to do the christin thing and we wont to live in piece.

When I read that note to Pa and Tom I felt the weight of time and the sorrows of the world had been lifted from my back. Our land was free and clear again for us to work on. I felt as if I could hardly keep my feet on the ground. I guess I was shouting.

"It's just a smudged little note," Jewel said.

I was so happy I hugged Jewel before she could back away.

CHAPTER SEVENTEEN

Baby Fay was born in October. She was the littlest of my younguns, dark skinned like the Peaces. "Small as a cricket," Tom said when he saw her. And that was what he called her, his little cricket. Crickets was out then. As I laid in bed I could hear them in the grass outside, and when the baby was sleeping I had nothing to do but listen to night sounds. For some reason I couldn't hear katydids, and thought maybe a early frost had killed them. I hadn't heard anything about a frost, but then I had been busy with the baby.

As I laid in bed I knowed Fay would be my last baby. It wasn't only that I was almost forty, and it wasn't just that there didn't seem any way Tom and me could patch up our quarrel this time. I felt different after he had got the gun and shot it in anger. And he acted different too. I think he was afraid of hisself. I think he was worried what he might do next time he got riled. But beyond any of those reasons I just felt Fay was to be my last. As I held her and nursed her and washed her in the dishpan, I thought, This is the last time I will do these things. And I thought, I had better do a good job. This is my final chance to raise a youngun right. And I thought how I would teach her to read before she went to school, and I would take her to church and meetings with me. And we would pack a picnic in the egg basket and take it down to the rocks on the river.

It appeared to me I had not been a very good mama. All my worry and thinking about the services when there was a meeting had tired me out. It didn't seem possible two good things could get in each other's way, but I saw they had. I made up my mind I was going to work harder raising Fay, no matter what happened.

Listening to the sounds of night I could hear a fox bark on the hill. And the waterfall at the mill rung like a bell that held minute after minute. But there was something else I heard through the open window, like a squawk that turned into a laugh. It come from the pines by the pasture, and went off into the dark like somebody chuckling. I thought, Was it an owl? But no, it didn't sound like a screech owl. And it didn't really sound like a squirrel. It was something laughing in the dark. It was laughing at me because I was awake to hear it. And it was laughing at the whole world. That moment I saw it was right. We was all foolish and making a spectacle of ourselves. Wasn't anything to do but laugh with whatever it was. I found myself chuckling, until I stopped for fear the baby would wake up.

It was the driest fall anybody had ever seen. After the big snows of the winter, and the rains of early summer, the streams had been full and the ground wet. But then it didn't rain any more. All the water was used up. I had seen falls foggy and rainy and so wet leaves never got their color but just turned brown and fell. But this Indian summer was perfect weather, sunny and warm. I set on the porch rocking Fay in the afternoon sun. It seemed everything was turning gold under a perfect sky.

The summer couldn't seem to stop, but went on and on. I thought maybe there wasn't going to be a winter. Pumpkins shined bright in the fields. I thought, If it never rains the mountains will turn to deserts. Instead of trees there will be ridges of dust and sand. I tried to think what the slopes would look like all brown and blowing dirt every time a breeze stirred.

One day Tom come running into the house after dinner. "The pasture is on fire," he hollered.

"How did it catch?" I said.

"A spark from the furnace," he said. Him and Pa had been making a last run of molasses. I had never seen him so frantic. I reckon he was not only mad the fire had got out, but that he had, in effect, started it hisself.

Tom grabbed up mattocks and axes and shovels from the shed and started up the hill.

"Where's Pa?" I hollered. But Tom had already run beyond the junipers. I knowed Pa must be up in the pasture. But he was too old to fight fire.

I could see smoke on the hill, between the pines and the hickories. The smoke looked like the mane of a horse streaming to the clear sky. The smoke was too far away to smell, but I could hear crackling flames in brush. The broomsedge and scrub was dry as paper in an attic.

"You hold the baby," I said to Jewel. Her and Moody was playing in the sand in front of the steps with Muir.

"I want to come," Jewel said.

"I want to come too," Moody said.

"You stay here," I shouted. I handed Fay to Jewel.

"She'll get me dirty," Jewel said. Jewel was the neatest, primmest child I ever saw. Even when she played in sand she kept her hands clean and dress unwrinkled. And Fay needed changing. I had been meaning to change her when Tom run to the house. But I had to go help fight the fire. And I had to go look after Pa. He would get too excited if he tried to beat out the flames.

"I want to help," Jewel said.

"Did outlaws set the fire?" Moody said. "I'll go shoot them."

"You stay here. I mean it," I hollered back as I took out up the hill. I had fought fire when I was a girl and fire got out on the mountain. I wondered if I should carry a bucket of water up to the pasture. But I didn't reckon one bucket would do much good, not if the whole pasture was burning. I tried to think how you could put out a fire in a dry pasture. In the woods we had cut pine limbs and beat the flames. Would you try to shovel dirt on a grass fire, or cut a ditch in front to stop it?

"Pa," I hollered, after I crawled between the strands of the fence. My apron caught on a barb and tore a gash in the cloth, but I didn't pay it any mind. I saw Pa up the hill with a pine limb beating at the smoke. It appeared the fire was rolling across the pasture. The flames at the bottom of the smoke turned like bright wheels. But mostly you saw the tower of smoke rippling and boiling. There wasn't much wind, but the smoke leaned up the hill so thick you couldn't see a thing beyond it.

"Pa," I said, "you better not get too hot."

His face was red and sweat streamed down his temples. His sleeves was rolled up. Where he beat at the flames the fire disappeared, then sprung up again after he lifted the pine limb.

"Where is Tom?" I said.

"Over yonder," Pa said, and pointed right into the smoke. I figured Tom had gone to the upper side and was throwing dirt on the blaze as it climbed the hill.

"You go back to the house," I said to Pa. But he ignored me. He kept beating at the fire like he was swatting flies. "It come from the furnace," he said, as though he was taking the blame.

That's when I saw the way the wind was stirring. It was not pushing up the hill but swirling around it. The blaze had swung across the slope from the lower pasture toward the hickories and oaks. I figured Tom was trying to keep fire from reaching the woods. The fire moved sideways and uphill at the same time.

I needed to go help Tom, and I needed to look after Pa. I didn't know which one to do. "You'll get too hot," I hollered to Pa. It was like the heat from the fire was reflected and doubled by the hillside. In the bright sunlight you could hardly see the flames, but you felt the heat on your face.

"You go back to the house," I shouted, but Pa didn't answer. He acted like he didn't hear and kept swinging at the flames.

Where are the cows? I thought. I hoped they was in the lower pasture. If they had stayed in the upper pasture they might be drove by fire to the yon fence and trapped. "Have you seen the stock?" I hollered to Pa. I knowed the bull, Bill-Joe, was in the barn because they was going to breed the Waters's cow that evening. I tried to think where the cows would be.

Would they be standing in the shade switching flies and waiting for the cool of the day? Or would they be at the branch getting a drink? I hoped they was down toward the river. If they got scared by the fire they wouldn't give any milk for days.

The fire had a mind of its own. I watched it burn this way and that, swirling around and backing. It didn't always answer the breeze. Sometimes it would pause on the stalk of an indigo bush and run high, then leap to the next tuft of broomsedge. Then it would stop and go down to the roots. A piece of the fire started burning backwards in a patch of dried crabgrass and come almost to my feet. I kicked dirt on the flames and they smoldered out.

"Go back to the house," I yelled to Pa. I had to run to the left, to the end of the fire, and see what Tom was doing. But just then I looked down the hill in the blinding sunlight and there was Jewel holding the baby and Moody leading little Muir. They had come to the fence and stood watching us. Jewel held the baby like she was one of her dolls. Moody was aiming his finger like a pistol and making Muir fall down in the grass.

"Stay back," I hollered. But Jewel didn't answer. She was as stubborn and sullen as Tom when she wanted to be. "Stay out of the pasture," I yelled.

I could not see the end of the line of fire, and the trees and top of the hill was all hid by smoke.

"Tom," I hollered, as I run along the edge of the flames. Burning grass has a sweet smell, like baked dirt, and also a bitter taste, like the smoke of paper. I was out of breath from running, and the smoke made me cough. "Tom," I shouted, but all I could hear was the seethe and crackle of flames.

I run along the bottom of the fire to get around it. Little fires had spread into the grass downhill and I tried to stomp them. When I got to the end of the flames I saw Tom shoveling the sod. He had cut a ditch, throwing dirt in a belt that wouldn't burn. His face was red and he was soaked with sweat. He had lost his hat. He shoveled like he was trying to stop a flood.

"Tom!" I hollered. He pointed to a mattock behind him, which I grabbed and started digging. The ground was hard and dry under the grass. We was so close to the woods leaves had drifted into the pasture. There was dry leaves to burn as well as grass and broomsedge. I tried to rake dirt onto the leaves.

As the fire got closer smoke poured right into my face. I was sweating something terrible. The smoke stuck to me and sweat dripped into my eyes. The dirt was so dry I thought it might catch fire itself. If the ditch didn't stop the fire it would get into the woods. I didn't know how we would fight it there.

"Throw some dirt here," Tom hollered, and pointed to where the ditch was narrow with grass right to its lip. I dug deeper into the ground and raked the dirt onto broomsedge. But no matter how much dirt I spread over it the stalks still showed through.

The fire was so close now I could feel the heat pushing, though I couldn't see anything through the smoke. To get out of smoke I held my head down low. The whole day had clouded over.

"Get it there!" Tom said, and pointed up the hill to a place the fire was almost at the ditch. We run up there and while he throwed dirt on the foot of the fire I widened the ditch, chopping at the sod with the mattock. Again the smoke got in my face and I coughed so hard I had to stop for a second.

"Ain't no use," Tom said. He pointed to a place further up the hill where the fire was already at the rim of the ditch. We run up there and started throwing and raking dirt.

But the grass was so dry fire leaped whenever the wind hit it. Flames washed along the ground in a wave spilling from tuft to tuft. When wind hit the flames they rolled forward, catching the tops of stalks and burning downward as other flames leapfrogged over them. The fire was playing with us. When we attacked it one place, it swung around and jumped ahead somewhere else.

"There!" Tom said. He pointed to a fire that had caught on the other side of the ditch. I rushed to it and raked the spot bare. It was like trying to kill a wild animal that twisted and fought back. I scraped at the dirt till the fire was out.

"Yonder!" Tom hollered. We run back up the hill and attacked another spot that had started in the hickory leaves. Tom pitched one shovel of dirt after another on the smoking leaves.

The fire was so close we couldn't stay near the ditch. The heat was blistering. A rabbit run out of the brush to the woods. "It's too late," Tom said. Spots of fire was catching across the ditch. I was too out of breath to say anything. Tom stomped out a flame with his boots. "Ain't nothing to do," he said.

I raked at another little fire with the mattock. All up and down the line new fires was catching in leaves and broomsedge. The smoke was so thick I was going to have to run to get out of its way. There was no way to stop the fire from reaching the woods. I was going to holler at Tom to run, when I saw the smoke lean back from us. It had been in our faces and now it jerked away. The wind had changed and was pushing from behind. Leaves from the hickories poured out over the pasture. I rested on the mattock. It was providence that the wind had changed just in time. "It's an ill wind . . . ," I said and laughed.

"Maybe the fire will burn out," Tom said, "going back over its own track."

But the fire was not going back exactly the way it had come. It had run around the hill from below, and now it was turned and going higher still, like it had come to a switchback and was zigzagging. It was heading across the hill above the spring.

"We'll have to dig a new line," Tom said. "I figure the fire will cross the pasture just above the orchard."

"Maybe the road will stop it," I said. There was a wagon track that wound up the hill to the woods above Joe's house. We used it to haul in firewood. Tom picked up the ax and other shovel.

I thought of Pa. He had been fighting the fire almost on the other side. When the blaze turned did it rush back on him? He was too old to run. If he was confused by the smoke he might walk right into the fire. With smoke in his eyes and lungs he wouldn't think clear. I started running along the lower edge of the burn.

With the smoke leaning in the other direction it was like looking up the side of some high rippling tent. The smoke was silky and gray and billowed way above the pasture higher than any house. It looked thick enough to climb on.

"Pa!" I hollered as I run around the hill. Where the fire had burned, the ground was both black and white at once. The charred stalks was black and the ground was sooty, but the

ashes rippled light as petals of white roses. Roots and tufts still
smoldered.

"Pa!" I hollered again, but couldn't see anything but smoke
ahead. Where I had left him was all burned over. There was a
burning pine limb, but I couldn't tell if it was the one he had
been using. I saw a dead bird and a burned field mouse.

"Mama!" somebody hollered. It was Jewel. She had crossed
into the pasture and carried Fay up the hill. Moody and Muir
come right behind her. The baby was crying.

"Did you see the outlaws?" Moody said.

"Go back," I hollered.

"What are you doing?" Jewel said.

"Go back to the fence," I screamed.

But Jewel just stood there with the baby. I guess she had
never seen anything like the pasture on fire. If the wind
changed again the fire might burn the very grass where her and
the younger ones was standing. I throwed down the mattock.

"Go back to the fence," I shouted and pointed downhill. But
she just stood there, like she didn't hear me, like she was too
stunned to know what was going on. I bent down and grabbed
her shoulder. I found myself shaking her. "Go back!" I yelled.

"Bang, bang," Moody said, and pushed Muir down.

Jewel started to cry. But she did finally turn around and start
walking toward the fence. Moody and Muir followed her.

I picked up the mattock and run around the burned pasture
toward the orchard. There was little fires here and there.

"Pa!" I hollered.

I climbed through the fence into the orchard and run
through the cornstalks and Spanish needles toward the upper

end. Ears of corn hit my elbows and I stumbled on the terraces. The cows had got through the fence and was eating corn
under the apple trees. I reckon the fire had burned down part
of the fence.

As best I could tell the fire was crossing the hill. Wind had
pushed it along the side toward the holler where the spring
was. I thought maybe the fire would stop when it got to the top
of the hill. I didn't see any sign of Pa.

Just beyond the orchard was the pine thicket, which run
almost to the spring. I knowed if the fire got in the thicket with
all its sap and dry needles it would burn like hell itself.

"Pa!" I hollered again. I thought maybe he had drove the
cattle into the orchard. But I didn't see any sign of him. I
looked back down the hill, but he wasn't there among the
plums and pear trees either. I didn't see Jewel, and figured she
had took the younguns back to the lower fence.

"Pa!" I hollered again. I thought I heard an answer, but maybe
it was just the roar of fire, and busting pine knots. The sweat was
in my eyes so I couldn't hardly see. I rubbed my brow and saw
how black my hands was. There was a shortness in my lungs, as
if the sores from last winter, the scars, was irritated.

The pine thicket sounded like a furnace, or shoal water. I
run down the far edge of the orchard. If I could reach the road
I could get to the other side of the fire. Surely the blaze wouldn't
cross the widened road.

The spring was in a holler on the far side of the hill. There
was pines above and below the gully where the spring branch
run, but hemlocks stood right over the spring protecting it
from sun and undergrowth. Nothing much will grow under

hemlocks, though the needles will fill up the spring if you don't rake them out.

I wanted to get to the spring before the fire reached there. I figured Pa must have gone to the spring for a drink. The flames roared in the thicket like animals fighting. I run up the road to get ahead of it, but was too late. The fire had leaped across the pines and surrounded the spring. It looked like the hemlocks might be catching. Smoke rose from right around the spring.

"Pa!" I hollered.

The pines in front of me was burning and I couldn't get any closer. I tried to see through the smoke and flames, but it was too thick. The pines burned like kindling.

And then I remembered the spring branch. The branch was lined with willows and maples. They would not burn so fast. I run further down the hill and got in the branch. Knocking limbs out of the way I run right up the stream, splashing through pools.

When I got close to the spring all the leaves and bushes was burning. Fire had just reached the hemlocks and was climbing among twigs and limbs above the water. The big branches of the hemlocks hung too high for the flames to reach at first. The fire spread along the ground among sticks and little limbs.

"Pa!" I hollered.

Then I saw him. He was setting right in the spring. He had hunkered down and was flinging handfuls of water over his hair and down his back. Flames leaped across the branch, and it was like I saw him through waving flags. He was in a ring of fire, and I didn't see how to get to him. I thought he might smother on smoke, for the hemlock needles sent up a poison-looking cloud.

"Breathe through your handkerchief," I hollered. I knowed he always carried a handkerchief in his hip pocket. But I don't think he heard me at all. He was too busy sprinkling water over his shoulders and the fire was crackling loud in the brush.

"Lord, please save Pa," I prayed. I knowed he had gone to the spring because he thought the fire wouldn't come down into the holler. "Don't let Pa die in this hell," I said.

Smoke slapped into my face. The flames wasn't more than ten feet away and coming right toward me. The fire was busy in the leaves and undergrowth. There was black gum trees with crisp leaves along the branch. I had to decide where to run back down the branch and get away, or run forward to the spring. Brush was burning on both sides and burning leaves was falling all around me. To get to Pa I had to run between the flames.

I lowered my head and splashed forward, right between the burning bushes. I run under the smoke with my hand over my nose.

Pa didn't seem surprised when he saw me. But first thing he said was, "You should have stayed back." He was setting on a rock at the rim of the spring dripping with the water he had flung over hisself. His beard and hair was wet.

"Pa," I said.

"Get low and sprinkle yourself," he said.

I stooped down right in the branch.

"Splash yourself," he said. He threw handfuls of water at my face and hair. I rubbed the cold drops over my neck and shoulders. The water felt good, and melted the soot on my hands.

The fire was burning right to the bank above the spring. It was like we was inside walls of flames. Smoke reached over us and the air was full of sparks and burning leaves. I got down so my face was almost in the spring. Burning leaves and sticks hissed when they fell in the water.

"I done this once before," Pa said. "In Virginny, during the war." He talked calm as if he was setting on the porch. "The cannon shots set the woods afire. Wounded men, and men that was trapped, got burned up. I started running and bullets was flying through the trees. Cannons was blasting the tops of trees off. I crawled to stay out of the grapeshot. But the fire got so close to my butt I had to up and run. Wind was whipping the fire and I jumped right into a spring. I got down in the water and splashed myself. The fire roared over me. When it was gone the only thing burned was my eyebrows cause my wet hat protected my hair."

Smoke was all around us, and it didn't feel like there was any air to breathe, but Pa didn't seem scared at all. I put my apron over my mouth and breathed through it. "Put your sleeve over your mouth," I said. Pa started coughing and his face got red.

"Breathe through your sleeve," I hollered.

"The fire's done passed," Pa said.

I looked up and there was nothing but smoke all around us. I couldn't see any flames. But the smoke was thicker than ever. "Glory be praised," I said. But then I started coughing. It was as if the smoke went right to the bottom of my lungs. My eyes streamed and I coughed so hard I felt I was going to throw up.

Pa was coughing too. "Let's go," he said.

He was right. We was going to have to get out of the smoke or choke on it. We stooped low as we could and started wading down the branch. I held Pa's hand. The smoke was so thick I couldn't see anything. The ground on both banks smoldered and the air was nothing but dry, bitter smoke. I tried to hold my breath, but couldn't. I had to cough and couldn't help it. My lungs was being tore in two all over again. I wanted to stop, but I knowed if we didn't get out of the smoke I would smother or strangle.

Everything was white and full of sparks and ashes. My eyes was burning and my nose running. My throat felt like it had been raked with a saw. A piece of burning brush fell in front of me. I wet my hand and pushed it aside, burning my fingers a little.

Pa and me must have walked all the way down the branch before we come out of the smoke. My lungs was so raw they couldn't feel the sweet air at first. I bent over coughing, and then I throwed up. I lost my stomach right there in the sunny pasture while Pa patted me on the back.

I was so tired and dizzy it seemed I was going to fall when I stood up. If I had stayed in the smoke another minute I probably would have smothered.

"Mama!" It was Jewel coming across the pasture. She carried the baby and Moody and Muir run behind her. Their faces looked so clean and fresh in the sunlight I could not scold them. "Mama, your face is all black," Jewel said.

"How come you and Grandpa are all wet?" Moody said.

"You've got ashes in your hair," Jewel said. Jewel never could stand to get anything on her face or hair. It bothered her to see somebody else untidy.

"Where is your daddy?" I said.

"We ain't seen him," Jewel said.

"You ain't seen him at all?" I said.

"We heard somebody hollering up on the hill," Moody said. "We thought it was outlaws."

"We ain't seen nobody but you," Jewel said.

"I bet he's digging a trench on the hill," Pa said.

I looked around to see which was the fastest way to the top of the hill. The fire was burning to the right, in the thicket toward the old house place. I could try to run all the way around to the Schoolhouse Branch. Or I could go back to where the fire had already burned. I figured it was shorter to go to the left.

"Stay here with Grandpa," I said to the younguns. I started running back around the hill toward the orchard. I couldn't remember what had happened to the mattock, but I wished I had a stick of some kind to knock limbs out of the way.

I run through the black smoking trees and then into the pasture. The open ground had been singed like a plucked chicken. The pasture looked gray as ashes. Fire was still burning near the top of the hill. Smoke lifted through the trees and beyond, streaming across the sky as sun sparkled on its top.

"Tom," I hollered, and run on up the hill.

And then I saw two men throwing shovels of dirt on the fire. They worked fast as they could drive the shovels into the sod and fling their loads on the flame. They didn't resemble anybody I knowed. I wondered who had come to help us fight the fire.

When I got closer I saw it was Tom and Joe. Tom didn't look like hisself at all. His face was black and streaming sweat. He had lost his hat and his clothes was wet and stuck with ash. He worked like he was angry, fighting some animal or person. I wished I had brought him a drink of water.

"You better rest," I hollered.

"Ain't no use," he said. But I couldn't tell if he meant it wasn't any use to rest, or to fight the blaze anymore. Him and Joe had been digging a trench over the top of the hill. They had raked a belt of dirt bare, about five feet wide. The ground was so dry it looked like they had been hacking at chalk.

"If the wind would just stop," Joe said. He paused to lean on his shovel. Tom kept raking and pitching dirt on the flames.

"Is there another shovel?" I said.

"Ain't nothing but an ax," Tom said.

I looked around and saw the ax in the weeds. But it wouldn't do any good to chop it into the ground or try to cut away the broomsedge. Tom stopped digging and leaned on his shovel. Under the soot and dirt his face was no longer red but pale. He had turned a dirty green color.

"You better rest," I said. But he didn't answer. He looked too tired to speak. Black sweat run from his temples and down his neck, like he was crying all over his face.

"Better rest a while, Tom," Joe said.

I noticed the smoke wasn't pouring in our faces anymore. The wind had died down. You could hear the fire crackling in the grass and on stumps back in the woods. Crows was calling further out the ridge in the big pines.

"The w-w-wind has stopped," Joe said.

"Well thank the Lord," I said.

"It's too late," Tom said. "Won't make no difference now."

"You don't want the whole country to burn," I said.

"Nigh the whole place has burned," Tom said. He spit in the smoldering grass like he was too disgusted to comment further.

I took his shovel and throwed dirt on a tuft of broomsedge that had flared up again. The fire had just got to the ditch when it turned back on itself and went out.

"Let's go to the house," I said.

But Tom didn't answer. I turned and saw this odd look on his face. It was like he wasn't listening, but thinking of something different. Under the soot now his face was white as paper.

"Tom," I said.

Joe come up closer to him. "How you f-f-feeling, old hoss?" Joe said.

But Tom looked like he had been hit in the belly and couldn't stand up straight.

"You need a drink of water," I said.

"Better go set down," Joe said.

"I'm going to the house," Tom said. He started walking like his legs weighed a hundred pounds each. He stepped right through the smoldering brush and broomsedge as if he didn't see them.

CHAPTER EIGHTEEN

When Tom got to the house he went right to **the** toilet. He stayed in the outhouse for half an hour. Pa come back to the house, and Jewel and the other younguns. Joe went to round up the cows and put them in the barn.

I washed my hands and face on the back porch. And then I set down on the porch and took Fay in my lap. My clothes smelled like smoke and my hair did have flecks of ash in it. When I touched a flake it melted to dust. I nursed Fay for several minutes, and when I was finished Tom still hadn't come out. I thought I had better go down and see about him. Maybe he had gone and I hadn't noticed it. I told Jewel to take Fay and put her in the cradle.

"Tom," I hollered, but there wasn't any answer. Wind stirred high in the hemlocks and limbs swished on the roof of the toilet. "Tom," I hollered again. It sounded like something stirred behind the door. "Are you there?" I said.

"I'm sick," Tom said in a low voice.

"What's wrong?" I said, and opened the door of the outhouse. There he set in the dark with his overalls down over his knees.

"I've got cholly morbis," he said. Under the soot he looked gray. He was sweating again.

"You better come to the house," I said.

"I can't get up," he said. He said it like he didn't care, like he wanted to be left alone.

"You can't stay here," I said.

I run back to the porch and told Jewel to go to the barn and get Joe. When Joe come we had to pull Tom out of the toilet. That was hard because he was so weak and because we couldn't get inside the place. We had to first pull him over, to the right, in front of the door. After we got him lifted I pulled Tom's overalls up and buttoned them, and we got on either side of him.

Tom was heavier than I had dreamed. He had gained in the past two years, and was stout to start with. He could mostly support his own weight, but Joe and me had to keep him from falling.

"Cholly morbis killed my grandpa," Tom whispered, "after he got hot pulling fodder."

"Well it won't kill *you*," I said.

It took us several minutes to climb the steps to the yard, and then to cross the yard. Tom walked like it was an awful strain to move. He was trembling, and too weak to hold his hands steady.

"Go put some water in the kettle," I hollered to Jewel. I thought there might still be fire in the kitchen stove.

It must have took us ten minutes to get Tom into the bedroom. He had been sleeping in the attic for the past six or seven months, but there was no question we had to take him to the bedroom. We set him down on the bed, and I took off his boots. He laid down quick, too weak to hold his head up any longer.

When the water was hot I poured some in a pan and got soap and a washcloth. I figured Tom wouldn't feel any better till he was cleaned up. If the doctor come I didn't want him to find Tom all covered with soot and dirt. With the pan by the bed I washed Tom's face and neck, his throat and his chest. He had pieces of burned leaves and weeds stuck in his hair. His skin had broke out in splotches, white in places and red in others. Where he was tanned on his forehead, below the hat brim, the skin looked green again. I unbuttoned his overalls and pulled them off, jerking a little on one leg and then the other. He was shaking and looking at the ceiling. "You don't have to do this," he said.

I thought, If I don't, who will? But I didn't say anything. I had never washed a grown man before, and I sponged him off like he was a baby. I washed him all over, where he was smeared with diarrhea, and where his legs and feet was crusted with dust and soot that stuck to the sweat. As I washed him he kept jerking, his teeth chattering. I wrapped him in a blanket. I was sweating in the hot room, but he was shivering like it was below zero.

"Do you want something to drink?" I said.

"No," he said, and closed his eyes.

I tried to remember what you give for cholly morbis. It was usually something that babies had in hot weather. It would kill them in a day if it wasn't stopped.

Joe was standing at the door when I come out of the bedroom. "Burnt l-l-liquor is what the old folks used," he said.

I went to the medicine shelf and got the jug. I poured a full cup of corn whiskey and set it afire. It was the scorching that was supposed to stop the cholly morbis. The flames leaped from the cup like it was a torch. I let it burn ten seconds before blowing it out. The liquor was warm when I took it into the bedroom. "Here, drink this," I said to Tom.

"Ain't thirsty," he said.

"This will help," I said. "This is the only thing that will."

His forehead was hot as a stove. It was like the fire he had fought had gone into him. I raised his head and put the cup to his lips. I reckon the liquor burned him, for he jerked away. "You've got to drink it," I said, "or you won't get better."

He took a sip, and then another. As the liquor went down the jerking stopped a little. I held the cup to his lips the best I could and he drunk most of it.

"Give me some more of that blessed good medicine," he said as the liquor took effect. He didn't sound like hisself.

But the liquor didn't make him cool off. As he laid in bed he felt hotter and hotter. I was scared the fire in him was fed by the liquor. I set by the bed and put my hand on his forehead. He just laid there burning like a coal.

Later, after I fixed supper and washed the dishes, I asked Pa what else you could do for cholly morbis. Pa had tired hisself and didn't even read the paper as he set in the living room.

"You could try blackberry juice," he said.

"I thought that's for ordinary diarrhea," I said.

"Might help," Pa said.

I took a lamp down to the cellar and got a quart of blackberry juice. It was the color of wine, but thicker, thick almost as ink. I give Tom half a cup of the cold juice, and it made his lips and tongue black. He seemed to be getting hotter still.

Sometime that night I must have put the children to bed. I guess Jewel helped, and I nursed the baby before she went to sleep. But I don't remember. All I can recall is setting by the bed and watching Tom get hotter. Late at night was supposed to be the worst time for the fever and it wasn't even midnight yet.

Pa looked in before he went to bed. "You better get some sleep," he said.

"I can't," I said.

Pa was wore out from the day's excitement. His shoulders slumped more than I had ever seen them, and his face looked hollow. "Joe done the milking," he said.

After the house was quiet Tom drifted to sleep for a while. Then he woke and looked around. "Are the cows all in?" he said.

"Joe got the cows in," I said.

"I didn't pull no tops for them," he said.

"You don't need to," I said. "The cows are done fed."

He drifted off after that and I started getting drowsy. I was thinking about fighting fire and running through the thicket looking for Pa. It seemed the faster I run the quicker the flames burned behind me. It was like my running fanned the flames.

"Stomp on it," Tom said. He appeared to be talking to me. He was hollering a warning. "Stomp on it," he yelled.

I woke and saw Tom was talking in his sleep. He was twisting, with a terrible look on his face. "Throw dirt on it," he said.

Tom moved his head from side to side as if he was trying to get loose from something. He was straining in an awful way.

"Tom," I said, "you're just dreaming."

"I won't let you burn it down," he said, like he was talking to hisself. "I won't let you burn down all I have done."

"Wake up," I said.

"You won't destroy me," he said.

"What are you talking about?" I said.

"This is the baptism of fire," he said, and chuckled. His eyes was closed but rolling around. His hand reached out and fell back on his chest.

"Tom, you are dreaming," I said.

"You and Pa will not destroy what I've worked for," he said.

He kicked the covers partly off. I reached to pull the sheet back and he pushed my hand away. But his eyes was still closed. He didn't know what he was doing. "You got to stay covered up," I said. I felt like Tom was a little youngun I had to look after.

I nursed the baby at midnight, and carried her around the living room until she belched. The house was still except for the creak of wind pressing the roof. I still smelled like smoke.

After I put Fay down I went back to the bedroom. As soon as I brought the light into the room I saw Tom had his eyes open. "You ought to sleep," I said.

"Ain't nobody going to stop me," he said, looking around the room as if he didn't even see me.

"Nobody is trying to stop you," I said.

"I ain't going to quit," he said. His voice was vague, as though he was saying one thing and thinking of something else.

"Quit what?" I said.

"I'll get a dollar for wood and hew more crossties," he said.

I saw he was out of his head. It was a new plan he had to make money that winter. The railroad had advertised it would buy crossties a dollar each if they was made from sound chestnut wood. It took a day to hew a good one, but in winter there wasn't any other way to make money. He had bought a new ax that fall.

"Ain't nobody going to stop me," Tom said again.

I pushed the covers back to his chin. The cholly morbis seemed to be over. I guess the burnt whiskey had stopped it. Or the blackberry juice. The old-timers had knowed what would work. But Tom had took some kind of fever. I figured he had got so weak and overheated something else had attacked him besides the cholly morbis. He was red hot. I could smell fever in the room.

"I'm going to get two dollars for the molasses and split some more rails," Tom said.

In the fever his worries was all magnified and multiplied. I guess he was remembering his fears. "Mama, we got fifteen cents and a gallon of cornmeal," he said.

"I know where they's a rabbit," he said.

The anger and spite went out of me. Looking at Tom laying there I thought I'd be sick myself if it would make him well.

I tried to think what to do for fever. There was still whiskey in the jug. And there was pneumony salve, but I didn't know if it would help. I tried to recall what folks said about fevers. The Indians made willow-bark tea. But I didn't have any willow bark. I went to the medicine shelf to see what was there.

Pa had tincture of lobelia for snake bites. And he had some powders for when his back was killing him. There was kidney pills Dr. Johns had give him, and yellow root I give the younguns for worms. There was a bottle of camphor, and cough syrup of honey and raspberry juice. There was Epsom salts and mineral spirits.

I got a pan of cold water from the kitchen and took it into the bedroom. The only thing I could think to do was sponge Tom off. There wasn't anybody to ask for help, and nobody awake but me. I turned the lamp up a little and pulled the covers back. Unbuttoning his nightshirt, I washed off Tom's chest like I had before. But this time I went slow, using more water to cool him.

"I'll take fifteen cents for the rabbit," he said.

I washed his arms, wetting the undersides and the insides of the elbows. I wet his wrists, because I knowed you could cool yourself off by chilling your forearms.

"Tom," I said, "roll over." I figured if I could wet his back and the back of his neck that would cool him off more than anything. But he didn't hear me. He was so heavy I didn't think I could turn him over by myself.

"I won't give a cent," he said. "I wouldn't give a cent for such carryings-on." He was talking to me, or about me. He was still thinking about the money I had give to the preacher.

"Turn over," I said. But he didn't pay any attention. He kept muttering like he was dreaming, but his eyes was open. I thought maybe if I could get a hold I could turn him over. I needed something to brace my foot against. I needed a place to grab him. I got on the other side of the bed and pushed my foot against the wall, and I stuck both my hands under his shoulders. I raised the shoulder some, but not high enough to roll him over. He fell back and his belly quivered. He was heavier than a big sack of meal.

"Roll over," I said. I tried again, and still couldn't get him turned. There was no way I could lift his shoulder. I was going to have to give up. Then suddenly he turned over like somebody rolling in their sleep to try a fresh, cool side of the bed.

I washed his back, and held the cloth to the back of his neck. I figured that might cool him a little. It seemed to work. He quit muttering and closed his eyes. After I took the pan to the kitchen I felt his forehead and it was cooler. His face was still red, but not as splotchy. He was asleep and not talking to hisself. I was so tired I set down and closed my eyes. After I drowsed a while, I got on the bed myself and went to sleep.

The next morning Pa brought me a letter from the mailbox. It was from Locke. I set right down by the bed and read it.
"Dear Ginny,

"You know my big mouth always has trouble squeezing itself into the point of a pen, like a camel going through the eye of a needle. But I wanted to write, as much as the rich man probably wants to go to heaven. I meant to write soon as I got your letter, but then they transferred us to California. And no sooner had I got here than we had an earthquake and nothing has been the same since. I've read your letter several times in the past few months, and I've tried to think of something useful to say. Maybe your letter has helped me more than I can help you.

"The night of the quake I started to write, but was too tired to concentrate. I had worked a twelve-hour shift at the hospital here. We've had a bad run of flu some say the soldiers brought back from Manila, and I've been working extra hours. The wards are full of sick soldiers and we are more shorthanded than ever. I had the tablet of paper and pencil on the table beside my bed, but I couldn't get started with my letter. I sleep in an annex of the hospital. I was so tired I kept going over your words, but they got twisted up with the faces of boys I'd been tending. Seventeen had died in the past week, and we had another hundred who could die. The flu kept spreading through the barracks.

"Finally I gave up and turned out the light. I must have slept four or five hours, dreaming of your letter and Pa and the place on the river. I thought I heard Mama speaking. You know what a deliberate voice she had. But she was talking about the flu and the boys in the ward. She was saying prayer alone wouldn't be enough. And as she spoke I was sliding away. I washed up and away on a wave, then rocked the other way. It felt like the building and earth under was melting. That must have been when I woke and heard the roar. It sounded like a train going underground and through the hospital. Timbers and brick walls crumbled. But I couldn't get out of bed. I was caught in a fluid that pushed this way and that. The bed slammed against one wall, then the other. I was scared as a baby would be if its mama had a fit. The solid stuff of the world had turned to plunging, shoving jelly.

"After a minute the awful rocking stopped and I let go of the bed and tried to find my clothes. There was screams and sounds of the building crumbling. It was dark and I tasted dust. Through the window I saw fires. A gas main exploded and lit up the sky.

"Ginny, I won't go into details about what followed. You can imagine how the hospital looked. Some of the walls and floors had fell and the wards was full of sick and dying, terrified, confused about what had happened. Many died that night of shock, or thirst. I worked eight hours straight carrying patients out of the rubble. I was lucky to be alive myself. Four nurses in a room next to mine got killed by a falling timber.

"Ginny, your letter has helped me more than I can ever help you. Your words reminded me of the family and the *peaceful*ness of Green River just when I needed them most. I have been weakened by the earthquake, and by the horror on the sick men's faces. To somebody in a fever an earthquake must seem like the flames of hell itself unleashed on their face. Everything that is solid and certain gives way. Earth has lost its firmness.

"Only now are things beginning to calm down. The electricity and water was restored to the hospital in less than a week. But it will be longer before the burned and collapsed sections are replaced. I feel weak as somebody with the flu. Worrying about the patients instead of myself has kept me going.

"Now that I've started I might as well tell what I've been thinking. You know what a binge talker I am. I think the biggest problem we all have is our fear. We live in fear of sickness and pain, and big losses. That's natural, the most natural thing. And in the mountains we are afraid of snakes and flash floods, spiders and panthers. We fear lightning and hailstorms. We are afraid of outsiders and strangers, of the law and government, and of change. We live in terror of damnation and hellfire.

"The special thing that humans have is thinking. We remember the past and plan for the future. But that knowledge of the possible makes us fearful and anxious. Almost everything we do is for reassurance. I guess what Mama feared most and Tom fears most is loss of control and reason. It scares them to see a husband or wife go out of control. If somebody that close to them can lose their willpower and dignity then they might also.

"We never understand another person's ecstasy. Watching intense joy in somebody else is repugnant to us, even somebody eating with extreme relish or drunk and singing to themselves. Somebody else's sexual pleasure is unsavory to us. And a fit of ecstasy at a service, the loss of control in speaking in tongues or rolling on the ground, must seem embarrassing as watching somebody in the spasms of sex. It could be seen as a loss of humanness, of the faculties that make us human.

"For somebody like Tom that is a price too great to pay. All his life he has felt little control over anything except his work. Sister, no one wants a spouse to escape to a place of their own, separate and sufficient, where they can't go themselves. It is a kind of denial of marriage. Would you be pleased if Tom had another farm he went to at times to work and cherish? Would you resent it if he loved to hunt as much as Joe does, and vanished for days or even weeks into the woods beyond the Long Holler? I don't know the answer, but it is the kind of thing you could think about. What if he had a passion for prospecting and was gone looking for minerals, though he never seemed to find anything but the enthusiasm for searching?

"But I think your kind of joy is a gift too. Not everybody can experience such pleasure, even if they wanted to. I'm not sure most of us have the capacity to feel what you do at the services. You and Pa and Joe must be blessed that way.

"You know as well as I do there is no greater pleasure than in giving, and in finding out what we have to give. That's where we find our asylum from the horror all around.

"Now here is my idea, Ginny. I want you to think about what Tom has give you. Think of where his joy is, his enthusiasm. Think of what he has brought to the place, and to Pa, to you and Jewel and the younguns. Consider what his talents are, and what his truest pleasure is. And if you think where his strength is, and his greatest fear (for they are close related, wouldn't you guess?) then you might see if you have been resisting his gifts. Have you been so busy that you have refused to accept what Tom has offered? Have you wanted to give more than to receive?

"This is my idea of the moment. Maybe I will have another one tomorrow. You know how I tear on once I start. Right now I have to go on my shift. The California sun is bright after a little rain. That's all the weather we get here, a rain from time to time that washes down dry streambeds and makes flowers bloom along the banks. It has made me feel better writing to you, and thinking about the place there on the river, and the family. Now I must get to the ward before the sergeant comes looking for me.

Love,
Locke."

That morning Tom still had a low fever. I give him spring water and sassafras tea. But the fever wouldn't go away. I knowed as the day wore on he would get hotter. All fever patients are cool in the morning. Whatever Tom had was still working in him. But the fever was hiding in the morning.

I sent Pa for Dr. Johns before dinnertime. I didn't know what else to do. The doctor and Pa come back in the doctor's buggy just as I got dinner ready.

"Looks like you had a little fire," the doctor said.

"It was fighting fire that give Tom cholly morbis."

"And he ain't got cholera morbis now?"

"He's got fever now," I said.

The doctor frowned. Doctors hate it when you tell them what's wrong with a patient. I guess they're afraid they'll have to disgree with you.

"He'd be dead by now with cholera morbis," the doctor said.

"He got over it," I said.

"But he's still sick?" the doctor said. When we talked it was as if we was still teasing each other, the way we had when I was a little girl. I invited him to have some dinner, but he went on into the bedroom. I took the jug of whiskey back in, for I knowed he would give Tom some and take a drink hisself.

The doctor bent over Tom and listened to him breathe. He sniffed his breath like he was a cook sniffing soup. "Take a drink of this," he said to Tom.

When the doctor come out of the bedroom he turned to me. "He has typhoid," he said.

"It's too late in the year for typhoid," I said.

"It's been a warm fall," the doctor said.

I felt I'd been slapped. "Typhoid comes in summer," I said.

"Typhoid comes when it comes," the doctor said and drunk from the jug. I set down, and couldn't think of anything to say.

"Typhoid is different every time," the doctor said. "It can last three days, or months. It can be walking typhoid, or it can kill you."

"What makes the difference?" I said.

"Everybody is different, and every fever is different."

Before he left, the doctor said to pull the curtains in the bedroom and keep the door closed. The house must be absolutely quiet. Tom would need dark and quiet. The children would have to stay away from the room. When the fever was high he could not be disturbed in any way. "Even a little commotion might push him over the edge," the doctor said.

I shut the door of the bedroom and closed the curtains. I hung a blanket over the window to make it darker still, sealing the room like it was some kind of secret vault.

The doctor had told me to give Tom oranges, if he would eat them. Squeeze oranges and give him the fresh juice. I sent Pa to the store for a bag of oranges. We hadn't ever bought them but at Christmastime. I made orange juice and poured whiskey in it. The bedroom smelled of oranges and spirits. And there was still the smell of burned broomsedge and weeds no matter how many times I washed Tom or bathed myself. It was like the stink of the fire was in my head and I couldn't get it out.

"Play in the yard," I said to the children. "Or stay in the kitchen and be quiet." If Fay was crying I carried her to the porch. I took her with me when I went to the springhouse.

It would not be fair to say that I was thrilled by Tom's sickness. And yet, the worse off he got the more sweetness I found in myself. It was like a new love, to be his nurse. I scrubbed the bedroom and washed him off. I carried the bedpan out to empty and wash on the back porch. I felt alive in a new way. I was strong and quick and had a freshness flowing through me and out of me. I can't explain it, except to say it was like I was now Tom's mother. No matter what he said in his fever it didn't rile me. When he cussed and fretted, when he repeated I was a religious fool, I let him rave. "Tom, you are sick," I said.

"You and your land be damned," he said.

"Tom, it is the fever talking," I said.

Pa peeled some willow bark by the river and I tried to make tea. But the outer bark was too dry to steep, and the inner bark was too green. I don't know how the Indians made willow tea. I tried to give Tom some brewed from the green bark, but he wouldn't drink it. It did look and smell like poison.

I had never had such energy, even when I was a girl. I didn't sleep more than four hours a night, and yet I didn't seem to miss sleep. A peddler come by selling sheets and blankets from a wagon and I bought new ones for the bedroom. I washed everything in the room twice a week. It was like I was inspired.

Florrie come over one day to offer her help, and I smiled sweet and thanked her. I told her I didn't need any help. "Well if you do you can always ask me," she said.

I found I wasn't mad at her anymore. I was too busy and strong-feeling to be mad.

"You're working too hard," Florrie said.

Joe walked down and did the milking every day. Him and Pa finished the molasses, but they let the batch overcook, too dark and rubbery. People from all over the valley come to buy molasses and ask about Tom. They did not get near the house, but stood in the yard and handed Pa their money and took the jugs theirselves from the smokehouse. Everybody was afraid of typhoid.

It surprised me how much I wanted to do for Tom. It pleased me to bring him juice and to wait up by him. I washed the bedsheets and the nightgown. I was completely in charge. Maybe I should have been a nurse, I thought. Maybe that's what I was called to do and never knowed it. Maybe Locke and me had more in common than I had thought. I was alert to when he started to get hot every day, and when he would cool off in the early morning. I got familiar with the small hours, which I never had before.

It felt as if the latest hours and earliest was the most sacred time of day. In the small hours it was just me and the fever awake. Sometimes I would pray, but mostly I set there thinking it was my will and work against the typhoid. We was fighting, and the fever was a mystery deep in Tom's body. I couldn't see it to attack direct. I could only give him juice and whiskey, and cool him with a washcloth, then change the bed.

But it felt like the fever saw my will pushing against it. I had to be patient and outsmart it. The sickness was evil that had got in Tom's flesh. It could see me but I couldn't see it.

Sometimes, for an instant, a lonely ache swept through me as I set by the bedside. But it was a normal loneliness that made me want to work harder than ever. I reckon if people didn't feel lonely they would get lazy. It is the ache, and the fear of the ache, that gives us starch and keeps us alert and planning. As I watched him laying there in the grip of fever I thought how lonely Tom must have been in his years on the river. When we was quarreling he didn't have any friends at all. His only companion was his work. I hated to think how hard it had been for him.

"Typhoid gets in you and likes to sleep for a while," Dr. Johns said. By the fourth day after the fire I saw how right he was. "Pneumony will build to a crisis and then either break or kill you. And the bad kind of flu will do the same. But typhoid will build up to a crisis and seem to go away. Some people have light cases and get well in a few days. And some die after three or four days. And others have it a month and then get better."

There was a night—I think it was the fifth night after the fire—when Tom got worse than he had before. It was the night the weather changed and you could hear wind in the hemlocks and feel cold soak through the walls and window. The house creaked and was quiet. I tried to give Tom water, but he was too weak to drink. He was way out of his head. I wet his lips with my finger.

"The molasses are dark," he muttered. I leaned close to him. "The river field . . . hawks," he mumbled. I couldn't make any sense of what he said. I reckon he was dreaming something terrible.

"Tom," I said. But he didn't hear. He was way off in the fever.

Something creaked way up in the top of the house, like there was a nail giving way. And then a weight fell in the attic right above, as if a piece of ham meat or even a body had slammed on the floor where Tom's pallet was. I felt I had been shoved by the noise, and listened to see what happened next. Had Pa or Jewel gone up to the attic? Had a big animal climbed up there? Had we hung something from a nail that give way in the middle of the night? I tried to think what was hanging up there between Tom's pallet and the chimney. There was some tobacco that was curing.

For some reason I thought of all the people that had died in our room. Mama had died there when I was a girl. And Grandpa and Grandma Peace had died there too. And the little baby born before Muir had died there. Other people had died in other parts of the house. The Revis boy died in the kitchen after he got shot on the mountain and they brought him in to operate on the kitchen table.

While I was thinking such mournful thoughts something knocked on the side of the house. It sounded like a fist hit the weatherboarding. It was loud as if somebody with a stick had slammed the wall. And nothing will get your attention like a knock. It was a little after two in the morning, for the clock on the mantel had just chimed. I set bolt upright and listened. Had somebody come and tried to get in? I almost hollered out, "Who is there?" I looked at the window but the blanket was over it.

Was somebody playing a trick on me? It was close to Halloween. Maybe it was Halloween? I had lost track of the days. But everything was quiet except for the wind. I thought maybe the house had cracked because it was turning colder. You know how a house will groan and snap when a freeze comes. That has to be it, I said. I turned to Tom and wet the rag again in cold water.

Just then a knock come from further down the wall, about where Pa's room was. It was not so loud a knock, just an easy knock like somebody had arrived and politely rapped on the boards. And while I listened another come from still further down, toward the corner of the house. And then there was a tap from the end of the house. Whatever it was was going around the house and tapping on the walls. The clapboards rung as if struck by a silver-headed cane. Knock, it went, and then knock, and knock again.

The fact the knocks was so regular made them more scary. I tried to imagine why somebody would walk around the house hitting the wall. Was it just a silly prank? Was it Florrie doing something to spite me? It didn't make any sense. Halloween stopped at midnight, if it was Halloween.

The knocks kept going around the house. I heard them on the porch and then on the kitchen wall. Whoever it was kept going. Could it be an animal jumping up on the wall? I thought it might stop at the door, but whatever it was didn't pause at all. The knocking went on regular as clockwork.

"I'm getting to the bottom of this," I said. I put the washcloth in the pan and took up the lamp. Quiet as I could I rose and eased toward the door. But just when I twisted the doorknob Tom mumbled something. I stopped to see what he said. He murmured so low it was hard to make sense of it. I walked back to the bed and listened. "Don't," he whispered. I leaned closer to him. "Don't," he said again.

"Don't what?" I said. But I couldn't tell if he was talking in a dream or to me. His eyes was closed and his face red as a coal. "Don't go," he said. It was as if he knowed about the knocking, though he hadn't showed any sign of awareness before.

"I won't," I said. I didn't know what else to do. If he didn't want me to leave him I couldn't, much as I needed to find out what was hitting the side of the house.

Tom's lips was dry and I had to give him more water. Once he drunk I'd go refill the pitcher and see what was making the noise. I put the lamp down and poured cold water into the cup. The knocking was coming on around the house, first at the back porch, then the living room. It went past the fireplace chimney.

"Drink this," I said, and held the cup to Tom's lips. His lips looked like old paint that was scaling off. Some of the cracked skin had turned black as if he had been eating huckleberries. I was careful not to let the water spill on his chin.

The knocking come around the corner of the house on the eastern end. It had not speeded up or slowed down, but was steady as a bell tolling. It knocked on the living room wall.

Tom's mouth wasn't really open, but I poured in some water anyway. A trickle run down each side of his chin. I think he got a little of the water on his tongue. I poured in some more, and then a little more. He was so hot his face looked swelled up. I didn't know a body could stay that hot and live.

A knock rung on the wall by the window, a single rap, like somebody wanted to remind they was there. Just a firm reminder.

I put the cup down and pulled the covers back. I unbuttoned his nightshirt and put the wet cloth on his chest. The water steamed off his skin. I washed his shoulders and his neck and tried to wet the back of his neck without turning him over. I wet his temples and I put his hand into the water. Last I pushed the covers all the way down and rubbed his legs with cold water.

Tom had fell off a lot since he got sick. His legs looked almost skinny. I washed him around his navel and private parts. But he didn't seem to have cooled any. Suddenly his legs started jerking, his arms twitching. His eyes was open and his face had this awful look, like it was pulling away from something. I thought he must be dying. His mouth made gagging, spitting noises. It sounded like he was going to choke. And then it come to me he was having a seizure. He was so hot he was having a fit.

I grabbed the whiskey and poured some on the cloth. I rubbed the liquor on his chest and throat. The fumes filled the whole room so strong they seemed blinding. I rubbed his legs and belly, his chest again. Some splashed on the bed but it didn't matter.

When I finished Tom felt a little cooler, and the jerking had stopped. He laid still and his eyes closed. His forehead wasn't burning so bad. Of course it was getting up toward four o'clock in the morning, the time when the fever usually started down. It was hard to guess how much good the rubbing had done.

I don't know when the knocking stopped. I was so busy trying to cool Tom off I forgot about it. But the knocks must have gone away while Tom was jerking, though I couldn't be sure. Just then wind shoved against the house and the ceiling creaked, and I saw it had been nothing but the old house getting cold. The knocks was boards shrinking. I wrapped Tom up in the blankets, and laid down myself. The house still creaked in the wind.

The next day it was cold and clear. The Indian summer was over. It looked like every leaf had been stripped off every tree during the night. The kitchen fire felt good. Pa already had a fire in the fireplace, and I put some rocks on the hearth to heat. When they got real hot I would put them under Tom's bed.

After I nursed the baby and washed up the breakfast things I went back to look at Tom. At first I couldn't see anything in the dark room, after the bright light of the kitchen. Mixed with the whiskey smell and the fever smell was another scent I couldn't describe. It was like the smell of musk and rotten leaves. I had kept Tom clean and didn't think it could be any dirty smell. It was a deep, dank smell, like straw that has been in a ditch a long time. It come to me that was the smell of the typhoid.

Tom was sleeping now, but I knowed the fever was waiting its time. The room was so still you could hear his faint breathing. I took his wrist and it was a second before I could feel any pulse. He was sleeping somewhere far away from me, floating in deep darkness, completely still. I went to the kitchen and squeezed an orange. There was almost a cup of juice, and I broke a raw egg into it. When I had mixed it all up I took it to Tom.

"Tom," I said, "you've got to drink this." But he was too weak to have much interest. He took a little juice between his lips and swallowed. I poured more in his mouth, and juice run down the sides of his chin. I knowed he couldn't go on like that. Either he was going to get better, or he was going to die. It seemed the fever could hear me think, and I could feel it listening.

People come and went all that day. Dr. Johns stopped by and told me I had done all I could, but that I should give Tom more whiskey to stimulate his heart. "The next forty-eight hours will tell the tale," he said. Dr. Johns had a talent for conferring dignity on sickness and a sickroom. Sometimes I think it was his best talent. He could talk of bowel movements and pus with such ease and confidence you always thought he had helped.

Florrie walked over before dinner and brought a pudding. She stood in the living room talking to Pa until I come out of the bedroom. "You have had a hard time, Ginny," she said.

I looked her directly in the face before I went on to the kitchen. "The fever has got to break," I said. "He can't go on like this much longer."

I didn't want to encourage Florrie to stay, because I didn't mean to go too far in making up with her. Better go slow and just be nice, treat her like a neighbor. Let more time pass.

Joe come after dinner with a load of wood. He took the horse and drug several chestnut logs into the yard and sawed them with the crosscut. He split the pieces with a go-devil and wedge. Before he left he piled a week's supply of wood on the porch.

It was cold when I went to milk, but not windy. There was a sunset spread from the mountains in the south to the mountains in the north. The west was salmon color, and the sky got pink overhead and purple in the east. The sky was so bright it looked like the world was burning up. It felt like the end of an era. I don't know what all I thought as I stood at the barn with the buckets in my hands. I walked a ways toward the Sunset Rock.

The valley to the west was laid out in red light. The river shined in places like beat gold and the sky was the color of a great rose petal. I thought if I could just keep walking west I could put away from me all the sickness and crying children and dirty dishes, and the bitter quarrels. I was suddenly so tired of the long days and nights of waiting in the sickroom. People don't think women dream of wandering away just like men do.

I've never seen a painted picture as pretty as the mountains to the west. It was like I was looking at something dreamed. And it was almost under my feet. But I turned around with the buckets and started to the house. There was a lamp on in the kitchen. I knowed the fever would be coming back in Tom by now. It always woke up at dark. The fever was a demon of the night.

"Mama," Jewel called as soon as I walked in, "Daddy's coughing." I put the buckets down and run to the bedroom. What I heard was a groan and rattle. Tom was trying to cough but couldn't get his breath his chest was so tight. You've heard that grinding racket people make in their throat when they're struggling to cough. It was a terrible sound. I knowed he had got so weak with typhoid he had took pneumony.

First thing I did was pour whiskey in a cup and mix it with water. I held it to his lips, but most of it spilled. I run to get the honey jar. Sometimes honey will soothe a throat and stave off the next cough. I opened the sourwood honey and dug a spoon deep enough to raise a gob. "Take this," I said to Tom.

"Is he worse?" Pa said, standing in the door of the bedroom.

"He is," I said. Tom just barely opened his lips, and I put the honey on his tongue. Just then a cough rolled in his chest and shook in his throat. The honey run out the side of his mouth.

"That don't sound good," Pa said. I could hear Jewel and Moody fighting in the living room and Muir crying. Fay had to be fed and the milk had to be strained and carried to the springhouse.

"Sounds like the death rattle," Pa said, bending to the bed.

"It ain't the death rattle," I said. I was suddenly so mad my voice was almost a hiss. "It's pneumony. Can't you hear the wheeze and whistle? Don't bury him before he's dead." I had not talked so sharp to Pa since before I was married.

Pa backed to the door and went out. I was astonished at myself, but not a bit sorry. I knowed I'd be sorry later, for Pa was old and got confused about things.

Tom tried to cough again. His chest sounded full of water. If something didn't help him he would drown. He was so weak he didn't have anything left to fight the pneumony with.

"Give me a nickel for the pumpkins," he whispered.

I reckon he was thinking about the pumpkins scattered over the cornfield and shining like lanterns now the weeds was killed by frost. Before Halloween he had meant to carry a wagon-load to the village to sell. On a frosty morning the pumpkins shined like stars and planets rising among the dead stalks. His voice was just a hoarse mutter.

There was a knock at the door. It was Jewel who stuck her head into the dark room. "Mama, Fay is crying," she said.

"Pick her up and rock her," I said.

"She won't shut up," Jewel said.

"Carry her around," I said, and waved her away. The door closed and I set in the dark with the lamp turned low. I had to think what to do. There wasn't anybody to help. If I sent for Dr. Johns he would just come and tell me to give Tom whiskey and honey. That's all he had to prescribe. Didn't anybody know what to do for typhoid, or pneumony.

I set there thinking. Tom had been sick too long to have any fight left in him. Didn't seem anything I could do for him, or about anything. Things just happened as they did. It come to me how little I had prayed. During the past week I had prayed only once. All the feelings from the meetings and brush arbors didn't seem to have anything to do with this pain and trouble. I had hardly thought about prayer. I saw how strange that was, and felt ashamed. I said a quick prayer, and I said the secret name Dr. Match had give me. I said the name over and over.

I pressed Tom's pulse and it was so low you couldn't hardly tell it was there. He was breathing in little gasps, as if there wasn't room in his chest to take in air. It was a pain to listen to the short intakes, one after another. He was trying to get air, and there wasn't any place to take it in.

All through the week I had tried to cool him. Now it seemed the only hope was to make him sweat. If he was too weak to sweat there wasn't anything I could do. I run to the door and called Pa and Jewel. "Put all the rocks and bricks in the fire," I said.

The house was filled with the crying of Muir and Fay. Moody had knocked Muir down. Fay was screaming in Jewel's arms.

"She's hungry," Jewel said, holding the baby out to me.

"I'll take her in a minute," I said. I tried to think where there was some more rocks. I grabbed the lamp off the mantel and run out on the porch. My flowerbeds and herb garden in the yard was lined with rocks Tom had hauled from the river. Tearing the weedstalks and grass away I carried about ten to the porch. The rocks was cold as great balls of ice. One by one I toted them in and set them in the fireplace. When I had finished, the hearth and sides of the fireplace was covered with rocks and bricks.

"You'll put the fire out," Pa said.

"Put more wood on," I said.

I nursed Fay a little bit and then give her back to Jewel. I was afraid to leave Tom any longer, and I was almost afraid to go back and look at him. Those little gasps made me shudder. The room was getting cold. I put another blanket on the bed, then I run back to the kitchen and put on the kettle to boil.

As I worked things got clearer. I saw I had to stimulate Tom's chest. I had to get his heart and blood moving faster. I had to put something in him to make him fight. I wrapped some warm salve in a cloth and took it to the bedroom. It felt like hot jelly in my hands and smelled brighter than any pine resin. I thought of the gifts of the Wise Men, and pulled back the covers to place the cloth on Tom's chest. He jerked with the shock, but I knowed the salve wouldn't burn him since I had been holding it. Hands are tougher than other skin, but I thought the shock of the heat might stir his lungs and heart. Soon as the poultice begun to cool I put a towel over it and pulled the covers up again.

Next I lifted Tom's head and poured whiskey into his mouth. "No," he whispered.

"You've got to drink this," I said.

"No," he muttered.

He needed something hot inside him. I should have thought of that before. I run back to the kitchen and poured hot water into a cup and mixed in sassafras bark and whiskey and lemon juice. I tasted the drink and my face broke out in sweat from the steam.

"No," Tom whispered when I lifted his head up again.

"You drink this," I said, like I was talking to a child. He turned his head away slightly, but with my fingers I pulled it back. I held his head in the crook of my wrist, and poured the hot drink into his mouth. He swallowed some and coughed. I waited a few seconds and poured in more. The hot whiskey and lemon juice and sassafras was loosening his throat a little.

After he had five or six drinks I put the cup down and run to get the rocks. They was so hot I was afraid they would burn a towel. I had to lift them into pans with the tongs and shovel. Pa had built up the fire something terrible with hickory wood.

I carried the rocks one at a time in pans and canners and put them under Tom's bed. The rocks was so hot they burned my face just to get near them. I hoped they wouldn't set the bed on fire. "Get out of the way," I yelled to Moody when he come toward me. "Don't touch the rock."

By the time I got all the rocks under the bed I was dripping with sweat. The bedroom had heated up like there was a stove in it. I closed the door and pulled the covers back.

Tom was gasping now in such short breaths you couldn't hardly hear them. His eyes was closed, his skin hot and dry. I poured whiskey into hot water and begun to wash him with it. I washed his face and neck and throat. I washed his arms, first one and then the other. I lifted the poultice and washed his chest with hot whiskey. And then I rubbed his legs and thighs. His legs looked like he hadn't walked in months.

Where the heated whiskey touched him the skin got red, and then turned pale again. His mouth was a little blue. All the time I worked a sentence kept running through my head. "Service is also praise," a voice said. It was a sentence so sweet, and an idea so sweet, I kept saying it. The words shined in my ears. "Service is also praise," the voice repeated. I guess it was my voice. It sounded clear and helpful.

After I had washed Tom all over with the heated whiskey I got so hot I had to rest. The room was warm as summer, and smelled strong of lemon juice and sassafras and whiskey. The dark air was lit with the smell of salve and liquor. I filled the cup again and poured some more of the mixture in Tom's mouth. His breath was so low you couldn't hardly tell he was taking in any air.

There wasn't anything else I could do. I covered him up with the blankets and set down by the bed. Another sentence run through my mind. I don't know where it come from. I just heard the voice saying it. It was repeated several times before I listened. The voice said, "Human things are all we know."

I couldn't think what it meant. I wondered if Pa and Jewel had put the children to bed, for the house was quiet. I didn't know how late it was, for I had been working too hard to listen to the clock. The wind in the hemlocks sounded cold. But the room was warm as a stove. "Human things are all we know," the voice said.

And then the same voice said, as though from right inside my head, "The tabernacle is with men." The sentence was from the Revelation. And it meant the same as the other sentence. It was my voice, even though it sounded like silver. "The tabernacle is with men; former things are passed away," it said. It was the most beautiful sentence I had ever heard. In all the years since I have never heard one more beautiful. And I knowed partly what it meant. That's why I was saying it to myself over and over.

I was drowsing and hearing the sentence again and again. When I woke I looked at Tom and his forehead was damp. In the lamplight it looked like dew had settled on his skin. His face glistened in the weak light. Was he was beginning to sweat? I reached out to touch his forehead and it was cold. I took his hand from under the covers and it was even colder. There was no painful breath coming from his chest.

CHAPTER NINETEEN

When I saw Tom was still I thought of laying right down on the bed beside him. I wanted to get close to him and be a part of him. I wanted to lay on top of him and mix my flesh with his. I put my hand on his chest and it seemed impossible that his heart was absolutely stopped.

The touch was gone. All the years of our marriage the connection had been there when we got close and met flesh to flesh. The room was warm from the rocks and bricks under the bed, and all the heat was in the air. It did not seem possible he wouldn't respond. I wanted to get under the covers and warm his body with mine. But the touch now told me he was not there.

I got down on my knees beside the bed. The heat from the rocks come right out from under the springs like a breath of summer raising in my face. I thought what a waste all that work of carrying the rocks had been. But the floor was cold even through my dress. The boards was slick with cold. "Lord," I prayed, "if it is your will to bring Tom back I beg that you will. Though we have quarreled and been bitter I don't know how to go ahead without him on the place, and I don't know how to raise the younguns on my own. I don't know any longer how to be myself without him to lean on. I don't know how I can face the next hour or the next day on my own, and the years coming one after the other. In all my joy of meetings and all my pleasure in worship I never thought I would have to bear this."

I stopped and pushed myself up and set in the chair. I felt Tom's neck for a pulse, but it was colder now. I took his hand and placed my fingers on the wrist. The skin was smooth and cool as ivory. I lifted the covers and placed my hand on his chest again.

Now the awfullest thing come over me. I can't explain it and I've never heard of anything like it. Of course if other people have had such happen they probably wouldn't tell. You don't know what things go on that people never talk about. But this anger poured into me suddenly. It just seemed to shoot up through the floor, out of the ground and all the way from hell.

I set in the chair so mad I felt dizzy. The anger roared inside my head like nausea and laughing gas combined. Tom, I thought, what a sneaking thing, to desert me. After coming here and courting me and making me fall in love and then taking over the place so my life was changed around and I have these children to raise. What a blackguard thing, to go and leave me. To make me depend on you, to take my youth, and then to go and leave me.

In my fury I thought how strong I was when single. I was prepared to live my life with reading and sewing and going to services and taking care of Pa. I had a balance then, and a delight in little things, a view of the world that was all destroyed by falling in love with Tom. Yes, I had a way of seeing then clearer than any I had had since. Recalling the simplicity of my years before meeting Tom brought tears to my eyes.

There come to me a flood of things I disliked about Tom. I hated the way he never had the enthusiasm to go hunting and trapping the way most men in the family did. I hated the way he would nod when I read to him, like he was listening even when his mind was on the firewood he would sell in the village or the terraces he was going to make in the orchard to level the steep ground into shelves.

It made me shiver with anger to think of the way he left his shoes by the hearth. As Pa and me set by the fire I had to smell them. I hated the way he hung his pants on the bedpost and you could smell sweat on them and the scent of work. It embarrassed and revolted me to think how he would set with company, silent and dumb as a rock unless somebody asked him a question. He never had an opinion about anything. He never entertained people with a story or kept up his end of a conversation.

This is what made me maddest of all, to know that I was sounding like Lily. It made me angry at myself to think of the way Tom folded the cloth he had put over seedbeds. He wrapped the cloth in tight squares as though in a military ceremony. He placed his tools in the shed on the right nail or hook, like he thought he could own the earth just by keeping it in order. When he didn't have anything else to fix he would cut weeds along the fences and take old harness apart to save rings and brads and rivets. He nailed boxes to the wall of the shed where he sorted screws and nails and steeples. He would sift through a box of trash to save pins and pieces of string. I often wondered what he thought he was saving such things for. Did he think he was going to live forever and could accumulate the wealth of the earth?

There was tears streaming down my cheeks and dripping on my wrists and hands. I had set there crying while anger thundered and roared in my head. The storm kept coming, but I tried to brush it away. What good was it? All the rage I could imagine wouldn't undo a single thing we had done.

I looked at Tom laying there and it seemed that as long as nobody else knowed he would not be dead. If Pa come in and saw him it would be over, or if one of the younguns woke and come to the bedroom I would have to tell them their daddy was gone. But as long as it was only me that knowed, it wasn't real, wasn't final. I set in the chair and thought it must have been three in the morning. And then I heard the mantel clock strike four. Time was moving on so fast I felt it flowing through me. I could almost hear the swishing and lapping of the waves rushing by and above me. I thought if I set silent and kept still long enough I might slow the river down, maybe even stop it. But the current swept through me and the room begun to cool off.

This is already my widowhood, I thought. I set there studying Tom's face getting white and lips turning blue. And it felt like somebody else looking at him through me. I shivered with the icy feeling of being hollow and clear enough for somebody to see through. It was like they was behind, seeing through my eyes what I saw. They was just inside, where the sense of myself was, there beside the me in myself.

Is it the Holy Spirit? I thought. Is it the guardian angel watching over Tom? Is it the other people who have died in this room? I shuddered and blinked.

Suddenly I saw all the things I had hated about Tom I could just as well have loved. Maybe that was me seeing through other eyes. Maybe Locke was right about me refusing to accept Tom's gifts. I saw what fools we had both been. All our quarreling had been such a waste. "The tabernacle is with men; former things are passed away," I quoted. But it would have been impossible for Tom to have changed. I thought of his shoes by the hearth and fresh tears come to my eyes. The saddest thing of all was I saw that people couldn't be any way but what they are. Even when doing right they are apt to be doing something else wrong.

The pile of chestnut logs Tom had sawed and left to season for crossties set between the barn and orchard. That was the place where he split rails and it was covered with chips and splinters. Now there was nobody to hew the crossties, unless it was Joe, and Joe would be too busy walking his trapline and hewing his own crossties. I could do most any man's work, but I would never be able to lift those heavy logs and hew them into crossties.

And then I thought of the road up the ridge to the mountaintop orchard. Tom had kept the haul road mowed, and the weeds and brush cut back around the orchard itself. Places that had been all growed up when I married Tom had been opened and took care of while I hardly noticed. Once he started doing it Pa and me took for granted that weeds along the pasture edge would be trimmed, and weeds around the smokehouse and springhouse and along the trail to the branch would be cut so you could see a snake before stepping on it. Tom even mowed the path to the Sunset Rock two or three times a year.

Often after finishing up in the field, or returning from selling produce in the village, he took his scythe from the shed and whetted it bright in the late sun. Working in a steady rhythm he would lay flat weeds between the apple and pear trees, and big pokeweeds below the hogpen. He did it so regular I hardly noticed. When weeds was cut in the sun they sent up an aroma of oils and incense rank as ether. I would walk where he had mowed and smell the wilting fragrance and not even think of the work he had done to keep the ground clear. I had never been able to mow with the scythe. It was too heavy to swing, and too awkward to balance the long handle and blade with the weight in my shoulders. It would be years before Moody or Muir could mow either. The place would grow up the way it had before I married.

The same might be true of the new ground Tom had cleared by the river. Without him to do the plowing and hoeing we could not cultivate so many acres. His long hours and steady work was the equal of three or four hired hands. But it wasn't just the work he had done we couldn't replace. It was his planning and thinking about what might be done. Wherever he looked he saw possibility. Every piece of ground was an opportunity, as every hour and day was. It was his "idea" about what to do that I would find the hardest to replace.

I thought of the gates Tom had built and the road he had widened. The road would have to be worked every year to keep it in the fine shape he had left it. The ditches would have to be opened and the puddles filled. New gravel would have to be spread in the low places. The steps down to the spring would have to be kept clear of leaves or they would be buried in a year or two.

There was the strawberry bed up by the spring, where Joe's Poplar stood. Tom had kept the vines separated and the red dirt bare of weeds. It was the kind of job you had to do on your knees, and it took days. But Tom did it once in the spring when the berries bloomed and once in August. Every shoot and sprout had to be sorted and cut back and every tore root reburied.

We had never rented any of the Peace land. Since my great-great-grandpa had cleared the place it had been worked by the family. A lot of sweat had went into the dark loam by the river where Tom put his watermelon vines and tomatoes. I reckon some of that ground had been cleared by Indians for their little patches. But most had been maple swamps that had to be cut and drained. When the bottomland was wild it was covered with poison oak and poison ivy, and weeds that caused milk-sick when the cows eat them. Where Tom laid off his long straight rows had once been vines and sinkholes and snake dens. Tom laid off the straightest rows I had ever seen. A furrow he made run like a rifleshot to the yon end. I never understood how he could make a horse stumble over the clods and dips in such a straight line.

To farm all the acres Tom had, I would have to hire help, at least until Moody and Muir got bigger. Or maybe I should rent some of the land? I could sell off some cows since I wouldn't be able to milk the four or five Tom had. The burned-over pasture might not support so many head.

As I set in the stillness by Tom's body it occurred to me I did not even know where he kept his money. Many a time I'd seen him count the day's earnings into the cigar box and close it. Sometimes he carried it upstairs where he slept on the pallet. It was just a pasteboard box that he used to put under the bed when he was sleeping with me. I had never paid it much attention, but I knowed he kept the money near where he slept. I would need the box to pay for things. But I did not want to climb the ladder in the dark and maybe wake Pa and the children.

I looked under the bed and of course the box was not there. The rocks and bricks was cooling, and I shuddered at the sight of them. Dirt still clung to the rocks and give off a strange baked smell. Where else might he have put the cigar box? I looked around the room and saw the chest of drawers. Only two of the drawers was used by Tom for his socks and underwear. I opened the drawers one after the other. I found the little jug Dr. Match had give me long ago, but there was no cigar box there. A pain went through my chest when I saw Tom's washed and folded underclothes.

The cedar chest set just under the window and I lifted its top as slow and careful as I could. The smell of the cedar rose in the dark like a vague memory. I felt among the quilts and blankets and my wedding dress, and found a silver spoon Pa had give me as a little girl. The spoon was cold as ice.

I stood and looked at Tom on the bed, and then I looked around the room again. The wardrobe loomed in the shadows almost to the ceiling. I opened the creaky door and felt among the shirts and suspenders on the shelf above the hanging clothes. There was the cigar box. With trembling hands I slid it from under the shirts and carried it to the lamp. The box was heavy as a clock.

When I opened it the cigar box give off the fragrance of metal, of nickels and silver, of copper and folded bills that had mildewed. I was almost afraid to touch the contents. The money was Tom's most private covenant. There was many twenty-dollar gold pieces and stacks of five and ten dollar bills tied with thread. There was a lot of silver dollars and dimes also. There was a big faded bone button, and I knowed what it was. It was the button from Tom's daddy's uniform that had been brought back from the prison camp in Illinois with the gold watch. All those years Tom had kept that button and never told me he had it.

I counted more than four hundred dollars in gold pieces. And then I saw a piece of yellowed paper under the coins. It was a clipping from an old newspaper. I opened it in the lamplight and saw it was a wedding announcement. "Mr. Benjamin Peace of Green River announces the marriage of his daughter Virginia to Thomas Powell. . . ." It was just a square of paper cut from the *Hendersonville Times* after our wedding and kept by Tom. The paper was ragged from the wear of the coins.

I put the cigar box on the table and looked at Tom. His face was gray now and his lips almost black. I thought of all he had give me, of the joy of his loving, and the children, of the work he had done to the house and the place, and the box of money. I thought of the terraces he had made on the orchard hill to hold back the topsoil in the worst rains, and the jugs of golden molasses in the smokehouse. He had give me more than I had even dreamed of. Locke had been right. I had thought I had give the Peace land to Tom, but the truth was he had give it to me.

It was such a waste that we had fought all those years. But saddest of all was that I could never repay him, or thank him, or tell him that I loved him. I wanted to tell him we was in his debt, not him in ours. I wanted to say I accepted his gifts.

I decided it would not be fair to wake Pa so near daylight. He would get up anyway soon to make coffee and read his Bible in the kitchen. Why not let him sleep as long as he would? There would be plenty of time for him to learn Tom was gone and to walk over the hill to tell Joe and Lily and Florrie and David. They would all come down and try to help and comfort me. The house would be crowded for several days. Joe would start building a coffin out at the shed where Tom had made one for the baby. Florrie would be rushing around the kitchen, and thanking folks that brought dishes. For days people would be condoling me and patting me on the back. Somebody would have to write to Locke.

I took a long deep drink from the whiskey jug and set in the silence as though it was a cool bath on a hot day. Silence is the language of God, I thought. He prefers to speak to us that way, and through our own voices. I wanted to wait a while longer and study about things. I might not be able to think this clear again for a long time. I wanted to figure it out a little more, to see if there was some way I could understand what had happened to me. What did it come to? Soon there would be light outside. Birds would start making a racket in the junipers and hemlocks. As quick as I heard Pa stirring I would get up and tell him, and begin working. There was a lot that had to be done before Florrie arrived and ordered me to set down and rest.